D0170108

THE POINT GUARD

Jeannie,

Thanks for your support.
Enjoy the read

THE POINT GUARD

A NOVEL

EDWIN J. SPRAGUE

iUniverse, Inc.

New York Lincoln Shanghai

THE POINT GUARD

Copyright © 2007 by Edwin J. Sprague

iUniverse books may be ordered through booksellers or by contacting:

iUniverse
2021 Pine Lake Road, Suite 100
Lincoln, NE 68512
www.iuniverse.com
1-800-Authors (1-800-288-4677)

Because of the dynamic nature of the Internet, any Web addresses or links contained in this book may have changed since publication and may no longer be valid.

This is a work of fiction. All of the characters, names, incidents, organizations, and dialogue in this novel are either the products of the author's imagination or are used fictitiously.

ISBN: 978-0-595-40559-6 (pbk)
ISBN: 978-0-595-84924-6 (ebk)

Printed in the United States of America

To Jo,

You are my inspiration.

Love Always

Chapter One

"Violence is tearing apart the very fabric of our society," states the leader of the most powerful nation in the world. The president of the United States of America addresses his nation on a frigid January evening from the once secure and impenetrable walls of the White House.

That statement, near the end of his television address to the nation, is perhaps the most understated of his presidency—there have been several acts of violence committed against the White House, and countless others have been promised. The president has also spoken on health care and the economy this cold evening, but violence is the focus of his efforts. With the economy making only small gains and his new health care plans near disaster, the president is trying to improve his sinking approval rating. Under these unfavorable circumstances, the president unveils his plans to protect the law-abiding citizens and punish criminals.

"It's time for us to get tough on violent criminal offenders. The days of revolving-door justice are over," the president says. "It's time to show those who break the law that this administration means business!"

"*Three strikes and you're out!*" warns the president as he defies criminals and attempts to comfort the law-abiding. At the same time, he preaches to the taskmasters of law their responsibility to round up undesirables and to imprison them in the dungeons of reform using his Three Strikes policy. His exhortation, broadcast live, sounds like bad dialogue from a Hollywood B movie.

The president's plan is to incarcerate three-time violent offenders and throw away the key. However, Americans are left to fend for themselves when a two-time violent offender is set free to commit a predictable third offense.

Staring steely-eyed into the camera, the president emphatically repeats himself: "*Three strikes and you're out!*" He forcefully pounds the desk, driving home his point to the millions of distressed Americans watching their televisions inside their locked homes.

In Philadelphia, surrounded by friends, a mother sits sobbing as she watches and listens to the president outline his crime bill. Less than a year ago, her only child had been raped and murdered by a two-time convicted offender. Her daughter had been missing for thirty-four days, while her killer lived comfortably in a federally funded halfway house—watching television, working out, and enjoying freedom. The halfway house was designed to assist in the social mainstreaming of paroled and released prisoners of the state. While living in these facilities, ex-convicts such as this killer have a limited ability to roam among law-abiding citizens.

The paroled offender had been arraigned on dozens of charges over a seventeen-year period but had been convicted only twice. His third conviction had been for the rape of the sobbing woman's daughter, although he had actually murdered his victim. The prosecutor in the case had tried to convict him of murder, but due to possible evidence tampering regarding the weapon, the prosecutor was required to limit his efforts to the rape case. Surprisingly, in a signed statement to the police, the man had admitted to killing the poor girl, but during the trial proceedings, the thug recanted his confession, saying that he had been coerced by the police and the prosecutor during the interrogation. After serving only thirty months, he was paroled and once again placed into a taxpayer-funded halfway house where he could stalk his next victim by day and lay in comfort at night.

The mother's voice is weary as she asks anyone who will listen, "How many strikes did he say?" She turns in disbelief to face her friends. "How many strikes do they get before they go away?"

Her only child has been abducted, raped, mutilated, and discarded like a dog by the roadside. The woman's shoulders slump as her body goes limp, drained of nearly all its energy. She shakes her head from side to side. "There has got to be a better way," she mumbles.

The worn woman is sitting in a Philadelphia public school classroom with other surviving family members of violent crime victims. This is her new circle of unfortunate friends. They all stare incredulously at the television perched in the corner of the room above a dusty blackboard and repeat the president's words over and over again in wonderment.

"Three strikes … three strikes and you're out?"

"What in God's name does that mean?" asks Mike Lane, whose wife of seven years was gunned down by three teenagers in a drive-by shooting in front of his Philadelphia home. Mike Lane and the others in that classroom are members of a support group called STOP (Stop Turning Out Prisoners). Their group is just one chapter of a national organization composed of people from all over the country who have lost family and friends to violence.

Lane's face turns red with anger. "I'll be damned! Three strikes, my ass! What the hell good will that do? That's not a solution!"

Lane is a handsome and well-educated man with a lean six-foot-two frame. His slightly graying hair caps his sad, deep-set eyes. He has lost twenty-five pounds since the murder of his wife, and his dark suit, although tailored, drapes over him, giving him the macabre appearance of an overworked mortician. Nonetheless, he remains an attractive man. His timeworn looks are the result of a deterioration of spirit caused by the terrible tragedy that happened not so long ago.

Three and a half years earlier, Lane and his wife, Tina, were returning home from a dinner engagement at the house of one of Lane's clients, Senator Jeff Wheatly. Lane owned and operated an accounting firm in downtown Philadelphia.

It was a clear, cool, moonlit summer night, with stars dotting the deep black sky. Lane pulled into the driveway of their comfortable and spacious property and turned off the car engine. In the stillness of the peaceful night, they sat in their car like new teen lovers. They were in front of the garage—twenty-five yards from the brightly lit street. Leaning over, Mike gently kissed Tina's neck and cheek while caressing her soft hands. He whispered in her ear while he softly nibbled. "I love you," he said.

A tingle ran up Tina's spine as she smiled softly with approval at his smooth advance. Mike rested his head on the seat back, clasped her hands in his, and gazed into her sleepy eyes.

"Thanks for putting up with Jeff, honey. I know he can really be a pain at times, but he's a good client." Playfully touching the tip of her nose with his index finger, he grinned and said softly, "You, however, are a *fantastic* wife! And … a very sexy one."

Mike was always quick to compliment Tina, and his compliments were always sincere. Tina smiled again and stared deeply into Mike's eyes. Over the years, they had managed to sustain their teenage craving for one another. It was a mutual infatuation that had started with their first kiss.

Tina unconsciously and seductively twisted her hair between her fingers as she slithered across the seat and eagerly nibbled Mike's ear in return. Breathing heavily, she tempted Mike in a low, sultry tone.

"I'm going up to our bedroom," she said. "Don't keep me waiting too long!"

Tina slid slowly across the seat to the other side of the car. Her wanton eyes perused every inch of Mike's body, taking a moment to inspect his swelling bulge as she moistened her lips with her silky tongue. Mike fidgeted behind the steering wheel and watched her like a schoolboy ogling a *Playboy* centerfold. Tina pushed the car door open and let out a girlish giggle. Slowly, she swung her long, shapely legs out of the car and placed her feet—clad in high-heeled leather—on the driveway and rose from the car. Her exquisite body was firmly wrapped in a sinfully short black strapless dress that accentuated each of her curves. With her jacket in one hand and her purse dangling from the other, her sultry figure cast a long shadow down the driveway. Suddenly, her seductive allure was interrupted.

The sound of gunfire erupted from a passing car on the street. The racket of breaking glass and piercing metal thundered through Lane's ears as though it had passed through an echo chamber. A storm of bullets tore through the car and surrounding trees as Lane ducked beneath the dashboard. For a moment, there was an eerie calm broken only by the high-pitched tinkling of Tina's chain purse strap striking the concrete driveway. Helpless, Lane watched in horror as Tina's body shuddered repeatedly and went limp before falling to the ground where it lay twisted on the edge of the drive.

Tina had been shot twice—once in the chest and once in the head. She lay still as blood drained from her chest and head. Her eyes were still and wide, gaping into the bright light of the full moon.

Lane would never shake the memory of his wife lying lifeless in their driveway. After seven years of a grand marriage, he and Tina—she was thirty-two—had been about to start a family. But she was gone. After Tina's murder, the days seemed to get longer. Every day, there were more reports in the newspapers and on the evening news of a continual rise in the number of violent crimes against innocent people. Often, he would hear of terrible deeds against the innocent and wonder how their husbands, wives, and children were coping with their loss.

Shortly after Tina's death, a client of Lane's invited him to one of STOP's support meetings. Lane became active in their outreach program, helping others to cope with the gut-wrenching pain he knew all too well. Helping others became therapeutic for Lane, who had never come to terms with the murder of his wife.

Despite this difficulty, he vowed not to let her death have been in vain. In her memory, he began an intense one-man quest to reform the justice system.

In that Philadelphia classroom, Lane hears the words of the president and questions the logic of allowing three strikes—three chances. He begins to pace the worn and weathered floor like a caged cat, seemingly oblivious to the others in attendance. "Three strikes! Three strikes!" He grumbles repeatedly under his breath as he continues his self-absorbed prowl. He paces up and down the aisles separating the perfectly aligned rows of tiny desks and grows more irritated as the president continues to outline his plan to curb violence.

Then, with the fury of an erupting volcano, Lane explodes. He grabs hold of one of the desks in the middle of a row and shakes it wildly. He twists the entire row of connected desks; his shirt is yanked from his trousers, and his tie flies over his shoulder. Lane's face turns scarlet, and his eyes stay locked onto the desk. He is oblivious to the fact that everyone in the classroom is gawking at him. The distraught man finally breaks the desk free and hoists it high over his head. Sweating, he stands stiff as stone and surveys the classroom. He breathes heavily, and his head pivots to meet the terrified, tearful eyes of the dozen others in the room. Then he lets out a blood-boiling howl, runs fifteen feet toward the blackboard, and hurls the desk. The desk hits the blackboard with such force that shards of metal and splinters of wood, slate, and chalk fly as high as the television perched in the upper corner of the room. Lane then turns toward the others and, lowering his head, makes a quiet but sad departure.

Chapter Two

For three solid years following the incident in the classroom, Lane all but went into seclusion. After hearing the president's three-strike solution, he began to spend nearly every waking moment doing research at the University of Pennsylvania Law Library downtown. He wanted to learn, as quickly as possible, all he could about fighting violent crime and about the American criminal law system. Lane had taken a double major at Stanford University, graduating third in his class in accounting and receiving a master's degree in criminal law. He was well equipped to handle research in large doses. It became his dream to put an end to soft sentences and inequitable punishment for criminals. Over the years, he witnessed more and more people attending STOP meetings, while criminals who had not served just sentences paraded out of the prisons and onto the streets. It had become his mission to learn all he could and use his political contacts to write substantial and credible legal reforms that would reach the halls of legislature and put an end to revolving-door justice.

Since that evening in the classroom, Lane had severed ties with most of those who had been dear to him. He left his house only to go to the law library, take care of urgent business, and attend STOP meetings. Senator Jeff Wheatly—the client whom Lane and Tina had visited on the evening of her murder—began to express concern about him. The senator and his wife, Jane, invited Lane for dinner many times after Tina's death, only to have their invitations rejected.

The senator, a career politician, had known Lane since the inception of Lane's CPA firm. For Lane, a man of impeccable character, their relationship was more professional than personal. The senator displayed the typical behavior of a politician—he was a greedy man who filled his coffers with special interest and PAC money, which he used to further his own personal agenda. He was forty-one years old, five foot six, and 136 pounds—including his $2,000 Armani suit. He wore wire-rimmed glasses and had thinning, dyed-black hair. He was a pointy-faced mouse of a man.

Some years ago, the Wheatlys had met Mike and Tina Lane at a cocktail party at the home of Meg Kelly. Meg was Jane's best friend and lived directly across the street from the Lanes. Tina would see Jane from time to time when she visited Meg and occasionally at political events. Although they never became the best of friends, Tina and Jane had been very friendly to one another, and the Lanes had attended cocktail parties at the Wheatlys' home several times over the years. A professional relationship developed between Mike and the senator shortly after the two had met.

At his wife's urging, the senator continued to extend dinner invitations to Lane but to no avail. As time passed, the senator's invitations dwindled and finally stopped. In the three years following the incident at the STOP meeting, Lane devoted nearly sixty hours a week to the preparation of a legal reform document, spending weekends, the better part of his afternoons, and all of his evenings at the law library.

On one stormy evening, at about 9:30, the senator and his wife were reading in their well-furnished, plum-colored bedroom. Over the sound of rain pelting against a large picture window, they heard a dull pounding on the front door. Mrs. Wheatly, clad in silk pajamas, rose from her gold-upholstered antique armchair in the corner of the room and wrapped a long satin robe around herself. The stately, quiet woman walked down the hall and descended the wide, curving marble staircase with the grace of a princess.

The Wheatly children were away at boarding school, leaving the seven-bedroom palace cold and barren—at least, as far as she was concerned. Her husband loved the fact that he could afford the luxury of sending his children away, thereby giving himself peace and quiet for nine months of the year. He would have liked to send them to summer camp as well, but his wife always begged to keep them at home for the summer.

Mrs. Wheatly glided across the black-and-white marble floor of the foyer and whisked open the front door as if she had been expecting guests. Standing under the porch light in the driving rain was a drenched and weary Mike Lane. She welcomed him in a quizzical but sympathetic tone. Her voice was nearly drowned out by a thunderclap.

"Hi, Mike! Come in out of the rain before you catch your death!"

Lane entered and stood silent just inside the doorway. He acted as though he'd been sedated.

"So … How have you been, Mike?" she asked. Lane nodded toward her and noticed that the senator was making his way down the stairway.

"Where the hell have you been, Mike?" the senator joked.

Lane greeted the senator at the bottom of the stairway as Mrs. Wheatly helped him out of his wet coat.

"Damn, you look like you've been rode hard and hung out wet!" Wheatly continued. "You all right?"

Lane shook his head nervously as his eyes darted between the couple before fixing on the senator.

"I need your help, Jeff," Lane said. His voice was shallow and weary.

Obviously stunned by Lane's haggard appearance, Jane stood quietly holding his coat. His eyes were deep and black, like those of the dead. They slowly drifted from the senator's eyes to the floor. Senator Wheatly and his wife exchanged a glance.

"So, you say you need my help, Mike?" Wheatly asked awkwardly.

Lane nodded slowly and deliberately. Attempting to lighten the mood, the senator spoke in an uncomfortably upbeat manner. "Sure, pal! Name it!"

Lane lifted his head. His rain-soaked shoes squeaked on the shiny floor as he shuffled his feet. He nervously wiped his wet lips. Then, barely loud enough to be understood, he cleared his throat and muttered, "*Justice.*"

Again, the senator and his wife looked at one another, unsure of what Lane had said. Jane shook her head and shrugged as the senator leaned forward with a confused but polite and tolerant smile. "What's that you say, Mike?"

"*Justice,* Jeff. 'Justice' is what I said. I want justice to be served. It's a concept that seems to have escaped the American judicial system for the past three or four decades."

Lane looked at the ceiling. His hands slipped into his pockets, and he stood motionless for a moment. He got no reaction from the senator. He raised his voice as though he had been ignited.

"Justice, damn it! I want justice! I want those bastards to pay for what they did to my Tina. I want an eye for an eye! A life for a life! Let the victims and their survivors deal out the punishment!"

Lowering his voice, Lane settled down slightly but continued to vent his frustration.

"Get these sorry liberal civil libertarian bleeding hearts out of the way and start punishing these heartless, self-serving creeps." He shook his head and raised his voice again. "Lock them up and throw away the key! Treat these animals the way they treat their victims. Ha! *That's* fair!"

Lane nodded in agreement with himself as he paced across the Wheatlys' foyer. They witnessed his progression of emotions without interruption.

"Strip these dirtballs of their rights, their dignity, their dreams! They should be hung in public … humiliated in front of their friends and families!"

Lane swallowed hard and wiped the rainwater from his face with his palm. He seemed unaware of the senator and his wife as they stood quietly and listened.

"I want the streets to be safe again. I want to be able to go to the movies, or to the mall, or have a drink without fearing for my safety. I'd like to be able to stop and help someone on the side of the road without the fear of a scam or some conspiracy to attack me."

Lane choked back his emotions and stood stifled for a moment, and then he fixed his stare on the senator.

"Jeff, I want my wife back. I want the child we were going to have. I want all the dreams we had. Those bastards killed our dreams, and they got away with it!"

Lane squeezed his eyes tightly shut to hold back the tears and rested his hands on the banister.

"I want *justice*, not three strikes!" he said in a quivering voice.

The senator put a comforting arm around Lane's shoulder and walked him into the living room. "Have a seat, my friend," he said. "Jane is going to get us some tea." He motioned to his wife.

While the senator continued to comfort Lane, Jane prepared the tea in the kitchen. She brought it into the elegant living room on a silver tray. Lane sat uncomfortably quiet as Jane handed him a steaming cup. The fine china clattered in his hands, and his eyes once again welled up with tears.

"Look at me, Jeff. I can't stop shaking. I can't eat or sleep. Every time I close my eyes …" He dropped his head, held his breath, and spoke to the floor. "I see Tina's body lying in the driveway."

Lane raised his head to face the senator. A tear rolled down his cheek and plummeted into his hot, black tea. The senator and Jane looked at Lane woefully, and the senator suddenly realized that he had never really discussed the shooting with Lane. Though he had been aware of the results of the trial, the senator had never really concerned himself with any of its details. He crossed his legs to get comfortable in his chair.

"Did you clearly see the car the gunshots came from, Mike?" the senator asked.

Lane nodded. The senator slid out to the edge of his chair. "The color, the year, the type?" Once again, Lane nodded.

"Were you able to clearly identify the shooters?"

Lane let out a sad, sarcastic laugh. "Yeah, I identified them. Before Tina … fell, I ducked, and then I turned around. I saw them as they drove under the streetlights. I could see their faces as clear as day. They looked out the passenger-side window back at Tina and me. It happened in a moment, Jeff. But I *did* see them as they drove by. And I saw it was a black BMW."

Shaking his head, Lane added, "Earlier that day, the bastards had shot the owner of the BMW as they stole it. He lived. Huh. He was just fine. Hell, he even identified all three of them! He testified that they'd carjacked him. They were just kids, Jeff. Teenagers. Hell, I picked them out of a lineup.

"They'd been brought up on multiple charges in two different cases: murder and attempted murder against Tina and me and attempted murder and grand theft auto against the owner of the BMW. God, Jeff … they're all out walking the streets! Two of them were only fifteen! They didn't even have to stand trial as adults!"

Lane fixed his eyes on the floor as he continued. "They went to juvenile court, and when all was said and done, they were released to their parents and sent to a special school. The third one was sixteen—only two days away from seventeen. He was held over on the same charges, and eventually he was tried as a juvenile as well. He served twelve months in a juvenile detention center for shooting the owner of the BMW and stealing his car—*and* murdering my wife."

Lane shook his head. "When he turned eighteen, they let him out. The judge said he felt that these kids could someday be productive in society, so they wouldn't be tried as adults even though one of them was already seventeen at the time of the trial."

Lane sat upright and pulled his shoulders back, stretching his tense muscles.

"It was all part of a gang initiation."

He squeezed his eyes shut repeatedly. He had yet to touch his tea. All the while, Jane had been sitting uncomfortably still as she witnessed Lane's despair with a great deal of sympathy. The cup and saucer now steady in Lane's hand, he glanced over at her and saw her attempt at a sympathetic smile. After finally taking a sip, Lane placed the cup and saucer on the table and quickly became more animated. His eyes brightened as he looked directly at the Wheatlys.

"What the hell is wrong with our system, Jeff? It's crazy! These bastards killed Tina and got away with it! The judge felt they didn't *intend* to shoot that poor bastard while they stole his car and that they didn't *intend* to kill Tina. Ha! Do you believe that? Their intentions! I didn't *intend* to live my life without my wife, but what do I get? I get nothing!"

A silent moment passed as Lane watched the uncomfortable Wheatlys. And then he declared, *"It ends here!"*

The senator raised his eyebrows as if to urge Lane on.

"I've figured out a way to solve the problems of our criminal justice system. I've created a nonprejudicial system that will prevent liberals and thin-skinned lawmakers from allowing criminal defense strategies to revolve around intent, environment, mental deficiency, and God knows what else. A way to make these bastards fry for the horrific deeds they commit. No longer will they be able to blame it on broken homes or terrible things that happened in their childhood. No longer will they get off because jails are too crowded. Fuck them! Fuck them all! Put their sorry asses in jail and pull the switch! Hell, *I'll* pull the fucking switch!"

Lane wasn't accustomed to using such language. He looked over at Mrs. Wheatly. "I'm sorry, Jane."

Embarrassed by his outburst, he quickly rose from his chair and went for his coat in the foyer. The Wheatlys followed close behind.

"I'd better be going," he said abruptly. He grabbed his coat off the banister and made for the door.

"Where are you going, Mike?" the senator asked.

"Home," he said.

"Wait, Mike! What is it that you wanted me to do?" asked the senator.

Ashamed of his conduct and language, Lane had forgotten to ask the favor he had come for.

He opened the door and stood silhouetted against the stormy sky. The driving rain blew in and drenched the floor of the foyer.

He cleared his throat.

"I want you to get a legal reform on violent crime introduced in the Senate, Jeff. For me and for Tina and for all the Americans wondering whether they could be next."

Nodding, Wheatly said, "I'll talk to you tomorrow. Now go home and get some rest."

He patted Lane on the back and fought the wind to close the door behind him. This done, the senator turned to his wife and rolled his eyes. Clearly quite amused, he chuckled. "He's lost his fucking mind!" he said. He walked past his wife as though she were invisible and started up the stairs.

"What a fucking idiot," he mumbled to himself. "Change the system! Ha! What a nut!"

Leaning into the pelting rain, Lane hurried to his car. He wondered whether the senator—whom he knew to be a shrewd politician with cynical and self-centered tendencies—would help him.

Chapter Three

Lane dashed through the rain to his car and started the lonely drive home. It had been years since Tina's murder, but it seemed like it had happened only yesterday. The image of Tina's bloodied body stretched out on the driveway, illuminated by a lovers' moon, still haunted him daily. He often thought about that hideous evening—the full moon so calm and so beautiful, then, in an instant, their lives torn apart by unspeakable violence.

Lane knew that the tragedy of his wife's murder was repeated every day, all over the country. He thought about how the influence of judges and defense attorneys affected the outcome of trials and led to soft sentences and often to inappropriate defense strategies such as claims of temporary insanity.

Lane contemplated the notion of temporary insanity. "They're right," he thought. "They're nuts! Insane! No kidding … they shoot, stab, and mutilate people … they *must* be insane. All the more reason to lock them the hell up. I really don't care *why* they're insane once they've committed a crime … only how to stop them from committing another."

His headlights exaggerated the falling raindrops as he steered his car with his left hand draped over the wheel through dark tree-lined streets. As the windshield wipers slapped rhythmically, Lane reached down with his right hand and nervously flicked and fanned the pages of the immense judicial research document on the seat next to him. Now, after years of research, it was complete. The cover of the document read: "THE POINT GUARD."

Finally home, Lane parked his car in the driveway and then ran through the downpour to the front door. Before entering, he turned and surveyed his property and scanned the lighted street. This had been his routine since the murder of his wife. This particular night reminded him of Tina and what might have been if she were still alive. Tina had enjoyed lying in bed late at night, listening to a hard rain beating on the windows and on the leaves of the trees. After unlocking the front door, he stood uncomfortably still just outside his home. Tina had kept their home neat and friendly—all that was now gone. Since her death, Lane had put almost no effort into maintaining the property. The lawn needed mowing, paint flaked from the exterior, and the rugs and furniture were thick with dust. Newspapers, food wrappers, soda cans, and God knew what else littered the floors and tables—his home looked like a post party fraternity house. Their bedroom, however, remained as Tina had left it.

He hadn't slept in their bedroom since the night before Tina's murder. Framed photographs of her adorned the mantle and coffee table in the living room, and she stared at him through dusty glass every night as he lay sleepless on the old, worn sofa that she had owned before they were married. Their wedding album sat open on the seat under the bay window overlooking the uncut yard. Often, Tina would sit at that window and look through the album as she awaited Lane's arrival from work.

Now, Lane was usually unable to fall asleep until early morning, when, out of sheer exhaustion, he would manage to get a few hours of restless shut-eye. His diligence had produced a document that, if enacted and passed into law, might afford him and thousands like him the possibility of a peaceful night's sleep.

Lane's document, "The Point Guard," was his law—a just system for dealing with violent crime in America. It contained his understanding of how the law worked and how his new ideas would improve the current judicial system. The system involved reimagining the methods by which punishment was dispensed and maintained. Although Lane's plan followed the general course of the current system—the one that had been fostered and enacted by America's Founding Fathers—it also updated it and clarified gray areas as no other legal amendment had ever attempted. His system put justice in line with what the Constitution had been intended to do at the time of its inception hundreds of years ago. His was a system through which mandatory sentences would be issued without compromise. It was a system he thought brutally fair and nonprejudicial.

Lane reached inside and flicked on the inside and outside lights. He held his document tightly under his arm, and he peered cautiously into his house. His life had changed forever on that night of unimaginable violence. Like too many Americans, he found himself terrified in his own home. He painstakingly inspected the sad and lonely house. The inspection had become habitual, and it always ended in his and Tina's bedroom. On this particular evening, he stepped into the immaculate bedroom and stood at the foot of the bed. Looking around, Lane recalled some of the memories that the once warm and cozy room held. The trace of a smile formed on his tired face as he remembered Tina's playful antics. Her seductive smile and her need to be cuddled through the night remained fresh in his memory. They were memories that had made it impossible for him to sleep in their bed.

He sank to his knees. Exhausted, he rolled onto his side and clutched his document tightly to his chest. He gently rested his head on the soft carpet and stared at the wall. With the completion of the document and the prospect of help from the senator, it felt as though a weight had been lifted from him. For the first time in years, in a matter of moments and after a few deep breaths, he fell into a sound sleep at the foot of the bed.

It seemed to Lane like only minutes later that he was startled awake by the scream of a car horn cutting into his night's peace. He stumbled over his document as he rushed to the window. Peering out into the night from behind the shades, he saw that the street was empty and quiet. Seeing no sign of a car or commotion in either direction, he thought that perhaps he had imagined the sound. He staggered through the hall and down the stairs, along the way turning off all the lights he had left burning before he had collapsed on the bedroom floor. In the kitchen, he took an open can of flat soda from the refrigerator. The refrigerator light cut through the quiet darkness as he took one long sip and held the cold can up against his sweating forehead.

And again, the evening silence was broken by a burst from a car horn. Lane shuddered, and soda erupted onto his face and dripped to the floor. He ran to the front door and flung it open. He couldn't believe his eyes. There it was again. Its engine revved under the streetlamp, just where it had been on the night of the murder. It was the black BMW with three youths inside. They were laughing at him. Lane squinted, desperately trying to make out their faces. Exposed by the porch light, his heart pounding, he stepped outside. Daringly, yet still afraid, he made his way to the cobblestone walkway at the edge of the porch. As he fixed his bloodshot eyes on the car, he saw a gun barrel emerge from the front passenger window. Running along the walkway in front of the house, Lane saw the blank, staring face of the teenager who leveled the weapon at him. The jet-black Beamer's tires squealed and smoked like a dragster's as it pulled away from him. Lane continued his reckless dash toward the car, trying desperately to confirm the identities of the passengers and get a good look at the license plate number. Still burning rubber, the BMW approached another streetlamp near the end of Lane's driveway. Its interior brightened under the lamplight, and Lane saw, to his horror, that the kids inside were the same ones who had shot Tina. Dazed and confused, about fifteen feet from the driveway, Lane fell to the ground as the gunshots erupted again.

Sprawled helplessly on the walkway, Lane recognized the cadence of the gunfire and felt an overwhelming sense of déjà vu. Raising his head and looking toward the driveway, he realized the young thugs had not been shooting at him. Instead, he saw Tina being struck by the bullets, one violent impact after another; then she fell in slow motion to the ground only a few feet away. It was too painful to watch. Lane dropped his head onto the cold walkway and covered his face.

In a blinding flash of light, he awakened panting and drenched with sweat. Another nightmare. He sat up and propped himself up against the foot of the only bed he and Tina had ever owned. Closing his eyes and taking a deep breath, he realized that his battle had only begun.

Chapter Four

Gathering his wits, Lane blinked rapidly and focused on the Point Guard document that lay next to him. He picked it up and laid it across his lap. He drummed his fingers on its cover and stared off into space. He wondered whether his years of work on judicial reform would bring significant and much-needed change to what he felt was a failing judicial system.

Lane had been stunned and deeply hurt when Tina's murderers were issued such soft sentences. He had then become convinced that it was not only his obligation, but also his mission, to prompt a change in the system that had failed him.

He had spent troubled days and sleepless nights trying to determine how he could make a difference. Then, only two weeks after the trials, Lane had been driving on a busy downtown street when his mind began to wander. Temporarily oblivious to his surroundings, he had been pulled over for running a traffic light. He had been issued a ticket and appeared in court a couple weeks later, where he fought unsuccessfully to have the points associated with the violation removed from his driving record. On his way home from the courthouse, it had occurred to him that, although the ticket had been salt in his recent wounds, the point system for the traffic violation seemed very efficient and fair. His experience with Tina's trials, the timely traffic stop, his experience in accounting, and his master's degree in criminal law all converged to serve as his inspiration for writing "The Point Guard." The principle of the point system used in Pennsylvania traffic law became the backbone of his research and the foundation on which he would build his legal reform.

Lane learned during his research that the current system utilized a multitude of measures to determine prison sentences. Those measures included federal guidelines, judges' discretion, criminal intent, circumstances, mandatory minimums, and many others. He felt that the current structure on violent offenses left too much gray area between supposed mandatory minimum sentences and what an individual judge might deem an appropriate punishment. Lane believed that this ambiguity was one of the contributing factors in the soft sentencing of Tina's killers. He wanted radical change in courtroom procedure and concrete, predictable punishment for the convicted. But he recognized that his reform needed to be embraced by the current wardens of the American judicial system if it was to be adopted. It needed to be constitutional, so he was careful not to try to change the system entirely. He did write radical reform on violent crime, but he did so ingeniously.

The law described in Lane's document was based on a point system similar to the Pennsylvania motor vehicle system, which issues points against drivers who have broken traffic laws. His general idea was to give every violent crime on the books a published point value. Serious violent crimes such as murder were given the highest point value, while lesser crimes such as armed burglary were given a lower point value. Every person would start with a zero point balance representing indisputable innocence. A person's criminal account could not be "active" until a violent crime had been committed, reviewed, and tried and a verdict reached. A guilty verdict would result in a criminal account being activated and assigned an account number. A verdict finding the accused innocent would mean that no account would be activated. Once a criminal account exceeded a predetermined point limit, the convicted criminal would automatically go to prison. The length of incarceration would depend on how much the predetermined incarceration limit was exceeded. The predetermined point limit in Lane's system was 100 points.

Anyone whose account exceeded 100 points would go to prison immediately. In Lane's system, murder carried a 1,000-point penalty—leaving the murderer 900 points over the 100-point limit. Every 10 points beyond the 100-point limit would equal one nonnegotiable year of incarceration. In other words, if someone were to be found guilty of murder, he or she would receive a ninety-year, nonnegotiable prison sentence. Any convicted murderer could also choose to be executed. Any person with more than 2,000 points against them, however, would be executed within twenty-four hours of a guilty verdict.

There were no appeals, paroles, or federal sentencing guidelines in Lane's system—only published point values assigned to violent criminal offenses. His reform was focused solely on violent offenses such as murder, rape, and battery. He listed each of more than a dozen violent offenses, detailed each offense, and listed the points associated with it. If the accused were convicted, they would be issued their points and serve the full sentence without the possibility of parole. All issued points, however, would remain on file in the Point Guard judicial records for the life of the convicted, even after a sentence had been served in full. Nonetheless, after a convicted violent offender had served their time and had no other violent crime convictions for one year, their "active" account would be reduced to zero.

In the document, Lane illustrated how the system would function by describing various scenarios. In these examples, Lane examined actual cases in which the suspects had been tried and found guilty of their violent crimes under the current system, and he explained how his system would have applied to them. He also detailed how the Point Guard system would have ensured a fair and just trial in each case. His experiences during the trials of Tina's murderers had helped him understand how to prevent trials from being swayed by slick lawyers or high-profile media coverage. In short, Lane believed that he had developed a plan that would reform the judicial process on violent crime in the complex American legal system.

One of Lane's many sample cases was that of Robert Moore, who had broken into the home of an elderly man in the middle of the night. The elderly man lived on the same street as Moore and was known to Moore to the extent that they routinely exchanged hellos when passing on the street. Moore was unemployed and addicted to drugs and alcohol. He spent much of his time in the street observing the day-to-day habits of his neighbors—in particular, he had noticed the older gentleman's monthly trips to the bank to cash his Social Security checks.

One night, in desperate need of cash to feed his ravenous addictions, Moore waited until past midnight and then broke into the elderly man's home. The man was a light sleeper and was awakened by the noises. He confronted the thief. Moore beat him and stole his Social Security money. Soon afterward, Moore was arrested by the police and identified by the victim. Moore was eventually charged and found guilty of breaking and entering, assault and battery, and unarmed robbery.

Under the Point Guard system, points would have been issued to Moore in the following manner: for breaking and entering, 50 points; for battery, 100 points; and for unarmed robbery, 100 points.

The total number of points issued to Moore's account would have been 250. With a predetermined legal limit of only 100 points, Moore's account would be "overdrawn" by 150 points. At one year of prison time for every 10 points over 100, Moore would therefore receive a mandatory sentence of fifteen years in prison—without parole.

If Moore had points in his account previous to this criminal encounter— points that had not passed the one-year limit—they would have been added to the points his new crimes had accrued, thus lengthening his sentence further.

In this example, it was assumed that Moore had started with a zero balance. During his detailed research, however, Lane learned that, in most instances of violent crime, the convicted felon would likely have points already accumulated in his or her account. Under Lane's system, Moore would actually have had a total of 50 points in his active account due to prior convictions that had not yet passed the one-year limit. The previous points would have been charged for breaking and entering (50 points).

Under Lane's law, Moore's total points would have been 300 after his most recent conviction. Now he would have a 200-point overdraft, which, at one year of prison time for each 10 points, would equal twenty years of nonnegotiable prison time with no chance of parole.

Lane believed that the Point Guard system would have a greater deterrent effect than the current system because repeat offenders would know that once they reached the point limit, they would be going to prison—period. In another example, a criminal had 95 points in his active account—just 5 points from the limit—and was arrested and convicted of battery in a barroom fistfight. In this example, the convicted was given 100 points for the offense, which meant that he would have had to serve nine and a half years, since the total of his criminal points now equaled 195. One feature of Lane's system was that if criminals have a considerable number of accumulated points in their account, they would have to be careful to avoid violent behavior—otherwise, they would find themselves doing substantial jail time for relatively minor offenses such as a barroom fist fight, if it overdrew their account.

Lane's program combined a hard-nosed approach to punishment with a commonsense flair aiming to deter and incarcerate violent criminals. After years of studying the relevant statistics, Lane had concluded that most crime—especially violent crime—that sapped the current system's resources was committed by repeat offenders, not first-timers. Thus, besides acting as a deterrent for repeat offenders, his system would also serve as a clear signal to anyone who contemplated violent activity. Offenders would know exactly how long they would be imprisoned, if caught, before they even committed a crime. The system would be published and posted for all to see. It would also be required study in the country's schools, and an understanding of it would be necessary for graduation. This would make its provisions well known to the youth of America.

Lane knew that it would certainly be too expensive to enforce the program retroactively. Instead, whatever punishments the previous system had ordered would be carried out. However, if a released convict had not served the maximum sentence—if, for instance, he were paroled or released for good behavior—he would begin his freedom with an active account balance of 100 points and would be one offense away from returning to jail and serving the entire sentence. This, in Lane's estimation, was the best way to treat anyone who had not served his or her full sentence in the current system.

As Lane wrote the real-life scenarios into his document, he often found himself sickened by the tragic reality of his work. But he continued to write, determined to change the system. In one case study, two men had raped and murdered a young woman in a mall parking lot. Police apprehended the pair after they were spotted driving the woman's car several days later. During the trial, the assailants testified that their intention had been only to steal the car, but the situation had escalated when the victim resisted. Their attorney concocted a defense based on this and was able to negotiate reduced charges. Both men were found guilty: one served eleven years and was paroled; the other served thirteen years and was released. One of them had a criminal record of violent behavior, while the other had none and was a first-time offender. If they had been convicted under the Point Guard system, the first-time offender would have been sentenced to life with an option to be executed, and the other would have been executed within twenty-four hours of his conviction.

Lane had designed his system to be managed by an appointed official who would be known as the "Point Guard." This person would be the highest-ranking officer of violent criminal justice in America and would soon probably be regarded as the most influential servant of the law-abiding majority. Lane's system was designed to operate seamlessly within the current system—but exclusively with the point system. The Point Guard would take his or her place at the table alongside the current Supreme Court justices. The Point Guard would oversee the implementation, administration, and enforcement of the new violent crimes point system in every courtroom in the country. Every judge in America would be educated in the point system. Each of them would be appointed the "point guardian" of his or her own courtroom, whether it be county, state, federal, or Supreme Court. The Point Guard's tribunal of justices and their network would oversee all judges' actions. The network of judges—or point guardians—would be appointed by the tribunal to ensure that the system was administered consistently throughout the land. This network would be composed of judges that existed in the current system. But because of built-in efficiencies that would utilize the current system's resources, it would require no additional personnel. This would save taxpayers from having to fund the reforms.

There would also be significant changes to rules of procedure in the trials themselves. Perhaps one of the biggest changes—inspired by Lane's experiences during Tina's murder trial—involved when and how evidence was introduced to a jury. Unlike the current system—in which evidence was often introduced by slick, fast-talking defense attorneys who twisted fact into incomprehensible fiction for impressionable juries—the new system would make considerable use of video recordings.

Unlike high-profile cases today, which allow cameras and reporters into the courtroom, the entire trial would be held behind closed doors. The hearing would be open only to the attorneys, witnesses, plaintiffs, and accused and would introduce all of the evidence. The point guardian would oversee all activities in the courtroom, and the trial would be videotaped from beginning to end.

After the completion of prosecution and defense arguments, the videotape would be edited by a guardian board to show only the pertinent evidence. It would then be submitted to the jury, which would have been chosen by lottery. A three-person legal guardian board would edit from the videotape any remarks that were ordered stricken from the court's record and any testimony that had been ruled objectionable. The guardian would focus on the facts and remove the personalities that could sway a juror.

Another change in procedure concerned past criminal activity. Often, there are disputes about whether information regarding past activities or criminal conduct should be allowed in a new trial. In the current system, attorneys for both sides make their arguments on this subject, which bogs down trials and backs up the system. The Point Guard system would eliminate such delay tactics, thereby keeping the trial speedy and fair.

Lane wanted to build a system that was fair to both the victim and the accused. All the same, he knew that past behavior was certainly an indication of an accused's propensity to commit crimes. So, to protect the rights of the victim, it would be admitted into testimony that the accused had either a history of lawlessness or one of law-abiding behavior. To protect the rights of the accused, the *nature* of his or her past crimes would not be exposed. Only their life point total would be made known without revealing why the points had been issued.

Lane believed this would create fairness and openness for all involved. In a murder case, for example, a jury might learn that the accused had a life total of 215 points, but they would not know for what crimes these points had been issued. This would protect the victim because it would show the jury that the accused has had convictions for serious crimes and would protect the accused because it would not disclose the nature of those crimes.

Remembering what had happened to Tina, Lane had written the section on juvenile reform with a heavy heart. He had decided that any youth over the age of fifteen would be tried as an adult, period. Any youth under fifteen would be tried as a juvenile using the same procedures as those used for adults. Juveniles, however, would not be incarcerated with adults, and with the exception of cases of extreme violence such as murder or rape, points would be issued at fifty percent of their normal value.

Lane wanted his system to speed the judicial process and allow court cases to be seen and heard in a fraction of the time it currently took. A jury would be able to hear an entire trial—one that currently takes months—in just a few days. Shorter trials might last only hours. The money saved in this way, added to that raised through other capital-generating programs within the system, would go toward funding the system and its reconstruction. More prisons would need to be built because, under Lane's law, far fewer convicts would be released. Programs would be instituted to generate the funds necessary to keep the system financially feasible.

Lane designed his system to run on the sweat and toil of prisoners. Prisons would be retrofitted to have full-blown manufacturing capabilities. Lane considered that, with economic globalization, products were being imported from countries that did not support American policy but that *did* accept American financial and humanitarian aide. These countries, as well as those not in "favored" status with the United States, would experience stiff competition from the Point Guard system's manufacturing power. The Point Guard program would put inmates to work in order to pay for their incarceration as well as to help level the economic landscape in regard to lower overseas labor rates. The prisons would manufacture components at cost that had previously been made overseas with cheap labor. These components would then compete effectively with imported products from non-favored countries in the U.S. market. This program would also teach inmates marketable skills for life after prison.

Lane had designed the Point Guard system to ensure the incarceration of violent outlaws while removing the financial burden for the reform from the taxpayers' shoulders.

Chapter Five

At 6:45 on the morning following Lane's visit to the Wheatlys' home, Senator Wheatly was aboard the jam-packed Philadelphia-to-Washington Metroliner, bound for his DC office. Wedged into his seat and hidden behind his newspaper, he went unnoticed by the other commuters. The train gently rocked from side to side as it sped down the rails. Leafing through the pages, the senator paid little mind to the article about the over publicized murder retrial that was now being held—a judicial farce involving a good-looking, greedy young man who had murdered his wealthy father. The nineteen-year-old had purchased a handgun at local gun shop and had written out a murder plan to assassinate his father. During the trial, he admitted that he had gone into the living room and shot his father multiple times as the man sat watching television. Dozens testified that the hardworking parent had provided his son with a quality upbringing and luxuries that few ever get to experience, but those privileges had proved too little to satisfy the young man. He had been tried for murder, and after weeks of deliberation, the jury had deadlocked. The testimony of character witnesses showed everyone who had followed the trial that the defense had been completely fabricated. The defense had argued that the father had mentally and sexually abused his son for as long as the young man could remember. It was a defense that had yet to be proved and one that could not be refuted by the dead father.

Lane sat at his kitchen table sipping his early-morning black coffee. The sun shone through the back window and fell warm and soft on his lap as he read the newspaper. Unlike the senator, Lane's attention was fixed on the article about the murder retrial. Questioning the outcome of the first trial, he thought, "They couldn't find this punk guilty?" He was amazed. "He shot his dad and then sat around watching TV for a couple of hours before being discovered!"

He shook his head in disgust. "That jury must have been be filled with morally bankrupt morons! That's premeditated murder! Two thousand points! Execute him!" Lane was further repulsed by the basis for his defense.

"How could the jury see it as anything other than premeditated? He bought the gun in advance, wrote down the way he would carry out the deed, *did it*, and then went on a shopping spree with daddy's money. He could have moved out if he couldn't bear to live there—he wasn't a little kid. He could have accused his father of the abuse or put it all behind him by leaving and never returning—that is, if his claims were true. But if he had done that, he wouldn't have been able to afford the opulent lifestyle to which he'd become accustomed. He was *spoiled!*"

Lane thought about how the Point Guard system would have changed such an absurd outcome and eliminated the need for a retrial in this type of high-profile trial. His program was designed to take the instrument of justice away from the news media and away from the crafty lawyers who sought fame, spewed rhetoric, and cranked out outrageous bills. His program would put the judicial system in the care of people who could tell fact from fiction, legal process from grandstanding.

The senator's train rolled to a stop at Washington's Union Station. He stepped onto the platform alongside hundreds of other commuters who, shoulder to shoulder, inched their way in a massive wave toward the concourse. He worked his way to the outer fringe of the wave, where there was more room to move, and was approached by a homeless woman. Her unwashed bangs were matted to her wrinkled forehead; her tattered clothes were stained and smelled of urine. Her nose and mouth were black with soot; her bowed head was wrapped in a rag tied loosely beneath her chin. Years of suffering showed in her eyes. She smiled at the senator and extended a trembling hand.

"Please, sir, can you spare any change?"

The senator ignored the tiny woman and fixed his eyes beyond her as he tried to rush past. But because of the thick crowd, he and the woman were forced to move side by side in the direction of the concourse, like flotsam on a rolling sea.

Again, she begged, "Please ... please, sir, a quarter?" This time, the senator glanced down at the woman for barely an instant. Unsettled by her appearance, he turned and dashed through the turnstiles into the concourse leaving her behind. Never looking back, he headed toward the street, where his aide, Anthony, awaited his arrival.

The old woman stood unsteadily, jostled by the morning rush at the side of the turnstile. She watched sadly, as the senator drifted out of sight. Slowly, she turned and resumed her begging.

Anthony—a tall, good-looking young man—stood beside the senator's idling limousine, about twenty-five yards from the station entrance. He smiled anxiously.

"How was your trip, Senator?"

"When will they clean up this fucking city?" Wheatly answered. "Damn bums! Where the hell were you? I thought you were going to meet me at the train."

"Well ... yes, sir ... but ... I brought the car, and ..."

"Never mind. Let's go."

"Yes, Senator." Anthony seemed to cower a little as he held the door for the senator and then scurried around to the driver's seat. In a moment, they were cruising down Pennsylvania Avenue. After several minutes of silence, the senator spoke.

"Look, Anthony, I'm sorry for jumping all over you back there."

"I know ... it's okay," Anthony responded.

"What's my schedule look like for the rest of the week?"

Anthony spent most of every week in Washington minding the senator's itinerary. He screened all calls and slotted all activities. He had joined Wheatly's staff as an intern and now took care of all manner of things when the senator was at home in Pennsylvania or out of town.

"Well, sir, all day today you're at your private office. Tomorrow you're on Capitol Hill, and on Friday you have a publicity appearance."

The senator perked up. "Publicity! For what?"

Wherever there was an opportunity for good press, the senator was eager to attend. Anthony made sure to quell the senator's excitement before it advanced too far. "Uh ... Sorry, Senator, but it's not an opportunity you'll like. You'll be airing your views on that abortion doctor who was shot in the Midwest."

The senator shook his head and said, "Shit."

"Oh, and don't forget that you have a dinner tomorrow night with the president of the Textile Union," Anthony added.

The senator looked out the tinted window at the majestic buildings lining Pennsylvania Avenue and continued to shake his head. Although he was really a liberal Democrat, his views seemed to waver—he always favored the most popular and most lucrative side of every issue.

"What's with these fucking people anyway? Why shoot a doctor, for God's sake? He aborted a child from a woman who didn't want it. Hell, maybe the kid was going to be born with a defect or something. Maybe the mother had medical problems of her own. God, I hate addressing this subject." He chuckled. "Shit, I'd probably get voted out of office and be out one hell of an income if people knew what I really thought."

Anthony glanced at the senator in the rearview mirror.

"Anthony, I want you to phone my wife and tell her I need her here in DC tomorrow for the dinner with the textile people."

Anthony seemed annoyed. "What for? I thought I ..."

"Don't think, Anthony. Just phone her and send a car for her."

Anthony sheepishly acknowledged the senator's demand as he pulled up in front of the senator's private office building. The senator kept several offices, one in Harrisburg, one at a Senate office building, and a private office where he conducted both official and personal business.

"Yes, sir. Kathy has a detailed copy of your schedule. Your lunch will be brought in to you at 12:15. Is there anything else before I park the car?"

"No, thank you."

The senator stepped out of the car and ascended the weatherworn marble stairs to the Victorian row house that had been converted into his opulent offices. Anthony, clearly troubled, stomped on the gas pedal and made an abrupt departure.

Senator Wheatly swung open one of the eight-foot oak double doors at the crest of the wide staircase. His office was elegant, with high vaulted ceilings and a collection of fine art. Antique furniture sat atop polished floors and expensive oriental rugs. Inside, Kathy Nolan, his secretary, greeted him with a smile.

"Good morning, Senator."

"Hello, Kathy."

In fact, Kathy wasn't just a secretary; she was a political veteran. She had been an assistant to four different senators over twenty-eight years. At forty-nine, she was striking—a redheaded beauty who was as professional as she was attractive. She knew more about politics and the inner workings of Washington than most politicians could ever hope to learn. Totally committed to her career, Kathy had never married nor had any children. This was a pity, for she had all the attributes that would have made for a wonderful mother and wife—but perhaps these were the same attributes that had made her the best at what she did. She was intelligent, honest, generous, and sincere; she spoke from the heart, didn't mince words, and was never intimidated into withholding her opinion.

Over the years, she had received quite a bit of unsolicited attention from many senators and congressmen, but she had withstood their advances. Leaving aside certain rumors that stemmed from the beginning of her career, it was said she had never succumbed to any politician's advances—noble or otherwise. Those rumors, dated to the late 1960s, involved the Kennedy family, but Kathy had never confirmed nor denied them.

Kathy was, without a doubt, the most indispensable member of the senator's staff. Advisers on every conceivable issue surrounded him—experts in their fields wielding MBAs and PhDs—but it was Kathy to whom he most often turned for an experienced opinion before he made a final decision. She had seen it all over the years: Vietnam, Watergate, Iran-Contra—all of it.

Over the years, Kathy had learned to keep her professional relationships just that—professional. So, as a rule, she expressed neither approval nor disapproval of the senator's lifestyle or choices and kept her personal and professional lives separate.

"Can I get you a cup of coffee, Senator?" she asked cheerily.

"Sure, Kathy. Thanks."

Pouring him a cup, she said, "Your schedule is on your desk, sir. Your accountant has called twice this morning but didn't want to leave a message." She handed him the coffee. "He did say that he wanted to make an appointment to see you this week. I told him that you have a very busy schedule and you'd get back to him."

"That's fine, Kathy. If he calls again, put him through. He's been going through a tough time. He can't seem to get past his wife's death. She was murdered, you know."

He turned his back to Kathy, rolled his eyes, and muttered, "The sorry shit."

Kathy recalled the incident. "My God, the poor man. I remember when that happened. What a horrible thing to have to live with." She looked thoughtful for a moment and added, "I don't recall ever meeting Mr. Lane."

They walked into Wheatly's colossal private office. The senator sat at his desk in an imported Italian leather wing chair. It looked almost like a throne. His mahogany desk was antique, and behind it stood floor-to-ceiling handmade mahogany bookshelves. The floor was of dark marble, and between the bookshelves hung an original van Gogh.

"No," he said as he took a sip of his coffee, "I don't believe you ever have met Mike."

Lane sat on the edge of a sticky vinyl chair at his kitchen table. He leaned over a half-filled cup of coffee, nervously turning it and staring into the steaming black pool within. He realized that he had done all he could for now and that he needed the senator's help to continue. He entertained the thought of calling the senator's office a third time. While he waited, he couldn't help but contemplate what might be ahead for him and his Point Guard document. He knew that getting it to a vote in Congress would be a monumental task, but he was prepared to face the lengthy process. He truly believed that the Point Guard system would become law and that Tina's murder would be avenged.

He soon grew so impatient that he felt compelled to try to reach the senator once again. Hesitantly, he lifted the receiver and dialed. His stomach fluttered as the phone rang. One ring ... two rings ... He stood and paced, thinking that it might be overbearing to call so many times in one morning. Three rings ... four rings ... "Hello, Senator Jeff Wheatly's office."Lane's heart pounded, each beat echoing in his ears and preventing him from thinking clearly. He cleared his throat.

"Uh ... Mike Lane for Senator Wheatly, please."

"Hold one moment, Mr. Lane. The senator is expecting your call."

The soft Muzak leaking through the phone made the wait nearly intolerable as Lane tapped nervously on the rim of his coffee cup. Finally, Wheatly answered.

"Hey, Mike, how's it going?'

Relieved that the senator had finally taken his call, Lane relaxed just a bit.

"Good, Jeff. Thanks. I'm glad I got you."

"Must be important, pal. Kathy says that this is the third time you've called this morning. Does it have something to do with your visit last night?"

"Yes, it does. I want to show you what I've been working on for the last few years."

"Well, what is it Mike?"

"I'd prefer not to tell you over the phone, Jeff. I'd rather talk in person."

Immediately impatient, the senator's attitude hardened.

"Mike, I'm a busy man. I need to know specifically what you want to talk about. Is it a secret or something?"

"It's not really a secret, Jeff, but I do have to see you face to face."

"Listen, Mike, if I don't know what it's about, I don't know how much time to give you!"

"I don't know how much time I'll need with you, Jeff. Maybe I could meet with you later in the evening, when you're not quite so busy."

Trying not to annoy the senator further, Lane found himself pleading for even a brief amount of time. But the senator was obviously trying to distance himself from Lane's request.

"Has this got anything to do with that … system of justice you were talking about at the house?" asked Wheatly. "If it is, I can give you a contact that can help you out."

"Jeff, I don't want a contact! I want *you* to see this! How about tomorrow night?" He paused, but there was no response. "I'll come down to Washington."

The senator seemed to be pondering Lane's request for a moment. Secretly, he enjoyed this game. He savored making people squirm. He turned his fat-cat leather chair from left to right and back again, watching the ceiling spin above him. He took a deep breath, batted his eyes, and, with the beginnings of a satisfied grin, said, "No."

Lane fell back into his chair. He wiped his dry lips and pushed his coffee cup away. "Jeff … I need your help."

"I'm sorry, Mike." Wheatly leaned across his desk and shuffled through the lone, short stack of paper at its center. "But I've got a very busy schedule this week—union dinners, abortion debates, God knows what else."

Despondent, Lane made no effort to respond. He just sat. Uncomfortable with the silence, the senator finally made him an offer.

"Look, Mike, let me see how the week goes. I'll try to call you later in the week. All right?"

The senator had made the battered man feel as though he should justify his behavior. "Yeah, Jeff. Thanks. I'm sorry, but it's been torture without Tina. This thing that I've been working on for all these years gives me a feeling of hope. I'd really appreciate you calling me later this week." Lane nodded as though agreeing with himself.

The senator half-heartedly listened to Lane as he said good-bye, and then he began his day.

Chapter Six

The senator greeted his first guests that morning at 9:45 to discuss the school lunch program in his home state of Pennsylvania and the impact that federal mandates would have on the state budget. The senator's public position on the issue was that he was in favor of whatever was best for the kids. His private position favored anything that would get him votes, regardless of nutrition or child welfare.

At eleven o'clock, he met with the director of the National Endowment for the Arts and was persuaded to support its cause, ensuring millions of federal taxpayer dollars to protect, encourage, and finance film, dance, theater, and all other types of art. These funds would come from the pockets of hardworking Americans and be used to subsidize associations of artists, musicians, actors, and other entertainers.

The senator was easy to persuade regarding this cause—like many politicians on Capitol Hill, he too would have liked to be a part of the *real* entertainment business.

After his usual hour-and-forty-five-minute lunch break, the senator finished his day behind closed doors, discussing the issues of assault weapons and gun reform with representatives of the National Rifle Association. Although the senator appeared to take to heart the views of his constituents, he always supported the most powerful lobbies in the nation and voted in their best interest when required.

Near day's end, Senator Wheatly relaxed with his legs crossed on top of his desk. He asked Kathy through the intercom to get his wife on the phone. Moments later, Kathy buzzed him.

"Your wife is on line one, Senator."

Yawning after what he believed had been a long, hard day's work, he reached for the phone. Without so much as a hello, he began to speak.

"Jane, when you come down here on Thursday ..."

She interrupted him. "Down where, Jeff?"

"Here. To Washington," he said, speaking to her as if she were an idiot. "Where the hell do you think?"

"What in God's name for, Jeff?"

"For dinner!" Confused, he hesitated for a moment. "Didn't Anthony call you about Thursday night?"

"No," she responded. "I can't come down there Thursday, Jeff. You know my sister is coming in from Seattle."

He switched to a slightly sweeter tone. "Jane, honey, I *need* you here. We're meeting with the people from the Textile Union. They donate huge sums of money to my campaign!"

"But Jeff, I haven't seen Karen in nearly a year."

"So what? I haven't seen my mother in almost two! What the hell does *that* have to do with anything?"

"But Jeff, I want to see Karen. She's my sister! Can't you go without me? You're always ..."

Wheatly quickly spun his chair away from the open office door. He leaned forward with his elbows pressed against his knees and spoke with muffled rage through pursed lips and a clenched jaw.

"Listen, you live like a fucking queen without a worry in the world while I put myself on the hot seat every day. Day in and day out I deal with these assholes, kissing their asses so that they'll give us the financing we need."

He spun back around to face his desk and continued, "So you tell your fat-assed sister that you'll see her on Friday when you get home and stop acting like an ungrateful bitch."

He slammed down the receiver and, within a few seconds, calmed himself into appearing as though he hadn't lost his temper. After a single deep breath, he shouted through the doorway for Anthony. In a few moments, Anthony arrived to find the senator staring at him suspiciously.

"Yes, Senator? What can I do for you?"

The senator scratched his scalp. "Is there any good reason why you didn't tell Mrs. Wheatly about Thursday night's dinner like I'd asked you to?"

Anthony looked down at his feet. "Well, I thought that we … we …"

Like a father disciplining his son, the senator roared at Anthony before he could finish his answer. "We, we, we, what? What do you have, a fuckin' mouse in your pocket? Just do as you're told, do you understand?"

"Yes." Anthony responded meekly.

"Good. Pick up Mrs. Wheatly on Thursday. The dinner's at seven o'clock."

Without hesitation, he dismissed his timid aide.

Jane Wheatly struggled to cope with her tattered emotions. For years, she had endured countless volatile episodes with her husband. Her eyes now pooled and overflowed as tears trickled softly down her flushed face into a handkerchief she held tight and dabbed against her cheeks.

Over the years, Jane had come to despise politics and all that its trustees stood for. Over the same span, she had come to abhor the person her husband had become. She couldn't pinpoint the exact date she had begun to feel this way, but she knew that it was not long after he had been elected to public office. As the years progressed, her respect for him had waned as she witnessed him engage in increasingly unethical behavior.

Having risen to the top, her husband possessed considerable power—power gained through deceit, treachery, and blackmail. But she had never been tempted to confront him or reveal his true nature—and for good reason. A kind and considerate woman, Jane was afraid of what others might suffer if the world were to learn about the real man and his true behavior. She knew that her husband was the kind of spineless coward who would bring down everyone around him if it looked as though he were about to fall. She knew that he would do anything to save his own skin and that he would certainly turn on others to save himself. Jane would not have been able to live with the burden of the havoc this would create for the innocent families of the other ambitious men who ran in his circles. After all, she knew that sort of pain firsthand.

Healthy emotion and intimacy were long past in their relationship. Once a month or so, the senator demanded self-indulgent, essentially nonconsensual sex. Jane used to try to fight him off but had eventually learned to detach herself mentally and emotionally from the brief but agonizing act. She had grown callused to any horror she had once felt and generally absorbed the damaging blows of her abusive marriage.

Jane had been raised Catholic and was part of a generation that believed in sticking with a marriage under any circumstances. Her sense of loyalty and religious guilt kept her bound to an empty promise. And so she lived with her shame while never considering separation or divorce. Nevertheless, in the eyes of others, she always appeared to carry herself with grace and dignity.

At 6:30 on Thursday evening, the senator repeatedly looked at his watch as he paced his office floor, swirling some scotch in a crystal tumbler. Finally, Anthony opened the office door for Mrs. Wheatly. They had arrived only twenty minutes before the scheduled dinner date.

"Where the hell have you been?" Wheatly snapped. "We've got to get moving, or we'll be late!"

Before they could respond, the senator grabbed his wife by the arm, spun her around just inside the door, and briskly led her outside.

"I'll drive tonight, Anthony," he said. "Take the night off."

Just then, the office phone rang. After a moment of indecision, the senator returned to Kathy's desk and answered in an annoyed tone.

"Hello, Senator Wheatly speaking."

"Jeff, it's Mike."

"Yeah, Mike? I'm just leaving for dinner. What can I do for you?"

"Well … it's about our conversation the other day. I thought you were going to get back to me."

"Yeah, I *am*, Mike!" said the senator. Was this guy for real? "The week isn't over, for God's sake!"

"When can we talk?" pressed Lane.

"Look, Mike, I'll get back to you when I have the time. I have to go to a meeting. Good-bye!"

Giving Lane no opportunity to respond, the senator shook his head and hung up.

On the way to the restaurant, Jane asked her husband, "Have you been able to help Mike?"

The senator had been preoccupied with other thoughts and turned toward her, looking cross.

"What?"

She repeated her question.

While trying to keep his eye on the downtown traffic, the senator shook his head and shot Jane another irritated glance.

"Help Mike? He's my damned accountant. He keeps me out of tax trouble, and I pay him well for that. He thinks I'm his friend; *you* think I'm his friend … I'm not his friend! A pain in my ass is what he is to me! I've been nice to him over the years because of what happened to his wife—but hell, it's been years! Get over it! Shit, I feel sorry for him, but I'm not his psychologist. You know, he's called five times in under two days!"

Laughing, he grumbled to himself as if Jane weren't there. "He wants justice ... has a new plan ... an idea! As though he could make a difference. Like any one person could make a difference!"

He had stopped for a traffic light but still preferred to speak to the windshield than to Jane. "You've got to take what you can, while you can! Otherwise, someone else takes what you already have! *That's* how this game's played."

Sickened by his lack of compassion and his overwhelming cynicism, Jane turned and gazed out her window. She was sickened but not shocked. Nothing he said shocked her anymore.

They pulled up in front of Packy's, a high-end restaurant in the heart of DC. A valet weaved through a group of other guests at curbside and whisked away the senator's car. Inside, the restaurant's staff had gathered to greet the Wheatlys as if they were celebrities arriving on the red carpet. The senator and his wife were led with much deference to their corner table, bypassing a number of patrons who would have to wait considerably longer to be seated.

Carl Ziese, the president of the country's largest textile workers union, warmly greeted the Wheatlys. Ziese was fifty-two, a large, solid man with just a touch of gray in his otherwise jet-black hair and beard. Standing to greet the senator, Ziese extended his immense paw, which swallowed the politician's soft and petite hand as they shook. Ziese had a deep, deliberate, and scratchy voice.

"Senator! Mrs. Wheatly! How are you? I'd like you to meet my wife, Carla."

Carla greeted the Wheatlys with a sassy grin and offered her hand. "It's nice to meet you, Senator Wheatly. Hi, Mrs. Wheatly."

Jane smiled politely in return, but the senator only nodded his head almost indifferently. Carla was a thirty-year-old, blonde, blue-eyed bombshell and had been Mrs. Ziese for nearly two years. After exchanging pleasantries, the couples ordered drinks and dinner. Unexpectedly, two more guests then arrived at the table, placed two chairs behind Ziese, and sat against the wall. Surprised, the senator glanced inquisitively at Ziese.

"Oh, I'm sorry, these are two associates of mine," he said without breaking eye contact with the senator. "Mr. O'Mally and Mr. Cantoni. You could say that they're invaluable to me. They've accompanied me to many of my meetings as of late, but they won't be dinning with us."

Both ominous figures, O'Mally and Cantoni nodded and leaned forward to shake the Wheatlys' hands. They didn't utter a syllable.

For the most part, the dinner was uneventful and pleasant, even though the thugs sitting motionless and silent behind Ziese were a bit distracting to Jane. When coffee was about to be served, Mrs. Wheatly excused herself. After a nod from Ziese, Carla also excused herself and joined Jane as Cantoni escorted them to the ladies' room. Senator Wheatly slouched comfortably in his chair, dipped his finger into his after-dinner drink, and traced around the edge of the glass with his moist finger. He stared lazily at O'Mally. Then, the senator fixed his cocky eyes on Ziese.

"Okay, Ziese, why am I meeting with you and not one of your delivery boys?"

With a chilling look, Ziese eyeballed the senator. "Let's get down to business. You've been squeezing the union for some big money over the years. Now it's payback time. A certain bill's up for a vote in the Senate. If it's passed, it could seriously hurt our union. We want you to vote against it."

"And what bill might that be?" Wheatly asked.

"You know fucking well which bill! The North American Free Trade Agreement, NAFTA! That fucking bill will move thousands of union jobs to Mexico. We want you to spearhead an opposition campaign to kill this thing before it gains any momentum. We ain't gonna lose any jobs. That's why we have you in our pocket!"

Senator Wheatly leaned forward, grinning.

"Is that all? Hell, Ziese, why don't I kill the president's health plan and NASA while I'm at it?" He placed his drink on the table and stared at Ziese. "Who the fuck do you think you're talking to? I'm a United States Senator! Your fucking money doesn't buy you whatever you want! At best, all I can try to do is steer as much business to your union shops as I can … here in the States."

He shot a quick look over his shoulder; he was concerned about being overheard.

"If you people want me to meddle in international affairs," he lowered his voice, "it will cost you. A personal donation of, say, $250,000 should do it."

Ziese nodded to O'Mally, who immediately left to intercept Cantoni and the ladies before they returned. Settling comfortably into his chair, Ziese lit a long Cuban cigar as he appeared to digest the senator's statement. He sucked hard on the stogie and then released a horizontal mushroom cloud in the senator's direction. After a chilling moment of silence and another billowing puff of his cigar, Ziese made his intentions clear. His polite and deliberate manner disappeared as his eyes rolled slowly before locking onto the senator. He spoke as if they were standing in an alley discussing a mob hit.

"I'll tell ya who the fuck I think ya are: a fuckin' puppet! And I've got my hand right up your pansy ass! You'll do whatever I tell ya to do, or I'll turn ya inside out, ya little shit! The gravy train is in the station ... it's time for ya to pay for the ride. So I ain't givin' ya no quarter million bucks!"

Ziese pulled his napkin from his lap and placed it on the table. Returning to a polite manner, he pressed his tie against his shirt and added, "But don't worry, Senator. I won't turn the union books over to the Senate Ethics Committee. We wouldn't want to show them just how much money it takes to be a public servant. Let's face it, that wouldn't be good for anybody." He mashed his cigar out in the center of his dinner plate. "But don't you forget—I don't like to be pushed into making people cooperate. Now if you'll excuse me, Senator."

Ziese stood while the senator sat still and swallowed hard. His imposing figure loomed over the senator for a moment, and then he headed to the door to intercept his wife and Mrs. Wheatly, who were being guarded closely by O'Mally and Cantoni.

"It was a pleasure meeting you, Mrs. Wheatly," he said.

Ziese took his wife gently by the arm, and they left the restaurant, goons in tow.

After a hasty ending to their evening, the Wheatlys drove in silence to their suite at the Whitehall Inn. Jane knew that something was wrong but, not really caring what it was, asked him nothing. At 9:30, the senator phoned Anthony and asked him to drive Mrs. Wheatly back to Philadelphia. It was a long, tiring trip from Washington to Philly, but Jane had no say in the matter. In truth, she was pleased to be able to get away from her husband.

After Jane had left the suite, an uneasy feeling came over the senator. He sat in the dark and thought about the conversation he'd had with Ziese just before leaving the restaurant. Ziese had ties to organized crime, and Wheatly worried that he might have gone too far, might have pissed Ziese off. He thought the only way he could keep Ziese happy would be to do what he was told.

Unfortunately, agreeing to Ziese's request posed a grave problem for the senator. Only weeks before, he had expressed significant interest in the North American Free Trade Agreement and had been informed by the president that he would probably be called to head the campaign in favor of the agreement—the very campaign that Ziese wanted Wheatly to oppose.

Chapter Seven

At 9:00 AM on Friday, Lane paced like a nervous father-to-be through his untidy kitchen and dim dining room. Eager to get his plan rolling, Lane fought off panic and self-doubt. *Suppose the senator doesn't call today?* he thought. *Or Monday? Or the rest of the week? God, he's got to call.*

He expected the Point Guard system to be his revenge for Tina's murder and knew that he *must* get it into the hands of the right people. He knew that his long-time client was the best agent to promote his plan but feared that he might have been pushing the senator too hard. Nonetheless, he felt it imperative to press forward. He decided not to wait for the senator to call. Tentatively, he picked up the receiver and called the senator's office yet again.

"Hello, Senator Jeff Wheatly's office. How may I help you?"

Lane responded to Kathy as calmly as he could.

"Hi, this is Mike Lane. Is the senator in?"

"Yes, Mr. Lane," answered Kathy cheerfully. "Just hold on one second, sir."

Kathy couldn't help but wonder about the pain that Lane must still have felt at losing someone so close in such a horrible way. Although she was undoubtedly a strong woman, Kathy's compassion was unmatched. She buzzed the senator.

"Sir, Mr. Lane is on line one for you."

"Lose him!"

"Pardon me, Senator?" Kathy was confused by what she thought she had heard.

"I said lose him!" he said more forcefully. "I don't want to talk to him. I have enough to worry about."

Kathy sat speechless and stared at her desktop for a moment after she hung up. She had to gather her thoughts before picking up the phone again.

"Mr. Lane, I'm sorry, but the senator must have stepped out."

Lane held the phone tightly to his ear. "Do you expect him back today?"

Kathy hesitated.

"Er … Yes, he'll be in and out today and probably throughout the weekend."

Having worked her entire adult life in the political arena, Kathy was quite accustomed to disposing of unwelcome callers. This, however, felt much different. She instinctively knew that it involved an intimate personal matter, and for some reason, this made her extremely uncomfortable. With heartfelt concern, Kathy tried to soften the senator's sentiments.

"Maybe you should try to reach him around noon. He might stop in around then."

Lane sensed the truth behind Kathy's disheartened words but agreed to phone back later.

*　　*　　*　　*

Carl Ziese stood fifty-five stories above Chicago's streets, behind a barrier of plate glass. From a spacious conference room outfitted with dark cherry wood-paneled walls and a massive matching conference table, he stared out across the city. Beneath his feet was a polished black marble floor and above him, a crystal chandelier. He could see, about six blocks away, the national headquarters of the Textile Union. Spellbound, he couldn't help recalling his days of running the streets as a young man trying to work his way up to the position he held today. Becoming the president of one of the largest unions in the world was not an easy task. He sometimes regretted some of the actions he had taken to get where he was, but his hardness ensured that his regrets were few and short-lived, a common trait in men like him.

The door of the conference room swung open, pulling his attention away from the skyline and his memories. Mr. Barletto entered the room. He sat in a chair at the boss's end of the conference table and comfortably crossed his legs.

Mr. Barletto, the son of Italian immigrants, had been born in America. He was in his early fifties but had a lean physique; his hair was dyed an unnaturally dark black. His tanned fingers, wrists, and neck were adorned with gold and diamond jewelry, but he dressed casually in cuffed black knit slacks and a fitted black T-shirt. He wore expensive Italian loafers.

"Carl!" he said in a rough working-class accent. "How the hell ya been? Ya look like that young bride's been feedin' ya too much pasta."

Rubbing his belly with a wide grin, Ziese agreed.

"So, how's everybody?" Barletto asked.

"Everyone is fine, Mr. Barletto. How are your wife and family?"

"They're doing just great," Mr. Barletto said as he motioned for Ziese to be seated. "Little Anthony's in high school now, do ya believe that? He wants to play football, but his mother's makin' a lotta noise about that. Robert and his sister are gonna go to Italy for awhile, you know … to see the family." Smiling. "Hell, you don't want to hear all this. Sit down."

With Barletto seated at the head of the conference table, Ziese sat to Barletto's left with his back to the Chicago skyline. Looking over Ziese's shoulder toward the city, Barletto lit a cigar. He offered one to Ziese, who gladly accepted.

"You know, Carl, I remember when I was just a kid, standing here next to my papa." He gestured toward the sky, making the sign of a cross. "God rest his soul. He and I used to look out over the city for hours. He knew what was going on in every building. I remember that one day he said, 'This city will be yours someday, son.' Damn if he didn't make sure I got it. I'd like to pass it on to my sons one day."

He sucked on his cigar and blew a swell of smoke to the ceiling.

"Taking care of business … that's what I do." He waved his cigar in Ziese's direction. "How about you, Carl? Have you been taking care of business?"

"Yes, sir, Mr. Barletto, I have."

Barletto smiled and leaned toward Ziese, offering him the flame of a diamond-studded lighter. Ziese bent toward the flame and lit his cigar.

"So what's goin' on with that pissant Wheatly?" asked Barletto.

"He tried to play the big shot, like you said he might. The little shit told me that it would cost us a quarter million." Grinning, he blew smoke toward the ceiling. "I straightened him out. I'm sure he'll see it our way."

Barletto shook his head and snickered. "He's a piece of fuckin' work. They all are. These crooked politicians are so predictable: they accept our money and then think they're doing us favors. He's in the Senate because I wanted him there. I paid his way with blood money—*my* blood money."

Bounding out of his chair, Barletto walked over to the window and looked through his own reflection at the overcast city. "Unless we remind these guys," he said, "they forget that we own them. From the minute they take our money, *we own them*. They think they make policy. We paid the money!" He raised his voice. "*We* make the fuckin' policy!"

He laughed and turned to face Ziese. "That little fuck actually thinks he's in control! You made his position clear, right?"

Ziese remained seated, with his hands folded comfortably over his stomach. He slowly nodded his head, now half enshrouded in cigar smoke.

"Good! That's good," Barletto nodded his head and laughed again. "They got the balls to call us 'organized crime.' Look at the organization *they* got. They stick it up the public's ass and then give themselves a raise. They set policy, but they ain't gonna live by it. They take hundreds of thousands—even millions—from special interest groups who are supposed to be legit and line their pockets. And they call *us* organized crime! At least we got the balls to admit what we are—the Mafia. They call themselves the fuckin' *Senate*." He bit his cigar and looked at the ceiling. "That little rat bastard. What good is he to me if he doesn't do what I ask?"

Barletto slowly walked along the windows, then around the conference table back in Ziese's direction. Directly across from his lieutenant, he stopped. He slammed his palm down on the table with a noise like a thunderclap and pointed the cigar in his other hand at Ziese.

"Carl, make sure that Wheatly runs the opposition campaign to the NAFTA bill. *Make him cooperate!*"

Ziese approved of Barletto's style. He stood, walked around the table, and hugged his boss. Their stogies dangled between their teeth as they parted company. Nothing more needed to be said.

"Senator, it's the president's office on line two."

"Thanks, Kathy. Put it through."

"How are you, Jeff?" said the voice on the line.

"Very well, Mr. President, thank you. And you?"

"I'm fine, Jeff. I just wish I could get more support from Congress. It looks like it's going to take quite a bit of persuading to get some of these deals through. But I know I can count on you and your continued support. The last time we spoke, you pledged your support for the NAFTA campaign. Well, congratulations, Senator! I'm putting you in charge of it! The bat's in your hand."

Wheatly's stomach began to ache as the president continued.

"You're the right man for the job, Jeff. I want you to garner support among key Democrats and help me gain some momentum on this thing. Eventually, we'll get the rest of Congress to follow suit. My staff and I are going to write up an agenda with the details. When I have a clearer view of the whole picture, I'll get back to you. After that, there will be a press conference to announce you as the committee leader for the NAFTA program.

"Now go get 'em, Senator!" The president sounded enthusiastic. "Let's get this thing done!"

"Uh ... Mr. President ... I'm not sure that this is a campaign I'd be interested in running. It seems that I ..."

"Listen, Senator." The president's tone was now forbidding. "You *will* do this. You've already given me your word, and you already have a relationship with the Textile Union. We're going to need that relationship because, sure as the sun shines, they're going to oppose the NAFTA bill, and we're going to need you to make them feel that everything will be all right."

The senator winced. If the president only knew how much the union opposed NAFTA! If he only knew what they were willing to do to the senator if he didn't vote against it!

"You're my man, Jeff; you know that. There is no backing out of this, like it or not. There's no one in politics who can press an issue like you. And that's why you're going to do it for me! Head up this campaign successfully, and you move up the ladder, make it to the next stage. Bail on me, and your political life will get rocky ... at least as long as I'm in office. Do we understand each other?"

As though his mouth were filled with razor blades, the senator was afraid to utter a sound. By leading the campaign—going against Ziese's warning—he'd be walking a high wire without a net. But Wheatly had no choice but to go along with the president, at least for the time being.

"You can count on me, sir," he said reluctantly.

He hung up the phone and prepared to leave his office. For the first time in his political career, he realized that he'd found himself firmly in the center of a lose-lose predicament. Whichever route he chose, the consequences were dire. If he held true to his commitment to the president, he would face a potentially violent response from the union. If he refused to head the committee for the president's NAFTA campaign, he would have to deal with the president's threats. Of course, his biggest concern was for his life, which the union was very capable of taking, if he were to support NAFTA. Therefore, he decided that he would focus on extricating himself from his promise to the president.

The senator's relationship with the union had begun early in his career. He had encountered Mr. Barletto at various political functions—in those days, Barletto could often be found lobbying for the union's cause in Philadelphia as well as in Chicago and other major cities throughout the country. After several meetings, Barletto had convinced Wheatly—a city council member at the time—to run for the Senate with the support of the union. It had been common knowledge that Barletto was tied to organized crime, but Jeff Wheatly's desire to move up the political ladder had been so strong that he had allowed Barletto to befriend and sponsor him.

Within months, Wheatly had accepted nearly $200,000 in legitimate campaign donations from Barletto and his associates and had been promised that his path to the Senate, to the governor's mansion, and possibly even to the Oval Office, would be paved in due time. In addition to the legal contributions, Barletto had illegally forwarded $200,000 in cash to Wheatly, which had not been reported to the IRS. In other words, the Barletto family now owned Wheatly.

Less than two years from his first meeting with Barletto, Jeff Wheatly had become Senator Wheatly, and the Textile Union had become as strong in Philadelphia as it was in Chicago. Senator Wheatly had taken great pains to ensure the union the lion's share of government contracts and to persuade private industry to deal with the union in Pennsylvania. For his part, the senator received $50,000 cash per month, which was delivered to a trash can beside his house by a mob-run garbage disposal company.

Familiar with the gear-grinding motion of political process, the senator knew that time was on his side. Perhaps he even had enough of it. The president would have to organize an agenda and staff before he would publicly name Senator Wheatly as NAFTA's committee leader. Wheatly was sure by that time he could concoct a plan to have himself discharged from his duty to the president.

"I'm going to lunch," he said as he walked past Kathy's desk.

Her phone rang. Before Wheatly could make it out the door, Kathy raised the receiver and gestured in his direction. "Sir, it's Mike Lane again."

The senator shot her a disgusted look and continued out without speaking. Kathy was disturbed by the senator's reaction and felt he had put her on the spot again.

"I'm sorry, Mr. Lane," she said. "You just missed him … he just stepped out."

Lane was at a loss. "Uh … it seems as though Jeff is avoiding me," he said. "Do you have any suggestions as to when … a … when … it's a good time to …?"

"He's a very busy man, Mr. Lane," Kathy responded uneasily. "Shall I try to have him phone you?"

"No … no … never mind."

Lane hung up the phone. He was sitting at the cluttered desk in his home office. He had often worked at home on weekends before Tina's murder and had spent as much time with her as possible.

Lane had started his CPA business the day he received his accounting degree. Tina had never doubted that he could turn a one-man business into a thriving firm. She stood steadfast by his side, encouraging him every step of the way. He recalled how patient she had been and how she had never pressured him while he pursued his double major in college.

As time passed, Tina had become more involved in the day-to-day affairs of the business. Eventually, she had left behind her own work as an X-ray technician to help build a successful enterprise with the man she loved. When the firm had begun to earn a profit, they saved up enough for a small wedding. They couldn't afford anything fancy, but they couldn't afford to be without each other. Mike's parents had passed away, while Tina's didn't have the resources to finance a wedding. So they married in a small church and celebrated with a few friends and their immediate family at a reception in the garden of a wealthy client's home.

At the time, Lane could not afford an engagement ring. All of their money had been tied up in the business they had worked so hard to grow. He dreaded having to tell Tina, but she handled it in her typical manner, saying, "Mike, *you* are my engagement ring. It's *you* I want. No ring or money could make me any happier than I am right now."

Thinking back on those days, Lane lifted a dusty framed photo from his desk. It was of Tina's face and was accompanied by a poem she had written for him on their anniversary.

> It's my life, my life, for me to give.
> To be happy, to be merry or sad,
> Nonetheless, my life to give.
> It's to you I give it, my love,
> My heart, my soul.
> Yes, it's my life to live.
> And to you, my love,
> I lovingly give it all.
>
> All My Love Always,
> Tina

Lane thought about the days before that anniversary. Tina had hidden the rough drafts of the poem in her dresser drawer. She must have written four or five pages to come up with the right words. Her attempts at composing and framing the poem were even more touching to him. He recalled how she would cover her handiwork or shield it from him with her body whenever he approached. Tina had never been known for her artistic abilities, but she put considerable effort and time into it nonetheless. This had made the gift that much more special.

After reading the poem several times, he sat quietly behind his desk and stared out the window into the bright blue midday sky. A trace of a smile crossed his face before he lowered his head and wiped away a single tear.

"Hhh …" he sighed. "I miss you."

It seemed like only yesterday that Mike and Tina had gone on the anniversary weekend when Tina had presented him with her poem and the photo. They had rented a small cabin on a lake in the Poconos. Mike had wanted to surprise her with a little gift of his own. They spent the first day skiing and playing in the snow like two love-struck teenagers. After nightfall, they drove back to the cabin on moon-drenched Lake Harmony. Upon arrival, Mike raced past Tina through the snow to the front door and made her wait just inside as he waltzed across the room, spinning and joking. He could still hear her giggle. "What the heck are you up to?" she had asked. She would soon find out. Mike lit a fire and turned off the lights, leaving only the bouncing blue and orange flames to light the room. From a silver bucket he had prepared before they left, he produced a bottle of chilled champagne and two sparkling crystal glasses. Tina was overcome with emotion when she realized these were the same glasses with which they had toasted on their wedding day. She thought they had been lost years before, along with the champagne. They had been gifts from her parents.

Mike remembered everything: the sound of the cork popping, the sound of their glasses clinking as they toasted, and the smell of the fire. He recalled walking across the room to Tina and gazing into her eyes. Words had been unnecessary. He gently kissed her soft, sweet lips, a kiss that felt as wonderful as their first. They had the kind of love that felt like adolescent infatuation, complete with butterflies in the belly. Mike whisked Tina across the room, softly lowered her onto a silky fur rug stretched out in front of the glowing fireplace, and poured out the champagne. The flames flickered and crackled seductively as he lay down next to her. He kissed her neck and whispered into her ear as she smiled with pleasure.

"I love you."

He turned her gently onto her stomach and slowly removed her clothes, stopping only to give her sips of champagne. Straddling her, he brushed her long hair to the side and massaged her with the scented hot oil he had prepared earlier. He slowly caressed her neck and nibbled lightly on her ears. His hands firmly rubbed her shoulders, back, bottom, and inner thighs. Tina spread her long legs as she writhed and purred in response to his touch. He worked his way down her body using his lips and teeth to tug gently at the soft, sweet flesh along her back and bottom while his fingers tickled and probed her. Tina enjoyed his strong hands kneading and tempting her as goose bumps rose all over her body. Intoxicated by a carnal yearning, Tina pitched herself forcefully over onto her back, exposing her tantalizing breasts to her lover. He kissed her hard and long and then poured oil in a continuous stream from her throat to her soft mound. He now removed his own clothes, revealing his lean muscular frame. He slid himself down her slick body. He spread the river of oil out to her breasts and around her nipples, and his hand massaged her firm bosom.

Tina could feel the heat from his erect member as it pulsed against her inner thigh. He continued to work his way down, spreading the oil evenly across her quivering body. She took hold of his hand and sucked on one of his strong fingers. Finally, Mike sent her into deep, convulsing orgasms as his searching tongue explored her soft silky mound. Tina could no longer take his tempestuous seduction. She forcefully pulled him on top of her. He mounted her firmly and thrust hard into her as she arched her back and bucked wildly beneath him.

Hours later, Mike and Tina lay quietly cuddling together as the fire crackled and danced nearby. When Tina was nearly asleep, Mike rolled her onto her stomach and massaged her neck and shoulders. She lay content and smiling. Moving from her shoulders, he worked his way down her left arm toward her hand. Turning it, he massaged her palm, her thumb, and each finger in its turn. Pausing at her ring finger, he spun her wedding band several times. Suddenly and seemingly producing it from thin air, Mike slipped an ice-cold golden ring onto her finger above her wedding band. It was adorned with a two-carat pear-shaped diamond.

Tina's eyes opened wide as she felt the icy band slide onto her finger. She lifted her head and weary upper body from the floor. She gawked at the glittering rock in astonishment. It sparkled like melting ice in the bright glow of the fire.

He remembered her reaction as if it had happened only moments ago. It had been a perfect opportunity to give her what he could not afford when they had become engaged. That night, he had proposed to Tina once again. The memory now brought tears to his eyes.

"Yes! Oh, yes, Mike!" Tears of joy tumbled down her warm, rosy cheeks. Tina would later say, quite often, that had been the most enjoyable, most romantic evening of her life. After agreeing to marry him once more, she had bounded to her feet and danced around the room. Her slim, sexy body and long, silky hair shone in the firelight like those of an angel. She was the most beautiful creature in God's creation. They slept peacefully that night, their bodies pressed tightly together as the fire burned.

When Mike had awakened the next morning, beside his head was a wrapped gift. It was her anniversary present to him. In rose-colored paper with a burgundy bow was the gift he would always treasure—the poem and the photo.

The memories were still painful.

Chapter Eight

Lane couldn't help but wonder why Wheatly had continued to avoid him. He was becoming consumed by his quest for judicial reform and had an itch to thwart the senator's avoidance. He felt the need to go to Washington that very Friday and confront him. It was about 12:30 in the afternoon when he set out for the capital. Depending on the traffic on the interstate, he thought he could reach Washington before the workday was over. He had sold himself on the idea that if he could corner the senator and pitch his plan face to face, he might have a chance of getting things started.

Lane arrived at the senator's office at 4:10.

"May I help you, sir?" asked Kathy of the fatigued-looking man who approached her desk.

"Yes, I'd like to see Senator Wheatly, please," said Lane.

"Do you have an appointment, sir?"

"No, I don't, but I'm Jeff's accountant. I'm Mike Lane."

Kathy had assumed that he had called from Philadelphia earlier and so was a little surprised to see him in Washington. But for some reason, she felt quite sincerely pleased to meet Lane.

"Well, hi, Mr. Lane! I'm Kathy. We spoke on the phone."

Kathy usually trusted her first impressions—Lane was ruggedly handsome but seemed vulnerable nonetheless. Lane grinned easily at her.

"Is the senator in, Kathy?"

Despite the senator's firm resolve to avoid Lane, Kathy felt compelled—knowing Lane's sad history—to help him.

"Well, Mr. Lane, he's out of the office until Monday."

Lane sighed and slumped forward.

"Are you okay, Mr. Lane? Can I get you some coffee or tea?"

Lane smiled weakly and shook his head.

"Na, I just need to see Jeff." He laughed sarcastically. "He's avoiding me."

Lane stepped back and unbuttoned his overcoat. He wearily sat in a chair opposite Kathy's desk, leaned forward with his elbows on his knees, and cradled his head in his hands.

Kathy slid out from behind her desk and approached Lane.

"Mr. Lane, are you sure I can't get you something."

Lane lifted his head. "Call me Mike, please."

"Mike, can I get you a bottle of water?"

"No thanks."

"The senator told me that ... well, that as a result of what happened to you and your wife, you want to get some kind of judicial reform introduced to the Senate."

In truth, the senator had just muttered a few words in passing about Lane's quest—something he probably wouldn't even have remembered saying—but Kathy was far more perceptive than he had realized. Lane nodded.

"Well, I think that's great! And ... I'm very sorry about what happened."

There was a long silent pause as Kathy smiled at Lane. The uncomfortable silence was broken when Lane lowered his head, swallowed hard, and managed a pained smile.

"Thank you. That was some time ago."

Kathy sat on the edge of the desk and crossed her legs. She was a top-notch professional—she had never meddled in the senator's personal affairs—but somehow, this situation felt different. After establishing that none of the other staff were within earshot, she leaned forward and spoke in a hushed tone.

"Listen, Mike. The senator often stays in Washington on the weekends. Even though it's no secret, you didn't hear this from me, understand?"

Lane's attention was suddenly fixed on her every word. He nodded.

"Everyone in town knows that when he's around on the weekend he always stays at the Whitehall Inn here in DC, and he always gets the same suite ... 309. Just about every senator in town keeps a room like it." She paused as an intern walked past, then resumed. "The senator didn't give me any details about your plan, but I have a feeling that you want to make things better. You certainly can't make them any worse."

Kathy extended her hand. Rising to meet her, he smiled gratefully and gripped it.

"Remember, Mike ... you did *not* get any of this from me."

"I owe you one," he said.

"You'd better get going," she said. "He'll be in his suite sometime this evening, I'm sure."

Kathy's heartbeat quickened as Lane turned and left the office. There was no doubt in her mind that he was a real catch.

The Pulpit Pub was located across the street from the Whitehall Inn and was famous for its Friday-night happy hour's grand assemblage of senators, congressional representatives, bureaucrats, and reporters. Once a week, the pub became a neutral ground where little business was discussed, at least openly. It was a rare Friday evening that Senator Wheatly was not in attendance.

He sat at a corner booth toward the back of the crowded bar, sipping scotch and trying to unwind. He rested his feet on the seat across from him. One of his colleagues, Senator James Baily of Florida, approached. Baily was an adviser to the president's NAFTA project and had wanted to congratulate Wheatly unofficially on his impending committee appointment.

"Hey, Jeff! You look like someone stole your dog! You okay?"

"Uh yeah, I'm doing fine," he said absently. He abruptly excused himself, stood, and walked away in what seemed like a hypnotic trance. Stress, the Floridian figured as he stood by the booth with a drink in his hand. It happened to the best of them on the Hill.

Wheatly spent the next couple of hours hunched over the bar alone, sucking down multiple glasses of scotch. He felt a hand rest on his shoulder.

"Can I buy you a drink?"

Getting no response, the intruder leaned in front of him. It was Anthony.

"Nope," replied Wheatly, with a drunken slur.

"Man, are you all right, Senator?" Anthony asked in a jesting manner. "You don't look so hot!"

The senator appeared not only drunk, but also spent. His jaw was slack, and his eyelids drooped. His words tumbled into one another.

"Anth'ny, you dunno the halfuvit!"

Anthony usually stood at the snapping end of the senator's whip, but he remained ready to serve. He epitomized loyalty. No other person could possibly be more dedicated to the senator.

"Is there anything I can do, sir?"

The senator unsteadily placed his drink on the bar and tilted his head to look up at the ceiling. He pondered Anthony's offer.

"I dunno, Anth'ony. I jus' dunno."

Wheatly tossed back the remains of his scotch. Wincing, he wiped his lips and struggled to stand.

"C'mon, kid," he said, patting Anthony on the back "We got work to do!"

The senator composed himself and walked in as controlled a manner as he could muster toward the door.

"Office or Whitehall?" Anthony asked anxiously.

"The hotel. Let's get shaking."

They crossed the street, were greeted by the bellhop and desk clerk, and ascended to the senator's private suite, which was charged to the good tax-paying citizens of Pennsylvania. Once settled, the senator confided in Anthony, revealing to him selected details of his dilemma regarding the president and the Textile Union.

After the carefully edited account, Anthony asked, "I don't really understand. I don't know if there's anything I can do to help. Is there?"

Staring out the window, the senator responded, "I don't know just yet."

He paused and rubbed his nose and mouth uneasily. "I don't know what to do. I need to work this thing out."

Anthony sat quietly while the senator paced. Watching the powerful senator walk nervously back and forth rattled the aide.

"Why are you telling me this, Senator? I don't see how I can help."

"Oh, just fucking great," snapped Wheatly. "Now you're gonna run with your tail between your legs, right? You don't wanna be involved, right? You little fucking worm."

"No! No, nothing like that … I'm just confused."

Anthony rubbed his forehead as he tried to understand the severity of the senator's position.

"Are you telling me," said Anthony slowly, "that the president of the United States of America has told you to run the NAFTA committee … *or else?*" Wheatly resumed pacing. "And that you face some sort of threat from the Textile Union if you don't oppose NAFTA? Is this what you're telling me, Senator?"

The senator ignored Anthony's question and continued his self-absorbed pacing.

"Fuck the Textile Union!" Anthony blurted.

Wheatly was surprised by this out-of-character outburst. It was clear to him that Anthony was still a little green when it came to the business of politics.

"Who do they think they are," Anthony continued, "threatening a U.S. senator? You should do as the president asks, and then we'll straighten the union out! I realize that they contribute to your campaign fund and support your causes, but to threaten you is ludicrous. We'll expose their threat and bring charges against them through the attorney general. They'll have their asses hauled off to jail, and that'll sure as hell put them in their place!"

Wheatly crumpled into a chair and gawked at his naïve assistant.

"It's not that easy, Anthony. The union has given me more than just support over the years."

"What do you mean?" "Uh … the Union's been paying me to ensure that they get more than their fair share of the textile business in the state. It's a multibillion dollar industry. As time went on, the pay got larger, and so did their demands. It went from textiles to food to liquor … it didn't end. Hell, everybody does it! Every player in this town has somebody like them in their pocket. Shit, only God knows how many of us the Barletto family has on its books. It's the way the game is played. It doesn't matter who it is—the unions, the NRA, AARP, the mob— they all get what they want by giving *us* what *we* want: money!

"I guess you never expected to hear that these types of things were going on in the ivory halls of justice," he added. "Sorry, Anthony, but that's the way things are."

Anthony walked to the window and gazed out.

"Okay, I'm in," he said. "What do you need me to do?"

The senator seized the moment.

"You're a good man, Anthony! I *knew* I could count on you."

Chapter Nine

Considering the near-constant tongue-lashings he suffered, it was a wonder and a mystery that Anthony was capable of such loyalty to the senator. Wheatly had recruited him personally two years before, straight from the University of Pennsylvania. Anthony Kane was a real Ivy Leaguer, right down to his khakis and loafers. He had finished second in his class as a political science major and had lettered in varsity track and baseball. He had been voted the baseball team's most valuable player. Though the Mets in a late round of the draft had chosen him, he had no real desire to play professional baseball, preferring instead a career in politics.

Since he'd had such an impressive early life, many people wondered why he continued to work for the senator. Some thought perhaps he harbored an extraordinary case of ambition for a political ascent of his own and wished to employ the senator's resources to this end. Whatever the reason, he continued to absorb the abuse.

Anthony had all-American looks: light-brown hair, blue eyes, a tall, athletic frame, and a smile that lit up any room. Clean-cut and honest-looking, he seemed a natural for kissing babies on future campaign trails. On the surface, he seemed a bit of a hard-nosed young man, but he in fact lacked a strong will and was very concerned about others' perceptions of him. It was thought these characteristics would serve him well in a political career.

The senator asked for privacy as he reached for the phone.

"Who are you calling, Senator?" Anthony asked.

The senator scowled at him, annoyed with the simple question. Quickly changing temperament, like Doctor Jekyll to Mr. Hyde, he answered nastily.

"I'm calling my wife. Is that okay with you?"

"Okay, then, sir … I'll just head down the street to pick up some things at the store." Anthony was careful not to let the door slam behind him.

The senator punched the numbers and twisted the phone cord around his hand. Just outside, Anthony's ear was glued to the wooden door. He could barely make out what the senator was saying.

"Hi, honey." The senator was using his perfect husband voice. "I've run into some problems I need to take care of." He looked at the door and felt a twinge of insecurity. "Hold on a moment."

Anthony heard the senator's feet shuffling across the floor. He wondered where Wheatly might be going and then realized the footsteps were approaching the door. Anthony dashed the forty feet to the stairwell, not looking back to see whether he had been noticed.

At the door, the senator shook his head in annoyance as he twisted the dead-bolt lever. He returned to the phone.

"Hi. Damn Anthony … he never locks the door. He can't seem to get that into his thick head."

The senator rarely spoke kindly to his wife anymore, but tonight, his tone had changed a bit—perhaps because he needed the sympathetic ear of someone he once loved. Despite public appearances, the marriage had long been one of convenience for him and of a certain agony for her. He used her as a prop at his social and political functions—his constituents were under the illusion that he was a loving husband and family man.

On the other hand, she had lost her sense of self-worth. Once a proud, strong woman, she had become an insecure pawn in the senator's power game.

Tonight, he spoke unusually gently to his wife, but she offered no reply to his rhetoric. She was unwilling to oblige him. Normally, her husband rushed through brief, meaningless, one-sided dissertations without paying any attention to anything she might have to say, and she responded no differently to him tonight.

"Okay, then, good night, Jane," he said, before sheepishly adding, "I love you."

Jane could hardly believe what he'd just said, but still she offered no response and lowered the receiver to its cradle.

For a moment, Jane just stood in the kitchen with one hand on the phone and stared off aimlessly with her head cocked to the side. Her sister, Karen, walking into the kitchen, interrupted her hushed bewilderment.

"What's wrong?" Karen said immediately. She knew her sister well.

"What?"

"What's wrong?"

A confused look appeared on Jane's face.

"Jeff … he just told me he loved me."

Karen giggled. "You've got to be kidding me! That bastard."

The sisters were very close and had confided all of their troubles to one another over the years.

"The shit, he probably has one of his little Washington whores with him as we speak! I don't know how you do it. I'd shoot the little fuck."

Karen was Jane's youngest sister—they were separated by eleven years—and she was by no means tied to any misguided, old-fashioned, stand-by-your-man virtues.

"Oh, don't say that, Karen." Jane's face turned red from embarrassment and shame. Even in the most awful circumstances, she always tried to be diplomatic.

Karen rolled her eyes. "Come on, Jane! Don't tell me you wouldn't want to see that prick dead!"

Jane turned her back to Karen and mumbled something.

"What did you say? Come on, Jane … spit it out!"

Watching her sister endure a bad marriage had always bothered Karen immeasurably. At times, it had infuriated her.

"Come on, Jane! You *have* to let it out! It's obvious what he's been doing to you. For God's sake, look at yourself! Are you happy with your life? Are you happy with the person he's forced you to become? Do you think he'll ever change?"

Despite herself, Karen was becoming confrontational now.

"Wake up, Jane! This is as good as it will ever get if you stay with him. You need to end it!"

As Karen spoke, Jane grew ever angrier—not at her sister, but at herself and her husband. Suddenly, she made a tight fist and pounded on the kitchen wall.

"Of *course* I hate the way he treats me!" she shouted. "I wish he would stay in Washington and never come back. *Ever!*"

She began to cry—for her, even uttering those words to her kid sister had been a big step. Karen rushed over to hold Jane and didn't prod her any further.

Anthony made his way back to the hotel. Peeking through the windows as he passed storefronts and specialty shops, he strolled past a small deli, and there, sitting at a hi-top table facing the street, was Mike Lane. Paying little attention to what went on in the street, Lane stared out the tall plate glass window that stretched from the sidewalk to the awning above. He tried to organize his thoughts and muster the nerve to approach the senator in his hotel suite as he sipped coffee. Through the rising steam from his cup, the young stranger captured Lane's eye as he passed by. They smiled politely at one another, and they exchanged friendly nods.

Returning to the suite, Anthony twisted the polished brass knob and gave the door a push with his shoulder. To his surprise, it didn't budge. He produced from his pocket a duplicate key the senator had given him. Before he had received the key, Anthony would occasionally be left in the hall cooling his heels for twenty or thirty minutes if the senator was attending to serious business. This was the first time he had to use the key.

It occurred to Anthony that it might be fun to surprise the senator. He unlocked and opened the door as softly as he could and poked his head inside.

"Sen-a-tor, I've got a key, remember?" he said playfully.

But the senator was nowhere to be seen. Dominating the view was a room service cart holding a silver ice bucket containing a bottle of Dom Perignon and two sweating glasses. He heard the sound of running water coming from the bathroom and wondered whether the senator had a guest. But that made no sense; the senator would have told him about a guest. He crept down the corridor holding his body close to the wall. Pressing his fingertips against the door, he turned his head and listened. He heard nothing but the sound of falling water. He tapped lightly on the door.

"Senator?" he half-whispered.

No response.

He knocked considerably harder. "Senator, are you okay? It's Anthony."

Still no response. He reached down and slowly opened the door a crack.

"Senator?"

Wisps of steam escaped through the crack and spilled out into the hall. Anthony looked down the hall suspiciously and then pushed the door wide open. A billowing cloud gushed out and engulfed him. He squinted through the nearly opaque mist toward the glass-enclosed shower stall at the far end of the enormous bathroom.

"Senator, are you okay?" he asked loudly but unsteadily. He inched his way toward the shower door.

"Come on Senator, this isn't funny."

He felt through the mist for the shower door. It was fogged and dotted with water droplets. Anthony tugged on the door. It seemed stuck. He pulled again harder, and it opened. In a low, shaky voice, he called once more into the large enclosure.

"Senator?"

Wheatly stood alone and motionless under the showerhead with his back to his aide.

"Senator?"

Anthony stepped fully clothed into the large enclosure, and still there was no response from the senator. Anthony's black leather shoes were quickly drenched and interrupted the flowing swirl of water racing toward the drain. His Oxford shirt was saturated and clung to his muscular body like a second skin. Another step soaked his full head of hair and pushed his bangs down over his probing blue eyes. He flicked his hair away from his face. He reached out to his boss, and his voice deepened.

"Jeff?"

The senator swiftly spun round and pulled Anthony violently toward him. He kissed Anthony passionately as he tore at the younger man's saturated clothing. Water bounced off their bodies as the senator unbuttoned Anthony's trousers and ripped away his shirt to expose his aide's aroused athletic body.

"What took you so long?" said Wheatly. "I've been waiting for you. You know how I like it!"

Chapter Ten

Near the end of their sexual foray, Wheatly and Anthony lingered under the warm shower. Meanwhile, Lane rode the elevator to the hotel's third floor. The elevator glided to a swift halt as Lane's stomach leapt up into his throat. The doors shuddered and shook before they slid open and out of the way. He felt nervous and light-headed. Taking deep breaths, he walked down the brightly lit hall decorated with fresh flowers sitting atop antique hutches. He read the room numbers to his left as he advanced down the hall.

301 ... 303 ... 305.

His heart felt as though it was going to explode, and he could hear his rapid pulse in his ears.

307 ... 309.

He took one last deep breath as he stood in front of the door. Overcoming any remaining inclination to hesitate, he knocked three times on the heavy door. There was no answer. He knocked again, harder this time. Again, there was no answer.

Lane nervously surveyed both ends of the hall. There was no one around, so he cautiously pressed his ear to the door. Since the bathroom was at the far end of the suite, he heard nothing. As he strained to listen, he unconsciously fidgeted with the doorknob, wiggling it tenths of inches in either direction. Unexpectedly, the elevator bell rang down the hall behind him. Startled, he tensed and turned to face the elevator door. His hand instinctively squeezed tightly around the knob. It rolled over completely, and the door opened a couple of inches. Before the elevator's passengers appeared, Lane had swiftly slipped into the senator's private suite.

Lane stood inside with his back pressed against the door. He took in the grandness of the suite—plush carpeting, chandelier, recessed wall speakers ... room service cart.

The cart was draped with fine white linen, and it held a frosted silver champagne bucket. He was embarrassed to be inside without an invitation but still felt strangely compelled to announce his presence.

"Jeff? It's me, Mike!"

Neither Wheatly nor Anthony heard him.

Lane stepped deeper into the suite. He had come too far to deny himself; Point Guard was too important. He heard the running water in the bathroom. He paused indecisively. It would be very uncomfortable for both of them if he were in the room when Jeff came out of the shower. Now that he was fairly certain the senator was in the suite, he thought that it might be best to stand outside and knock on the door every five or ten minutes until the senator answered. Suddenly, another thought crossed his mind. What if the senator wasn't alone? Suppose Jane was in town and the two of them were in the bathroom together?

This uncomfortable thought made up his mind for him, and he turned to hightail it out of the suite. At that instant, the bathroom door flew open and crashed against the wall. The senator—dripping, naked, and giggling—pranced up the hall.

Before Wheatly even noticed him, Lane started to offer an apology.

"Jeff, I'm sorry ... I was just going to ... I mean ... I was ..."

Hearing a voice, the senator froze in his tracks. He hadn't been wearing his glasses. He wiped water from his eyes and squinted at the figure at the end of the hall.

Lane spoke up.

"I was going to leave you and Jane a note," he said. "You see, the door was open and ..."

The senator had realized who it was, but before he could react, a naked Anthony galloped out of the bathroom, dripping wet and swinging a towel over his head.

"Jeffrey! Jeffrey!" he yelled.

Anthony had run to within a few feet of the senator when he noticed a figure looming beyond the end of the hall. He stopped short and slipped on the polished hardwood floor. It looked as though someone had suddenly yanked a rug out from beneath his feet. His back slammed hard against the floor, but he lost no time in flipping over to his belly and trying frantically to get up. The floor being too slippery for the speed at which he was trying to move, his feet kept sliding out from under him, and he began to scramble back to the bathroom on his hands and knees.

The senator turned to watch Anthony make the pathetic retreat and then turned back and stood quietly facing Lane, covering his genitals like a child.

"Oh God … oh God!" Anthony cried as he slid out of sight into the bathroom.

The senator hung his head in shame. It was too late for an explanation. The last few seconds could never be taken back. Lane moved to escape from the suite as fast as possible. Wheatly stood still as he watched Lane close the door behind him.

Wheatly tried to steady himself against the wall as the suite started to spin. His stomach ached; his face and hands felt numb; and he collapsed into the puddle of water beneath him. Goose pimples rose all over his clammy skin. He slumped forward on his knees, covered his face, and wept. In the bathroom, Anthony lay in the fetal position on the cold marble floor of the shower stall. He was sobbing as well, his muffled moans echoing off the ceramic tile walls.

Lane almost sprinted down the corridor to the elevator and pressed the button repeatedly.

"Come on … come on, damn it!" he mumbled.

The elevator didn't seem to be moving—it seemed to be stuck on the twelfth floor. He noticed a lit exit sign further down the corridor, hustled to the doorway underneath it, and ran down the dismal, empty staircase, two and three steps at a time.

He could hardly believe what he had just seen.

He thought, *My God, Jeff is gay! What about Jane? His kids?*

He jumped down to the final landing, stretched both hands out in front of him, pressed the panic bar on the metal fire door, and entered the inn's lobby. Wiping the perspiration from his forehead, he tried to pass the front desk without arousing suspicion. Cocking his head to one side and scratching his eyebrow, he sailed by the desk clerk, who wished him a good evening. He nodded in response and escaped to the sidewalk.

He wondered who the young man was whom he had seen with the senator. Then it occurred to him—he, Mike Lane, might well have been the only person who knew that the senator was having an affair with a man.

Reeling from the experience, Lane drove back to Philadelphia.

The exposed lovers spent the night apart, silent and deeply troubled.

The senator and Anthony had met at the university, where Wheatly had given a lecture to a group of third-year political science majors. At the time, Anthony was responsible for setting the department's activities and had met the senator during the course of these duties. Throughout Anthony's junior and senior year, the two cultivated an intimate relationship and rendezvoused at secret locations.

Although Anthony had never had a homosexual encounter before he was first seduced by Wheatly, neither had he had a heterosexual one. As a teenager, he dated only girls—but he often thought about boys. He tried hard to keep his feelings concealed, but after the senator's masterful seduction, he thought only of men as appropriate partners. Even so, he still found his own sexuality alarming. If anyone were to find out about it, he didn't know what he would do. He was a textbook closeted gay man. This might explain why he tolerated the shabby treatment he received from the senator.

But the senator, too, had a secret that only Anthony knew—that they were lovers.

So, they were bound by their secrets to one another.

Early the next morning, Senator Wheatly, draped in a silk robe, got up from the sofa where he had spent the entire sleepless night. He pulled the curtains closed, choking off the morning sun. He walked to the desk and listlessly tapped out his home number on the telephone. His thinning hair was matted down and dark circles bulged under his eyes.

"Hello?"

The senator cleared his throat.

"Jane. It's me."

Anthony, fully dressed, trudged down the hall toward him. His garment bag was tossed over his shoulder.

Without further explanation, the senator informed his wife that he would not be home until Sunday evening and hung up.

"Where are you going?" Wheatly asked his aide.

Without responding—without even making eye contact—Anthony walked past him toward the door.

The senator raised his voice. "I said, where are you *going*?"

Without a word, Anthony opened the door. Wheatly sprang up and slammed it shut. Pressing his arm on Anthony's back, the senator pinned him against the door.

"Where are you going, Anthony?" he whispered in his ear.

Anthony dropped his bag to the floor and rested his forehead against the door. He winced and tried to smother his tears.

"I don't know. Out of here, I guess."

The senator—a master of deceit—had worked out a plan to defuse the situation.

"Look, sit down. Everything is going to be okay."

He reached up and massaged Anthony's neck. "I promise you that it will be all right. The guy that was in here last night is a friend of mine."

Anthony closed his eyes for a moment as if to approve of the senator's touch and his promise. Suddenly, Anthony snapped out of what seemed to have been a hypnotic trance. He spun around to face the senator, kicked his bag out of the way, and raised his index finger to the senator's face.

"Everything's going to be all right, you say?" he lashed out. "We were just caught ... if that guy had come in fifteen minutes earlier he would have actually caught us having sex, for God's sake!"

His face turned red, and he stalked across the room.

"I'm telling you, Jeff, if ... if ..." Anthony ran his fingers through his hair. "I'll kill you!"

The senator stiffened and stood in silence, believing that Anthony did not really mean what he said.

"I will! And that fuckin' friend of yours, too!"

Confused and emotionally exhausted, Anthony collapsed into a chair and began to weep. "I swear ... I will."

The senator edged toward Anthony as the young man whimpered into his cupped hands.

"Don't cry," Wheatly said as he stroked Anthony's head. "I can make sure that he doesn't tell anyone."

Anthony raised his head. His eyes were bloodshot, and his cheeks were streaked with tears. "How?"

"Mike needs a favor from me. He wants me to sponsor some kind of bill. It's very important to him. I'm sure he'd do anything to get it to the Senate floor. All I have to do is make sure it gets there."

"And if you don't? Or can't? Or if it isn't enough for him?"

The senator smiled. "Don't worry about that. I'm the best at bringing motions to a vote. But no matter what happens, Mike won't tell anyone. Not a living soul. I promise."

Chapter Eleven

At eight o'clock on Monday morning, Lane sat at his breakfast table drinking his coffee and chewing on a piece of toast. The morning sun shone through the window, casting his lonely shadow onto the floor. He imagined Tina's shadow moving next to his, as it used to.

"Maybe this weekend we can drive out to Lancaster and go to the markets," he imagined her saying.

She had loved to visit the Amish countryside in the fall—to see the brilliant leaves and buy freshly baked goods. He could smell the vanilla perfume she wore.

The phone startled him out of his reverie.

He picked up the receiver and cleared his throat. "Hello?"

"Good morning, Mr. Lane. This is Kathy from Senator Wheatly's office. How are you today, sir?"

"Oh ... Hi Kathy, I'm fine. How ..."

Kathy, a little excited, interrupted him. "The senator would like to schedule an appointment with you at your convenience, Mr. Lane."

For a moment, Lane wondered why Kathy was speaking so formally to him after her friendliness the week before. He then imagined how angry Wheatly would be if he were to discover that Kathy had been the one who had told Lane about the hotel room, and he understood.

"How about tomorrow morning at 10:30?" he asked.

"That will be fine. We'll see you tomorrow, sir."

Lane hung up the phone and leaned back against the counter. A faint grin found its way to his lips.

"It's going to happen, honey," he said aloud. "We're going to make a difference."

At precisely 10:30 on Tuesday morning, Lane entered the senator's outer office with his Point Guard document packed securely away in a leather briefcase. He wore shiny, wing-tipped shoes, a perfectly-fitting new black suit, a crisp white shirt, and a blue tie. He had an air of confidence. There seemed to have been a magical transformation in the man whose suits, just a few weeks before, had hung loosely on him. Hope had breathed new life into him.

Despite the gratitude he owed her, Lane knew better than to treat Kathy in anything but a strictly professional manner, especially since she knew nothing of what had transpired in the suite.

"Good morning, Mr. Lane!" She smiled warmly. "How was your trip?"

"It was just fine, Kathy, thank you."

They shared a mutual twinkle of the eye.

"Is Jeff in?"

"Why yes, he is, Mr. Lane. Can I get you a cup of coffee?"

Lane declined and followed Kathy to the senator's office. She knocked lightly on the door and gently pushed it open.

"Senator, Mr. Lane is here for his 10:30 appointment," she said.

Lane walked past her into the office. The senator's desk was easily twenty-five feet away from the doorway. Wheatly stood and extended his hand across the large gap that separated them. The senator seemed relaxed, but Lane noticed, upon shaking, that his hand was cold and clammy. Kathy closed the door, leaving the two men alone.

"How the hell are you, Mike?" He sounded like he was greeting a long-lost friend and betrayed no hint of embarrassment or remorse. "Have a seat! Can I have Kathy get you some coffee?"

Lane pursed his lips as they sat across from one another.

"No thanks."

The senator shrugged his shoulders and settled back in his chair.

"I just want to discuss my plan with you, Jeff," said Lane.

Lane did not intend to mention what he had seen at the hotel on Friday night. He knew that the senator would not want anyone to know his secret and felt this trump card was better left buried in his hand.

"Listen, about Friday night ..." Wheatly said softly.

Lane leaned forward and locked eyes with the senator. Wheatly's gaze shifted to his desktop.

"It wasn't what it looked like," he continued.

Lane reached down into the briefcase and tossed his thick document onto the desk.

"Don't even try it, Jeff," he said. "I know what I saw."

Lane fanned the pages of the document for a couple of seconds before speaking again.

"I call it Point Guard," he said. "Basically, it's a point system that I've come up with. It's designed to deal out justice impartially, without prejudice or malice. It's revolutionary, Jeff. The current system was fine for its time—when there were only a few million people in the country and issues weren't so complex. Times have changed, Jeff! We need a more decisive, speedy, and impartial way to try criminals. We need a system based on sound values. And without appeal! Jeff, my system takes the salesmanship and media out of the courtroom; it puts control into the hands of law-abiding people—peers and victims. No more early release! No more loopholes! This is the kind of system our Founding Fathers would have expected us to adopt to maintain our dignity as a free society."

Lane slid the document across the desk.

"I want you to read it, Jeff. I want to change the way our judicial system deals with violent crime."

The senator picked up the document, looked at Lane, and took a deep breath.

"Look, Mike," he said, "things take time in Washington. I don't know if I can do anything about this."

"You've got to be kidding me!" Lane surprised himself with his own vehemence. "I've been keeping your books and doing your taxes for years! And all that time, you've been pretending to be a friend."

Lane shook his head and stood up. He placed his hands on Wheatly's desk and leaned toward him. He barely managed to keep his voice down.

"I don't believe it will take too much time at all, Jeff," he said. "You're fucking around with a college kid or something! I don't know what anyone else would think of that, but if I were you, I wouldn't want anyone to know about it."

For a split second, Wheatly felt certain that he was going to puke.

"Easy, Mike!" he said. "I didn't say that I wouldn't help. I said it would take time."

He sounded humbler than Lane had ever heard him and certainly humbler than he felt.

"Now sit down, and tell me more about this plan."

For the better part of an hour, Lane explained the Point Guard system. Throughout his summary, the senator asking pointed questions and even making helpful remarks interrupted him. It seemed to Lane that Wheatly was sincerely interested. Toward the end of their meeting, the senator sat on the windowsill overlooking a small garden behind his office. He nodded and tapped a pen against his lips.

"Mike," he said, "you might have something here."

Lane smiled. "Yeah, I think I do."

"Can you leave the document with me?" Wheatly asked as he slid off the sill.

"Yes." said Lane. "I have another hard copy for myself and, of course, a copy on my computer. I'd planned to give you this one."

"Have you presented this to anyone else?" Wheatly asked as he moved toward the desk.

Lane raised his arms above his head and stretched.

"No," he said.

"No?"

"No, Jeff. Just you."

Due to his expression of interest in Lane's plan, Wheatly was quite sure that his secret was safe for the time being. He was beginning to feel self-assured again. Straddling the corner of his desk, the senator rolled down his shirtsleeves and clipped on a pair of expensive cuff links. He looked down his nose at Lane.

"Okay, Mike, you have my interest piqued. Let me tell you what I'm going to do for you. I'm going back to Philly for the rest of the week. I'll take your document home and study it. You know, get a better feel for it. I'll phone you by Friday and tell you what I think."

Wheatly went back to his chair, sat down, plucked the document from the desk, and put it inside his briefcase. "Now, I can't promise you anything, Mike," he said dismissively. "But I'll read it and do my best."

The senator grinned and reached across the desk.

"Do we have a deal, Mike? I'll read your document, and *you* have never been to the Whitehall Inn. All right?"

Lane stood and ignored the senator's hand. He pulled his jacket from the back of his chair and headed for the door.

"Just read it, Jeff. I'll call you on Friday."

Lane was new at this game, but he was a quick study.

Chapter Twelve

Senator Wheatly returned to Philadelphia and began to study the document as he had promised. The more he read, the more impressed he became with Lane's work. Nevertheless, he had been a part of the political process for many years and knew that such a drastic change to the country's most fundamental laws would be a monumental undertaking. After all, the criminal justice system had been in place for over 200 years. Still, in view of the public's growing concern about violent crime, he realized that—even if it never became law—Lane's plan was intriguing enough to create quite a stir if Wheatly could somehow bring it to a vote. He easily envisioned a scenario in which such a stir translated into personal popularity for himself. The Point Guard system seemed so brilliantly fair that surely every red-blooded American would support him.

The plan had been written out in great detail—it was nearly 1,100 pages long. Every conceivable type of court proceeding and legal action associated with violent crime was discussed. As the senator pored over the document, it became evident to him that Lane had a firm grasp of the criminal justice system—perhaps even knowledge as extensive as Wheatly's own. Over the next couple of days, the senator spent every spare moment engulfed in Lane's work.

On Thursday evening, Lane's phone rang as he watched television.

"Hello?"

"Mike, it's Jeff. How are you?"

Lane fumbled with the remote, turned off the television, and scooted out to the edge of his sofa.

"Fine. Fine, Jeff," he said eagerly.

"Listen, Mike, I really got into this scheme of yours over the past couple of days."

Lane hadn't expected to hear from Wheatly until the following day. His call was a promising sign.

"What did you think?" Lane asked.

"I think it's good. I'm going to need a little more time to really understand it, absorb it. You know what I mean." He tempered his enthusiasm. He didn't want to let Lane know just how good he thought the plan really was. "It needs a lot of work, of course … but it has potential. I think it's worth putting some effort into it. I think that we can try to make it a reality. I think that, with my help, you can get this thing moving."

Wheatly was a shrewd negotiator but didn't allow himself to forget the power Lane had over him.

"Give me about a week," the senator said. "I want to consult with someone who can give me better insight into the criminal justice system … someone who can help me take the proper steps. Is that okay with you?"

Lane pumped his fist.

"Is that okay, Mike?"

Lane restrained his excitement.

"Yeah, that will be fine, Jeff. Should I call you tomorrow?"

"No, that won't be necessary. I'll call you next week. I'm going to need some time to set up some meetings and get things in order."

"I understand," said Lane.

"Now, I'm going to work on getting you security clearance. That's going to take some time. I want you intimately involved in this thing. Down the road, I'll need you to sit down and discuss your system with other senators and congressional representatives, just as you did with me. In the meantime, I'd like to keep this as confidential as possible. Are you with me?"

"Yes." Lane was still struggling to contain his excitement.

"Mike, who all knows about this?"

"Nobody, really."

"Nobody?"

"Well, I've asked for some advice over the years from some of my clients. You know, people like yourself. But nobody had a clue as to what I was working on. Truth is, no one ever asked."

"Okay. We'll communicate by phone for now. I don't want anyone else getting wind of what we are working on. Do you understand?"

"I *understand*, Jeff. I'll be sure to keep it between us."

After hanging up, Wheatly sat and thought. There were countless positive effects that Lane's plan could have on his career. Of course, it would require changes before it could be presented. That would pose no problem—it was the sort of thing he did well. But what *really* interested him—at least in the short term—was how this document could disentangle him from the NAFTA committee. If he could convince the president that Point Guard was a worthwhile endeavor and that *he* was the man to administer it, the president would release him from the NAFTA campaign. At the very least, this would ease the tension between him and the Textile Union.

Lane pulled his copy of the document from a file drawer in his home office. He gave some thought to the senator's concern for confidentiality. He also thought about his own threatening behavior in the senator's office earlier in the week and what kind of impact it may have on Wheatly. He sensed that he should consider being a little cautious and store his work some place less obvious than a file drawer. Lane looked around the cluttered office. He was checking out the bookshelves behind his desk when the perfect hiding place came to mind. With the document cradled in his arm, he quickly walked through the house and headed toward the basement door. Years ago, when Tina had talked about starting a family, Lane began converting the basement into a massive playroom. Getting pregnant had taken much longer than they had anticipated. Tina was almost certain she was pregnant by the time Lane had completed the playroom—just before she was murdered. She'd had an appointment scheduled with her doctor for the day following the shooting and had hoped the happy news would soon be confirmed.

The pregnancy was verified during her autopsy. Lane had never discussed with anyone the fact that he had lost Tina and his baby on the day of the shooting. It was just too painful.

The wood of the rarely used cellar door had swelled, and it took him several tugs to pull it open. On the third tug, the door flew open, and a musty odor assaulted him as cool air rushed out of the darkness toward his face. He flicked the switch at the top of the stairs, and a single dull bulb in the center of the room illuminated the basement playground. He jogged down the steps; at the bottom, he paused and thought of the promise of happiness the room once offered. The playroom was dusty but undisturbed. It was the start of a child-sized fantasyland—less the toys. He had built a wooden playhouse with a cedar-shingle roof and shutters. Inside it was a large chalkboard for drawing, and behind it, he had painted a lawn, bushes, and driveway on the floor. Beside the playhouse, he had erected a mini carport with a bright red roof. Parked beneath the port were two small pedal cars, one pink and one blue. A thick coat of dust had obscured the cars' once-brilliant finishes.

Lane closed his eyes tightly and tried to banish futile wishes and painful memories. He anxiously rushed across the basement floor past the playhouse. He stooped down, pulled the toy cars out from under the carport, and then knelt and crawled under it to the painted driveway. He lifted the lid of an empty toy chest he had built into the front of the carport, placed the Point Guard document inside, and slammed the lid shut. He crawled out, carelessly shoved the cars back into place, and hurried up the stairs. After he had shut off the light and forced the basement door closed, one car lazily rolled forward from beneath the mini carport, and then all was still.

With his back pressed against the basement door, he took a deep breath and turned to face the mess his home had become over the years. Charged with the exciting news that the senator was going to help, he decided to put the energy to good use and started to tidy up the house. After more than an hour of cleaning, he plopped down on the sofa exhausted, and he fell asleep in front of the television.

Early Friday morning, the senator went to Washington. As usual, Anthony met him, but this time Anthony was considerably more anxious to see him than usual. Anthony was waiting on the busy railway platform and reached for the senator's briefcase mere seconds after Wheatly stepped off the train car.

Anthony raised his impatient voice above the din.

"*Jeff!* Did you talk to your accountant friend this week? Did you work everything out?"

Without even making eye contact, Wheatly rushed past Anthony toward the main concourse. On the street, he spotted his limo through the drizzle and swiftly wound his way to it through the other parked vehicles. Anthony rushed to keep up and arrived at the limo just in time to shut his boss's door behind him. Anthony scurried around the car and took his place behind the steering wheel. Fidgeting, he looked at the senator in the rearview mirror.

"Did you hear what I said in the station?" he asked.

The senator's unexpected response was immediate.

"Don't you *ever* fucking call me Jeff in public, do you understand me?"

Anthony lowered his eyes and said nothing as he pulled into traffic.

They had nearly reached the office when the senator broke the silence.

"Yes, I did talk to my friend."

He stared blankly out the window, and Anthony's eyes flitted back to the mirror. "We have nothing to worry about. Like I told you before, he needs me to do something that is very important to him." Wheatly shrugged. "I do him a favor, and he keeps quiet. It's as simple as that."

This was hardly reassuring to Anthony. The windshield wipers swung back and forth across the misting glass, and their insistent rhythm seemed to intensify Anthony's panic. His mouth felt dry, his palms felt clammy, and his doom felt imminent. He pulled the car to the side of the road and rolled to a smooth but quick stop. Reaching his arm back and placing it on top of the seat back, he pressed down hard on the brake pedal to boost his body up and give himself enough leverage to turn around and face Wheatly.

"That's it? Suppose he decides to tell someone anyway?"

The senator was almost entertained by Anthony's naiveté. "Now, do you think I'm going to leave anything to chance, Anthony? Do you think I haven't already thought of that? I've already told you don't worry. I'll take care of this!"

Anthony kept his arm across the seat back for a few seconds, then sullenly turned away and resumed the commute. He wondered how Wheatly could be so sure of himself. He started to feel queasy—it had been a regular symptom since that night at the inn. The limousine pulled up in front of the office.

Upon entering, the senator instructed Kathy to contact the president's office and arrange a phone call—he wanted to discuss NAFTA.

At 11:45, Wheatly was tying up some loose ends before lunch when Kathy buzzed through on the intercom.

"Sir, the president is on line one for you."

He looked at the intercom as if it were going to bite him. It buzzed again. "Sir? Are you there? The president is on line one."

"Okay, Kathy. Put him through."

After a couple of deep breaths, he pressed the flashing button and picked up the phone.

"Good morning, Mr. President. How are you today?" he said nonchalantly.

Wheatly tried to begin with a few pleasantries, but the president nipped them short.

"You wanted to talk about NAFTA, Jeff. What's going on?"

"Well, Mr. President, I have a situation that I feel you would want brought to your attention. It could affect my participation in the NAFTA campaign, but it's a matter of great importance."

"Jeff, we already spoke about you being the committee leader. I don't see any reason to discuss it further."

"Yes, sir, I understand that, but I think you're going to want to see what I have. It may change your opinion."

Wheatly spoke quickly, as he knew a sudden rejection could come at any time.

"Sir, I won't kid you. This could very possibly make it impossible for me to spend any time on the NAFTA committee, but I think it'll be worth it. In fact, I know that this is something in which you're going to want to be involved. I think that it could even guarantee you another term in office."

The president contemplated the senator's words for a long moment.

"What do you have, Jeff?"

"I'll need some time alone with you to discuss it. Any time. Tonight, this afternoon … now?"

The president was intrigued by the tone of urgency in Wheatly's voice—as well as by the possibility of improved prospects for his own reelection. He agreed to meet with Wheatly at 4:00 PM in the Oval Office.

Delighted with himself, Wheatly headed out for lunch at the Pulpit Pub. He sat alone at a booth and ordered a corned beef sandwich with extra mayo as well as a scotch with Perrier on the side. As he waited for his lunch, he leafed through the *Washington Post*. He stopped to take notice of an editorial comic strip about the president. He had been drawn as a giant straddling the Unites States–Mexico border. He had one foot in Texas and the other in Chihuahua, and there appeared to be a strong southern wind blowing his hair over his eyes. His shirttail flapped, his clothes looked tattered, and tumbleweeds piled up against his boots. Between his legs, a tiny convoy of Mexican trucks carried duty-free goods across the border into the United States. As each truck rolled by, the president tossed cash into the back. Heading in the other direction on the same road were Mexicans driving brand-new luxury cars. They smiled broadly and waved to the president as they drove past unemployed Americans who stood dumbfounded by the roadside. "NAFTA—it's good for American trade," the caption read.

In the midst of his chuckling, he was startled by a bullish figure sliding into the booth with him. The man bulldozed Wheatly into the corner, crumpling the senator's newspaper beneath him. Wheatly tried to turn his head to face the intruder, but he had been jammed in so tightly that he could hardly move. Finally, the pressure eased, and he was able to identify his antagonist.

"Hey there, Mr. Senator! Havin' lunch?"

The senator recognized the thick Irish accent. It was O'Mally, one of Carl Ziese's thugs.

O'Mally was a beast of a man—a hardened Dubliner with cauliflower ears and a nose smashed tight to his cheeks. Each of his hands was thick and hard like bricks. His fingers were crooked and pale—rough as sandstone and ribboned with raised scars at the knuckles. He had no remorse for any damage he had ever inflicted on another human being. He was a particular favorite of Mr. Ziese and took advantage of his boss's generosity—as coarse a man as he was, O'Mally was always dressed to the nines, usually wearing imported Italian suits that were custom tailored to fit his powerful frame.

"I was asked to come down and see how t'ings were movin' on the NAFTA situation," he said.

He reached into his breast pocket and pulled out a pack of Camels. Stretching past the senator for a pack of matches lying at the end of the table, he crammed Wheatly even more tightly into the corner of the booth. A waitress approached with another scotch and bottle of Perrier. O'Mally struck a match and lit a cigarette as the waitress stared oddly at the two men. Grinning from ear to ear, O'Mally nodded casually at her. She put down the drinks, offered nothing else, and quickly moved away from the table.

O'Mally blew a plume of smoke toward the ceiling and returned his attention to Wheatly.

"What do ya have for me, Mr. Senator?" he asked. "What can I relay to the boss?"

Having been in tight squeezes before, the senator was surprisingly calm, though he was naturally very concerned by O'Mally's presence.

"You people don't give a guy much time to do his job, do you?"

O'Mally only grinned in response.

"You just tell Barletto and Ziese that I'm working on it. All right?" He squirmed in an attempt to gain some breathing room. "Tell them to cool it. It takes awhile to get these things done."

Wheatly worried about whether any of his colleagues could see what was happening. "Listen, if you keep doing this kind of shit, I won't be able to help you people at all! I'll be out of politics. You coming here and acting like this can ruin me!"

O'Mally nodded, lifted his bulk from the senator's body, and slowly slid to the end of the booth. Just before standing, he dropped his lit cigarette into Wheatly's scotch.

"You have a nice day now, Mr. Senator."

O'Mally tugged on the bottom of his jacket, smoothed his lapels, and left.

Senator Wheatly tried to smooth out the wrinkles in his own clothing, with considerably less success. *Shit,* he thought, *I'd better get the president to release me from the NAFTA committee today—before Barletto's crew finds out that I'm supposed to be the leader of the damn thing!*

Pushing the polluted scotch away and staring down at the table, the senator pondered his quandary. Even though he might be able to get off the NAFTA committee, he was still expected by the textile mob to oppose and shut down the bill—a prospect to which the president would surely take exception.

Suddenly, someone else slid into the booth, this time across from him. He looked up alarmed, but it was only Anthony. The aide made a sour face at the tainted glass of scotch.

"What's up with this?"

"Don't ask," the senator replied.

Chapter Thirteen

Back at the senator's office, Kathy was speaking on the telephone with Mike Lane. He had called to thank her for the help she had given him the previous week.

"You definitely pointed me in the right direction," Lane said. "I was finally able to introduce my work to him. I can't thank you enough."

"Well, you're more than welcome," she replied in a low tone.

Had Kathy known the real reason for the senator's newly accommodating attitude toward Lane, she would surely have been shocked.

"I hope that I might be able to repay you somehow."

"That's not necessary, Mike," she said rigidly.

Sensing Kathy's discomfort in talking to him from the office, Lane decided to cut the call short. It was obvious she was concerned the senator might suspect it was she who had told Lane about the inn. In fact, due to the traumas Wheatly had suffered of late, he hadn't considered how Lane had found out about the hotel in the first place.

"Well, listen, Kathy, I don't want to keep you. Don't worry, our secret is safe."

"Thanks, Mike." She sounded sincerely relieved.

Before hanging up, Lane felt compelled to add, "Kathy … I don't know why you went out on a limb like that for me … but I think I should tell you that Jeff asked me whether I've told anyone about my plan. I said no. Anyway, I'm just trying to say I didn't even tell him that I'd spoken to you."

"Thank you, Mike. I can't even begin to imagine how important this must be for you. Trust me. I'm really pulling for you." She then surprised herself by speaking impulsively. "Uh … I'm heading up to New York to spend the weekend with my sister and her family. Philly is on the way … maybe if I stopped and met you someplace, we could talk and have a drink."

He wasn't sure how to respond. He hadn't been alone with a woman in any way since Tina.

"Well … er … I don't know. You see, I … um …"

Kathy felt that she had clearly overstepped her bounds, and she interrupted him. "You know, on second thought, I should probably drive straight through, and …"

"How about eight o'clock at my house?" he blurted out, surprising the both of them.

"Okay," she said simply. A smile flashed across her face.

He gave her directions, and they said good-bye.

Lane stared at the phone for quite some time, feeling a little nervous and unsettled. After all, he had never played host to another woman at the home he and Tina had once shared.

At precisely four o'clock, Senator Wheatly was escorted across the White House main lobby by a towering marine. The senator was forced to hustle a little in order to keep up with the thick-necked marine. They crossed over an enormous presidential seal laid into the marble floor and approached a bulky twelve-foot door. The marine robotically opened the door with his white-gloved hand and held it open for the senator. Wheatly glanced up uneasily at the leatherneck as he passed him and took notice of the light reflecting off the black, patent-leather beak of the marine's hat.

Inside the Oval Office, the senator placed his briefcase on a chair in front of the president's desk. He walked over to the windows situated behind the desk and stood there fantasizing about being commander-in-chief. He envisioned himself wielding the mightiest sword on earth. His reverie was interrupted when the president entered the room.

"Jeff! You made it!"

"Yes sir," said Wheatly. "I greatly appreciate you seeing me so soon, Mr. President."

"Hell, Jeff," the president said. "Now what kind of boss would I be if I couldn't take time out to see my NAFTA right-hand man?"

Wheatly smiled half-heartedly.

"Well, sir, I'd like to talk about that."

The president sat in the wingback leather chair behind his grand, uncluttered desk. "Okay, Jeff, let's talk about it," he said. "I'll go first. You know I need you and want you on that committee."

"Yes, I know, but if you were to look *this* over ... you might see things a little differently." He snapped open his briefcase, removed the thick manuscript, and placed it on the president's desk.

Wheatly started the most important pitch of his career.

"First off, sir, you know that there are a lot of qualified people out there who can head the NAFTA committee."

The president opened his mouth to respond.

"Sir, I know what you're going to say: that you want *me* to do the job. I realize that, and I'm flattered. All I'm asking is that you look at this. I'm telling you, if you were to spend a few hours with it, you'd find it worth my pursuing with great tenacity. *Well* worth it."

The president leaned over the document and read the cover aloud.

"The Point Guard."

"It's judicial reform. It's brilliant, sir." Wheatly pointed at the document. "This will get you reelected." Raising his eyebrows, he looked up at Wheatly. "You know, Jeff, you've been a good soldier ever since I took office ... I'm sorry, I can't say that I'll take you off the committee, but I suppose that the least I can do for you is take a look at this thing. But you should know, Jeff, that I've finally chosen the staff I want you to work with on the NAFTA project." The president stood and ended the meeting abruptly. "But I guess I can hold off on notifying them about your appointment for a couple of days. I promise that I'll take a quick look at this thing. But this is the last delay. After this, we get down to business."

The senator squeezed the president's hand. He was unsure of his success, but it seemed as though he still stood a chance.

"I really appreciate it, sir. I'll be at the Whitehall Inn all weekend if you have any questions. Suite 309."

Wheatly closed his briefcase and turned to leave. He hesitated and then faced the president once more.

"Sir?"

The president raised his eyebrows.

"If the Point Guard becomes a reality, you'll go down in history with the likes of Washington, Lincoln, and Kennedy. It will revolutionize a significant segment of our judicial system, and you'll be the man who gets the credit for it!"

The president looked surprised but intrigued, and the senator took a brief, lusting look around the Oval Office before letting himself out.

Ziese and Barletto sat smoking cigars in a conference room overlooking Chicago. A couple of Barletto's bodyguards milled around the fringes of the room.

"So, Carl, what's up with that little fuckin' prick Wheatly?" asked Barletto.

"He tells us he needs a little time. That it takes time to line his ducks up."

Barletto cocked his head to the side. "Is that what he said?"

Ziese shrugged. "That's what he says."

Calmly, Mr. Barletto pointed at Ziese with his cigar.

"Carl," he said, "you get paid to keep an eye on dirtballs like Wheatly, right? You get paid to get them to do what *I* want them to do, not what *they* want to do. Right?"

Barletto's tone became progressively more impatient and disturbed.

"Do you feel that you've been keeping a close eye on Wheatly? Do you feel like he's operating in our best interest?"

"Yes," said Ziese, squirming a little. "I think that once he gets his ducks in line he'll do as he was told."

Barletto slammed his fist down on the conference table, capturing the attention of everyone in the room.

"Bullshit!" he yelled.

Ziese was astounded at this outburst. He had always been one of the most productive workers in Barletto's brutal organization. It was suddenly obvious to him that there must be a problem that he was not aware of concerning the senator.

Ziese raised his arms, and his cigar sagged between his lips.

"What?" he said.

"Whaaaat?" Barletto mimicked, exaggerating Ziese's word and his pose.

The two stared silently at each other for a moment, and then Ziese glanced at the bodyguards. "What the hell's going on?" he asked.

"Carl," said Barletto, "you're supposed to *know* what the hell is going on in your own backyard! I found out that your little fuckin' senator has decided not to work with us on the NAFTA shit. Even worse than that, I found out that he's been appointed as the head of the president's committee to turn the fuckin' thing into law!"

Ziese knew better than to doubt that Barletto was telling him the truth, and he knew better than to make any excuses. He sat quietly for a moment with his jaw tightly clenched.

"I'll take care of the motherfucker," he finally said.

Barletto laughed. "You ain't gonna take care of anything. How the fuck could you not see this coming?"

Ziese said nothing.

"Tell me!" Barletto demanded.

"Mr. Barletto, I thought we had him under wraps. It's obvious to me now that I was wrong." Ziese was simultaneously pissed and alarmed. "How do you know this, Mr. Barletto?"

"We got an informant in Senator Baily's office ... his aide." Barletto spoke more calmly now. "He told us that Wheatly was appointed to the committee by the president after a recommendation from Senator Baily. So, how did this happen, Carl?"

Ziese dropped his head and mumbled. "Wheatly, that little jerk-off."

"I know that Wheatly's been notified about the appointment," Barletto said, "but, for whatever reason, he hasn't turned it down. I have had *enough* of that prick."

He got up, walked over to the windows, and gazed out over the city. He tapped lightly on the sill for thirty seconds.

"I guess we can't buy his vote," he said calmly. "So we'll have to take it away from him. Whack him."

Ziese was eager to redeem himself. He got up and swiftly left the room.

At 7:30 that evening, Wheatly and Anthony met in the suite at the Whitehall Inn. The senator began by explaining that Lane needed his help in trying to get the Point Guard up for a vote.

"Mike needs me," he concluded, "to try to get his work committed to law. In exchange, he says he'll remain quiet about you and me."

Anthony sat nervously at the dining table as Wheatly walked circles around it.

"Now, the problem that I see with this arrangement has to do with when he doesn't need my help any more. What if his plan passes into law? It's human nature to forget all your ties when you find success. I'm concerned that Mike could become too big to manipulate, and I don't know whether he's trustworthy enough to keep our secret."

Anthony felt nauseated as he imagined his family and friends discovering that he was gay.

"On the other hand," the senator continued, "Point Guard could be rejected. In that case, Mike might become despondent—or worse, vindictive—and there would be nothing preventing him from telling everyone what he knows, despite our deal."

Anthony slumped in his chair. He was noticeably shaken. His sunken eyes had dark circles under them and were bloodshot from lack of sleep. The entire ordeal had sapped the life out of him. He had also learned that he lacked the guts to kill himself. Just a couple of days before, at his parents' house in Philadelphia, he had stood in the bathroom holding sleeping pills in his clenched fist. He had stared at the mirror and had been ashamed of the image he saw. He had raised the pills tremblingly to his mouth but had been unable to push them past his quivering lips. Instead, he had dropped them into the sink and fell to his knees. He had then muffled his tears and moans behind cupped hands, so that his sleeping parents would not know of his pain.

"There *may be* one way that Mike won't tell anyone."

Wheatly felt as though he were dangling a piece of string in front of a kitten. Curious, Anthony turned to listen. But before the senator could resume, the phone rang, and he answered it. It was the president.

"Okay, Jeff," he said, "you have my attention. What I've read of your document has more than intrigued me. This point system is ingenious, and I think it could actually work! Of course, I'll need to study it further, but I think it's worth having you pursue it. I'll hold off on naming you to the NAFTA committee for now."

"I thought you would see it that way, sir." Wheatly smiled broadly.

"Are you alone on this one?" the president asked.

"Not exactly, sir."

"What do you mean?"

Looking over at Anthony, the senator turned his back and lowered his voice.

"Sir, perhaps we can talk in more detail after you get a little more acquainted with the document?"

There was a moment of silence, as the president seemed to be pondering the senator's response.

"Okay, Jeff. Let me review this thing with one of our constitutional experts and get back with you."

"Sounds like a good plan, sir."

After hanging up, he turned toward Anthony. He slapped his hands together and rubbed them briskly. "Things are looking up!"

Anthony was unaware of what had just transpired and was unable to join the senator in his enthusiasm. He gazed at the floor, desperate to solve the problem that had weighed so heavily on his mind for the past week.

The senator, now pumped, moved in to finish the job he had started before the president's call. He pulled a heavy crystal decanter from the bar and approached Anthony from behind. He gripped the decanter's neck with one hand and massaged Anthony's neck with the other.

"You're tight!" he said. "I'm telling you, don't worry. I have everything worked out."

Anthony's head fell forward, accepting Wheatly's touch. The senator raised the decanter above his aide's head and asked, "Can I pour you a drink, Anthony?"

"No thanks."

The senator walked around to where his glass sat on the table and filled it with scotch. After taking a sip, he resumed his position behind Anthony.

"As I was saying," he said, "I think I know a way to keep Mike Lane quiet." He leaned closer and whispered in Anthony's ear. "Mike has the only other copy of the Point Guard, I'll find out where he keeps it, and then *you* will sneak into his house ..." Anthony's eyes gaped wide, and he recoiled from the senator's touch. "And you'll steal it!"

Anthony quickly turned to face the senator. "Steal it? What for? No way! Get someone else?"

"Get someone else? I'm a fucking senator! What do you want me to do, find a thief in the Yellow Pages, for God's sake?"

"I don't see how stealing his document is going to help anything. You already have a copy," Anthony said.

The senator took a big swig of scotch from the glass and swirled it around in his mouth before swallowing.

"You want our secret to stay a secret?"

"I'm not stealing anything, Jeff!"

"I've fucking had it with you!" The senator slammed his glass on the table. "You act as if you're the only one who got caught. If it gets out I'm having a relationship with you, my career is fucking done!" He leaned and yelled within inches of Anthony's face. "Do you understand me?"

Horrifying visions rushed through Anthony's mind as he shook his head. He tried to stand, but the senator pressed down on his shoulders and persisted.

"Listen to me. I can make Mike our best friend."

Anthony squirmed and shook his head in disapproval. The senator pressed on.

"All I have to do is convince him that he needs to be wary of the people I will be introducing to his work. Once you have stolen his copy, he will assume that it was them. This really isn't a big deal. What are we stealing? Something we already have?" Wheatly continued, "I'm not going to talk to any of my colleagues until after we have his copy and we're convinced that he feels we are indispensable."

Anthony now seemed to be ignoring the senator. "Are you listening?" Wheatly shook him. "Are you listening to me?"

After ensuring that he had reclaimed Anthony's attention, he explained while stalking around the room.

"You see, like you said, I have a copy of his document. He would never suspect me. All I need to do is tell him that I met with my colleagues, who are very powerful and shrewd men, to get started on his work. Some of them, I'll explain, would do anything to claim the fame and power that goes along with authoring powerful reform like the Point Guard. I'll warn him. I'll make him paranoid over the whole damn thing. He may be reluctant at first to trust me, but once the document is stolen, he will look to me for guidance and protection far beyond what we are doing right now. He'll trust me."

Anthony leaned on the table and anxiously rubbed his forehead.

"Anthony, we need to do this as soon as we can. Tomorrow, I'll call Mike and try to find out where he keeps his copy without raising any suspicion of me. I'll strike up a conversation that will give me an idea of when he may be out of the house over the weekend. When he's gone, you'll break in and steal the document. You will need to destroy everything on his computer and find anything related to Point Guard and take it. It needs to look like someone took everything, and I mean everything, as if they knew what they were looking for. After you finish, bring everything back to the inn. Try to be as inconspicuous as possible. You should spend the night here. That way, you'll have an alibi, and I'll be your witness to it just in case. There should be no reason to suspect you, but as an added measure of insurance, I'll call my wife at around the time you'll be carrying out your task. I'll pretend to be speaking with you here in the suite while I'm on the line. I will also get room service for two.

"You see, Mike reassured me that nobody else knows about the Point Guard. I guarantee you; he will contact me when he discovers that his work has been stolen. That's when I'll go to work and reassure him that I have his back. At that point, he will know that I'm the guy that can prove he is the author, the founder of the Point Guard system. After all, I have a copy to prove it."

The senator bent down and moved close to Anthony's face.

"Understand this, I can't afford to have anyone know about you and me, and I'm willing to do anything to keep it that way."

"I can't do this," Anthony whined.

"Unless you want to be out of the closet, you better come up with a better plan. And you better come up with it right now."

Anthony's fear of being uncloseted overrode both his common sense and his good-heartedness. He had never committed a dishonest or hurtful act but now found himself blinded by desperation. The senator had strung him along as well as could any puppeteer. In the end, a tired and confused Anthony reluctantly went along with the senator's plan without realizing what he was really getting into.

Chapter Fourteen

Lane spent the better part of the early evening hours cleaning his house, making sure that it was presentable for Kathy's visit. As he cleaned off the kitchen table, the phone rang.

"Hello?"

"Mike, it's me, Jeff."

"Hey, Jeff. I didn't expect to hear from you until next week."

"I just wanted to keep you in the loop Mike."

"Great. What's up?"

"I've had a few confidential meetings with some colleagues to discuss your Point Guard."

"Yeah?" Lane took a seat on the sofa.

"Yes, and it went very well. I feel *fairly* certain that they will keep it confidential. These guys are ..."

Interrupting the senator, "What do you mean, you feel *fairly* certain?"

"Like I was going to say ... these guys are very ambitious and powerful men, Mike. I've worked with *some* of them in the past, and they understand the necessity for confidentially in matters like this ... but they are ruthless men."

"What do you mean?"

"Look, Mike, now that we're moving ahead, there are going to be some *very ambitious* people involved. Trust me; they'll see the potential in this thing. Hell, who ever is associated with bringing your system to fruition will gain significant political power."

"Who are the people we're talking about? Politicians?"

"Some of them, yes."

Lane was quiet. He hadn't counted on this.

"Mike, this will eventually take an army of people to get done. It'll need to go through all types of legal process, and all manner of people will work on it. That's why it's so important to have confidentiality early on. We'll need to get the right people involved. We'll have to choose who we want to work on this *very* carefully. As soon as that's done, we need to rush to get it out in public."

"Why?"

"Like I said, there is an awful lot of power connected to this type of reform. Who knows what people would do? *Plagiarize it … maybe just imitate it. Maybe even attempt to steal it!* So the sooner we announce this and get it out in the public … the less chance there is of anyone trying to claim it as their own."

Lane was quiet again.

"You maintained confidentiality on this, right?" asked the senator.

"Uh … yeah."

"Good. Make sure it's in a secure place."

"I did that."

"You have?"

"Yeah."

"Are you keeping it at home?"

Lane considered Wheatly's question very carefully. He had already taken the precaution of not keeping his document in an obvious place because of concerns about the senator. He felt he had sufficient reason to somewhat trust the senator, especially since he considered the information he had about Wheatly's private life to be an unbeatable trump card. However, this call gave him serious reason for concern. But who should he be concerned about most, the senator or his colleagues?

Lane answered the question.

"In the basement."

"Good. We'll need to move fast on this. Will you be available this weekend?"

"I can be," responded Lane.

"What does your schedule look like tomorrow?"

"I can meet you whenever you want, Jeff."

"That won't be necessary. I can work around your plans. I just want to talk about the next steps. I can do that over the phone."

Lane nodded, "I had planned on going to a STOP meeting."

"What time is that?"

"Six."

"How long will you be tied up?"

"They last about three hours."

"I'll tell you what. I will call you on Sunday at around noon. How's that?"

"Sounds good."

"We'll talk then. Mike, be careful."

Lane hung up the phone, and for several minutes, he sat staring at the table while he considered the senator's warning. He had an hour before Kathy was due to arrive, so he finished picking up the house and got dressed. Right on time, the doorbell sounded, and he took several deep breaths to calm his nerves before opening the door.

Before long, Lane and Kathy found themselves sitting on the sofa with cocktails and telling one another about their lives. They felt none of the discomfort that normally accompanied a new friendship. It was the first time that anyone else had been inside the house since the night of Tina's funeral, when friends and family had gathered to console him. Alone every night since then, he hadn't realized how much he had been missing the company of a woman to whom he felt an attraction. Having spent so much time alone, Lane was happy to have Kathy over and was as excited as a schoolboy at the sophomore dance.

The two quickly hit it off. They talked comfortably and laughed much.

"You're a funny man, Mike!" Kathy said. "That is, when someone gets to know you."

Lane never did take a compliment very well. He just nodded his head. Thinking of Tina he said, "Yeah. I've been told that by someone before."

There was a brief pause and a momentary hint of sadness. The feeling quickly dissipated as Lane's shy smile caught Kathy's eye.

After several more drinks and a great deal of conversation, their attention turned toward work.

"So, Mike, what about this law thing you're working on? Is the senator interested in it?"

Lane smiled and said, "Oh yeah, very much so."

"That's fantastic! Congratulations!"

They raised their glasses for a toast and looked into each other's eyes for an electric moment. They both then glanced away awkwardly. In an attempt to lift the slight air of embarrassment, Kathy resumed the conversation.

"That's great, Mike. So the senator likes your ... thing?"

"Yeah. Thank God."

"Would you mind if I asked exactly what it is? This law project you're working on. I'm sorry if I'm prying. It's just that I feel as though I might be able to help. Don't get me wrong—I've never involved myself in the senator's business. Nor anyone else's, for that matter."

A little buzzed, Kathy felt as though she were botching her attempt to qualify her interest in Lane's work. Lane could see her embarrassment. He smiled.

"I trust you," he said. "I'd be happy to tell you all about it."

For about twenty minutes or so, Lane gave her an overview of his plan.

"My God, Mike!" she said once he had finished. "That's brilliant! I can see why the senator is interested."

"Listen, Kathy … Jeff said that I shouldn't discuss it with anyone. But because I … well, because I'd already told you what I was trying to do and because I couldn't have got it into Jeff's hands without you, I feel that it's okay to tell you about it. Just don't repeat any of it to a soul, all right?"

Kathy mimed locking her lips and throwing away the key.

"You have my word, Mike."

Lane instinctively knew that he could trust her.

For the second time that evening, they found themselves gazing into one another's eyes, saying nothing. They both felt a glow of energy, a twinge in the belly, and more than a little light-headed. Kathy moved her leg close to his. He felt her aura softly warm his knee. Slowly, he lowered his nervous hand to his knee to feel the sensation. Kathy reached out. He accepted her hand with his. Tightening their grip, an unsettled Lane looked down toward the floor. Kathy leaned forward, trying to keep her eyes locked with his. She reached her other hand up to soothe his head, but before she touched him, the phone rang.

"I'd better get that," Lane said as he motioned toward the kitchen.

Kathy smiled and nodded. The phone rang again; Lane sat there and admired her smile.

"I'll let the machine get it."

Kathy still smiled.

"Mike, it sounds like you're on your way. That must be exciting?"

"It is," he said modestly.

Kathy bounded to her feet and stretched her arms wide to give him a congratulatory hug. He then stood and returned her enthusiastic squeeze. As they embraced, they instinctively moved in unison, as though in the middle of a slow dance. He closed his eyes as his face brushed lightly against her hair. Smelling the sweet fragrance of her silky mane, he found himself lost in the moment. Kathy leaned her head back to look at him, and she brushed her hand softly against his cheek. Lane cupped her face in his hands, and he slowly lowered his lips to hers. Their lips touched softly and pulled apart, and then again, and again, and then they pressed their mouths hard together and kissed passionately. Lane lowered an arm around the small of her back and pulled her tight against him. She went weak from the combination of his firm grip and the sensuous kiss. Then, suddenly, Lane pulled away and took her by the hand. She opened her eyes dreamily as he touched her face. Lane appeared to be confused.

"What's wrong, Mike?"

He turned away and shook his head.

"Kathy, I can't … I just can't … It's been …"

Nothing more needed to be said. Kathy knew that he was the type of man who dedicated his heart completely to the one he loved and that it would not be easy for him to be with another, even though his wife was gone forever.

She placed her hand on Lane's cheek and nodded.

"It's alright," she said "I understand. It's about time I got on up to see my family anyway."

She moved toward the door and grabbed her coat from the old wooden garment tree in the foyer. Lane made a clumsy attempt to help her.

"You're a good guy, Mike," she said.

She turned quickly and let herself out. Lane stood in the open doorway. He had been unsettled by her quick good-bye. He felt his anxiety build with each step she took away from the house. Suddenly, he called out to her.

"Kathy!" She stopped and turned. Lane stepped outside. She met him halfway.

"Don't leave, Kathy," he said. "Stay … please."

He wrapped his arms around her and spun her inside. With an impassioned swoop, he closed the door and pressed his body against hers. They stood in the foyer, locked in a long, tempestuous kiss. He then tried to explain himself but was hushed by Kathy's whispers. "No, don't speak." She panted and ran her hands through his hair. She kissed him uncontrollably and climbed his body as they both gasped for air. Lane pushed her onto the carpeted staircase and thrust his hips into hers as he kissed her face and neck. Kathy groaned with approval, her hands exploring his shoulders and back. Lane paused to gaze into her eyes and then started to unbutton her blouse. After allowing him to expose her full breasts, Kathy pulled him down on top of her, wildly kissing him and tearing at his trousers. Finally, undressed and intertwined, they made fiery love at the base of the stairs.

Early the next morning, Kathy and Lane sat smiling at each other over coffee at the breakfast table. They confessed the attraction that each of them had felt during their first meeting at the senator's office. They also admitted that they were glad things had worked out as they had.

As Kathy took her last sip of coffee, she slid across the table a piece of paper with her phone number and address scribbled on it. She then informed Lane that she really did have to get on the road to New York. He reached across the table and took hold of her hand.

"This has been very nice," he said. "I hope that we'll be seeing each other again soon."

Kathy smiled and nodded. "You can count on it," she said.

Before Kathy's departure, they agreed that it would be best to keep their romance a secret from the senator. Lane wanted to be sure that Wheatly would not connect his appearance at the Whitehall Inn with Kathy. Lane also felt that it would be best not to tell Kathy about the senator and Anthony.

Their relationship began veiled in secrecy.

Lane then went about his day—a Saturday so different from other Saturdays recently gone by. There was a sense of increased optimism in the air caused by a combination of the good news about Point Guard and the rejuvenating feeling of a budding relationship. Due to all the work he had been doing on the Point Guard document, he had not attended a Survivors of Violence meeting for some time. But because he felt better about both his own future and that of his work, he thought perhaps he could be a positive influence for someone else. So he had made up his mind, as he had told the senator, and would attend the meeting.

That afternoon at the Whitehall Inn, the senator gave Anthony some last-minute instructions.

"The document is in the basement," Wheatly said.

Anthony sat motionless, staring at the floor. He felt on the verge of being disabled by fear and didn't utter a word. The senator paced back and forth, dictating his plan like a football coach going over strategy in a locker room.

"Once you have it, be sure to retrieve any computer disks and hard files. Be sure to get into his computer and erase any files that appear to be associated with the document. And be sure to check out the rest of the house for any evidence of the thing. He's very meticulous with his work. I'm pretty sure that he'd keep everything in the office—but check anyway."

Anthony continued to sit quiet and still.

"Are you hearing anything I'm saying, Anthony?"

Anthony slowly nodded. He could barely allow himself to believe that he was about to commit a crime in order to cover up his gay relationship. He was beginning to believe that what he was about to do was actually worse than coming out of the closet.

"Pull yourself together, Anthony. I need you to be focused. Imagine what would happen to our careers if anyone were to find out about us. What would it do to your parents if they found out you were gay? How would your friends see you?"

Anthony continued nodding listlessly.

"Anthony, once we have the document in our possession, you'll have nothing to worry about. Now ... when you leave the inn, be sure that no one—and I mean *no one*—recognizes you. Take the stairs and the service exit. Remember that I'm your alibi. I'm going to say that you never left the room today. Lane should be at his meeting by six o'clock. He said that they usually last about three hours. That should give you plenty of time. When you get back to Washington, enter the inn the same way you left it—being careful not to be noticed. I'll expect you back here no later than midnight."

Anthony rose from the chair and grabbed a black duffel bag that held a change of dark clothing, gloves, a ski mask, and tools. Without saying anything, he left the suite. As the door closed behind him, he could hear Wheatly's faint voice.

"Good luck!"

Chapter Fifteen

Lane received a warm welcome from his friends at the STOP meeting.

"Good to see you! Where have you been?" they asked.

Meanwhile, Anthony's drive north on the interstate was going terribly slowly. He came to a complete halt due to an accident ahead and was only a few miles from the exit he was to take. Now forty-five minutes behind schedule, he was growing progressively edgier. Cars were lined up four lanes across for as far as he could see. His leg bounced nervously. Suddenly, he swung the car onto the empty right-hand shoulder and darted past the stagnant traffic until he could see flashing blue and white lights in the distance. He then reentered the traffic and forced his way, an inch at a time, to the far-left lane. He drove past the accident scene, and his stomach did flips as he witnessed firefighters frantically using cutting tools to free a victim from an overturned car that had come to rest on its roof off in a ditch. Being witness to this mishap only heightened his trepidation. He turned away from the accident and looked down anxiously at his watch.

He finally rolled into Lane's neighborhood and crept past the accountant's house, inspecting the property a couple of times. The driveway was empty, and the house was dark. He noted some overgrown bushes and foliage along the edge of the property that led right to the side of the house. He would use the greenery to get to the house without being noticed. Although he was behind schedule, he was still concerned that there was too much daylight. He decided to wait until nightfall and parked inconspicuously a few blocks away. Waiting for sunset made him all the more nervous. Finally, it was dark enough; he reached into his black bag on the passenger seat for a black hooded sweatshirt with a kangaroo-style zipper pocket on the front. He pulled it over his head. He straightened his hair with nervous hands and then reached into the bag again for some tools and the ski mask, all of which he jammed tightly into his belly pocket. He reached beneath the steering wheel to the floor and tied his sneakers tight with trembling hands. Taking several deep breaths and exhaling hard, he could feel his heart pounding like a hammer. He left the car and trotted down the sidewalk toward Lane's house, masquerading as a jogger. He looked at his watch again. It was already seven-thirty, so he picked up the pace from a jog to an outright sprint.

Swiftly approaching Lane's property, Anthony dashed along the sidewalk past neighbors' houses and then suddenly slowed and made a hard right turn onto Lane's lawn. He gathered speed again and bolted along the row of seven- or eight-foot-high overgrown bushes. He jackrabbited across a small gap to an evergreen tree that pressed tight against the side of the house. He quickly dropped to his knees and crawled under the tree. Anthony gasped and tried to recover from the sprint. His legs quivered, his lungs burned, and his heart pounded deafeningly.

After several minutes of recovery, he pushed through the undergrowth to the side of the house. A few inches above his head and concealed by the tree was a window. The novice thief was fortunate, for he could work on the window undetected by passersby. Pausing at the window, he listened and waited to be sure Lane wasn't home. Then, reaching over his head, he pushed on the window. It was locked. He fumbled through the pouch pocket and pulled out a small jeweler's hammer, a cloth, and a pair of black leather gloves. He put on the gloves and wrapped the cloth around the head of the hammer. He gently tapped on the window. His first tentative strike produced no results. He struck harder with each successive blow. On the fifth blow, a small piece of glass fell onto the carpet at the end of the ground-floor hallway inside the house. Anthony plucked pieces of glass away from the window and placed them on the ground. Before long, only the window frame remained. Using the tree to boost himself, he slid through the window and fell to the floor.

Allowing his eyes to adjust to the dark, they widened like silver dollars. He started to navigate through the unfamiliar house. He crept up the hall, through the living room, and into the dining room in search of the basement door. He was very aware that he did not have as much time as had been originally planned to complete the job, so he moved swiftly, albeit clumsily, through the house. Eventually, he pulled on the sticking basement door. After a few tugs, the door opened. By this point, he was beyond tense. He licked his dry lips and groped for the light switch. He found it and flicked it, and the light seeped up from below.

The narrow and shadowy staircase spooked Anthony, and his skin tingled as he hustled down the stairs. At the bottom, he stood beneath the single bulb and looked around the dusty cellar. He assumed that the office would be in the basement and was confused to see only the massive playroom. He peeked around the wall to look beyond the stairs, only to see the furnace. Considering the senator's instructions, he decided to start his search. He worked the room in a sweeping pattern. He walked deliberately and methodically, first to the left and then back to the right, walking deeper into the room with each pass. He looked for anything that could hold a thick manuscript.

Anthony looked at his watch. It was 8:15, and he still had a lot to do. After inspecting all the open floor space, he began to look behind and under everything, not bothering to replace anything. Unable to suppress his jitters, he kept tugging at his gloves and wiping away the sweat that ran down his head and face. He crouched down and rummaged through the wooden playhouse; then through the playhouse window, he saw the carport and toy cars. Something clicked, everything seemed to be meticulously situated, and he noticed that one of the cars appeared to out of place.

Anthony scrambled over to the carport. He dropped to his knees and noticed that the thick coats of dust that covered the cars appeared to have been recently disturbed. He shoved one car to the side and pulled the other from under the carport. In front of him, he saw a toy box. He quickly lifted the lid and fumbled around inside the deep dark box. He was relieved to find the document. Not wasting a moment, he crawled out and jumped to his feet. He bolted up the stairs, the large document secure in his arms.

Since he was feeling the crunch of time, his search became progressively sloppier. He left the basement door open and the light on. He needed to find the office the senator had told him about. He hustled through the living room and stood by the front door for a moment as he considered where the office might be. He looked down the hall toward the widow where he had entered and then shot down and opened doors as he progressed. He peeked first inside a laundry room, then a bathroom, and finally the office at the end. He entered the modest office. It was 8:45. He saw the lit streetlamp outside through the slits in the open blinds. He had been leaving lights on all over the house. He placed the document on the center of the desk, pulled the blinds closed, and turned on the office light. He sat at Lane's desk in front of the computer monitor. He turned on the outdated computer and rifled through nearby drawers and file folders, where he found a couple of disks labeled "Point Guard," which he stuffed into the zippered pocket of his sweatshirt. He then began to examine the computer files. This was perhaps the only aspect of his mission that he was actually qualified for—Anthony was something of a computer whiz.

Meanwhile, Lane had left the STOP meeting—earlier than Wheatly had expected he would. Lane was tired from all the excitement of recent days. As he drove through the dimly lit streets of West Philly and approached his neighborhood, Anthony was accessing the Point Guard document. Anthony was aware that time was tight but felt he would still be able to complete his mission and escape from the house before Lane came home.

Anthony found multiple files and input a command that would initiate their deletion. He watched intensely as the computer screen indicated a systematic deletion of all information relating to the Point Guard document.

Suddenly, his concentration was diverted by the sound of a key entering the front door lock at the far end of the hall. He sat petrified for a moment that seemed much longer than it was as he listened.

Lane turned the doorknob. Anthony leapt to his feet in a fright, rushed into the office closet, and pulled its louvered door closed behind him. He hadn't even had time to turn off the computer. Shivering with terror, he could see, between the slats of the door, the computer screen on the desk. File after file of the document flashed past as the computer expunged them from its memory. Anthony shook severely as he reached into his front pocket and quietly pulled out his knit ski mask. He struggled to pull the mask over his head and face and did his best to fight off hyperventilation. The mask restricted his view, but he hoped that it would keep him from being identified—assuming he would be able to find the courage to flee when the opportunity presented itself. He peered out into Lane's office with what felt like tunnel vision and waited.

Stepping inside, Lane immediately noticed the lights were on. He first assumed that he had left them on before going to the meeting, but as he turned and bolted and chained the door, he began to doubt this rationalization. He slowly pivoted to face his home's interior and examined the house more suspiciously than usual.

Since Tina's murder, he had become hyper-aware of his surroundings at home. He took a few cautious steps into the living room, passing the hall where Anthony had entered the house and which led to his office. Cautious and troubled, Lane proceeded deeper into the house. He took two more steps and saw the basement door. It was open. His heart jumped and began to pound like a bass drum. His eyes widened as he tried to rationalize the situation. But he knew that there was no way he had left the basement door open. As he approached the top of the staircase, he was alarmed to see that the downstairs light was on. All doubt vanished. Someone had broken in. As he stood at the top of the stairs, it dawned on him that whoever had broken in could still be there. He froze and listened hard for about thirty seconds.

Meanwhile, Anthony tried desperately to determine where Lane was and what he was doing. From the cramped closet, he could see only the desk and computer screen. The machine was still eliminating Lane's document file by file. The closet was becoming claustrophobic.

Lane crept down the basement stairs as quietly as he could. When he was on the third step, he heard a series of beeps coming from the front of the house. He thought that it sounded like his computer—did this have anything to do with Wheatly's warning? It *was* the computer. Its antiquated software caused it to emit a series of beeps to signal that it had finished deleting one of the many document files. It would pause before moving on to the next.

Both men in the house had been startled by the sound. Anthony gritted his teeth, and Lane stood erect, holding his breath and waiting to hear if the sound would repeat itself. But no sound would follow until the next file was deleted. Confused, Lane turned back and made his way toward the front door. Within a few feet of it, he looked down the hall to his left and saw that his office door was partially open and that the light was on. He stepped softly down the hall and paused outside the office door to inspect the sliver of the room that he could see. He heard his computer click and whir. He gently pushed the door open. The back of his black leather office chair obstructed the view of the computer screen. Baffled and rather afraid, he entered the office and stepped into full view of Anthony. Lane's back now restricted Anthony's view of the screen. Lane could see that his old monitor was flashing madly as files repeatedly disappeared from the screen.

Suddenly, he noticed his hard copy of the Point Guard document sitting on top of his desk. He squinted as he focused his attention on the computer screen. At the bottom of the screen, a program command flashed: "Delete/Point-Guard;files." A sickening feeling overcame him. He quickly leaned forward and desperately worked his fingers across the keyboard, trying frantically to halt the malicious command when he felt he heard something coming from the closet. Pausing, he thought he might have heard something again as Anthony accidentally rubbed lightly against the door. Lane turned and slowly walked toward the closet as Anthony held his breath and watched him approach. Terrified, Lane got within two feet of the closet and stopped to listen again.

There was only the sounds of the computer when suddenly, like a claustrophobic bear escaping from its cage, Anthony kicked violently on the closet door, knocking it off its hinges. He flew out and crashed into Lane. They both slammed onto the top of the desk and tumbled to the floor. The keyboard and pages of the document crashed down with them. Anthony picked himself up and made a dash for the front door. As the computer continued its systematic eradication of the files, Lane lifted himself to his knees, quickly reached under his desk, and withdrew a pistol hidden there.

He had purchased the weapon a few days after Tina's murder but had never used it. It had been slung for years untouched, in a holster screwed to the desk. However, it was loaded and ready for use.

Lane instinctively gave chase. Anthony was now desperately fumbling with the chain on the front door. Lane ran down the hall, gun at the ready. He flew toward the intruder and bowled into him, sending both of them across the room and crashing onto the coffee table. As Lane became tangled with the table, Anthony jumped to his feet, ran to the door, and tried again to unlock it. Lane kicked the table away and vaulted to his feet. He raised the gun, squeezed it tight, and pointed it at Anthony.

"Don't move!" he screamed. Spit flew from his mouth.

His hand shook as he took aim, pointing the dusty gun barrel at the center of Anthony's back. Still, Anthony kept trying to open the door. Lane inched toward him. Finally, Anthony unhooked the chain and tugged hard on the door handle. It turned, but the door didn't budge. An inside deadbolt—installed as an extra safeguard after Tina's shooting and which required Lane's key to unlock—held the door firmly closed.

Anthony continued to pull on the door in vain. Lane shouted at him again as sweat ran down his face.

"I said don't move! I swear to God I will fucking shoot you!"

Neither man was built for such violence, and accordingly, both were scared half to death.

After a few more seconds, Anthony stopped pulling on the door and turned to face Lane. Anthony's ski mask gave him a frightful look, and Lane's gun hand grew even more unsteady at the sight of the masked man. He panted heavily and raised his other hand to the gun in an attempt to steady it.

"What do you want?" Lane shouted.

Lane took an unsteady step forward and quickly glanced down the hall to his office. His computer was still grinding through the Point Guard data. He edged toward the office while keeping the gun pointed at Anthony. "What are you doing?" he asked.

Anthony just stood there, mutely terrified.

"Who sent you?" There was still no response. "Why are you destroying my files?" Lane wanted desperately to terminate the deletion process. He continued to move slowly toward the office, hoping to halt the extermination of his files while continuing to hold the thief captive.

He backed down the hallway. Only a few feet from the office, he turned his head for an instant to get his bearings. At that moment, Anthony bolted out of sight, across the living room, and toward the back of the house. Abandoning his plans to reach the computer, Lane again gave chase. Being more familiar with the house's layout, Lane gained on Anthony quickly. As Anthony reached for the back door's knob, Lane crashed into him again, this time driving both of their upper bodies through the panes of glass in the back door. They both rebounded and fell backward onto the kitchen floor. The ski mask prevented Anthony from being cut, but Lane suffered a large, deep gash that stretched from the top of his forehead to below his chin. Blood spilled everywhere. It gushed from the massive wound onto Lane's face and into his eyes as he struggled to keep Anthony in view and hold a firm grip on his weapon. Anthony scrambled to his feet and tried to step over Lane, who reached up, grabbed Anthony's leg, and sent him sprawling to the floor once more. Anthony's mask twisted around, and he could only see through one of the eyeholes, which were now down near his nose. Unable to free himself from Lane's hold, Anthony turned to fight. He threw himself on top of Lane. They had been struggling for less than three seconds when the gun discharged with a loud bang.

They thrashed around on the floor for a short time after the shot. There was a gurgling sound as the two men finally separated. Anthony staggered to his feet and pulled off his ski mask. He looked down in utter horror. Lane thrashed about on the floor while clawing at his throat and grasping at the air. Blood gushed from his throat, and he attempted in vain to halt its steady flow. He jammed his bloody fingers into the gaping hole made by a bullet from his own gun. Pools of blood spread over the now slick linoleum floor. Anthony's stomach heaved, and he tried to suppress the vomit welling up in his esophagus. He staggered away from the sickening sight and back to the office, leaving behind a trail of bloody footprints. Frantically, he picked up the keyboard with his bloody gloves and placed it back on the desk. The computer had finished deleting the files and had requested a final command. At the bottom of the screen, he read: "save: c:\point guard?(Y/N)."

The cursor flashed under the letter N, insisting on an answer. Anthony pressed the N repeatedly, and all traces of the files were gone. Panicked, he gathered up the pages of the document and stuffed them under his arm, but not before grabbing the computer and quickly smashing it on to the floor.

He ran back into the kitchen. Lane's foot fluttered as though he were being electrocuted. Stepping over him, Anthony accidentally kicked the gun that lay on the floor near Lane's leg. He stood dead still at the back door as he watched the gun slide across the bloody linoleum floor. Undecided on what to do, he stood there and starred at the weapon for a few seconds. Suddenly, he darted over to the gun and stuffed it in his pocket before he unlocked the back door and slipped into the moonless night. He sprinted along the back of the house with Lane's document sloppily wedged between his arm and ribs. His movement into the empty backyard set off a motion detector, which turned on a set of floodlights that lit up the yard and the rear of the house. Running toward the bushes, he squinted as he looked up into the lights. Before he was able to get to cover, he was noticed by a neighbor of Lane's, an elderly widower who stood by his kitchen window washing dishes at this time every night. Suspicious of the noises he had heard and noticing a stranger carrying something through his neighbor's backyard, he immediately phoned the police, who would take several minutes to arrive. In the meantime, Anthony stumbled through unfamiliar backyards in the dark as he made his getaway. He pulled off his sodden, blood-soaked gloves, and shoved them into his pouch, along with the ski mask and the computer disks he had stolen. Bolting out onto the sidewalk, he breathed heavily as he approached his car and climbed in.

Chapter Sixteen

A police cruiser pulled into Lane's driveway. One of the officers stepped swiftly from the car and started to examine the property as the second officer radioed to inform the dispatcher of their arrival.

Meanwhile, Anthony was heading toward the interstate. On the highway, he made certain to keep his car moving at precisely fifty-five miles per hour. He constantly checked and rechecked his speed. He looked repeatedly into his rearview mirror—almost to the point of distraction—to see whether he was being followed. This caused his vehicle to swerve out of his lane from time to time, which added even more stress to his situation.

The meaning of the evening's events sank in as he drove. His mind felt stunned, and his body felt as though it was overwhelmed by nausea. He tried to shake the image of Lane wallowing in his own blood and gasping for breath but couldn't. He rolled down his window in a panic and dry-heaved into the night air, all the while struggling to keep his car centered on the four-lane highway. He swerved again, this time nearly into another car. Steering the car back into his lane, he suddenly spewed vomit onto the steering wheel and dashboard. Recoiling, he swerved yet again. This time, an alarming blast from a tractor-trailer air horn rocked him as the rig nearly collided with the side of his car. Gathering his wits and control of his car, Anthony suffered a continuing barrage of convulsive dry-heave bobs and gags as he continued his getaway.

One of the police officers knocked loudly on Lane's front door and got no response. The other quickly proceeded around the residence, inspecting it more closely. They both checked nearby trees and bushes with their flashlights and discovered nothing suspicious. They peeked through several windows and saw no one inside. It was apparent that there had been some sort of disturbance on the ground floor of the home—there was obvious damage and disarray. They made their way to the rear of the house, where they saw that the glass of the inside back door had been broken and the outer door had been left open. This meant trouble. The officers drew their weapons and proceeded with caution. Before entering the house, each of them instinctively looked over his shoulder. They saw Lane's neighbor standing in his kitchen, framed by the window and silhouetted by the light behind him. They stepped closer to the door, illuminating the area ahead of them with their flashlights. Bloody footprints were clearly visible on the metal threshold inside the storm door. Careful to avoid stepping on Anthony's tracks, they entered the kitchen.

Almost immediately, one of them called for assistance and an ambulance with his shoulder-mounted radio. He had seen Lane's motionless body lying facedown in a pool of blood. One of the officers rushed past Lane to secure the rest of the house, while the other bent over Lane's still body.

A few hours later, Anthony reached the suite undetected after parking his car on the street. He wore a leather jacket that concealed the vomit-and-blood-soaked sweatshirt underneath.

Anthony let himself in and could make out the senator lounging on the sofa in the dark. Wheatly wore nothing but a satin robe and stretched out comfortably while sipping wine. The suite's shades were drawn, and the flickers emanating from the porno video Wheatly watched dimly lighted the room. Anthony closed the door behind him and leaned against it. His face was pale and sweaty, and his sunken eyes seemed even darker than they had been earlier in the week.

Upon hearing the door close, the senator jumped off the sofa, secured his robe, and rushed over to greet Anthony. Anthony started for the bathroom but was intercepted by the senator before he reached the hallway.

"God, you stink!" said Wheatly. "What the hell is that smell?"

Anthony stopped, looked over the senator's shoulder, and saw the porno film playing on the television as well as the bottle of wine. The light from the television lent an ominous aspect to Anthony's appearance, an aspect that may have been heightened by the loathing he felt for the senator at that moment. Anthony placed the disheveled document on the desk at the end of the hall, pulled the computer disks from the stained sweatshirt hidden beneath his jacket, and tossed them on top of the document.

"That's all of it," Anthony said, his voice cracking.

Without another word, Anthony disappeared into the bathroom. The senator, who felt amused and content, sat at the desk and started to thumb through the document when he noticed traces of blood on the cover. He had an odd look on his face when he grabbed hold of the disks. But he was quickly distracted by the television. He pursed his lips in approval of the scene that was playing and toted everything that Anthony had stolen to the sofa.

About fifteen minutes later, Anthony emerged from the back of the suite with his bags in hand and headed straight for the door. His hair was wet from the shower and was slicked back tightly to his head. Not intending to engage with the senator, he had been reaching for the doorknob when Wheatly emerged from the living area and asked, "Did everything go as planned?"

Anthony dropped his bag and turned to face the senator.

"No," he said expressionlessly.

"What went wrong? What happened?" Wheatly read something strange in Anthony's eyes.

"He's dead," Anthony said.

"What?" said Wheatly, as though he didn't quite understand.

Anthony looked past the senator and spoke in a monotone.

"He's dead."

The senator rubbed his head, squinted, and walked across the room. Turning back around, he approached Anthony with a blank look.

"What do you mean, he's dead?"

Anthony looked down at the floor and then raised his eyes to meet the senator's eyes.

"Just what I said." Anthony spoke slowly as anger rose within him. "He ... is ... *fucking* ... *DEAD*!"

Wheatly started to walk rings around the dining room table. As he circled, he tried to organize his thoughts. After the third or fourth lap, he stopped and looked at Anthony.

"*What the fuck!* This wasn't part of the plan," he said, rapidly shifting from confused to deeply angry. He pressed Anthony against the door and stretched his neck in an attempt to meet Anthony face-to-face.

"How the *fuck* did he end up dead?" Wheatly yelled.

Anthony closed his eyes and swallowed hard as he struggled to fight back tears of shame and anger.

"Don't you start crying, you fucking faggot," said Wheatly.

Anthony couldn't hold back and began to sob.

"Did you kill him?" the senator persisted.

Anthony couldn't answer.

"I *said* did you *kill* him? *Did you kill Mike?*"

Anthony lurched toward the small, badgering man and locked his hands around his skinny throat. Letting out a howl, he drove Wheatly into the living room. The senator struggled to break the aide's grip as he tried to maintain his balance, but he was no match for Anthony's athletic power. Anthony slammed the helpless politician onto his back and continued to choke him. Anthony's bloodshot eyes bulged, and spit dripped from his mouth onto the senator's face.

"Yes! *Yes*! YES!" Anthony shouted.

The senator tried with all his might to loosen Anthony's grip. Out of control, Anthony pounded the senator's head against the thickly carpeted floor. Wheatly's face turned a reddish purple. In under a minute, the senator stopped struggling, and his eyes bulged like those of a rat caught in a trap. The only sounds in the suite were the moans and screams of the characters in the porno film.

Just as the senator was about to lose consciousness, Anthony snapped out of his fit and released his hands from Wheatly's throat. The senator gasped for air, coughed, rolled over onto his stomach, and crawled away from his aide. Blowing heavily, Anthony went to the door and grabbed his bag. Before leaving, he turned toward the senator and spoke one last time.

"I should kill you, Jeff," he said. "You used me."

Wheatly did not attempt to stop him from exiting the suite.

The senator dragged himself up to the sofa and massaged his throat, trying to restore normal breathing. When he had finally recovered from Anthony's rampage, he began fanning the pages of the Point Guard document as he fondled the computer disks absently. He sat for some time, considering his options, and giving thought to a new plan.

He decided that he would drive home to Philadelphia. He would have plenty of time to think during the drive. He gathered his things and checked out of the inn, even though it was after midnight. Wanting to ensure that he was noticed, he stopped and engaged in idle chitchat with the night desk manager before leaving the property.

Wheatly arrived home at almost three o'clock on Sunday morning. He turned on some lights, poured himself a scotch on the rocks, and ascended the grand staircase to the second floor. Jane was awakened by her husband's inconsiderately loud arrival. As he approached their bedroom, she could hear the ice in his drink jingle against the cold glass. With each step he took, the annoying noise grew louder. The sound ceased when he stopped outside their bedroom and resumed after he had turned the doorknob and stepped inside. He made his way to the bed. Jane lay still, pretending to sleep. Her unwelcome husband turned on the lights.

The senator had been aroused by the evening's activities. Murder, porn, and a near-death experience had stimulated his perverted senses. Plus, he had the great pleasure of knowing that his secret was secure. With Lane dead, there were suddenly limitless opportunities in regard to the Point Guard. If he could find an angle, Anthony's blunder had the potential to be a good thing for the senator.

He sat on the end of the bed, swirled his drink, and guzzled it down. He then lay back on his side and rubbed his body against Jane. Jane lay near the edge of the bed on her side, facing away from her husband. He leaned over, pushed his lips close to her ear, and whispered, "I know you're awake."

She squeezed her eyes tightly shut and prayed that he would leave her be. The stench of liquor and cigars pouring from her husband's foul mouth turned her stomach. He reached around and slid his hand underneath her soft nightgown. She rolled onto her stomach, acting as if she were tossing and turning in her sleep.

"I know you're awake," he taunted.

He propped himself up on his elbow, pulled his hand from under her gown, and ran his finger up and down her back.

"Come on ... Daddy wants some cookies," he said. He licked his lips and chuckled.

She still refused to respond.

He suddenly pulled the covers away from her and slid her silk gown easily up her legs, exposing her bottom. Increasingly frustrated by her disregard, he became forceful.

"Come on!" he yelled. He forced his hand between her legs, trying to separate them. Jane tried to hold her legs tightly together and turned back onto her side.

"No, Jeff! Please! I don't want to!"

He laughed and unbuttoned his trousers.

"No? Who do you think you're saying no to? I'm your husband!"

With his pants around his knees, he roughly climbed up her legs and straddled her buttocks. She could feel him trying to force himself into her from behind. She rolled onto her back, writhing and trying to throw him off.

"Please, Jeff! No!"

Ignoring her, he rolled over on top of her and tried to drive her thighs apart by jamming one of his legs between hers. She squirmed underneath him. He reached back and slapped her ferociously across the face. However, this only made her more determined to keep him—her own husband—from raping her. Jane fought off his attack for about fifteen more seconds, after which he was able to pin her arms to the pillow above her head. She continued bucking and resisting, screaming into his face for him to let her go.

Suddenly, he smashed the top of his head into her face, dazing her and bloodying her nose. She felt him lift his weight from her arms, but she was too disoriented to put up an effective defense. He tore her nightgown away from her body. Jane scratched and clawed weakly at her husband, trying to dig her nails into him. Before she could inflict a wound on his face, he balled his hand into a fist and punched her squarely in the jaw, rendering her semiconscious. The senator now took what he wanted from her staggered, bruised body. Jane was conscious of what he was doing, but she could no longer stop him. She lay still and wept as he continued the heartless deed while tears streamed from the corners of her eyes and dripped onto the bedsheets.

In less than two minutes, he had consummated his act and rolled off his wife. He sat at the end of the bed and said nothing—he didn't even look back at her. Jane lay naked on her back—she was cold, in shock, and whimpering. The senator stood up, grabbed a robe, wrapped it around himself, and went downstairs. He sat on the livingroom sofa, lit a cigar, and puffed away. He reached for a pad and pen from the end table. As cigar smoke drifted past his eyes, he scribbled on the pad:

> Rape—200 points; 20 years.
> Accessory to murder after the fact—150 points; 15 years.
> Conspire to break and enter—50 points; 5 years.
> Total—400 points.
> Allowable points—100 points.
> Overdrawn—300 points/Total 30 years.

He smirked as he jotted down the totals. "What a fucking system!" he said. "Ha!"

Jane shifted to the fetal position, sunk beneath the covers, and lay motionless. Her drying tears tightened the skin around her cheeks and eyes.

She felt helpless. She knew that she would not report his actions to the authorities. She believed no one would listen. No one would believe that her husband had raped her. Jane stared coldly at the ceiling for hours and tried to make sense of a marriage that had strayed so far off course.

Chapter Seventeen

After lying awake all night, Jane slowly and timidly went downstairs at around eight o'clock. She entered the living room and found her husband sound asleep on the sofa as if it were any other Sunday morning. Feeling very sore, she stepped gingerly through the foyer toward the front door. She gently opened the door and gathered the morning newspapers from the porch. Despite her best efforts at silence, Wheatly was now awake. He lifted his head from the sofa and said nothing as his wife disappeared into their kitchen. Jane placed the papers on the breakfast table, brewed a pot of coffee, and started to cook some bacon and eggs. The hardy odor of the morning meal wafted into the living room, prompting Wheatly to make a move to the kitchen. Standing in the doorway, the senator suspiciously watched his wife go about her normal Sunday routine. He hadn't really known what to expect from her after the previous night's brutal attack. He grabbed a section of a newspaper and sat at the table. He offered his wife no apology or excuse.

Jane felt anxious and terrorized and decided not to cross her husband this morning. She had chosen to retreat within herself and say nothing to upset him. She intended to go about the morning as though nothing had happened at all, and he intended to let her do so.

As the unhappy couple ate breakfast, Wheatly worked swiftly and uneasily through the papers, searching for a story about Lane's death. There was none.

Jane picked quietly at her breakfast, seemingly mesmerized by her full plate. She didn't once lift her swollen eyes and bruised nose in her husband's direction.

It was obvious that he was scouring the newspaper for something in particular, but she wasn't about to ask him what it was.

He was a little surprised to find nothing at all about Lane in any of the papers. Perhaps it had happened too late to make the morning editions.

Jane started to clean up the dishes. He watched her closely, like a guard dog. Her nightgown hung sloppily loose; her slippers dragged across the mosaic tile floor. Her hair was knotted and uncombed; her nostrils were swollen and caked with dried blood. Wheatly pushed his chair roughly away from the table, and she jumped. He laughed at her reaction and left the room.

"I'm going into my office to phone Anthony," he called out to her.

Jane heard him but didn't respond. He stopped in his tracks and went back to the kitchen, where he found her placing dishes in the dishwasher.

"Did you hear me?" he demanded roughly.

She nodded tightly.

"Then acknowledge me!" he shouted.

Her shoulders bristled. She grimaced and began to shake.

"Now ... I *said* ... I'm going to call Anthony."

She felt that it would be better to say something rather than provoke another outburst, so she mustered a stiff smile and tried to appease him with trivial banter.

"I ... I ... saw Anthony yesterday," she said.

His face went blank, and the hairs on his neck stood on end. He moved closer to her.

"What did you say?" he asked tersely.

"What?" Jane responded. She was scared and confused.

He rushed toward her and raised his voice.

"What did you say?"

Jane cringed and stood anchored to the floor. She tucked her chin into her chest, and cowered. She had been holding two dishes in her hands, and she now dropped them both. They smashed against the floor, and shards of imported china flew in all directions. Wheatly gripped her shoulders and shook her violently.

"Where? *Where* did you see Anthony?"

Jane had finally been driven to the end of her rope. She began to cry uncontrollably and went limp. She was expecting more of the same treatment she had received the night before. He asked her the same question repeatedly, but she was unable to respond. She was nearly paralyzed by fear. Seeing that his methods had become counterproductive, Wheatly tried to change his tone. He removed his hands from her quivering shoulders, wrapped his arms around her, and pulled her unreceptive body close to his.

"Everything will be all right," he said soothingly. "Now just calm down."

He repeated his question once more, this time gently.

"Now, honey ... where did you see Anthony?"

"I saw him when I was over at Meg's house," she said, sniffling between words. "By Mike Lane's. When Meg and I were having dinner."

Meg Kelly, Jane's best friend, still lived directly across the street from Lane. Meg had never married, and so Jane and Meg often enjoyed dinner together when the senator was out of town. The previous evening, as she sat on Meg's enclosed porch having a cup of tea before dinner, Jane thought she had recognized Anthony's car as it slowly cruised down the street. A few minutes later, it had driven past a second time, and she had been able to see Anthony clearly at the wheel. Considering the professional ties between Jeff and Lane, Jane had given Anthony's appearance very little thought.

After hearing Jane's explanation, Wheatly pulled his arms away from her, turned away, took a couple of steps, and then turned back to face her.

"You mean Anthony? *My* Anthony ... my aide? You saw him near Mike Lane's house?"

Jane nodded as she wiped tears from her eyes with the palms of her quaking hands. She had no idea why her husband was behaving this way.

Reeling from Jane's alarming disclosure, the senator hurried off to his home office, which was situated underneath the staircase, to phone Anthony. In his haste, he paid no attention to the fact that he had left the office door slightly ajar. He quickly pounded out Anthony's phone number.

Seconds after the senator had left the kitchen, Jane took a deep breath and headed for the stairs, leaving the shards of the broken dishes scattered over the floor. Emotionally and physically drained, she struggled to lift her legs one at a time up the stairs. She couldn't help but overhear her husband talking on the phone. It was clear that he was furious with Anthony. Her curiosity overcoming her anxiety, she stopped midway up the staircase and listened for a moment. She then proceeded to the second floor and squatted beside the banister, firmly gripping its spindles. She was now directly above his office door and could make out most of what her husband was saying.

"Damn it, Anthony, my wife saw you! Do you know ..."

Jane missed the end of the sentence, but then Wheatly's voice rose.

"It fucks up the alibi if you ever need one, you stupid shit!"

Jane's knuckles whitened as she squeezed the banister spindles ever tighter. Why would he need an alibi for something? Suddenly, the phone slammed down. An instant later, the office door flew open. Jane jumped to her feet and scurried down the hall to her bedroom. Wheatly emerged from the office and looked up to the second floor. Had he heard a sound coming from up there? Though Jane was now out of sight, he was able to catch a glimpse of her shadow retreating down the hallway wall. How much had she heard?

The senator ascended to investigate. He found Jane drawing a bath in their oversized Jacuzzi tub. The bathroom was at the far end of the bedroom—and was larger than most people's bedrooms. It was outfitted with fine Italian marble, floor-to-ceiling mirrors, twin vanities and sinks, and private toilets. In the corner, there was an immense glass-enclosed shower with built-in marble stools that could accommodate four people. He stood in the doorway of the bathroom watching Jane as she slapped at the water running from the spigot and adjusted its temperature. She wasn't aware of his presence. Once the water temperature was to her liking, she slid out of her dressing gown and dropped it to the floor, exposing her bruised but exquisitely tall and thin body. Jane bent over the Jacuzzi and stretched across to turn on the television recessed into the wall above. She then turned and was startled by her husband. She stood stark naked without saying a word. He stared at her at length distrustfully. He still wondered what, if anything, she had heard. He glanced up at the television.

"I'm going downstairs to watch the news," he said, and turned to leave.

Jane took a deep breath. It seemed as though she had been standing in front of the tyrant for minutes, but it had actually been only a few seconds. She sat on the edge of the Jacuzzi and brushed the knots out of her hair before sliding into the warm, soothing water.

Lounging on the sofa downstairs, the senator impatiently surfed from channel to channel in search of news regarding Lane, but he found none. He picked up a cordless phone and called Anthony again.

"Have you seen any news about it yet?" Wheatly asked.

"No," said Anthony despondently.

"Shit!" The senator switched off the phone without another word.

Upstairs, Jane soaked in the tub with a warm washcloth draped over her face and eyes, trying to relax. The television was tuned to a local network, but preoccupied as she was with her own emotions, she hardly noticed the newscast begin. The confident voices of the anchors resonated in the humid room as she reclined into the steamy suds in search of a few minutes of welcome oblivion.

Downstairs, the senator had finally ended his surfing on the same local news broadcast that was on in the bathroom. Wheatly sat on the edge of the sofa for ten minutes before he saw what he had been waiting for. On the screen, he could see police officers and patrol cars swarming all over what he recognized as Lane's property. Wheatly moved closer to the television as he glanced toward the stairs.

"A West Philadelphia man was shot yesterday in his home," the newscaster said. "Police believe that it may have been the result of a robbery attempt, but this has not yet been confirmed."

Jane fidgeted a little as she tried to reposition herself and resoak her comforting washcloth. She was now paying a little more attention to the broadcast. She lay back, covering her eyes once more.

Wheatly remained charged with anticipation as he listened closely to the report. He remembered that Jane had turned on the bathroom television and wondered whether she was tuned in to the same broadcast.

The story continued: "A neighbor who was an eyewitness reported that he saw a man walking through the victim's yard earlier in the evening. The victim was taken to Lankenau Hospital, where he was pronounced dead several hours later. The victim, an accountant named Michael Lane, was the city's ninth homicide victim this month."

Upon hearing Lane's name, Jane shuddered and floundered. She tried to sit up. Water crested over the side of the tub and soaked the tile floor. Her eyes snapped open, and her first instinct was to look in the direction of the bathroom doorway and out into the bedroom.

She pieced together everything that had transpired since last night, and it all made a sickening kind of sense to her.

Cautious and afraid, Jane climbed out of the tub. The beads of water and suds that cascaded down her body sparkled in the bright lights. She tiptoed across the marble floor, leaving a foamy trail behind her. From the doorway, she saw the bedroom door across the room. It was open. She stepped onto the bedroom carpet, trying to ignore the shivers of cold fear that coursed over her body. Now, she finally knew of what her husband was capable. She dashed across the room toward the bedroom door.

Downstairs, at about the same time Jane started to climb out of the tub, Wheatly threw down the remote and rushed up the stairs to the bedroom.

From the bedroom, Jane could see her husband climbing the staircase two steps at a time. At the top of the stairs, Wheatly saw Jane making her way toward the door. They were both about the same distance away from it, and they now raced to reach it first. Wheatly broke into a sprint and streaked down the hall.

Jane was unable to maneuver around the bed in time, and she found herself at the doorway just when he reached it. Standing nude and dripping wet in front of him, Jane shivered and tried her best to act as if nothing unusual were happening. In an act of self-preservation, she made an unconvincing attempt at comforting her husband, but her act was transparent to him. She reached out with a trembling hand to touch his chest and forced out an edgy smile. The senator responded with a stare as cold as death. He took hold of her hand and gave it a crushing squeeze. Jane whimpered. He tightened his grip and twisted her arm into an excruciating position. Her silky, nude body bowed in pain as tears fell from her terror-filled eyes.

"Jeff, please, please stop, Jeff," she cried.

He raised his fist high above her head and crashed it down into her teeth, shattering them. Her lips split and blood erupted from her mouth.

Because of the adrenaline flooding her veins, she hardly felt the massive blow at all, but it had struck her with such force that it knocked her flat to the floor. She attempted to crawl away, and he repeatedly and unmercifully punched the back of her head with all the force he could summon. Each blow was intended to kill.

Somehow, she managed to absorb these blows and continued to crawl across the floor. Wailing horrifically with each of his punches and kicks, she managed to scratch and paw her way under the bed. Hiding like a petrified pet, she covered her head with her hands and panted wildly.

Wheatly sat on top of the bed, breathed heavily, and wiped the sweat from his face. He looked as though he were taking a break from a tennis match. His feet rested flat on the floor just inches from Jane's head. He lowered his head between his ankles, looked at his wife upside down, and laughed. Blood rushed to his head, causing his veins and eyes to bulge. It gave him the appearance of the deranged man he had become.

Jane saw his upside-down purple face and spun toward the opposite side of the bed.

Wheatly bounced off the bed, reached underneath, and grabbed one of her ankles. He yanked her kicking and screaming from her hiding place and dragged her toward the bathroom.

Every inch of the way, Jane reached for and grabbed at anything she could. She knew that she was now fighting for her life.

At the bathroom door, she hooked her hands onto the doorframe and tried to resist his jerking pulls. He had hold of both of her legs now, and his mighty tugs caused her thin body to rise off the floor as she refused to relinquish her grip on the doorframe.

The senator's lungs burned from the extreme exertion. Saliva drooled from his mouth. His weary arms let go of Jane's ankles after one more hard jerk, and her flesh slapped loudly against the cold tile floor.

With what little energy she had left, Jane tried to shimmy away from him as he tried to catch his breath. Too tired to do anything else, Wheatly threw his body over hers, pinning her to the floor and keeping her from retreating into the bedroom. He wheezed deeply as he tried to recharge for another attack.

Jane was also too tired to fight. Both of them lay entwined and motionless; each was out of breath and was awaiting the other's next move.

After fifteen or twenty seconds, Wheatly staggered to his feet and straddled his wife. Jane took advantage of this move by attempting to race across the floor on her hands and knees, but the senator snatched at her hair and viciously jerked her head back. He struck her directly on the nose with the side of his fist. Her body went limp, and she fell to the floor again. She was now too dazed to put up a fight. He dragged her easily across the wet floor to the full Jacuzzi.

Almost subconsciously, Jane still put up a feeble resistance. She moaned and tried to communicate with him as her head bobbed spasmodically. The senator spun his wife into position beside the Jacuzzi. He reached beneath her armpits and hoisted her onto the tub's edge, but her nude wet body was too slick to handle, and she kept sliding from his grip. As Wheatly repeatedly tried to improve his hold, Jane began to regain some of her senses. She wanted to resist, but she was still so terribly dazed that she could not.

Finally, by pressing his knee against the center of her back, the senator was able to pin her against the side of the tub, facing the water. He grabbed her neck with one hand and a fistful of her hair with the other. The reflection of Jane's beaten face stared back at her as he held her head above the water. She reached up behind herself in a final effort to grab at his face, but her position and grogginess did not allow her to succeed. With her upper torso folded over the edge of the tub and her head in his hands, she was now at the complete mercy of the father of her children.

For several seconds, he just held her in that position. There was a brief hint of reconsideration. Then his expression changed, and he appeared emotionless as he plunged her head and shoulders into the water.

Jane battled weakly to raise her head, but she could only lift it high enough to catch one last short breath. There was a gurgling sound as he drove her back under, this time deeper. She struggled for only a short time before her body went completely limp.

The senator continued to hold her head underwater even though he knew that she was dead. His clothes were soaked; his shirt and trousers were torn. A look of desperation flashed across his face as he stared down at Jane. Her hair fanned out and floated to the surface.

He eventually rose from her lifeless body like a sleepwalker, left the bathroom, and settled on the edge of the bed. He sat quietly, and his mind wandered. From the bathroom, he could hear the television and the soft splash of water against the sides of the tub. Jane's head and shoulders bobbed in rhythm with the roll of the water.

The phone rang. Wheatly sat unresponsively through seven or eight rings before picking it up. Without even muttering a greeting, he held the receiver to his ear.

"Hello? Hello?"

"Yeah," Wheatly said lifelessly.

"Is everything all right, Jeff?"

"Oh ... uh ... Yes, Mr. President."

The president then spoke like an excited schoolboy.

"Jeff, I've been reading this Point Guard document all weekend, and I've got to say that it's pretty damn intriguing!"

The senator was unable to share the president's enthusiasm.

"I've talked this over with one of my legal experts to be sure something like this can be legally implemented. The good news is that it can. The bad news, and I'm sure you know it, is it's a huge undertaking. Now I haven't talked about it with anyone else as of yet—and I don't think you should, either. I think it would be best if we kept this under our hats for now. I'm telling you, Jeff, this really excites me!"

Uninterrupted, the president gushed about the plan for about five minutes before wrapping up his call. "Jeff, I want to start on this immediately. Now, you're alone on this, right?"

The senator was silent. He thought about the president's question. This was his opportunity.

"Right, Jeff?"

"Uh ... yeah," said Wheatly as he considered his answer.

"The other night you told me 'not exactly,' what *exactly* does that mean?"

"Uh ... I mean ... I talked to some people as I developed it. But nobody knew what I was actually working on, except for my aide, Anthony Kane."

"Listen, Jeff, I will get you on my schedule this week. I don't want to get my staff involved in this until I get a firmer grip on it. I'll have my legal expert keep it confidential as well. I'll also let my staff know that you and I will be meeting to transition your appointment from the NAFTA committee to someone else. That will buy us some time so we can get our strategy set on this. So, just you and me for now ... no staff or aides, understand?

"Yes, I understand."

"It will take a lot of work to get this thing where we want it, but I think that we can eventually get it to Congress for a vote." He paused and thought for a moment. "We'll need to sell the Supreme Court justices the idea that they'll have a significant role in this thing if we are going to have a chance at pulling this off. It's a big chore, but I really think it can happen! Regardless, the whole concept will cause enough excitement among the public to get me reelected, just because I'll be doing something that appears to make sense!"

"Yes, sir, I agree."

"We're in this together, Jeff. It's on to bigger and better things for you, and if all goes well, perhaps a second term for me. Now have a good night, and I'll see you later this week."

"Bye ... Mr. President."

Still sitting on the edge of the bed, the senator took a mental inventory of the carnage of the previous twenty-four hours. He stared directly at his wife's corpse in the bathroom as a busy tone screamed from the receiver he still held loosely in his hand. He had always been able to justify his past sins to himself. But murder? Could he draw another line in the sand?

He placed the receiver back on its cradle and then paced the floor as he considered the problem of Jane's body. Certainly, he could think of no scenario that would explain away her fate as an accident. Her death being the work of an intruder was also unlikely—their home was not only burglarproof, but it also received considerable attention from the police due to his political clout.

"Come on, Jeff, think!" he muttered. *"Think!"*

Finally, his pacing ceased. An idea had occurred to him. He went downstairs, closed all the shades and curtains on the ground floor, and returned to the bedroom. For the next couple of hours, he cleaned and straightened the bedroom, which had come to resemble a war zone. After finishing with the bedroom, he headed for the bathroom.

By now, the water in the tub was perfectly still and had turned a translucent pink after mingling with Jane's blood. Her body looked almost peaceful, as it lay bent over the edge of the tub. He moved her hair and then reached down into the water and unplugged the drain, causing Jane's head to roll as the water poured out. He grabbed her body under the arms and gently pulled it away from the tub. He placed it on the floor and proceeded to clean the bathroom. Turning to the tub, he stepped over his wife's body to find a reddish ring circling its interior. A large quantity of Jane's hair had clumped around the drain. He wadded up some toilet tissue and rubbed vigorously to remove the ring of blood. He then scooped her hair from the drain and flushed it down the toilet.

Once he had scrubbed the entire room with bleach and had returned the bathroom to its normal state, he slid his wife's body across the floor into the bedroom and started to dress her. It took quite awhile for him to choose the clothes, and it was nearly impossible for him to dress her limp, uncooperative corpse. Once Jane's body was fully clothed, he propped it up against the bed. He considered applying makeup to her bluish face but was too disconcerted by her dead, open eyes to manage it. Instead, he climbed behind her and tried to brush her hair into something approximating the style she normally wore.

His grisly work had lasted the better part of the day, and he needed to rest. He went downstairs and sat staring at the television while Jane's body, seated on the floor next to their bed, stiffened.

At about eight o'clock that evening, Wheatly went back upstairs and changed his clothes. Once dressed, he went over to his wife's body, hoisted it onto his shoulders like a firefighter, and staggered toward the hall. He carelessly banged the body repeatedly against the doorjamb and then against the wall as he descended the staircase. Finally, he stumbled into the living room and plopped Jane onto the sofa. Wheezing, he lost his balance and fell across her lap. He was surprised that his wife's thin, lifeless body was so difficult to handle. He lay against her, trying to catch his breath.

He was beginning to feel sick and tried to swallow, but his mouth and throat were too dry. He pushed himself up off Jane and walked to the kitchen. Twisting the faucet, he dipped his mouth underneath the tap and sipped from the stream of cold water. He dried his face with his sleeve and returned to the living room.

Wheatly was wearing one of his most expensive suits. It had been his intention to create the appearance that he and Jane were heading out for a late dinner, which they often did on Sunday nights.

Once again, he struggled to lift her onto his shoulder. He carried her to the garage, placed her in the passenger seat of his car, and got behind the wheel. He revved up the Mercedes Benz S500 sedan, pressed a button on a remote to open the garage door, and backed out into the night. He drove down dark side streets, avoiding major roads. The car's windows were tinted, ensuring that Jane's state would go unnoticed by anyone who glanced in their direction.

After what seemed to him like an age, he turned onto Kelly Drive, a winding riverfront road that followed the Schuylkill River. His pulse rate increased with every passing second. Kelly Drive had the river on one side and a very steep and jagged rock cliff on the other. In the daylight hours during the summer months, the drive was filled with cyclists and lovers walking hand-in-hand. Years before, he and Jane had been one of these couples. The thick foliage that bordered the road shielded most of the drive's streetlamps. Because of its geography and its dimness, Kelly Drive had seen its share of serious auto accidents.

The senator drove up and down the scenic route several times, for several miles in each direction. He was looking for the best opportunity and location to send his car off into the deep river. He knew the area well, and before long, he had identified the dangerous curve he would use—it featured a man-made retaining wall that acted as a riverbank and a flight of concrete steps that led down to the river's surface.

As he neared the fatal bend, adrenaline coursed through his veins. His pulse raced, and his hands shook. He struggled to control his bladder. About two hundred yards from the curve, he pulled to the side of the road and idled beneath a dark tree, gathering his courage. After about a minute, he turned off the lights and ignition and took several deep breaths.

The night was crisp, quiet, and very clear. He could hear the river as it roared past its banks nearby. He knew that he had to consider every detail. It was important to make the accident look as real as any that the police had ever seen.

After one last deep breath, the senator reached over and disconnected Jane's seat belt. He placed his right hand on the back of her head and his left around her chin and throat. He looked around to make sure that no other cars were nearby. He then thrust her head with great force against the windshield, trying to duplicate the impact of a collision. The result sounded like a melon smashing on a sidewalk. Her head left a crackled impression in the safety glass and rebounded forcefully toward the headrest. Wheatly settled in once more behind the wheel. After taking a few seconds to steel himself, he squeezed his eyes shut, reared his head back, and slammed it hard against the steering wheel. He inspected his forehead for traces of blood and found none. In fact, he hadn't done himself any visible damage at all. Unsurprisingly, he had used less force on himself than on Jane. Twice more he bounced his head off the wheel, but to no effect. He clearly didn't have the nerve to strike hard enough to break his own skin.

Discouraged, he opened the door and got out. The car's interior light illuminated Jane's ghastly face—she looked more like a Halloween prop than a human being. Wheatly rummaged around the car for one of the heavy gray stones that littered the area. Finding one and taking it in hand, he dimpled the glass by striking the windshield with it at the point that his head would likely have struck in a collision.

He dropped the stone and then once again prepared to inflict self-injury. This time, he pressed his somewhat swollen forehead hard against a corner piece of car door molding, and with one long swipe, he dragged his flesh against the sharp trim. To his satisfaction, this produced a gaping wound across his forehead that spilled blood profusely onto his face and over the front of his suit. Although he felt no pain due to the adrenaline high, the blood pouring from his wound soon brought him to the verge of panic.

He climbed back into the car, turned the key in the ignition, and accelerated toward the chosen curve. He wiped blood from his eyes as he tried to concentrate on the road ahead.

Wheatly leaned toward the center of the car to a position that enabled him to see through an unshattered portion of the windshield. He gripped the wheel with one hand and the door handle with the other. Entering the curve, he purposely swerved the car sharply, causing it to fishtail and leave skid marks behind. Sliding into the curve, he unintentionally hit a raised section of curbing, and the car shot off the road prematurely. He was actually now out of control. The car flew across a grassy bank toward the river, now only thirty feet away. Wheatly hit the roadside faster than intended, and without the restraint of a seat belt, he was sent airborne inside the car. He bounced from the driver's seat onto Jane's lap. The senator's panic increased as he realized that he might be unable to leap out of the car before it plunged into the black river. Desperately, he tried to stretch his foot across to the brake pedal. The car raced toward the river's edge, churning up sod and soil. The senator and his wife were tossed around the interior like rag dolls as the car rumbled over tree roots and bumps, sounding like a train careening down a broken track.

Suddenly, there was an abrupt end to the clamor. All went silent as the car launched itself off the bank. For a long moment, the Wheatlys and their Mercedes took flight.

The car broke the deep river's dark surface with a heavy splash. The terrific impact sent the senator forward to the floor, pinning him beneath Jane's feet. Her head and shoulders were thrust forward and were now wedged in the windshield. Her stiff body pressed down on her husband. The car leveled off on the river's surface for several seconds and floated swiftly downstream. It then took a sudden nosedive and began to fill with cold and murky water. The senator struggled frantically to push Jane's feet off him, as his head sank under the rising flood.

From under the water and through the side window, Wheatly had a blurred view of passing traffic on the Schuylkill Expressway across the river. He continued his desperate struggle as the car sank deeper into the darkness. Within thirty seconds, the car had all but disappeared—all that could be seen from the surface was a pair of taillights fading into the depths. Finally, there was no trace of anything at all.

On Kelly Drive, all was quiet. A few cars drove by after the senator's car had taken its plunge—but by then, no trace remained of the incident. Only the skid marks on the road and the tire tracks on the grass were left behind.

About thirty minutes later, a police cruiser drove past the scene. The officer inside noticed the skid marks, but since kids often raced recklessly on Kelly Drive, he didn't think them worth closer inspection. He drove by without stopping.

Several miles down the road, close to the city's edge, the officer noticed a figure sitting slumped against a lamppost. He drove up to the man, who remained motionless and unresponsive to the cruiser's high beams and spotlight. The officer turned on his red-and-blue flashers. He exited the cruiser and, gripping his baton, carefully approached the man. He fixed his flashlight on the man's face. The man flinched and then shielded his eyes from the bright light.

"Are you okay?" the police officer asked.

There was no response.

The officer moved closer. Another cruiser pulled in from the other direction.

"Sir, are you okay?" the officer repeated.

As he got closer, the officer could see that the man was wholly drenched. A puddle had formed beneath him.

The man shook uncontrollably, and he lifted his head.

"I'm Senator Jeff Wheatly," he said. "There's been an accident."

Chapter Eighteen

At eight o'clock the next morning, the dozens of reporters crowding the sidewalk outside the senator's private office caught Kathy off guard. She walked past several news vans and was approaching the steps when reporters started to ask her questions about the senator and his wife. She weaved her way through the mob and jogged up the stairs. The media followed close behind, yelling questions and pushing microphones and cameras into her face. Annoyed by their aggressive behavior, Kathy held up her arm as she passed quickly through the throng. She picked up the morning paper and jammed it under her arm before rushing inside and locking the door behind her. She took a deep breath and headed directly to her desk, wondering why the press seemed particularly excitable this morning.

She tossed the paper onto her desk. It landed face up, but she didn't look at the headlines. She hung up her coat, sat down, and settled into position at her desk when she noticed that there were seventy-one messages waiting on the office answering machine.

She wondered what in God's name had happened.

Then she finally noticed the newspaper's front page.

"SENATOR ESCAPES," it screamed. "WIFE DROWNS"

Kathy read the story in shock while members of the press knocked on the door, begging for any morsel of information they could get.

"Senator escapes the jaws of death," the article began. "Pennsylvania Senator Jeff Wheatly and his wife, Jane Wheatly, had been driving down Kelly Drive in Philadelphia Sunday evening when the senator's car went out of control ..."

Kathy's telephone rang, and she answered while trying to continue reading the article.

"Hi, Kathy," the solemn voice bled through the handset.

"Senator! Are you okay? There are reporters everywhere!"

"Yes, Kathy, I'm fine." His voice cracked in a manner that he hoped demonstrated sufficient grief. "There's been a terrible accident … Jane is dead … she drowned."

Kathy offered her heartfelt condolences. For the first time since meeting the senator, she called him by his first name. "I'm so very sorry, Jeff. I'll take care of everything here at the office. Don't worry about a thing. If there's anything that I can do, just ask."

Kathy didn't particularly approve of the way the senator handled his day-to-day affairs nor did she consider herself a personal friend. But her desire to make this trying time a little easier for him was completely sincere.

"Thank you, Kathy. I'll talk to you later."

After hanging up the phone, she promptly finished reading the newspaper article and then turned on the early television news, where she was able to get the rest of the story before starting what would turn out to be a hectic day.

Kathy spent most of the day returning phone calls and delegating various responsibilities to other staffers. By afternoon, the office had become very busy, and the day seemed to fly by. When she finally took a break, she decided to call Mike Lane to thank him again for the lovely evening they had shared on Friday.

The Philadelphia police had been investigating the Lane shooting for nearly two days. Standard procedures had been set in motion; one of them was to tap Lane's phone and record his messages, one of which might provide them with a lead.

"Hi, Mike!" Kathy spoke cheerily to the answering machine. "I had hoped to hear from you by now. You may not have been able to get through to our office today. It's been crazy here. I guess you've already heard about Jeff's wife. Anyhow, I just wanted to thank you for Friday night. It was wonderful. I'll try calling you tonight. Bye-bye!"

*   *   *   *

In a West Philadelphia police precinct, Detective Frank Farrel sat propped against a break room wall in an old wooden chair on its unsteady back legs. He was five foot eleven, average build, wore his graying hair in a crew cut, and had a rugged face. He puffed on an unfiltered cigarette. He had been assigned to the Lane case.

The room reeked of stale smoke from many years of police gatherings. Paint peeled from the gray walls, exposing patches of white plaster, some of which had fallen to the floor around the perimeter of the dismal room. The 1950s-era lime-green floor featured gaps in the tile that exposed a soot-stained concrete floor.

Farrel was a thirty-year veteran of the force. He had started out on a street beat in a tough section of North Philadelphia and had worked his way up through the ranks before finally making detective. Strong and rough around the edges, Farrel was a street-smart cop and a damn good detective, despite the fact that he was usually disgusted with the justice system. He was handed a note by the shift sergeant, a burly Philadelphia-Italian cop.

"Hey Frank, some woman left a message on dis guy Lane's machine. She says she was wit' him on the Friday night before he got popped."

Farrel let the front legs of his chair pound down onto the floor. He gave the note a quick scan as his cigarette dangled from his lips. His years of experience had taught him that the earliest leads were usually the most fruitful. He had made it a practice to follow up on them immediately. He crumpled the note and stuffed it into his shirt pocket. He dropped his cigarette to the floor and mashed it with his heel.

Farrel had already found out about the death of Lane's wife, Tina, and knew that the two shootings were definitely unrelated. Her murder had been an act of random violence, plain and simple. The meager punishment the perpetrators had received in that case sickened him. Maybe this case would turn out differently.

While Farrel thought about the mystery woman's message, his partner, George Lewis, stepped into the break room with his coat on and Farrel's in his hand.

"Let's go, Frank!" He tossed the coat to his partner. "Let's get back over to the Lane residence and see if we missed anything. Maybe if this woman calls while we're there she can shed some light on this thing."

"Let's hope so," Farrel mumbled.

"What?" said Lewis.

"Nothing. Let's go."

∗   ∗   ∗   ∗

Friends and family arrived at Senator Wheatly's home to offer their condolences. From time to time, the senator would sob aloud and take short breaks alone in his and Jane's bedroom. It was less than twenty-four hours after the Mercedes had crashed into the river, and the book on the case was already closed. Investigators had ruled that the senator had lost control of his car on Kelly Drive, as so many others had done in the past. The official cause of Jane's death was drowning, which had been verified by the coroner. No further investigation was planned.

Farrel and Lewis sat at Lane's kitchen table and went over the case as they waited for the phone to ring.

They had been partners for about three years. Unlike Farrel, Lewis had entered the force at the level of detective after training at the Police Academy. Lewis was an incredibly broad man—he was six foot two and weighed a beefy 265 pounds. He had a fantastic sense of humor and was a sharp dresser.

On the other hand, Farrel dressed adequately at best. He wore the same color and style of clothes every day. He owned seven or eight identical outfits, including suits, shirts, slacks, and shoes. He wore them because he liked them he said—but it drove the fashion-conscious Lewis nuts.

The two detectives constantly ribbed one another and even threw racial slurs at each other (Lewis was an African American and Farrel was white) in the course of normal conversation, but neither of them ever took offense. They had become the best of friends.

"Why would someone want this guy dead?" Lewis asked, tapping his fingers on the table.

Farrel chuckled and straightened his tie. "Who says anyone wanted him dead? Maybe it was a robbery, sweet and simple, and Mr. Lane walked in on it."

Lewis shook his head. They were engaging in one of their frequent games of devil's advocate. It made them question every angle in their investigations.

"Nah. I don't think so," Lewis said. "There was cash in the dining room hutch that the perp uncovered and more in the bedroom dresser, but he didn't take it. I think he was looking for something."

"Maybe," said Farrel. "Like what?"

"Maybe some fuckin' outrageously expensive piece of jewelry or something."

"I don't know about that." Farrel made a face. "Look at this place. It doesn't look like this guy is doing that well."

Lewis shrugged. "How much cash are we talking about?"

"Hundred and twenty bucks … Hell, George, *you* wrote the report! You know how much cash was there!"

"Shit, Frank, what's a motherfucker want with a c-note and two when he's pulling off a jewel heist?"

Farrel laughed.

"What's with the fucking Shaft impersonation?" he asked.

"Fuck you, Frank!" Lewis grinned.

Farrel mimicked his partner: "C-note and two, my brother … I'll take a Colt Malt Liquor and a bag of jewels to go … Give me a break, Don Cornelius."

"Listen to your old-cracker, no-rhythm, needle-dick, Soul-Train ass playing this thing like you know what the fuck went down. The money's still in the hutch. How do you figure a robbery?"

Farrel laughed but did not respond to the question. He got up and went through the dining room toward the living room.

"Maybe this guy was into drugs," Lewis yelled from the kitchen, "and someone broke in to get his stash."

"Do you know a junkie who'd pass up a nickel, let alone a hundred and twenty bucks?"

Lewis followed Farrel into the living room.

"Alright, Frank, so he isn't into drugs. That doesn't mean he doesn't keep any expensive jewels or collectibles around the house. I mean, I don't want to go fishing in an empty hole, but maybe it's more than just a random robbery."

Farrel collected his thoughts and tried to rationalize the case.

"All right," he said, "the guy's an accountant—not exactly a prime target and …"

Farrel turned to Lewis.

"Hey! Maybe that's it!" Farrel said.

"What's it?"

"He's an accountant! Maybe whoever broke in wasn't looking for money or jewelry. Maybe they were looking for records."

"What the fuck are you talking about? What kind of records?"

"I don't know … accounting records … stocks, bonds, investments, taxes!"

Lewis raised his eyebrows.

"Okay," he said, "so he handles other people's money and tax records. I guess that could be a possibility."

Farrel turned and walked briskly toward Lane's office.

"Maybe someone felt he knew too much about their financial affairs and wanted to do something about it!"

The detectives surveyed Lane's work area, which was still in a shambles.

"I bet the answer's in here somewhere," Farrel said. He gestured toward the smashed computer. "On that computer or among his files. We'll need to subpoena all his records. Chances are that whoever did this erased their account from his computer and took whatever files they needed. We'll check with computer forensics and see if they can salvage anything from this mess."

The news that the senator's wife had died had reached Barletto in Chicago. He phoned Ziese and called off the hit on the senator. He knew that the authorities tapped his phone from time to time, so he spoke carefully.

"Carl, let's forget about those plans for our man, for now. He's had some unfortunate family circumstances, so the timing's not good. We'll let him sizzle for a while. We'll keep an eye on him and reevaluate the situation in a couple of weeks."

Ziese, as usual, abided by his boss's wishes.

Farrel and Lewis finally got the call for which they had been hoping.

The detectives had decided to allow any callers—including the mystery woman—to leave a message. They thought that she—or anyone else—might leave enough information for them to do a background investigation before the caller became aware that he or she was being checked out. However, it was also decided beforehand that if it seemed like a caller was not going to leave sufficient information, they would pick up the phone and start a conversation immediately. Kathy was the first caller of the evening, and she gave them what they had hoped for without them having to speak to her. "Hi, Mike. It's me again ... Kathy." She spoke apprehensively. "I guess you've been pretty busy this weekend. If you get a chance, you can call me if you like. You can reach me at work ... or at home. Jeff probably won't be in for the rest of the week, so maybe we could go for lunch if you're in town. Bye-bye now."

"Good," Farrel said.

He was pleased. That phone number would tell him a lot. "George, find out who this woman is, where she lives, her relationship to Lane ... you know, the usual shit."

"Why do I have to do all the grunt work?" Lewis said, feigning offense. "Shufflin' through files and researchin' shit while you sit at your desk smokin' them coffin nails and pickin' your nose!"

Farrel blew out a cloud of smoke that enveloped Lewis's head.

"Because," Farrel said, smiling, "I'm the pitcher, and you're the catcher."

Farrel knew that Lewis had only been trying to rattle him. Lewis turned away and snickered.

"Motherfucker," said Lewis.

Back in their car, Lewis mused on what he thought was an unrelated subject.

"Who do you suppose will get the Wheatly case?"

"Ha! You kiddin' me?" said Farrel. "No one! The blue-and-whites handled it."

"What do you mean?"

"I mean, there *is* no investigation. That's what I mean! The uniform guys said that it was a case of accidental death. The captain agrees, and the book is closed. Nighty-night, sweet prince."

"Well, shit," Lewis said in disbelief. "They *have* to investigate it."

"It's a matter of semantics, George. It gets passed across a detective's desk on its way to a closed file. He signs off on it, and therefore, it was officially investigated! Wheatly's a fucking senator—senators don't get investigated."

Farrel rolled down his window and flicked out a cigarette butt. He exhaled his last drag into the whipping wind.

"I know ... it sucks," he shrugged. "But there isn't a thing we can do about it. I'm sure that there wasn't any foul play involved, but it should at least be investigated."

"Huh," Lewis sarcastically shook his head. "If that were you or me or, God forbid, a brother on the street, we'd have to endure an investigation as the prime suspect. The police would be in our shorts for God's sake. It seems like these guys are all above the law and don't get as much as a slap on the wrist. Hell, these guys pocket campaign funds ... get preferential treatment from everyone and break laws without so much as a ..." Disgusted and obviously frustrated, Lewis struggled to find the words. "Not only do they get away with this shit, they keep their jobs ... *they get reelected!*"

Lewis shook his head.

"That's bullshit," he concluded, as they pulled up to the station house. "Justice is only for those who can afford it."

Lewis steps out of the car mumbling to himself. "No investigation, what a joke."

Farrel waves as he drives off. "See you tomorrow."

By the middle of the following afternoon—Tuesday—"Kathy" had been identified, and a subpoena had been issued to obtain Lane's records.

Still on duty, Farrel slouched on a bar stool at his regular watering hole and sipped on a cold beer. The door swung open, and Lewis appeared out of the blinding bright sunlight. Farrel waved his partner over and, with his foot, shoved out a neighboring stool for him.

"Hey, slim. What's up?" asked Farrel.

"A chicken's ass when he's eatin'," cracked Lewis.

Farrel laughed as Lewis slapped a file folder onto the bar.

"I got the information you asked for."

"Now?" Farrel asked. "It's the end of the day. It can wait until tomorrow."

Frank Farrel had been jaded by years of down-and-dirty police work in a flawed justice system and had decided it was best for his physical and mental health that he kept his job and his personal time separate. He didn't think that the long hours he had worked in the past had amounted to any significant difference in the grand scheme of things. He had therefore decided to work as little overtime as possible. However, he remained the best at what he did and still took pride in his work—he had simply become a realist. Farrel desperately wanted the system to change but realized that at the investigative level at which he operated, it was impossible to affect the judicial process. Like every police officer, he wished that the system were less liberal and that punishments were more equitable.

"Yeah, Frank, this *could* wait until tomorrow," Lewis said, "but according to my watch, we're still on the clock *today*. Besides, you're going to want to hear what I found."

Farrel pushed his empty bottle away and motioned to the bartender for another.

"What do you have?" he asked.

"Her name is Kathy Nolan. Never been married, no children, and no priors. Clean as a whistle. She could be Lane's girlfriend or something." He hesitated for dramatic effect. "But there *is* something extremely interesting about her."

Farrel looked over at Lewis and took a swig of his fresh beer.

"What?" he asked impatiently.

Lewis opened the file folder. "Well …" He raised his brow, and Farrel took another swig. "She works for Senator Jeff Wheatly!"

The beer bottle froze against Farrel's lips for a few seconds. He swallowed and then slowly placed the bottle down on the corner of the file and pushed his bar stool back on its hind legs.

"Senator Jeff Wheatly?" Farrel repeated.

Lewis nodded slowly.

"Of Pennsylvania?"

"No, of the planet Neptune!"

Farrel's stool fell forward, and he reached thoughtfully for his beer.

"That's not all, Frank. Guess who's a client of Mike Lane?"

They stared at each other for a moment and then said in unison, "Senator Jeff Wheatly of Pennsylvania."

Farrel lit a cigarette and took a deep hit.

"Does anyone else know about this, George?"

"I don't know. I didn't tell anybody."

"Are there any copies of this file yet?"

Lewis shook his head.

"You didn't tell the captain?"

"No fucking way, Frank. What do you think I am … brain dead? The shit would hit the fan if the brass thought we were trying to rock Wheatly's boat. I mean, let's face it, any links between Mike Lane, Kathy Nolan, the senator, and his wife could just be a colossal coincidence. I think we'd better get more facts before we say anything to anyone, or we'll find ourselves pushing pretzel carts down Market Street for a living!"

After thirty years on the job, Farrel knew that coincidences were rare. "And what if the links *mean* something, George?"

Lewis massaged his temples. He couldn't recall his partner ever asking a question in such a serious tone.

"Man, I don't even want to think about that, Frank. If any of this ties together … and I mean *any* of it … this would be some deep shit." Lewis leaned forward. "Frank, if anyone in the department found out that I was digging up info about the senator … shit, especially this senator … they'd cut our balls off and feed them to us at our bon voyage party. Shit, Frank, you know as well as I do that the people in our department … hell the entire city, think Wheatly walks on water! I say we give it to the top dogs and let them turn it over to the feds. I say we wash our hands of it."

"Take it easy, George," said Farrel calmly. "We don't even know if there's a connection here or even what it could be."

"That's right, Frank. And I don't *want* to know—you understand me?"

"George … what happened to the guy I was talking to last night? The guy who was sick and pissed off about people like the senator being above the law? About them being immune to investigations?"

Lewis backpedaled.

"Hell, I'm not saying to sweep it under the rug, Frank! Like I said, turn it over to the captain. Let him pass it on to the feds. If there *is* something to the situation, let *them* solve it!"

"You know as well as I do," Farrel argued, "he's a heavy hitter. He carries some serious political clout. If this gets into the hands of the brass too early and the senator is guilty of anything, it *will* be swept under the rug. Remember, if we just turn this over to the captain now, we'll still be in the middle of it. If the senator's hands *are* dirty, whoever ends up with the investigation—whether it's the FBI or whoever—face it; they're not just going to let the two cops who got it started just waltz off the case!"

Farrel raised his voice.

"We're *involved*. Whether we like it or not! So let's just hope that it's a coincidence, so that we can get on with the Lane investigation. But if it's *not* a coincidence, I'd rather be in the driver's seat and get the facts firsthand through our own investigation. I don't want to be yanked around by the feds—or anyone else—for that matter."

Lewis nodded reluctantly.

"No thanks, bud!" Farrell continued. "I'd rather get all the facts first and then decide who we should tell them to. If the senator's not involved, we include it in our investigation as an interesting lead that didn't pan out. If it turns out that there is a connection, we'll decide on what to do at that point. In the meantime, let's keep it quiet. So, are you with me, partner?"

Lewis sighed, and Farrel took this as a "yes."

"Frank, I've got a bad feeling on this one."

Farrel stood up, placed a ten-dollar bill on the bar, and grabbed the file.

"So do I."

They walked toward the door.

"Was computer forensics able to pull any financial files from Lane's computer?" Farrel asked.

Lewis raised his eyebrows and nodded.

"Were they able to recover Wheatly's?"

"Yeah," said Lewis. "I pulled his out and put them in the file."

"Good, I'm going to take this file and show it to an old friend of mine … Mike Taylor. We can trust him. He was an assistant to the city auditor. Aside from being a financial whiz, he's a tax expert and now works for the state. He has access to state tax records. I'll have him look at the senator's tax returns and compare them to Lane's files. If there are any discrepancies, Mike will find them. If the senator's hiding anything, Mike will sniff it out."

"Are you sure we can we trust him?" Lewis asked.

"Definitely," said Farrel. "We grew up together. Plus, he owes me a couple of favors."

Chapter Nineteen

On the following morning—a bright and crisp Wednesday—Jane Wheatly was buried. The senator's office closed for the day, and his entire staff attended the ceremony at the suburban Philadelphia cemetery. A hundred yards away, partially concealed from view by a massive oak tree that stood alone in an open field of headstones, were Frank Farrel and George Lewis. They observed the sad occasion through field glasses. It was quite a sight. More than two hundred personal friends and family had come to see Jane put to rest at the private ceremony. The mayor of Philadelphia was in attendance, as were many senators and lesser politicians, the better part of the police brass, and the chief of police himself. The senator was a huge supporter of the force and had earned their support in his time of grief.

"Look at all those big guns out there, Frank. I'm telling you ... I hope we don't find anything on this guy. All those people out there will want to hang us if we do. Shit, they either love him or owe him—you know where that leaves us."

Farrel lowered his binoculars, looked at Lewis, and shook his head. He didn't know whether he was more amused or annoyed by Lewis's nervousness. He then resumed watching what appeared to be the end of the ceremony.

The mourners filed past the casket, which was ivory white and trimmed with gold—it was fit for a queen—that was suspended above a cold, gaping grave. Each person placed a single white rose on top of the coffin and then paid his or her respects to the senator. He received each of them with a grateful handshake or a tearful hug. He wore a dark suit and topcoat as well as a brimmed hat that partially covered the white bandage protecting the self-inflicted gash across his fore-head.

Jane's family, including her sister Karen, was among the first to approach him. When Karen reached him, she screamed and struck him hard several times.

"You did this, you *bastard*!" she said.

Stunned relatives quickly subdued her—she had been the only soul privy to Jane's torment at the hands of her husband—but she continued to yell at Wheatly as she was virtually dragged away. Her words echoed across the quiet cemetery.

"BASTARD!"

The detectives at the base of the oak lowered their binoculars and raised their eyebrows.

"What the fuck is up with that?" Lewis wondered.

Farrel shrugged.

Everyone present who witnessed Karen's outburst was stunned at her behavior. The general sentiment was that she must be in shock. After all, no one hated Jeff Wheatly.

At the senator's invitation, many of the mourners returned to his house for refreshments. Once there, he brought his staff into his office for a brief private meeting. He thanked them for coming and gave instructions regarding business matters that couldn't wait. He dismissed them after ten minutes but requested that Anthony stay. A minute later, the two were alone.

Anthony stood still at the door and stared at the floor. He made no attempt at eye contact. As far as he was concerned, his relationship with the senator was no longer voluntary. He knew that Wheatly would dangle Lane's shooting above his head indefinitely.

The senator swaggered across his office, reached out, and lightly lifted Anthony's chin. He smiled as he spoke.

"See, Anthony? I told you everything would work out. Now, can we get back to being friends again? It'll be easier now. Mike Lane can't tell anyone our secret, and Jane is gone. We can spend more time together at the house, and no one will know."

He tugged playfully on his aide's tie. Anthony turned his head away.

"What's wrong? You're not still mad at me, are you?"

Anthony pushed Wheatly's hand away and spoke in a low voice to not be overheard.

"It's over between us, Jeff!" His face reddened. "By God, I wish I had choked you to death when I had the chance." He fought back tears. "You make my stomach crawl. I wouldn't be surprised if you killed your wife!"

He hesitated for a moment.

"I'm resigning from your staff," he finally said. "I don't ever want to see or hear from you again."

In his agitation, Anthony had walked behind the senator's desk. Wheatly now followed. The senator leaned close to Anthony, grinned crookedly, and spoke in a hushed, threatening tone.

"No … it's not going to work that way, Anthony, my boy. It's not. I'm the only one who knows what you did. Now, I didn't want it to be this way, but it seems as if you insist on it. You see, I'd hoped that we could go on with our relationship as it was, but …" He fondled Anthony's tie once more. "If you force me to, I can have you put behind bars for the rest of your life! If you're lucky."

His tone changed to one of mock seriousness. "You *do* realize that you could get the death penalty for what you've done, don't you?"

Anthony opened his mouth to respond, but the senator crushed his impending argument.

"After all, you have no alibi."

These words hit Anthony hard. He knew it was true. He would only have an alibi if Wheatly agreed to provide it.

"Point Guard document aside, Anthony … you murdered Mike Lane, and I know it."

"You're part of this too, Jeff!"

"Says who? *You?* Ha! I know what you're thinking, Anthony. You're thinking that we're in this together. That it was my idea to steal Mike's work. That we'll both go down for this. That won't happen!"

He paused as though waiting for Anthony to press him for an explanation. Anthony said nothing, so he continued.

"It *won't*, because for anyone to know that you and I were in this together would mean that they would know that Mike was murdered by *you*! And believe me; I *will* be sure they find that out. So, unless you plan to let the world know that you're the man who shot Mike Lane, you'd better start listening to me. And before you start to get any ideas, I think I'd better tell you a little more about your alibi. Or should I say lack thereof?"

Anthony felt as though he were suffering an endless nightmare.

"You see, I thought I might need a little insurance … so I never did place an order for room service for two, like we'd planned. As for Jane, well, she's dead …

so, your alibi consists entirely of my word as a respected senator. You're in a sticky situation, my boy!"

The senator placed his hands on his aide's shoulders. Anthony's eyes fell. Wheatly's grin widened.

"You know, Anthony, Mike's Point Guard has a lot of potential ... possibly for the both of us."

There was a knock at the door. They quickly separated, and the senator turned toward the door.

"Come in," he said.

It was Kathy.

"Sorry to bother you, Senator," she said, "but I really should get going. I know I keep saying it, but I'm so sorry about Jane. If there's anything I can do, please call."

Kathy hadn't seen anything unusual between the two men, but she did sense a strange vibe between them that made her uncomfortable. She turned to leave and seemingly casually—although, in truth, with a great deal of forethought—asked about Lane.

"By the way, I thought I might meet your accountant friend today ... um ... Mike Lane, was it? Couldn't he make it?"

Kathy had begun to wonder if perhaps Lane wasn't as kind and considerate as he had seemed. Was he trying to avoid her?

Wheatly nervously patted the bandage that covered his forehead and looked down at the floor. At the same time, Anthony's throat constricted, and his heart raced. It was clear to Kathy that she'd hit on the wrong subject, but she didn't understand why. The senator cleared his throat and spoke sadly.

"Oh God ... with everything that's happened, I nearly forgot about Mike."

"What about Mike?" Kathy asked anxiously.

He shook his head, "He was killed Saturday night."

Kathy wobbled and reached for the wall to steady herself. She tried to regain her composure before the men could detect the depth of her shock.

"How?" she asked. Her voice quivered, and her eyes glazed over.

"He was shot."

Kathy turned her head toward the wall and acted as if there were something in her eye.

"My God!" she said. "How did it happen? Where?"

"All I know is that it happened in his house on Saturday. We found out about it on Sunday when Jane ..." The senator choked up but recovered quickly.

Anthony turned and rolled his eyes as the senator continued. "Anyway ... I for-got about the whole thing."

Kathy tried to say something meaningful, but she could only manage two words.

"He's dead?"

"Yes, I'm afraid so," said Wheatly. "Shot in the throat at point-blank range. He didn't have much of a chance."

Kathy's voice cracked as she said good-bye and immediately exited the office. She sped through the senator's house with her face aimed at the floor. She rum-maged quickly through the closet, grabbed her black wool coat, and let herself out unnoticed.

Due to their own preoccupations, neither the senator nor Anthony had paid much heed to Kathy's reaction. Wheatly motioned toward the door.

"You may leave, Anthony," he said formally, "now that we understand one another."

Anthony left the house hastily as Wheatly went to mingle with his guests.

Kathy was only able to drive to the end of the senator's block before she was forced to pull over and turn off the engine. She slumped her head and arms over the steering wheel and cried. It was the first time she had realized just how much Lane had meant to her. After several minutes, she raised her head and looked at her reflection in the rearview mirror. She turned the key with one hand and rifled through her purse with the other. She pulled out a tissue and used it to wipe away the mascara-blackened tears that streaked her cheeks.

She never really knew why she did what she did next. For whatever reason, she wanted to be at Lane's house, and that was where she went.

Farrel and Lewis followed not far behind.

Kathy was one of the last people to have seen or heard from Lane before he was shot—that much was clear from the message she had left on Lane's answer-ing machine. The detectives were hopeful that she might lead them to some sort of useful clue.

Kathy had only been to Lane's house once—and only knew one route that would get her there—so she had to find her way back to the interstate and then turn around and proceed from there. After awhile, Farrel and Lewis began to wonder if she was lost. Her route had traced out the greater part of a circle, and she was now not far from where she had started.

For the detectives, Kathy's involvement had been nothing but speculation. It had just provided another place to dig while they waited to learn about the sena-tor's finances. Maybe she didn't even know he had been shot. Or did *she* shoot him and leave that phone message as a smokescreen? Either of these—or anything in between—could have been true.

The detectives were surprised when she finally led them to Lane's house. She pulled into the driveway and stared at the house for several minutes. A little way down the street, Farrel and Lewis sat and watched. Kathy got out of the car and slowly walked up to the house. She was hoping that the senator had been mistaken. It seemed denial was the least painful option open to her now. She looked around the front yard of this house that had seen so much tragedy. She knocked on the door.

"Frank, I don't think she's a suspect. I mean, look at her. And it wouldn't make sense for her to come back here."

"Unless she's trying to make it look like she doesn't know what happened," said Farrel.

"Nah," said Lewis. "She doesn't know we're here. And like I said, look at her. If she's not devastated, she's the best actress I've ever seen."

"I think you might be right, George," he said. "Let's see if she can help us out."

They parked behind her car and proceeded up the walk. Kathy was still standing at the front door.

"Excuse me, Miss Nolan." Kathy appeared startled. "My name is Frank Farrel, and this is George Lewis." Lewis nodded. "We're detectives with the Philadelphia police." They showed her their badges. "Do you mind if we ask you a couple of questions?"

Over her surprise, Kathy inspected the badges and nodded. She wiped away a stray tear.

"Why don't we go inside, Miss Nolan?"

She smiled politely. "Call me Kathy, please."

Lewis unlocked the door.

Kathy was confused and shaken further by the state of the interior. It had been jostled around a bit after the investigators had done all that they needed to, but it certainly appeared as though a significant struggle had taken place inside. Farrel led her to the sofa where she had sat so comfortably only a few days before—when she had been touched and kissed so tenderly by Lane. Again, the tears welled up. She now knew that a real romance had been brewing. And now it was gone.

Lewis handed Kathy a glass of water from the kitchen, and as sensitively as he could manage, Farrel began to question her. The water glass trembled in her hands. She steadied it and listened.

"Kathy, we know that you were a friend of Mr. Lane's. We've heard the messages that you've left on his machine over the past couple of days."

Kathy nodded.

"How did you know Mike Lane?"

"From the senator's office. He's Senator Wheatly's accountant. He came to the office a little while ago."

"Forgive me if I seem to be getting too personal," Farrel said, "but from the tone of the message you left on his machine, it seemed that you were quite close to him."

"Yes ... I am ... I mean not really." Kathy wasn't quite sure how to frame her response. "Mike was a really nice man, and we hit it off." An embarrassing laugh slipped out. "I didn't actually know him all that well ... this is silly." She stopped and wiped her nose. "I'm sorry."

"That's okay," smiled Farrel.

"We had sort of a ... date on Friday night. It was kind of a secret. The senator would be upset if he knew that I was seeing his accountant. He frowns on that sort of thing. I ... I'd appreciate it if you didn't mention this to anyone—especially the senator."

Kathy kept her pact with Lane and didn't describe how she had sent him to see the senator at the Whitehall Inn.

"I have no intention of sharing anything you tell me with Senator Wheatly," Farrel said. "And if I ever need to, I promise that I'll tell you about it first. Okay?"

Kathy returned a sad smile and nodded.

Lane's phone rang, and Farrel gestured for her to wait a moment. They watched Lewis pick up the receiver near the kitchen doorway.

"Hello? No, this is Detective George Lewis. Uh, no. We don't really know. We knew he belonged to an organization called STOP. Yes, we're suggesting people send donations to that organization. No, he had no immediate family that we knew of. Good-bye."

"Oh God, he told me he had no family left," Kathy said. This made her even more upset as tears streamed down her cheeks. "What about his burial?"

Farrel answered gently as he reached into his pocket, withdrew his handkerchief, and handed it to her. "His estate will take care of it."

"My God," Kathy said, "he was alone! That's so sad ... a wonderful man like him being put to rest all alone."

"I'm very sorry, Kathy." Farrel reached out his hand to comfort her, although this gesture made him feel uncomfortable himself.

"Now," he resumed his questioning. "You say you just started dating Mr. Lane?"

She fixed her eyes on the floor and nodded.

Farrel looked up behind the sofa and noticed Lewis gesturing to end the questioning. Kathy was an emotional mess, and it appeared obvious that she was nothing more than a love interest.

Abruptly ending the interview, "I don't think we need anything else Kathy. Are you going to be okay to drive?" Farrel asked.

She nodded again.

Farrel took Kathy by the hand and helped her off the sofa. Handing her his card, he said, "If you think of anything that might help our investigation, you can reach me at this number."

She looked up at Farrel through bloodshot eyes.

"Mike was all alone."

Farrel nodded and smiled in an effort to comfort her as he and Lewis escorted her to the door.

Kathy continued, "The poor man ... he must have suffered terribly."

Farrel and Lewis both became curious.

"What do you mean?" Lewis asked as he followed behind.

Kathy turned around. "The way he died."

"I'm sorry. What about the way he died?" asked Lewis casually.

Kathy looked at Lewis as though he were being unusually callous.

"Well ... having been shot in ... in the throat! He must have died a *horrible* death!"

"And how do you know that he was shot in the throat, Kathy?"

"I didn't, until just a little while ago. Senator Wheatly told me ... or was it Anthony? At the senator's house today, after Jane's funeral. 'Point blank in the throat' they told me."

Farrel opened the door and hesitated, "Anthony who?"

"Anthony Kane, the senator's aide."

Nodding, Farrel held the door as he raised his eyebrows at Lewis.

"Okay, Kathy," he said, "that's all for now. We'll be in contact if we have any other questions for you. All right?"

Farrel thanked Kathy and closed the door. He turned toward Lewis to see his animated face.

"Why didn't you ask her to try and remember who *specifically* told her that Lane was shot in the throat?"

Farrel seemed preoccupied. "Patience," he mumbled. He walked to the bay window and watched silently as Kathy walked to her car and drove away.

"George, you did keep the press locked out of this, right?"

"Yeah. You told me not to disclose anything to the press ... only that Lane was dead."

Farrel closed the shades. "She said that the senator—or this Anthony guy—told her about it. How do you suppose they know that, George?"

Lewis shrugged.

Farrel put his hinds in his pockets. "Of course, it *could* all be a smokescreen—maybe *she* knew it and was trying to implicate the senator."

"Come on, Frank! You saw her as well as I did. She had no more to do with this murder than I did. You're barking up the wrong tree, pal. Plain and simple, she was doing the nasty with the bean counter, and that's that!"

Farrel had merely been playing devil's advocate but saw no reason to continue. "Okay," he said, "then either someone leaked the information to them, or they know it firsthand."

"I don't think it's a leak, Frank. Think about it. Too many coincidences. The night before the senator's wife dies in a car accident, his accountant is shot, the accountant's girlfriend is the senator's secretary, *and* the senator has insider knowledge about the Lane shooting? *Way* too many coincidences. I hate to say it, Frank, but Senator Wheatly should be put under a microscope. Shit, it's time to turn this over to someone else." Shaking his head, "I don't want to be involved."

"Too late, Nipsy, we're in it," Farrel joked.

"Nipsy?"

"Yeah. Nipsy Russell. I see a resemblance."

"Ah, fuck you, Frank!" Lewis retorted and laughed.

Farrel used his cell phone to contact Mike Taylor, and Lewis went into Lane's office to see whether he could find anything that they might have missed. Lewis was seated comfortably in Lane's swivel chair when he heard his partner yell, "Jackpot!"

"What?" asked Lewis, as Farrel appeared in the doorway.

"Mike says that it looks like the senator's tax returns have been doctored. He said he was able to compare Wheatly's filed state returns to his income state-ments, tax ledgers, and tax forms that Lane prepared. It seems that the senator's made a lot more money than he's reported to the IRS."

"So Lane was helping the senator evade taxes?"

"Maybe, maybe not. This is where it gets good, buddy. You see, Mike says that it usually works this way. Lane does the senator's accounting, and at the end of the year, he compiles his earnings, his assets ... you know the usual shit, and then prepares his tax documents. Typically, an accountant signs the returns and sends them to the client for a signature, and he includes all the envelopes so that the client can mail them in to the IRS himself. So, it's possible that the senator could have doctored ... or maybe even replaced the taxes entirely before sending them in! He'd be betting that the IRS would never dare audit a senator, and he'd probably be right."

"So, you're saying the senator changed his tax returns without Lane's knowledge and then sent them in with bogus information on them so he could pocket some cash?"

"Yeah, Mike says it looks that way. And the fact that Lane is a CPA and does lots of politicians and executive-type returns, no one would suspect any hanky-panky, especially when it comes to the senator."

"All right, Frank," said Lewis, "that's all fine, but it doesn't tell us who shot Mike Lane, and it certainly doesn't make the senator the shooter. It just means he doesn't pay his taxes."

"Stick with me, George. Suppose Lane somehow becomes aware of the senator's fiddling. Suppose he confronts the senator and tells him to come clean, or else he goes to the authorities!"

Farrel became even more animated, and Lewis could tell that his partner really believed he was on to something.

"*Or*," Farrel continued, "maybe Lane wanted some of the money that Wheatly had been pocketing. What if he was blackmailing the senator with the knowledge of the tax fraud? He might even have been involved in it. What if ... *what if* he was getting kickbacks from the senator and wanted a raise? There are tons of scenarios here, George, but I'm sure that we have a man with a motive!"

"I don't know. It's one thing to have a motive and another to kill a man over something like ..."

"Listen ... let's just say that for one reason or another Lane and Wheatly got into a confrontation about the senator's tax tampering. You and I know damn well that *if* that confrontation happened, it could lead to a shooting."

"Yeah, Frank, but that's a big 'if.' You know what they say: '*If* the dog didn't stop to shit, he would have won the race.'"

Farrel ignored his partner's ill-timed humor.

"Maybe so, George. But it's all we've got right now."

George couldn't argue with that. "Okay, Kemo Sabe, what do we do next?"

"Well, Tonto," Farrel shot back. "Among other things, I think we try to get Kathy Nolan to help us out. Maybe she can be a source of information. I think we get to know her and—"

"*Frank, are you out of your fucking mind?*"

"No. Based on what I just saw, I'd bet she'd like to see Lane's shooter brought to justice. If we are able to gain her trust …"

"Gain her trust? You *are* out of your mind. Frank, I think—"

"Listen to me, George. She's around Wheatly every day, so who knows what she might learn. She probably knows everything that goes on there. There is no telling what she hears."

Lewis sighed. "That's not the point, Frank. We don't know anything about the woman. Shit, for all we know, she's having an affair with the senator."

"What? You saw her yourself. She looks like she's in love with Lane."

"Maybe she *was,* Frank, but he's dead now, and she hardly knew the guy. Anyhow, it's a significant stretch to think we can get her to listen in on the senator or be a source of information. *Or … or* do whatever it is your pea-sized brain is working on."

Farrel shrugged his shoulders and raised his voice. "At this point, it's the best way to find out what kind of relationship Wheatly and Lane had." He mumbled under his breath, "I've got to get something now."

"What?" Lewis said.

Farrel shook his head and answered, "Nothing."

Lewis pressed, "What did you mumble?"

"I was just thinking that we need to get this thing moving."

"What happened to patience?"

For a moment, Lewis stared at Farrel in disgust. He knew Farrel well enough that when his partner had made his mind up to do something, it couldn't be changed.

"Frank, how in the hell are you going to get Kathy Nolan to trust you when you don't even know her?"

"I don't know yet."

Bobbing his head, Lewis said, "I don't suppose we're going to ask the captain for permission to recruit Miss Nolan as an informant? After all, that would make it an out-of-state federal case, wouldn't it?" He closed his eyes and pinched the bridge of his nose as if he had a headache. "And we're not going to tell him that we're investigating the senator either, are we?"

Farrel rolled his eyes and cracked, "You ask the dumbest fucking questions, George!"

Chapter Twenty

After leaving Lane's residence, Farrel and Lewis spent the rest of their day strategizing and reviewing the files they had compiled on the Lane case. It was clear by now the senator was their prime suspect. However, the motive was not yet clear. Nonetheless, they agreed tax evasion was the best, if not the only, option to pursue at the time.

At ten o'clock the next morning, the senator was seated in front of the president's desk. He was in the middle of a conference with the president, who was pacing excitedly.

"Jeff, I've got to tell you," said the president, "this Point Guard system makes a lot of sense! We need to mold it into shape, of course, but I love the way the system removes all the gray areas regarding sentencing. It allows only the facts. The slogan writes itself: 'Know the Time before the Crime!' I love it!"

"It's pure genius!" he continued. "It will certainly decrease crime and should deter most ex-cons from reoffending. It'll sure make them think twice when they realize that the next crime they commit could put them away for five, ten, twenty years ... maybe even life!"

"Or death," Wheatly added helpfully.

The president sat down and leaned up against his desk. He adopted a commanding tone. The senator leaned forward and listened closely.

"I can't move ahead on this without any help. I know you're the best at getting things like this put together, Jeff, but it's just too big. I'll need to assemble an advisory staff and a team of legal and constitutional experts that you can lead." The president shook his head and then looked toward the ceiling. Thinking aloud, he said, "That may take weeks … and I'll need to keep it all classified." Consumed by thought, he lowered his eyes and stared quietly at the senator for several seconds. "Listen," he said, "for the time being, I won't be discussing this with anyone but you … at least until I figure out who to put on this. Do you understand?"

"Yes, sir."

"You and I will work on this thing alone. We can get some of the logistical bugs out before we turn it over to the constitutional experts. While we do that, I'll start putting a team together on paper. All right?"

Barely able to contain his excitement, Wheatly nodded.

"All right then. Just the two of us until we get everything squared away. We'll amend it to my Three Strikes program. You'll probably win the thanks and admiration of the entire nation—and I'll get another term."

The president stood and paced again. "If we pull this off, Jeff, we'll become the two most admired men in the country!"

✳   ✳   ✳   ✳

Lewis leaned on Farrel's desk and tapped his pen on a file folder.

"Okay, Frank," he said, "we can build a case around tax evasion. But that's not the case we're supposed to be working on. We're supposed to solve the Lane murder. We need to tie the senator to Lane in some concrete way or give up and hand it over to the feds."

Farrel nodded. "We got a gift from Kathy Nolan when she told us about her conversation with the senator and his aide. Eventually, we'll need to press her on *exactly* who it was that told her."

Lewis chuckled. "*Eventually?* … Like I told you when we had her at Lane's house, 'we should have asked her then.' I still don't know why you wanted to wait."

"Where the hell is she going?" Farrel snapped. "She's a phone call away for God's sake. Besides, I wanted to be sure that we hadn't released any details to the press. I didn't want her to know that. Not only that … didn't you say for all we know she may be having an affair with the senator? We don't need to tip our hand this early on."

"First of all, I was being facetious, and second … how would asking her to tell us who *specifically* told her about Lane's shooting tip our hand?"

"Pressing her to remember who *specifically* told her could raise some questions in her mind. That just *might* lead Kathy into a conversation with Kane or

Wheatly. I don't want them to know prior to our questioning them that we learned that one of them knows the details of the shooting. Does that make sense?"

Lewis stared at Farrel for a second. He looked convinced.

"Patience, George, patience. Do I have to teach you everything?" Farrel quipped.

"Kiss my ass, Frank."

Farrel suggested they sit on the tax information for the time being and begin surveillance of the senator and Anthony.

An extensive background search on Anthony revealed that he was a model citizen whose primary address was in Philadelphia. They knew that he returned to Philadelphia regularly to visit his parents, and they decided to pay him a visit the next time he was in town. They didn't think that talking to Anthony would raise undue suspicion—since Anthony was the senator's aide and Lane was the senator's accountant, their visit would be considered a standard interview of someone who might have been a business acquaintance of the victim. They would tell Anthony they were planning to interview the friends and associates of Lane's other clients as well.

Farrel and Lewis believed that they would have to conduct covert surveillance in Washington, DC, before questioning either Wheatly or Anthony. The detectives wanted to get an idea of their day-to-day routines before knowledge of police interest could lead them to alter their behavior.

Both procedure and law dictated that the crossing of state lines for the purposes of an investigation required the detectives to inform their superiors beforehand. Their superiors would have to supply the Washington, DC police and the FBI with the pertinent details. In this case, Farrel convinced Lewis that they should inform neither their lieutenant nor their captain. Of course, if their violation were discovered, they could be suspended, fired, or even jailed. Their plan to avoid such punishment involved taking turns on the Washington stakeout—one of them would conspicuously show his face around the precinct house while the other was in the nation's capital. They would keep up this charade as long as it took.

At the start of the investigation, Senator Wheatly was its main focus. The detectives spent countless hours alone in various locations, keeping a close eye on him. Farrel and Lewis often found it difficult to maintain the surveillance with all the Secret Service activity they encountered around the White House—Wheatly met with the president a fair amount. Nevertheless, they managed reasonably well—from their car, from nearby buildings, and from simple strolls along the street. They noticed that every day on which the senator had a meeting with the president that he carried a large leather briefcase. Wheatly spent most of his nights at the Whitehall Inn instead of taking the train home, and this made for long, lonely nights alone in their car for the detectives.

Late at night, Lewis was speaking to Farrel on his cell phone. He was parked about half a block from the inn, keeping a close eye on its lobby. His car had become a rolling trash can after several days of sleeping and eating in it without the benefit of a shower. The seats and floors were littered with food wrappers, coffee cups, and soda cans.

Lewis had often seen Anthony accompanying the senator to the inn. On rarer occasions, Anthony would go in alone after the senator had arrived. Anthony's movements this evening were somewhat unusual—whereas he typically left the building between eight-thirty and nine o'clock, it was now well past ten, and he still hadn't appeared.

Anthony felt trapped—he had been compelled to continue assisting the senator. On this particular evening, Wheatly was trying to convince him to stay after their work had been completed.

Anthony was now a mere shell of the young man he used to be. The events of the past several days had taken their toll. He had lost several pounds and had become skittish—he was worn out.

He was sitting at the dining room table snapping closed his briefcase when the senator approached him from behind.

"You know, Anthony," Wheatly said, "it's been awhile since we've … spent any time together … outside work."

Anthony rolled his tired eyes and said nothing.

"What, are you going to be mad at me forever?" Wheatly grinned confidently. "Now that everything has worked itself out like I told you it would, I'm sure that we can be friends again."

Anthony slumped forward onto his briefcase, and Wheatly bent down to face him.

"Don't you miss me?" Wheatly whispered.

Anthony was nauseated. He squeezed his eyes shut and turned his head away.

Standing, the senator continued, "I told you that everything would be okay. We're on our way up! The president loves the Point Guard plan. It's just a matter of time now."

Wheatly reached out to touch Anthony's shoulder, but his aide's temper flared.

"Take your fucking hand off me!" he shouted and swatted the senator's hand.

The senator cowered. Anthony jumped up from his chair and stepped into Wheatly. His lips turned down and his voice shook.

"*Don't you ever touch me!*" he yelled. "You may think you own me … but … don't you ever touch me!"

The senator retreated, but Anthony moved forward and pressed his finger into Wheatly's chest.

"I let you ruin my life!"

"Listen, Anthony … everything will be okay. Just listen to me."

"*I've listened to you enough!*" he said as he choked back his tears. Dropping back down into the chair, he shook his head, "I've listened to you enough."

The senator sat down across from Anthony. "Look, everything is going to be fine. The president is sold on the Point Guard plan. This makes me indispensable to him. He will—"

"*Jeff!* Listen to yourself! You're talking as if you're the author of the damn thing. My God … you've lost your mind. What would the president do if he knew we killed Mike Lane and you … you … stole his work?"

The senator shook his head as if it were not true.

"We did Jeff! We killed Mike Lane!"

The senator bounded to his feet. "*We* didn't kill Mike Lane. *You* killed Mike Lane!" He started to pace alongside the table. "And you're going to help me get this fucking thing done. Do you understand me?"

Despondent, Anthony couldn't muster the energy to respond.

"Now, here's how this is going to work. *You* will do what I need you to do. You will work on the Point Guard, and if I need you to vouch for me as the author of the fucking thing, you will."

"I'm—"

"*Shut up!*" The senator shouted. "Shut the hell up!" he repeated as he approached him. "You killed a man, and I'm the *only* person who knows it!"

Exhausted, Anthony propped his elbows up on the table and rested his head and face behind his hands. His voice was muffled. "What are you going to do, Jeff? Tell someone I killed Mike Lane?" Anthony said. "Wouldn't that expose you? Wouldn't that mean everyone would learn that you're not the author of the Point Guard? How does that all end? I'm the *only* person that knows you're not the author."

The senator rubbed his forehead. It was a stalemate.

Wheatly sat back down on the edge of his chair and stared at Anthony for a moment. "Okay, what are we going to do?"

Anthony shrugged, "I don't know."

"We better figure it out."

"Yeah … I guess so," Anthony said hopelessly.

Anthony hung his head. He put up a good fight. But he knew that he was still on the hook for murder. He knew that if and when this all unraveled he would be fingered for the murder of Mike Lane and that could always be held as collateral by the senator.

Anthony looked up at the senator and sighed. He pulled his briefcase off the table and grabbed his coat. He left the suite without another word.

Lewis was still talking to Farrel on his cell phone when Anthony finally exited the inn's lobby at 11:45. Anthony barely lifted his feet as he walked and looked as though he had just been in a fight.

"Here he comes," Lewis said. "He looks like shit."

"Yeah?"

"Wheatly must work this poor kid to death."

Lewis had never seen anything unusual at the senator's hotel and had no reason to believe that tonight would be any different. So he and Farrel decided that instead of Lewis keeping watch at the Whitehall Inn that he would follow Anthony. He didn't lead them anywhere interesting—he drove back to his Washington apartment, where he would collapse from exhaustion on the sofa and awake in the morning fully clothed.

Despite the absence of new leads, this would start a new pattern for the detectives. They decided that they would now tail Anthony every night instead of sitting outside the inn. The next couple of days were uneventful. The long meetings between the senator and the president continued, and each night Anthony appeared in the Whitehall lobby looking progressively worse than the previous night.

"Man, what are they, lovers or something?" Lewis joked aloud as he sat alone in his car. "What the hell do they do up there?"

Anthony left the inn early on Friday night—and Lewis once again followed him. He eventually headed north on I-95, and it was soon apparent that he was going home to Philadelphia. Lewis was glad about this—not only did it mean that he was heading home himself, but he and Farrel had also been waiting for an opportunity to interview him in Philadelphia, thereby not raising any suspicions about their illegal investigation. When he arrived in Philly, Lewis phoned Farrel about the good news. They agreed that it was too late in the evening to interrogate the senator's aide and decided they would do it on Saturday morning.

Early on Saturday morning, back at the Whitehall Inn, there was a loud knocking at the door of the senator's suite. Wearing nothing but a pair of boxer shorts, Wheatly squinted with a bleary eye through the peephole. He sighed, rolled his eyes, and unlocked the door.

"Don't you have anything else better to do, O'Mally?"

The towering brute pushed Wheatly aside, entered the suite, and proceeded to inspect the premises. Annoyed, yet curious as to what he was looking for, the senator shadowed the massive Irishman. O'Mally was peering down the hall, with the senator following his gaze, when suddenly O'Mally reeled around, grabbed Wheatly by the throat, and violently slammed him to the floor. O'Mally tightened his clutch with the one hand and pulled a .45 from under his suit jacket with the other.

Before Wheatly could plead for mercy, O'Mally jammed the cold barrel of the gun into his mouth. The taste of the oiled steel terrified the senator, and his teeth chattered against the metal.

The senator had known that he had to cross this bridge eventually, but he hadn't expected to reach it so soon.

Wheatly knew why O'Mally was there. Barletto must have found out that he was not promoting the union's interests regarding the NAFTA bill. The senator tried to explain the situation to O'Malley—that he'd gotten off the NAFTA committee—but the gun barrel made his words unintelligible. His desperate attempts to speak only heightened O'Mally's amusement. The thug pushed the pistol deeper into the senator's mouth, gagging him. Wheatly's eyes teared up. O'Mally grinned. The senator balled his fists, and his lips turned white from fright. He cried, whined, and prayed as he waited for O'Mally to pull the trigger.

The door of the suite crashed open, and Carl Ziese entered the room. He closed the door gently and looked around the suite, nodding in approval of the decor. He nonchalantly unbuttoned his long leather overcoat and parted it to reveal a shimmering silver-grey suit. He dragged a dining room chair over to the pinned senator, sat, and lit a cigar. Wheatly had followed Ziese with his eyes but had been careful not to move his head an inch lest O'Mally accidentally blow it off.

Ziese reached down and patted O'Mally on the shoulder. In response, O'Mally dragged the senator to his knees by the throat. O'Mally continued to press the gun into Wheatly's gaping mouth, driving the senator's head back and forcing him to try to focus on the relaxed Ziese over the top of his own twitching lower eyelids. O'Mally made a disgusted face as the senator's drool oozed onto the thug's wrist and shirt cuff. O'Mally looked at Ziese as though he were waiting for the order to squeeze the trigger. Wheatly grunted and panted heavily while pulling frantically and uselessly on O'Mally's trouser leg.

"Are we to do this?" O'Malley asked.

Ziese smiled and nodded. Wheatly bit down on the barrel and screamed. Urine dripped from his suddenly soaked shorts.

O'Mally pulled the trigger.

There was a loud snap.

O'Mally let go of Wheatly's throat, and the senator collapsed like a rag doll into the puddle of urine beneath him. He wept like a child.

Ziese stood and buttoned his overcoat.

"You have been given a reprieve, Senator," he said. "Forget about the NAFTA agreement." He and O'Malley headed toward the door. "By the way, we know about your queer relationship with your aide. We also know quite a few other things that might surprise you."

Wheatly weakly lifted his head to face Ziese.

"But don't worry, Senator! Your secrets are safe with us."

They left as quickly as they came.

Though Barletto had been tipped off about Wheatly's appointment to the NAFTA committee, he had decided to have the senator followed anyhow. A smart and patient man, Barletto learned all that he needed to about Wheatly's professional and *personal* life. Wheatly rose to his knees, looked down at his urine-soaked boxers, and palmed the tears away from his face. He angrily realized how effortlessly Barletto could reach him—how easily he could be wiped out. And if Barletto knew about Anthony, who knew what other horrible secrets lay open to the mobster? The senator now knew that if he was to have any chance against Barletto that he would have to become an untouchable.

He would have to be the Point Guard.

If he were to bring the Point Guard system to fruition and gain control of the most powerful judicial process in the country, it would make him bulletproof.

Not even Barletto would be able to take him down.

At around the same time Ziese and O'Mally had paid a visit to Wheatly, Farrel and Lewis pulled up in front of the Kane residence. It was nestled in a neighborhood of old row houses that seemed to have been untouched by time. It was the kind of place where tight-knit families kept an eye on one another, as they sat in front of their brick homes, playing cards and shooting the breeze on warm summer nights. This morning, the neighborhood was quiet. The detectives approached the house and knocked on the door.

Mrs. Kane was in her mid sixties and wore her white hair in tight curls. She answered the door in a pink-and-white calf-length housedress and a pair of fuzzy white slippers. She opened the door only partway.

"Can I help you?" she asked.

Lewis held up his badge.

"Yes, Mrs. Kane," he said politely. I'm Detective Lewis, and this is Detective Farrel. We'd like to speak to your son, if we could."

Mrs. Kane was surprised, but not alarmed. She knew that Anthony sometimes dealt with the police in conjunction with his job.

"Let me go wake him up for you."

She opened the door wide and invited in the detectives.

Normally, when staying with his parents, Anthony would be off at a local playground shooting hoops at this hour on a Saturday morning. But today, he was sleeping in, as he had been doing often of late.

Mrs. Kane disappeared up the stairs just as her husband entered the living room, where the detectives had been left standing. Mr. Kane had been in the kitchen and had heard voices. He was a retired pipe fitter and a more hardened man than most. The Kane's had lived in the small row home since they had married and had raised four children there; Anthony was the youngest.

"What can I do for you?" he asked.

The detectives detected considerable wariness in his voice, and Lewis was quick to ease his nerves.

"Your wife let us in, sir. We're Detectives Lewis and Farrel of the Philadelphia Police Department. We're here to speak to your son, Anthony."

Kane, who was wearing a flannel robe, nodded and took a sip of his coffee. He, too, had become accustomed to Anthony's dealings with the police and politics, so he wasn't alarmed.

"Well, have a seat," he said.

The detectives smiled and sat on the sofa next to the stairs in the tiny living room. They heard footsteps and turned to see Anthony coming down.

Kane excused himself. "I'll give you fellas some privacy," he said. "I'll get yas a cuppa coffee."

Anthony entered the room. He was barefoot and wore gym shorts and a T-shirt. His hair was sticking out in all directions, and he tried, to no avail, to tidy it.

He greeted the detectives nervously. They introduced themselves and shook hands with him. Both Farrel and Lewis noticed that Anthony's hand was clammy and saw it quiver when he withdrew it.

"What can I do for you fellas?" Anthony asked, as casually as he could manage.

"Well, we'd just like to ask you a few questions, Mr. Kane," said Farrel.

At that moment, Anthony's parents entered the room; Mrs. Kane carried cups of coffee on saucers for the detectives, while Mr. Kane carried the cream and sugar. They placed the china on the coffee table, stepped back into the kitchen, and strained to hear what was being said. Lewis thanked the Kane's and doctored a cup for himself.

"Sure," said Anthony. "What about?"

"It's about a shooting, sir," Farrel said. "Senator Wheatly's accountant was shot in his home recently, and we're following up on a couple of leads. You do know Mr. Lane, don't you?"

Anthony's stomach churned, and his chest tightened. Although he tried to act calm, he couldn't help but squirm.

"No. I mean … yeah. I mean … I don't *know* him. I've seen him in the office a couple of times. That's all."

"Uh," Farrel continued, "we're aware that he has been to the senator's office. That's why we wanted to question his staff. Maybe one of you could help us understand why anyone would want to shoot him."

The detectives could easily tell that Anthony was uncomfortable.

"Like I said, I hardly ever even spoke to the man … if ever."

"Is that a fact? Tell me, Mr. Kane, do you know anything about the shooting?"

Anthony shook his head.

"Nothing at all? Not how, or where, or anything like that?"

Anthony furrowed his brow and continued to shake his head. He had no idea what the detective was getting at.

"Are you sure?"

Lewis leafed through his notebook.

"Yeah, here it is, Frank!" Lewis pretended to read from a nonexistent entry. "While interviewing some of Mr. Lane's friends, we were told that Senator Wheatly had told them that Mr. Lane had been shot at point-blank range in the throat. And according to what they said, *you* were present at that time, Mr. Kane. Is that true?"

With all the stress he had been experiencing, Anthony couldn't remember the senator making that revelation. Since he hadn't seen any news reports about the shooting, he had no idea what details about it had or had not been revealed to the public. He accordingly considered this an excellent time to act both dumb and agreeable.

"Oh yeah, that's right!" he said. "I *did* hear that! But I'm not sure if it was from the senator."

"All right," said Farrel, "I guess that's all for now, Mr. Kane. Thank you for your time, and have a nice day."

Through the shades, Anthony watched the detectives drive off. He wiped a bead of sweat from his upper lip as his parents came in behind him.

"What was that all about, son?" Mr. Kane asked.

"Uh … just a … some local police business."

In their car, Farrel and Lewis discussed the interview.

"The kid knows something, Frank. Did you see the sweat on him?"

"Did I see it? I was swimming in it! And his hand was shaking like a leaf! I say we let him stew for a day or so. Then we'll bring him in and nail him down to exactly how he knows what he knows. Maybe we'll get somewhere with him."

Anthony sat on the edge of his bed and tried to organize his thoughts. This was not an easy task.

Okay, this is routine. They don't have anything … But what if they do? What if Jeff told them something? Oh, my God, what have I done? Think … Think … What could they have? They don't have a gun. I tossed it in the Susquehanna River. Shit … I'll be put away for life! Should I leave the country? Are they watching me?

He walked to his window, scanned the alley that ran behind the house, and drew the shade closed. He began to hyperventilate. He tried to think of some way to rectify the situation. But he knew there was nothing he could do. The crime he had committed had ruined his life. If they found him out, he wouldn't be able to escape on his own. He needed protection. There was only one person he could turn to, and the thought sickened him.

He needed his alibi.

He rolled nimbly across his bed, picked up the phone, and dialed the number for Wheatly's suite at the Whitehall Inn.

One ring. Two rings. Three.

"Come on, come on, pick up."

In the suite, its curtains drawn closed, the senator sat on the floor in his soiled boxer shorts, watching the phone as it rang. Anthony knew that the senator was there. The answering machine had not picked up, and Wheatly had always been very strict about turning it on when no one was in the suite.

Seven rings. Eight.

"*Come on*, Jeff. Pick up!"

With a blank look in his eyes, the senator reached over to the answering machine and switched it on. The greeting message played, and Anthony's frantic voice filled the room.

"Jeff! Jeff, pick up! It's me, Anthony! We need to talk! Let's work this out. I'll do whatever you want! Pick up."

Wheatly turned his head away but otherwise didn't move.

Anthony eventually hung up.

Both of them were stunned and petrified and stayed in their darkened rooms alone until the following day.

Chapter Twenty-One

Early the next day, Anthony made a rare appearance at St. Gabriel's church—the same church where he had been baptized as a baby. At the end of Mass, Anthony worked his way through the throng of parishioners toward the parking lot.

Detective Farrel intercepted him and smiled politely.

"Good morning, Mr. Kane," he said. "Do you mind if I call you Anthony?"

"Uh … hi … sure," Anthony stammered as he continued toward his car. Farrel walked along the edge of the curb beside him.

"Anthony, can you come down to the station house with us?"

Lewis pulled alongside in their unmarked car.

Without a word—without even asking why they wanted to talk to him again—Anthony quickly surveyed the crowd outside the church and then swiftly climbed into the backseat. Farrel slid into the passenger seat and shrugged at Lewis.

Typically, the detectives would not have reported to the station on a Sunday, but they felt this was the perfect time and place to interrogate the senator's aide formally. A man who'd just been to church might be more eager to confess whatever he knew, and Anthony looked as if he were on the verge of a nervous breakdown. Furthermore, the captain never worked Sundays, so they would probably also be able to keep their investigation on the down-low.

Farrel and Lewis hustled Anthony up the dingy station stairwell to the fourth floor and into an interrogation room. They offered him a cup of coffee, which he declined. The detectives then left the room for fifteen minutes, giving Anthony some time to be alone.

Interrogation is an art form for detectives and is rarely conducted without a strategy. A good interrogation is generally constructed to confuse a suspect. It includes setting traps, providing obvious escapes, and asking carefully planned questions designed to elicit the most accurate responses possible.

The room was dimly lit and smelled of mold. Anthony nervously tapped his fingers on the table in front of him. He pushed his metal folding chair away from the table, and its legs squealed as they scraped across the floor. He walked to the very large open window and stared four stories down into a grubby alley. Placing his hands in his pockets, he leaned over the wide windowsill to get a full view of the alley. He chewed on his lower lip. His foot tapped anxiously on the floor. He took his hands out of his pockets and put them on the sill. He leaned even further out.

"Don't jump!" yelled Lewis. He and Farrel laughed as they entered the room.

Startled, Anthony flashed them a rigid smile and then glanced quickly once more into the alley. The detectives wondered what he found so interesting down there.

Lewis motioned toward the metal chair, and Anthony sat down.

"So," Lewis said, "you were All-Ivy-League in baseball! Pretty impressive."

Anthony nodded.

The detectives took their seats at the table and spent a few more minutes discussing college baseball. The conversation then turned more serious.

"So how long have you worked for the senator?" asked Farrel.

"Since college"

"Do you like it?"

"Yes"

"What's the long-term goal?"

"I'm sorry. I don't understand."

"The long-term goal … Do you plan to be a senator one day?

"No," Anthony answered abruptly.

"All right. So, have you remembered anything about Mike Lane that you think we should know? Where you met him … anything strange about him … anything?"

"I didn't really know him."

"No? But you've met him, haven't you?"

Anthony swallowed hard.

"I don't recall. One time or another, maybe."

"So does that mean yes, you have met him?"

"I don't know."

"It's an easy question." Farrel's tone became a little testy. "Did you or did you not ever meet Mike Lane?"

Anthony looked defiantly at Farrel. He had been getting progressively edgier. "No!" he said.

Farrel looked surprised. "How about the senator's lawyer? Have you ever met him?"

"Yes."

"Where?"

"At the office."

"Has Mr. Lane ever visited the office?"

"Not that I'm aware." Anthony looked out the window.

Farrel tapped his pen on the table and looked over at Lewis. Anthony's curt answers were annoying them both.

"So the senator's lawyer *has* visited the office, and you have met *him*. But the senator's accountant has *never* visited the office, and you have never met *him*. Do I have that right?"

"I don't know," Anthony said.

"Yesterday you said you have seen Mr. Lane in the office."

This line of questioning lasted for about thirty minutes and produced no significant results. Anthony had decided that by not cooperating—by limiting his answers to "I don't know" and "no"—he stood the best chance of protecting both himself and his family from the shame of his actions.

Farrel was standing now. He circled behind Anthony and asked, "You said that you remember someone saying Mr. Lane had been shot at point-blank range in the throat. But now you don't remember who said it." He decided to twist Anthony's words a little. "But yesterday, if you recall, you said that it was Senator Wheatly. Isn't that right?"

Farrel stood over Anthony's shoulder. Anthony shook his head tightly but seemed slightly confused.

"Come on, Mr. Kane, surely you can remember! Was it the senator who said this, or was it *you*? Who said that Mr. Lane had been shot in the throat at point-blank range?"

Anthony twitched and stammered.

"Who was it? Was it you? Was it the senator? *Who?*"

"I don't know! It wasn't me."

"If it wasn't you, was it the senator?"

"I don't remember."

Wanting to protect Kathy's status as a possible source, Farrel couldn't come right out and say it was she who had told them about the slip and the circumstances surrounding it. What Farrel and Lewis were trying to ascertain was why Anthony was playing stupid and what he was trying to hide.

"How could you not remember?" Farrel continued. "How did you hear about it? You're an intelligent guy. Think!"

Anthony struggled for an answer that would implicate neither himself nor the senator.

"I can't remember! Maybe ... maybe I heard it on TV!"

Lewis leaned across the table, and his eyes bored into Anthony.

"Really? Where?"

"I don't know. I *must* have seen it on TV. I think that's where I heard it."

"Think, Mr. Kane. Are you sure?" Farrel asked.

Anthony's eyes darted between Lewis and Farrel.

"Yeah, I'm pretty sure. I saw it on TV."

Farrel imitated the sound of a game show buzzer.

"Wrong!" he said. "It wasn't released to the press. It wasn't on TV!"

Farrel raised his voice with each sentence he spoke.

"We never released any information to the press about the details of the shooting! Now, do you want to take another shot at this? Who said that he was shot at point-blank range in the throat? Was it you?"

Anthony shook his head.

"Was it the senator?"

Anthony felt sick as he realized that the detectives must know something. But *what* did they know? *What?*

He leapt to his feet, causing his chair to fall to the floor behind him. He pointed a finger angrily at Farrel.

"Listen," he shouted, "maybe I just heard it in passing! I don't know! But unless you plan to arrest me for something, I want to leave. And if you want to know about the senator, I suggest you talk to him!"

His lips trembled with fear.

"Can I leave now? Are you finished?"

Lewis got up and pushed open the door.

"We didn't make you come here; we only asked. You could have left any time you wanted," he said.

Lewis smiled politely as Anthony rushed past.

"We might have some more questions for you soon, Mr. Kane!" Farrel called after him as he walked toward Lewis.

"Whew!" said Lewis. "We struck a nerve there, Frank!"

"Oh yeah. He knows very well who said it. He's hiding something."

"So, what do we do about Wheatly? You *know* that Kane's going to tell him about this right away."

"We'll phone the senator and let him know that we questioned Anthony. We'll tell him that we've been planning to contact him as well, but we questioned Anthony first because he was in Philly. We'll tell him it's standard procedure, like we planned. He shouldn't be suspicious—unless, he has a reason to be suspicious. And I think he does."

Lewis chuckled. "Yeah, I'll bet that their story about the point-blank shooting gets a new twist."

"You know what they say, Nipsy."

"Here we go with the Nipsy shit."

Their mirth was cut short by the appearance of their captain in the doorway.

Captain Billy Carr was six feet, four inches of solid, beer-drinkin', hard-hittin', honest Philly cop. He was dressed in khakis and a golf shirt, and his badge dangled from a belt loop. Carr was a family man and was annoyed that he had been forced away from his wife and kids to track down Farrel and Lewis on a Sunday morning.

"Where in the fuck have you two been? You really think you're slick, don't you?"

"Captain—" Lewis started.

Carr pointed a finger at Lewis. "Shut up. I told the desk sergeant to tell me the minute he saw you two together—and you show up on a Sunday, of all days! Come on, Frank, when was the last time you worked on a Sunday?"

Farrel started to say something, but Carr cut him off. "So I figure something's going on that I should know about. Am I right, Frank?"

Farrel and Lewis bustled past Carr and tried to escape down the hall.

"Not really, Cap," Farrel said.

"Farrel! Lewis! In my office, now!"

The detectives froze in their tracks. They reluctantly turned and followed the captain to his office. Carr sat on the edge of his desk and waved the detectives into the ratty green vinyl chairs in front of him.

"All right, you knuckleheads, let's have it! What are you guys doing in here on a Sunday? And who was that guy you just let outta here?"

There was no immediate response, so Carr kept haranguing them.

"I haven't seen either one of you all week. All I know is that you've been sneaking in and out of here behind my back. Did you guys forget that I used to do your job? Now, what are you hiding?"

"Nothing, Captain," Lewis said.

"Don't give me that shit! I know better. Frank, I haven't seen you in here past five o'clock in years. Seeing you on a Sunday is even rarer. Now, you two start telling me what's up, or I'll bring that kid back in here, and I'll find out myself."

"Sir," Lewis said sheepishly, "our investigation has led us in a direction that involves Sena—"

Farrel anxiously interrupted his partner.

"Cap, if we tell you, I'm sure you'll pull the plug on it. Trust us. This is big."

Carr's face turned red as he stood and overshadowed Farrel.

"Trust you, huh? Listen, Frank, unless you want to be selling soft pretzels at traffic lights for a living, you'd better start briefing me on what's going on. And don't give me that 'afraid I might pull the plug' bullshit. I'm the captain, and unless you've lost your fucking wits, you know that means that I'm your boss. Now start talking, or I'll bust you two down to the records room!"

Farrel slid back in his seat, sighed, and fiddled with his watchband. Lewis simply sat still.

"We didn't tell you earlier," Farrel said, "because we knew you'd have to take it out of our hands."

"Yeah, Cap," said Lewis, "we *wanted* to tell you ..."

"I thought you were smart enough not to follow Farrel down the tubes, Lewis," Carr snapped. "Shut up and let him explain!"

"Uh," Farrel continued, "during our investigation into the Lane shooting ... You ain't going to like this, Cap. We came across some real sticky information."

The captain sat in his chair and folded his hands across his stomach. "Just tell me the story. I'll tell you whether I like it or not."

"The guy you saw leaving," said Farrel, "is Anthony Kane. He's an aide to Senator Jeff Wheatly. We've discovered that Wheatly was a client of Lane's and that his tax returns look funny. We suspect that the Lane shooting could be related to a possible tax evasion scheme involving the senator." Farrel rubbed his lips. "It started with what looked like an innocent coincidence. Someone from Senator Wheatly's office had visited Lane the night before the shooting. Because of the common tie to Wheatly, we decided to have the senator's financial records examined. You see, Cap, we think that whoever broke into Lane's house was not there to steal money or valuables. Lane being an accountant, it only made sense to check out his records. We started with Wheatly because of the coincidence.

However, after having his financial records examined, we had sufficient reason to include him as part of our investigation. We're still not sure that the cases aren't just coincidental. But it's an avenue I think we have to pursue. If it *is* coincidental … great, it was worth a shot! If it's *not* … we might be opening up a can of worms that we don't want to turn over to the feds. What I mean is … if it's not a coincidence, then who knows? Maybe Mrs. Wheatly's death wasn't an accident. Maybe it's another piece of the puzzle."

Carr gave the detectives a menacing look.

"I can hardly believe what I'm hearing, Frank," he said.

"I knew you wouldn't like it, Cap," Farrel responded.

"Shut up, Frank! So, do I understand that you two believe that Senator Wheatly murdered his accountant because Wheatly was evading his taxes?"

"In a nutshell, yes. Why not? Lane could have blackmailed the senator about the tax situation, and the senator wiped him out. At least that's one possible scenario."

"Damn, Frank, you're going way out into left field on this, aren't you?"

"It's a theory, Cap."

"Well, you better start working on some backup theories, Frank."

"This is the angle we're working on right now, Cap," Farrel shrugged.

"God! And you think that the senator could be responsible for his wife's death?"

Farrel shrugged again, and Lewis continued to listen quietly.

"What is this? The Keystone Kops, for God's sake?" said the Captain.

Unable to stay quiet any longer, Lewis squirmed and chimed in, "Captain, we have a credible source—Frank's friend Mike Taylor—who suggests that the senator is probably evading his taxes, and … and we found that either he or Mr. Kane—or both—are aware of some unreleased facts about the Lane shooting."

"What facts?" Carr asked.

"Mr. Kane was somehow aware that Mr. Lane was shot at point-blank range in the throat." Lewis shook his head as he spoke. "And he couldn't know that legitimately because that information was never released."

Carr shook his head in disgust.

"All right," he said. "You two are on the desk."

"Cap! You can't!"

"You're on desk duty for violating code," Carr repeated. "You know that all this information should have been turned over. I want a full, typed report on my desk by five o'clock today. If any of what you say is even near the truth, this is a job for the feds. And when they find out you two been investigating the senator without their knowledge, they're gonna come down on us so hard we'll be lucky to have fuckin' jobs."

"Come on, Cap," Farrel objected. "It's Sunday! We'll give you the report tomorrow."

"Today. Five o'clock. On my desk. And I'll be waiting here until I get it."

Farrel and Lewis trudged to their desks.

"Fuck ... fuck," Lewis muttered. "I can't believe this shit."

"Take it easy, George," said Farrel. "It'll work out."

"This thing's going to get turned over to the feds, Frank. I know it!"

"Let's just get the report to the Cap, all right?"

"I told you this was going to happen, Frank. I hope you're satisfied."

Farrel clenched his teeth. "Just shut up and do the paperwork, George."

At 4:30 that afternoon, as they neared the end of their task, a call was patched through to Farrel.

"Yeah?" he said into the receiver.

"Detective Frank Farrel?"

"This is Frank Farrel."

"Hi, this is Kathy Nolan."

"Hi, Kathy. How are you?"

"I have something you need to see."

"What is it?"

"I went away for a bit to visit a friend, and when I returned, there was a package waiting for me from Mike."

"What is it?"

From across the room Farrel noticed Lewis motioning for him to pick up the other phone line.

"It's a copy of Mike's work with a letter."

"What work? A letter about what?"

"His legal work ... I ... I don't know. He sent it to me to keep safe."

Again Lewis motioned for Farrel to pick up the flashing phone line.

"Can you hold on a second, Kathy?"

Farrel hit the hold button and yelled over to Lewis. "What?"

"You need to pick up that call."

Farrel hit the flashing button to let the other call come through.

"Farrel," he said into the receiver.

He listened quietly for ten seconds and then shot to his feet.

"Shit!" he said. "I'm on my way!"

He quickly picked up Kathy's line. "Kathy ... are you going to be around later on?"

"Yes, but I think ..."

Farrel interrupted her. "Kathy, what you have may be important. I have to handle something real quick, and then I want to talk with you as soon as I'm done. Is that okay with you?"

"Yes, but ..."

"Good. I'll give you a call back."

He hung up the phone, grabbed his coat off the rack, and motioned for Lewis to join him. Farrel could see that the captain was watching them through his open door. As they headed for the stairwell, Carr was in close pursuit.

"Whoa! Whoa! Where do you two think you're going?"

Farrel stopped midway down the first flight and turned to face the captain.

"Cap," he said, "either you come with us and let us explain on the fly, or you'll have to write us up!"

"Frank ..." Carr spoke in a stern, warning tone.

"Billy, we need your help. This is important to the case. Please. Trust me."

Carr had known Farrel for more than twenty years. He trusted Farrel more than he trusted any other man on the force. Although he had become a stickler for policy in recent years, he remembered from his long hours of grunt police work that instinct was an important tool for any cop.

"Let me get my coat," Carr said.

Lewis breathed a sigh of relief.

"Your white-bread ass ain't gonna be happy until I'm out of a job," said Lewis.

Ready with a comeback, Farrel was stifled by Lewis before he started. "And don't give me that 'take it easy Nipsy' shit."

Farrel shook his head and ran down the stairs as Lewis pulled on his coat and chased after him. "Slow down, Green Hornet! We'll get there," Lewis cracked.

Less than ten minutes later, the three of them rolled up to the Kane residence. The street was lined with police cars, and an ambulance was parked in front of the Kane's house. The three men rushed past curious neighbors who had gathered on the sidewalk, and they entered the house. They walked past police officers who were milling about inside. In the tiny kitchen, Anthony's father sat staring at the floor, taking no notice of the commotion around him. They headed down the dark and narrow basement stairs. They found Mrs. Kane seated on the bottom step, wailing into her hands. After maneuvering around her, they turned a corner to find Anthony hanging by the neck from a clothesline tied around a floor joist above. His body hung next to the clothes dryer and beneath a rusted and dusty light fixture.

Lewis shook his head and flared his nostrils. He turned to see whether he could comfort Anthony's mother. He gently took hold of the sobbing woman's arm, helped her to her feet, and escorted her up to the kitchen.

"Shit," Farrel muttered as he watched two forensics officers inspect Anthony's nude body. Farrel tried to ignore the terrible echoing wail of Anthony's grieving mother as he took a cursory look around the basement.

He wondered why Anthony was nude.

"Billy," he whispered to his captain, "that's three people dead who were associated with the senator. You think it's all a coincidence? Come on! I'm telling you, something big is going on here. This goes real deep."

"Shit, Frank," Carr responded, "let's get the blue-and-whites out of here. You get some investigators in here, clean this up, get back to the station, and finish that report. Add this to it, and try to make it as complete as you can. Do you understand?"

"Give me a couple more days, Cap! I have one more person to question. Then the report will be complete."

"No way, Frank."

"Two more stinkin' days, Billy!"

Carr stared at Anthony's naked body.

"Okay, Frank. I'll give you until five o'clock tomorrow. One day. But I want the report complete and on my desk then, so I can turn this over to the FBI on Tuesday morning."

Farrel slapped the captain on the back and rushed up the stairs to find his partner, who had been getting an update from the first officer to arrive on the scene.

"George, we need to clean this up and get to Washington. We have to talk to Kathy Nolan before the captain turns this over to the FBI. She's got something."

Chapter Twenty-Two

At around ten o'clock on Sunday night, Farrel and Lewis parked their car on the tree-lined cobblestone street in front of Kathy's Washington condominium; they hustled up the stone steps that led to her unit and knocked on the door.

After peering through the peephole, she unlocked the door and swung it open.

"Thank God. I'm a little nervous, guys."

Holding a small package in her hand, she invited them in.

"There's no need to be nervous," Farrel said.

"If you say so," she said facetiously.

"Is this it?" Farrel gestured toward the package.

Kathy nodded and handed it to him.

Kathy closed the door; she pointed toward the living room. Standing just inside the door, Farrel ignored her invitation and immediately reached inside the parcel. He pulled out a computer disk and examined it quickly. He dropped the disk back in the carton and then pulled out a short handwritten note. Lewis and Kathy stood patiently as he read it.

After he finished reading, he turned to Kathy and asked, "Are you okay?"

She nodded unconvincingly. Tears welled up in her eyes.

"You have no reason to be worried. No one but Detective Lewis and I know that you got this. Do you understand me?"

She nodded no more convincingly this time than the last. Farrel handed the package to Lewis and took Kathy by the arm to the sofa in the living room. He knelt down in front of her and with a comforting smile tried to reassure her.

"Kathy, listen to me. You are in no danger. Whoever did this to Mike Lane has no idea that you have a copy of this. Trust me. You have nothing to worry about."

She felt comforted by Farrel's confident manner. With an embarrassed smile, she said, "I'm sorry."

Lewis came into the room with the letter in one hand and the package in the other.

"It sounds like Mr. Lane trusted you."

She turned her head to the side before nodding. "Yeah. I guess he did," she said as she wiped a tear form her cheek.

"Miss Nolan, have you looked at what's on this disk?" Lewis asked.

She sniffled. "Your name's George, right?"

He nodded.

"George, please call me Kathy," she said, prompting a smile from him.

"No, I haven't, but I already know what's on it. It's Mike's work on legal reform." Trying to pull herself together, she offered the men coffee. They accepted.

"You know," Kathy called out on the way to the kitchen. "I wonder if I'm the only person Mike sent a copy of his work to."

Farrel shrugged. "I would have to say … yes … based on the note."

Farrel and Lewis stood in the middle of the living room while Kathy prepared the coffee. The room was brightly decorated and contained many lush plants and fresh cut flowers. Returning, Kathy offered the detectives a seat on her sofa. A fluffy mutt of a cat loitered under Kathy's antique cherrywood coffee table.

"What's your cat's name?" Farrel asked, as Kathy brought them their coffee.

"Nixon," she said, smiling.

"Nixon?"

"Yeah, it's strange, but I just adored Richard Nixon. I thought he was loyal to his country, right to the bitter end. Anyway … Nixon. Do you like cats, Frank?"

"I'm more of a dog guy," he said.

With that, Nixon jumped immediately onto Farrel's lap.

"He seems to like you," Kathy said.

Farrel was far from overjoyed, but he stroked the cat's head anyway.

Lewis interrupted. "Kathy," he said, "why do you suppose Mr. Lane wanted you to keep a copy of this Point Guard thing?"

Kathy raised her eyebrows. "I'm not quite sure. Like you said, he must have trusted me."

"Why? Why did he need to trust you?"

Kathy gave the question some thought but couldn't come up with anything other than the obvious.

"I don't know. I think he really liked me as much as I liked him."

"I get that. I understand his kind sentiments in the note … but the *tone* of the note implies concern for his work. It seems like he might have been concerned that someone wanted to steal it."

Kathy shook her head as Lewis paused for her response; she had nothing to add.

He looked down and read part of the note aloud.

It was an evening more enjoyable to me than you could ever imagine. Thanks.

Enclosed is a copy of the Point Guard on disk. It seems that my work is pretty popular these days. I would appreciate if you would continue to keep our conversation confidential and the enclosed copy in a safe place.

Suddenly, Farrel looked as though something had struck a nerve. His cup jerked in his hand, and coffee spilled out. He quickly grabbed a napkin and dabbed the spot on the rug.

Glancing at Farrel, Lewis then turned to Kathy.

"You don't know why he wanted you to keep a copy in a safe place?"

"I'm sorry. I really don't, George."

"Fair enough. Did you and Mr. Lane …"

Farrell interrupted Lewis. "Kathy, we're not sure that any of this is related to the shooting of Mike Lane. It is, however, another twist."

"What do you mean?"

"During the course of our investigation into Mike Lane's shooting," Farrel continued, "we've uncovered some things that may implicate some very important people. In order to make sense of the information that we have, we're going to need to ask you some questions. We're also hoping that you'll trust us and understand we're trying to bring to justice the person who shot Mike."

Her usual soft smile slowly transformed into an intensely serious stare. She nodded. "What do you need from me?"

"More than anything, your trust. We need to tell you a few things so that we can learn a few things. Okay?"

"Okay," she responded with concern.

Farrel detected a touch more apprehension in Kathy and gave her another reassuring smile before he continued.

"We have reason to believe that Mike Lane's shooting might have something to do with a client of his here in Washington. And if that's true, we have a federal case on our hands."

"I'm not sure I understand what you're saying," she said anxiously.

"Kathy, what do you know about the relationship between Mike Lane and Senator Wheatly?"

She slid out to the edge of her chair.

"You … you think that the senator could be involved?" she asked.

Farrel shook his head. "No, we didn't say that. We're just asking you about their relationship. What do you know about it?"

"Um … n-nothing … other than the fact that Mike was his accountant."

"What about Anthony Kane?" he asked.

"What about him?" said Kathy.

"Do you know what kind of relationship *he* had with the senator?"

"He's pretty much the senator's right-hand man … gofer … researcher … even … um …" Part of Farrel's question seemed odd to her. "What do you mean 'had'?"

Farrel rubbed his forehead. He had felt an instinctive fondness for Kathy since their first meeting and wasn't comfortable telling her the news. But it had to be done.

"Mr. Kane was found dead this morning in his parents' home."

Kathy instantly broke into tears. She and Anthony had spent a lot of time together. He had almost been like a son to her.

"My God, how?"

"It looks like a suicide. His mother found him hanging in their basement."

As tears flowed down her face, Farrel reached out to comfort her again. As he had done at Lane's house, he offered her his handkerchief.

"Kathy," Farrel said, "this makes three deaths around the senator in a very short period of time."

Farrel moved to the edge of the sofa. "Now, like I said earlier, we're going to need you to trust us. Our only goal is to bring Mike's shooter to justice."

Kathy nodded.

"In the spirit of trust and in light of what we have discovered today," he pointed at the package and continued, "meaning the note and Mr. Kane's suicide, I feel it's necessary to tell you what we have discovered in our investigation into Senator Wheatly. It's confidential, and it needs to stay that way. Are you okay with that?"

"Yes." Kathy stifled her tears and listened intently.

"We suspect that the senator might have been doctoring his taxes after Mike Lane prepared them. Simply put, he might be guilty of tax evasion. We think Mike might have found out somehow and was afraid he might be implicated. Or perhaps he was involved in the fraud. We don't know. Either way, we suspect that the senator needed Mike out of the picture because he knew about the tax evasion."

Kathy suddenly looked as if something very serious had crossed her mind. As Farrel spoke, she sat up in an exceptionally rigid way and shook her head as Farrel continued.

"Kathy, what we need from you is any information about this. And … now … anything else you can tell us about this disk he sent you. Was there any conversation that you may have been part of or overheard in regard to Lane or the senator's taxes?" Distracted by her mannerism, Farrel stopped. "What's wrong?"

Kathy's eyes widened. She looked stunned.

"Mike had been calling the senator repeatedly for some time," she said. "He wanted to come in and see him about something that was very important to him. Senator Wheatly had become very annoyed with Mike's persistence and told me not to take his calls any longer. He was very cold toward Mike at that point."

Farrel stared at Kathy intently as he listened. Lewis glanced over at Farrel but said nothing.

"One day, Mike drove all the way down here from Philadelphia to try and see the senator, who had already left for the afternoon. I met Mike for the first time that day at the office. I had spoken to him a few times on the phone prior to that and had gotten friendly with him. Well, anyway, we … we kind of hit it off, and he confided in me as to why it was so important that he see the senator. There was this plan he had. It was a sort of justice system reform that he wanted to see passed by the government. It was the Point Guard thing, and he wanted the senator to introduce it. He was doing it in memory of his wife. She'd been murdered. But you probably know that. I felt compelled to tell him where he could find the senator. It was something I normally wouldn't dream of doing.

"I mean, I'd never betrayed an employer before. I have the best reputation in this town, but I'd probably lose my job if the senator found out that I sent Mike to his hotel suite. I felt compelled to help him."

She paused and shivered as she remembered Lane.

"Then things got strange. Suddenly, after Mike had met with the senator, the senator was having me phone him to set up appointments right away. It seemed as though the tables had turned in a single evening and that now the senator was pursuing Mike. Mike and I spoke in secret several times over the phone. I didn't want the senator to connect us—he might have figured out it was me who sent Mike to the hotel. Eventually, Mike and I set a date and met at his house on a Friday night."

She sat silently for a moment, remembering the gentle, passionate night they had spent together. The detectives didn't dare interrupt her. After a moment, she continued.

"We sat and talked and got to know each other. After awhile, he started to tell me about this Point Guard plan that he'd written, and he swore me to secrecy."

"What exactly is this plan?" asked Farrel.

"Well, it basically describes a set of laws—it's a brilliant idea, really—that would send criminals to jail based on a point system like the kind that exists now for traffic violations. I don't understand the entire thing, but I know that the senator was sold on it."

"Why do you say that?" Farrel asked.

"Because Mike told me," she said. "I'd rather believe that this all has to do with taxes, but I'm not sure that it doesn't have to do with the document on that disk."

Farrel took a deep breath and looked over at the disk in his partner's hand.

"Well," he said, "we can add this to the case file, can't we?" He stood and paced a little. "So you think that Mike's shooting has something to do with this disk?"

"Now I do!" she responded fretfully.

Farrel nodded and mumbled something to himself.

Lewis stretched out his arms and yawned.

"Uh … Frank," he said, "let's go to Mr. Lane's house and see if we can find any copies of this thing. If we can't, it may be the reason his house was broken into. If that's the case, there's another angle and one more reason to investigate the senator. That is, if Mr. Lane told no one but Kathy about the thing."

"I can assure you," Kathy said, "that no one but Mike, the senator, and myself knew about his work. He spent every waking hour doing research—all of it in memory of his wife. If he said that we were the only ones who knew about it, it's true."

"Kathy," Farrel said, "we've noticed that the senator has been spending a lot of time with the president. Do you happen to know what that's all about?"

"No. But I suppose it *could* be about the Point Guard plan. I know that the senator has talked to the president an awful lot lately."

"Does the senator typically speak with the president that often? I mean, *did* he before this?"

Kathy shook her head. "*Typically* … no. Not really, not as much as he has lately. I know from memos and rumors that the senator is the leading candidate for the NAFTA committee. Before that, the senator talked with the president only when the president wanted to talk to him, ... which wasn't that often. But ever since the NAFTA thing got started, he has talked with him a fair bit ... but ... lately he has been talking with the president quite a bit more."

A look of deep concern crossed Lewis's face.

"Frank," he said, "you're not trying to tie the president to this, are you?"

"No," Farrel laughed. "We don't even know if Mike's work has been stolen from his house."

"Shit, Frank, don't you think we should find that out before you start tossing the president into this? I don't even like to talk about that! Damn, you scare me! I think we should just write this into our report and turn everything we've got over to the captain right now, just the way it is. The tax information, Kathy's story, the disk ... everything."

Farrel shot an irritated look at his partner.

"Kathy," Farrel turned toward her, "do you trust us?"

"I do."

He smiled. "Will you cooperate with us and help us to bring the ..."

Lewis interrupted him suddenly and asked Kathy if he could have a word with Farrel in private. The detectives stepped into the kitchen.

"Frank," Lewis said, "have you got a fuckin' brain tumor or something? You want this woman to help us nail a senator, which might in turn—and we have no idea—domino us all the way into the president? Shit, you're acting as if this is a routine case, for God's sake. I'm telling you, let's turn it over to the captain and wash our hands of it."

"We can't do that, George, and you know it. We are where we were in the beginning of this thing, only deeper."

"What are you talking about? The stakes are higher. We may be talking about the president!"

"George," Farrel said seriously, "you're going to have to trust me. Can you hear what I'm saying?"

"Whether the Point Guard documentation is gone from Mike Lane's house or not, we're involved, George! I'm just trying to think ahead and prepare us for the worst. If it's there, then the case is probably tax-related, and we turn our report in to the captain. If it's *not* there, we're going to have to reconsider everything and ..."

"Bullshit! Why do we need to reconsider anything?"

Gesturing for Lewis to keep his voice down, Farrel explained.

"If we include any of this Point Guard thing in our report to the captain, we'll have nothing to work with, no edge; everything will go to the feds. They'll know what we do. You know we're going to be suspended the moment we turn our report in … no matter what. So let's just give the captain what we have on the taxes; he'll turn that over to the feds. Chances are they'll sweep it under the rug. Wheatly's a powerful guy; nobody will go after him on taxes."

"Then what?"

"Then, we investigate the theft of Lane's Point Guard work and continue on with our investigation."

"Why?"

"Because whatever the truth is, I want to get to the bottom of it."

"Who are you, fuckin' Dick Tracey? Do you know what you're asking me to do?"

"Yeah! Exactly what I'm *willing* to do. Carry on the fucking investigation into the theft of Lane's Point Guard after we are suspended. That is … if we confirm that it's been stolen."

"Listen to you … you want to work the case we're going to be suspended from!"

"George," Farrel said, "if we don't do this, this prick is going to walk. I can feel it; he's big-time dirty. You can feel it too, can't you?" Farrel urged his partner. "You want to see this guy get what he deserves, don't you? You know he's up to something."

"I do, but shit … I mean … shit, Frank. This is some pretty heavy shit we're getting involved in."

Farrel reached out to shake.

"What do you say?" Farrel pressed. "Are you in, pal? If we don't do this, we may never know what really happened."

Lewis stared Farrel in the eye as he stood quiet for a moment. As much as Lewis would have liked to disagree, he trusted his partner and valued his experience. He finally shook Farrel's hand.

"Okay," Lewis said, "but I don't like this."

"You don't have to, George. You just have to like catching the bad guys."

When they returned to the living room, they were surprised to see Kathy standing with hands on hips, confronting them with a look of intense determination. "Listen, guys!" she said sternly. "From here on in, no more private discussions. If the Point Guard work is missing from Mike's house, I want to know."

"So, I take it you want to help us?" Farrel smiled.

"What's the next step, fellas?" she asked.

"Just go to work as usual," Farrel said, "and keep your eyes and ears open. Just act normal and pay attention to what's going on around the office. Okay?"

"Yeah, I get it, Frank. Act normal," she teased. "It doesn't sound all that hard."

"George and I will head back to Philly. The first thing we'll do is check Mike's house. We'll phone you in the morning and let you know if it's missing. Then we'll turn in our report to the captain, like we promised him."

Farrel saw a look of concern return to Kathy's face.

"Listen, Kathy, there's no reason for anyone to suspect any involvement on your part. Once we turn in the report, we're probably going to find ourselves suspended for not reporting that we've been crossing state lines. If that happens—and I expect that it will—it'll give George and me a little more time to check out this Point Guard thing."

After another cup of coffee, Kathy led the detectives to the door.

"We'll call you tomorrow," Farrel said as he gently touched her hand. "Don't worry."

Kathy bolted the door behind them, leaned back against it, and sighed. She felt anxious but somehow secure knowing that Frank was on the case.

Before she left for work early the next morning, Kathy got a call from Lewis.

"Good morning, Kathy. It's George."

"Hi, George."

"We couldn't find anything about the Point Guard stuff."

"Oh my God."

"Are you okay?" Lewis asked.

"Yeah. Yeah, I'm fine."

"Okay, good. We'll be talking soon."

Later that day, Lewis and Farrel knocked on the captain's door. Their report was tucked under Lewis's arm. The captain was meeting with two other men whom the detectives did not recognize. Both of these men were about the same size—over six feet tall and weighing over two hundred pounds—had dark, slick hair, and wore dark suits, white shirts, and solid-blue ties. The men were nearly carbon copies of each other.

The captain motioned for Lewis and Farrel to enter. Lewis placed the report on the desk in front of Captain Carr.

"Thanks," the captain said. "Farrel, Lewis, these are Special Agents Andrew and White from the CIA. They'll be taking over your case."

The four shook hands and nodded politely, despite the automatic mutual suspicion and animosity usually felt between members of competing investigative units. Captain Carr lifted the report and passed it to Agent White.

"If you boys need any professional help," said Farrel, "don't hesitate to ask, okay?"

"I don't think we'll need it, thanks," Agent Andrew replied.

The agents opened the door to leave.

"Thanks for the cooperation, Captain," Andrew said.

The captain slammed the door shut behind them before losing his temper.

"Do you two know how much fuckin' heat I'm takin' for the way you nitwits handled this investigation? I contacted the FBI, and for God's sake, they sent out the CIA. You assholes really struck a nerve!"

Carr ran a hand through what was left of his hair. "Frank, you're on suspension," he said.

"But, Cap, I ..."

"No 'buts,' Frank. You know better. For God's sake, you were supposed to set an example for Lewis."

George tried to get a word in. "But, Captain, he ..."

"Shut up, Lewis. You're on desk duty. Now, both of you get the hell out of here."

This was not how Farrel expected it to come down. Now stuck on desk duty, George wouldn't be able to assist him in the investigation. But Lewis was a quick thinker.

"Shit, Cap, I'd rather take vacation than desk duty!"

"That's fine with me, Lewis. Put in for it, and get the hell out of my sight."

They hurried from the captain's office.

"Quick thinking, Nipsy. I guess you really *do* want to catch the bad guys."

"Fuck you, Frank."

Chapter Twenty-Three

That Monday—the same day Farrel was suspended and Lewis put in for vacation—the senator was a no-show at his office. He sat quietly alone in his living room. His children had returned to their respective boarding schools after spending some time at home for their mother's funeral. They had pleaded with their father to allow them to stay at home rather than return to school and mourn alone, but he had dismissed the notion and sent them on their way. Senator Wheatly had learned about Anthony's death and had been wrestling all day with his emotions and the ramifications of the suicide on both his personal and professional lives.

Farrel and Lewis wanted to be the ones to break the news to him. They wanted to be sure that at least one of them got to hear his reaction firsthand. The senator had hardly paid any attention to the name of the person who had notified him—all that had registered was that it had been a representative of the Philadelphia Police Department.

Lewis had encountered an odd reaction from the senator when he had phoned him on Sunday night. After a few seconds of phony shock, Wheatly's biggest concern was whether or not Anthony had left a suicide note. That was typically a concern limited to family members, spouses, and lovers—not an employer. When Detective Lewis had informed him that Anthony had not left a note, the senator had breathed a sigh of relief.

Although Wheatly had certainly enjoyed the relationship with his aide, there was no doubt that his death would mean one less thorn in his side. Of late, Anthony had only been a source of dissention and an unwilling participant in the senator's plans. Another advantage of Anthony's death was that now—as far as he knew—there were only three people who knew about the Point Guard document: himself, the president, and the president's classified legal expert. Yet another bonus was that now there was no link that could connect him to the shooting of Mike Lane. Anthony's unstable behavior since the shooting had been a serious concern of the senator's, and now it was gone.

Nevertheless, Wheatly couldn't help but wonder whether Anthony had indeed hung himself. Could he have been murdered? What if those union bastards had killed him? Wheatly needed to distance himself from those people. He needed to get the Point Guard program moving. Then he realized that the union killing Anthony this way didn't make sense. Wouldn't they have let him clearly *know* that it was a warning? Furthermore, it would have been more damaging to him for them to hang the gay relationship over his head. In any case, he knew that Barletto's people would be sure to contact him soon if they had a message for him. For now, he felt marginally comfortable with the facts as Lewis had presented them. It had been a suicide.

The next day, Wheatly returned to his office to resume business as usual. The recent tragedies had slowed the production of his office to a trickle, but now with the worst behind him, he was eager to continue working with the president and finish the Point Guard project.

On his first morning back, Kathy handled her usual daily responsibilities but kept a suspicious eye planted firmly on her boss. Early that morning, she and the senator had spoken briefly, behind closed doors, about Anthony's suicide. Wheatly was a skilled and crafty communicator, so he had left Kathy feeling uncertain about his involvement.

Later that morning, the president called the senator.

"Hello, Jeff. I know I've said it before, but I'm so sorry about Jane."

"Thanks, sir."

"But listen, Jeff. Everywhere I turn, I see something about you in the papers. First, Jane makes the news ... and now your aide. What's going on with this suicide?"

"It's a shame, sir. He was a nice kid."

"Yeah, I'm sure he was terrific," the president said callously. "Listen to me, Jeff. This isn't good."

"What do you mean?"

"Hell, Jeff, you've been in this town long enough to know that the press will jump all over this. God knows what those bloodhounds will uncover. You can be sure it won't be good. Let's face it. If there's a scandal in this, they'll dig it up! So, until I can be sure that there isn't going to be any fallout from this, you and I will need to cool off on our meetings. We'll work over the phone the best we can. Agreed?"

"Yes, sir," said Wheatly, despite his misgivings.

"Why do you suppose he committed suicide, Jeff?"

"You know, I really don't know. He was a great kid. But I must say … my wife would tell me, from time to time, that she thought he might be gay. He never really seemed to go on dates or show any interest in women. I must admit … after awhile, I, too, thought he might be gay. But I never approached him about it."

"Well, I'll tell you this, Jeff. If he *was* gay, then the media will focus on that. We have a lot to do, and with all that's been going on in your life lately, it might be good for the media to have a story to focus on other than you. If you know what I mean.

"Jeff," he stressed, "you'd better figure out how to get the spotlight off yourself so that we can do our work."

After a short discussion regarding Point Guard, they said good-bye.

The president had planted a seed in the senator's mind.

In fact, Wheatly knew *exactly* what the president was asking him to do. It was very clear. He should exploit the notion that Anthony had been a gay man struggling to come to grips with his sexuality. This might defuse any efforts by the media to unearth a scandal about Wheatly himself. The suicide would be explained by a simple case of confused sexuality—short and sweet.

Of course, the senator would have to upset the very people Anthony had been trying to protect, but Wheatly could care less. Anthony's parents were old-school Catholics and viewed homosexuality as immoral. The influence of their beliefs on Anthony over his lifetime—and the fact that there had been no other family members or friends in his circles with the same sexual orientation—had kept him in the closet. His masquerade had been so effective that he and his friends would often joke about gay people. In other words, the news of his homosexuality would come as a huge shock to his parents and friends.

So be it, the senator thought.

*   *   *   *

Senator Wheatly stood at a podium in a packed conference room at the Whitehall Inn. He was holding a press conference to deal with the suicide of his aide. Cameras flashed and videotape rolled as the journalists waited to see whether the senator would give them a story worth exploiting. Wheatly cleared his throat and looked somberly around the room at the familiar faces.

"Today," he said, "I would like to make a statement and then answer any questions relating to the death of one of my staff members, Anthony Kane. As you all know by now, Anthony was discovered in the basement of his parents' home by his mother on Sunday. There is an ongoing investigation being conducted by the Philadelphia police, but by all indications, it appears to have been a suicide. I cannot speak to the investigation; I can only say that Anthony Kane was an outstanding staff member and friend."

He looked around the room and stood quietly for a couple of seconds.

"Any questions?"

The room erupted as the reporters shouted simultaneously. Wheatly raised his arms above his head as though he were conducting an orchestra.

"Please, please!" he said. "One at a time." He pointed at a particular reporter. "Yes."

"Senator, why do *you* think Mr. Kane killed himself?"

"I think there's a lot of people wondering the same thing. I guess there is no way to know for sure."

"Was his suicide work-related?"

"No. Not that we are aware of."

Another reporter yelled out. "Senator, did Mr. Kane leave a note?"

"No. There was no note."

"Senator ... senator," yelled one reporter above the rest. "Was the death of your wife ruled an accident or was ..."

Instantly, the senator interrupted, "I will only say this one time." His face turned red. "*I will not answer any questions regarding the accident or the death of my wife.*"

The menacing reporter raised her voice and asked the question again. Wheatly was obviously disturbed. He turned away to ignore the journalist and pointed to another.

"Senator, has the police or anyone else for that matter speculated on why your aide committed suicide?"

"I guess, yeah."

"Can you tell us what that speculation might be?"

The senator stood silent and seemed to give the question some thought.

"Um, some suppose that it might have had to do with his sexual orientation and the struggles he faced in that regard."

"What do you mean? What was his sexual orientation?"

"He was gay."

Most of the senator's staff attended and was stunned by the revelation. They whispered among themselves as the conference continued. Wheatly pointed at another reporter.

"Senator, did you know that Mr. Kane was gay when you hired him? Was he having problems with his sexuality then?"

"Yes, I did know that he was gay, and he always seemed to have a problem dealing with his sexuality. I took Anthony under my wing and tried my best to counsel him." He looked down at the podium and paused. "He was like a son to me. From time to time, he would tell me that he was unsure about how to live his life. There were times when he even talked about suicide, but that was along time ago. Back then I tried to get him help, but … well, I guess he was more comfortable with keeping it a secret. The loss of Anthony Kane is a great loss for our staff and his family. I will miss him immensely."

For the next seven or eight minutes, the questions the senator was willing to take were carefully selected. Although many reporters had questions regarding gay and lesbian rights, the death of his wife, and a number of other subjects, he would only select reporters he had heard asking about Anthony's suicide. When responding to these questions, he said basically the same thing repeatedly, but in many subtly different ways. Finally, he raised a hand above his head, thanked the media, and exited the room.

The press conference seemed to have been a success. Wheatly was quite sure that he had managed to divert any press interest away from himself and onto Anthony.

Anthony's elderly parents were devastated by shame and sadness after they watched and read the reports about their son. His father became withdrawn and depressed, a state from which he would never recover. His mother, too, became severely depressed, and from the day of the press conference forward, she rarely left her cozy house even to stroll the friendly streets of her tight-knit neighborhood.

In Chicago, Barletto laughed while watching a tape of the news conference on CNN. "What a piece of shit this guy is!" he said. "His day's comin'. If he wasn't as hot as he is right now, I'd kill him myself!"

Shortly after the news conference, the senator's media celebrity subsided considerably. The president congratulated him on doing a fine job of defusing a potentially volatile situation. The two of them resumed their work on the Point Guard.

The detectives sat in Kathy's living room discussing the case. As usual, Farrel seemed to be driving the investigation, and Lewis and Kathy abided by nearly every suggestion or thought that he voiced.

"We need to be absolutely certain," Farrel said, "that Wheatly is responsible for the theft of Mike Lane's work. If that's what he and the president have been talking about, we need to know it. What we need … is a way to listen in on their conversations."

Lewis rolled his eyes. He had been feeling more and more uncomfortable every day with where Farrel was taking the investigation. Somehow, Farrel was always able to convince him to continue.

"Kathy," Farrel asked, "have you ever been present during any of the senator's conversations with the president?"

"On the phone?"

"Yeah."

"No, not really."

"Why do you ask, Frank?" Lewis questioned.

"I figure that Kathy might be able to confirm what Wheatly has been talking about if she were to hear the senator's phone conversations with the president."

Lewis nodded.

"But if she's never actually in the room she …"

"You know," Kathy interrupted, "the president is coming in to see the senator in a couple of days. Everyone is so excited; he has never come to our office."

"Really? What for?" Farrel asked.

"Nobody knows. The senator has kept it hush-hush."

"What if Kathy just walks in on one of their meetings?" Farrel suggested.

"Do you think it would work?" Lewis asked.

"Maybe, maybe not. Wheatly seems to be a paranoid little prick. It's possible that he would suspect something. But why would he?"

"I don't know, Frank."

"Shit, why would he be suspicious of Kathy? Why would her walking in on their meeting—as long as she had a good reason—make him suspicious?"

Lewis turned to Kathy.

"Do you just walk into his office normally?" he asked.

"Not if the door is closed, no. If the door's closed, I usually knock. But … when I know for certain what he's doing, I do … on rare occasions enter without knocking … like when he is alone working on something, I will walk in and offer him some coffee. However, he did specifically tell me that no one was to disturb him for any reason when the president comes in this week."

They all pondered the problem for a moment.

"Suppose I just walked in unannounced with coffee for them? I mean, I'm like a fixture in there sometimes. They might not even notice. I'd just step in and offer them some coffee, simple as that! I know the document well enough to know whether or not they're discussing it. It's worth a try. I don't see how it would raise any suspicion. Like I said, I do go in on occasion when the senator wants privacy and offer him coffee. The worst thing that could happen, as far as I can see, is that he gets annoyed and tells me to leave."

They thought it over again.

"All right, Kathy," Farrel said. "That's what we'll do! But be careful."

*   *   *   *

Senator Leonard King, the chair of the Senate Ethics Committee, was attending one of his frequent meetings at CIA headquarters. This particular meeting was highly confidential, since Agents Andrew and White were briefing him on the Wheatly situation. King was a former strategy expert and consultant to several Fortune 500 companies. He was also a longtime supporter and very close political friend of the president. He had been responsible for the CIA agents' appearance at the Philadelphia police station. After Captain Carr had contacted the FBI, the Bureau had contacted Senator King about the Wheatly investigation and potential ethics violations related to the senator's taxes. King wasted no time; aware of the president's close ties to Senator Wheatly and NAFTA, King immediately pulled some strings to gain control of the case and contacted the CIA, which was better equipped to work on confidential operations and where he had more influence and political connections. In fact, Andrew and White acted as double agents of sorts. They worked for the CIA but over the years had operated as covert agents for King whenever required.

Agent Andrew's summary was quick and concise.

"Senator," he said, "the Philadelphia investigation could implicate Senator Wheatly in the shooting of his accountant. There is some speculation that the accountant might have found out that he was involved in tax fraud. Further, because of the timing, there is some concern about his wife's death as well. Now, to top it all off, his aide has turned up dead—an apparent suicide.

"Sir," he continued, "I know that Senator Wheatly is a very powerful senator. And I know we are assigned to this case for damage control, but that was only for tax evasion. With the two other deaths, it's possible—at least as far as the Philly police are concerned—that tax fraud is only the tip of the iceberg." He hesitated for a moment. "We need some direction on this, sir."

King rubbed his forehead with both hands, wondering how to insulate the president from this mess. With all the circumstances and accusations surrounding Wheatly, King found himself with the makings of what could be a mammoth case. As the chair of the Senate Ethics Committee, King could have found himself obligated to proceed with an investigation into Senator Wheatly, even though Wheatly had close ties to King's friend, the president.

Over the years, Senator King was involved in many covert operations and was considered one of the best in the field. However, his primary job as head of the Senate Ethics Committee was not to cover up improprieties but to expose and investigate all unethical behavior in the Senate. Like many times in the past, he found himself with stakes on both sides of the fence—working in a quasi-covert damage-control role with the CIA agents and as head of the Senate Ethics Committee. In fact, shortly after hearing about the drowning death of Mrs. Wheatly, King had been briefed by CIA brass that a cover-up strategy had already been hatched in case there had been any improprieties on Wheatly's part. As it turned out, Senator Wheatly was not suspected in his wife's drowning, and King did not have to engage in what could have been a highly publicized and difficult operation to contain.

King was worried about the president's NAFTA campaign but unaware that Senator Wheatly was no longer the president's candidate to run the project. After digesting the agents' report and giving the matter as much thought as he could for the time being, King gave them their direction.

"Gentlemen ... leave the file with me for now. If Wheatly's guilty of tax evasion, it's no big deal. We can deal with that. If there's a murder in here somewhere—or more than one—that's a different story. Let me look the file over and brief the president. This is a decision that needs to come from the top. I'll be in touch."

The president and Senator Wheatly sat looking over stacks of Point Guard papers and other documents that were strewn across the senator's desk. Nearly three hours into the meeting, Kathy summoned the nerve to make her move. The senator's office was swarming with Secret Service agents. Of particular concern were two large men in dark suits who stood quietly but alertly at the door of the senator's private office.

Acting as though she had been expected to serve the president and senator, Kathy loaded a silver tray with a sterling coffeepot, a silver creamer and sugar bowl, and fine porcelain coffee cups and saucers. Nervously, though doing her best to look nonchalant, she approached the senator's door and nodded politely as she stepped between the two agents. One agent stopped her as she reached for the doorknob. She held her breath and tried to steady herself as the other agent made a cursory examination of the tray. Then, finally, one of them gave her a nod, and they retreated.

Breathing heavy, she turned the knob with her free hand. She had already begun her intrusion when the porcelain cups clattered against their saucers due to the shakiness of her nervous grip on the tray. She hesitated for a moment, gritted her teeth, smiled at the guards, and stepped quietly into the senator's office. The president and the senator were both sitting behind the desk. They were staring directly at her. She tucked her chin into her chest and raised her shoulders.

"I thought you gentleman might like some coffee. I won't bother you; I'll just set it up over here."

It hadn't gone quite the way she'd planned, but she was in. When the men didn't respond immediately, she decided to forestall any negative reaction by quickly moving over to a table in the corner of the office, where she began to prepare the coffee. After a couple of seconds, the men continued with their meeting as if she weren't there. As she kept busy with the coffee, she listened carefully and could tell immediately that they were discussing the Point Guard document. Kathy forced a smile as she carried two full cups over to the desk. They thanked her, and she left the room confident she had heard all she needed.

Later that evening, Farrel and Lewis met Kathy at her condominium. She told the detectives about her eavesdropping adventure. Kathy was charged with excitement as she sat at the end of her dining table with Farrel and Lewis on either side.

"You won't believe this! I walked in as I was supposed to—right past the guards, they're pretty big guys—anyhow, I walked straight in. And they were talking about Mike's work!"

"Are you sure?" Lewis asked.

"Absolutely! They talked about it the entire time I was in there. They were talking about how point totals could be printed on drivers' licenses and ID cards."

Farrel liked her style.

"Did Wheatly seem suspicious of you?" he asked.

Kathy shook her head.

"Not at all suspicious?"

"When a girl shakes her head," Kathy teased, "she means no, Frank."

He smiled. "Did the senator say anything to you?"

"No, nothing. I just gave them coffee, listened to what they were saying, and left."

Farrel was now convinced—and, more importantly, he had persuaded his partner—that the senator was probably the person who had destroyed Lane's files and had stolen the Point Guard document. He now attempted to get into the mind of a man like Senator Jeff Wheatly. Thinking aloud, he considered the crime and how it might have gone down.

"All right," he said. "For some unknown reason, the senator suddenly changes his attitude toward Mike Lane and decides to meet with him. Why, we don't know. Maybe he sees the potential of the plan and can see how it could help his political career."

Farrel circled the dining table as he went on.

"He steals the document and destroys any evidence that leads back to Mike as the author. Mike trusted him and never suspected that he was in danger, so maybe he told Wheatly everything—where he kept the document, whether there were extra copies, what was on the computer disks, and what he had on his personal computer—everything. Somehow, during the theft of Mike's work he gets shot. I don't think Wheatly could do that. He must have had someone else in on it."

"How about Anthony Kane?" Lewis asked.

Farrel gave the notion some thought. "Maybe he ..."

"No," Kathy shook her head and bristled. "Anthony could never kill somebody!"

Farrel glanced over at Kathy and smiled in a soothing way. "Listen, we can work on that later. Okay?"

Kathy nodded and settled down.

He continued, "I'm sure the senator did *not* know that Mike mailed a copy of the disk to you." Farrel glanced at her again. "For some reason Mike must have stopped trusting Wheatly ... or maybe someone else. That's why he mailed you a copy for safe keeping."

Farrel continued to pace around the table as Lewis stared straight across the room with his arms folded across his chest.

"So, Mike gets shot," said Farrel, "and as far as the senator is concerned, he has sole possession of the document. Then ... maybe ... just maybe ... his wife somehow gets wind of what he's done, and Wheatly kills her?"

"Now that's stretching it, Frank," Lewis said. "Killing his wife? I mean, sure, I think that there should have been an investigation into her death, but I'm not really convinced that he *murdered* her."

"Okay, maybe he didn't. Maybe that part was just a coincidence. Bad timing. But for the sake of strategy, let's assume the worst—that he killed her."

"Where does that play in? I mean, why would he do it?" Lewis asked.

"I don't know," said Farrel. "It's just a possibility."

He stretched his neck from side to side before continuing.

"Now ... and I'm sorry, Kathy, Anthony Kane, the senator's aide, commits suicide." He looked at George and raised his eyebrows. "That's three dead, an important document stolen, and now the document is in the possession of a powerful senator."

"This is complicated, Frank." Lewis rubbed his face and seemed aggravated. "The president, the senator, three dead, justice reform—we're out of our league! I mean, anyone that might have witnessed anything or led us to a smoking gun is dead! We need an eyewitness."

"That would help," Farrel replied. "George, let me ask you. *Now* do you believe that the senator stole Mike's work?"

"I hate to say that you're right, Frank ... but yeah, I think he did it."

"All right then." Farrel seemed positive about their prospects. "We'll figure it out. We'll get a break. Let's just keep digging."

Chapter Twenty-Four

A couple of days after the two detectives and Kathy sat at Kathy's dining room table and theorized about the investigation, Senator King sat outside the Oval Office. He had studied the file on Senator Wheatly's tax evasion and was now awaiting a scheduled meeting with the president.

"Senator King, the president will see you now," the president's secretary said.

The president was always pleased to speak to King but not necessarily thrilled to have the chair of the Senate Ethics Committee request an urgent meeting. King had told the president over the phone only that the meeting was urgent and that it concerned Jeff Wheatly.

"Leonard, how are you my friend?" said the president as he reached across the desk to shake King's hand. "I was hoping that I could go through the entire term without the need for an urgent meeting with you. So, what's on your mind about Jeff?"

Relaxed, the president settled back in his chair. He comfortably folded his arms across his chest as Senator King sat down. The president prepared himself for whatever bomb King was about to drop.

"Mr. President," said King, "there is currently an investigation being conducted regarding a charge of tax evasion against Senator Wheatly."

The president maintained his posture but fidgeted a bit in his chair. Not noticing the president's slight discomfort, King continued. "Sir, I know that you've been meeting with Jeff lately."

It was no secret that the president was meeting regularly with Wheatly. It was also known in political circles that Wheatly had been the president's first choice to run the NAFTA campaign—there had been no announcement yet that there was an impending change regarding that post.

"So I thought that I'd better come to you as soon as I understood the charges and circumstances."

The president felt uneasy about King's revelation but veiled his apprehension well.

"Leonard, you know I appreciate that. What do you have?"

"Actually, what I have is a mess. Evidently, during the murder investigation of a Philadelphia man, an accountant, it was revealed when records were subpoenaed that Jeff had been one of the victim's clients. He was a man by the name of Mike Lane. The Philadelphia detectives evidently ran a check on Jeff's tax returns, and they uncovered some questionable records. The Philadelphia investigation brings up the possibility that he may have committed tax fraud and then shot his accountant to keep him quiet. None of that's been proved, of course, but it's a messy situation. I cashed in some favors and took control when the FBI contacted me—it's standard procedure to contact me when there are accusations of Senate ethics violations. In an effort to get a handle on this thing, I had a couple of covert CIA agents whom I've worked with over the years take over the investigation until we decide on the best course of action. I know that Jeff Wheatly is one of your top guys, and I wanted to be sure that this got all the attention we could give it. But with all that surrounds it—his wife's death and now the suicide of his aide—it's certainly a bigger can of worms than we typically see. Unfortunately, your close involvement with him regarding the NAFTA project could show that your choice for the post lacks good judgment. Sir, with all due respect, I know that you've been meeting with him regularly. And, Mr. President, I'm not trying to be one of your advisers, but we have a case here that may go as deep as murder. Even if it doesn't—even if it's only tax evasion—we still have an enormous problem. And part of the problem is your close relationship with Senator Wheatly."

The president seemed annoyed with King's findings. He leaned forward on his desk, and his head slumped.

"You weren't shitting when you said this was a mess," he said.

The president tried to think of a way to rectify the situation. The Point Guard plan was vital to him and to the country, and he didn't want anything to derail his efforts to pass it into law. Searching for a solution, he took a long serious look at King. He squinted and leaned across his desk.

"Leonard," he said with a steady gaze, "I'm going to trust you to do something that you may find objectionable. But it's necessary. I'm working on something with Jeff that may perhaps be the most important thing to happen to our country in a long time. I can't tell you what it is yet, but I am going to need you to pledge your allegiance to the country and me … and to do what I ask without questioning me. Do you understand?"

King nodded.

"Leonard, your background in strategy will play large in what I'm going to ask, and your position as ethics chairman is going to be challenged as well. We've known each other for a long time, and you know that I wouldn't ask you to do anything that would compromise the security of our nation." The president paused at length but continued staring at King. "Leonard, we need the Wheatly situation to go away."

The statement threw King back on his heels a bit—but not entirely. He was already aware of the plan to cover up the senator's river accident and had a history of being involved in these types of affairs. However, he did have to keep in mind his ethics post.

"Um … Mr. President, are you sure that you want to be saying this to me?"

King smiled uncomfortably. He looked as though he might have thought the president was kidding, but he knew that this was unlikely.

"I mean, sir, what could be so important that it would lead us to conceal possible murder, tax evasion, and God knows what else? Hell, we don't even know if the senator *did* these things." King hesitated and then spoke searchingly. "Unless … we *do* know that Wheatly is guilty of these things?"

King stiffened and asked, "You want me to help arrange a cover-up with my associates at the CIA because you know that Jeff is guilty, don't you?'

The president gave no indication that he knew anything at all.

For several seconds, King looked into the unyielding stare of the president.

"Are you going to tell me anything about what you're working on?" King asked.

The president spoke with great respect for King but with a deeply concerned look on his face.

"I know this is a tall order, but I, and this country, need your help. If you play this by the book as it relates to your job with the ethics committee, you will ruin an opportunity to affect significant and much needed change to one of our nations most important issues." The president pursed his lips and shook his head. "But I am *not* going to tell you what it is."

The president enunciated every word of his next sentence with great deliberation. *"You will need to trust me!"*

Neither man said a word for a moment. Then, the president added, "With your strategy background, as well as your ties to the CIA, there's no one better to take care of this. You'd play an instrumental role in ensuring that what Jeff and I are working on comes to fruition. So, Leonard … can I count on you?"

"Sir, you're talking about murder. I can't say I'm comfortable without knowing more."

"I can't tell you much more, Leonard."

The president sat up and folded his hands on the desk. He looked at King as if he were about to issue a declaration of war.

Uncomfortable, King squirmed in his chair and shook his head.

"I'm sorry, sir." He swallowed hard and looked to the floor. "I know you feel I'm qualified, but I'm not the right man for this. The ethics committee …"

"Senator," the president demanded. "I'm asking you to do this for me … for our country. Don't make me go to someone else. I don't want to have to change my game plan."

King felt threatened. The president stared boldly and waited for a response. Getting none, the president prodded.

"Can I count on you, Leonard?"

King bowed his head in thought before looking up again. He stared at the president for several seconds.

"Yes … sir, you can count on me," he said reluctantly. "But sir, I have to say I don't like this."

Satisfied, the president nodded and launched directly into the matter.

"Can we isolate the tax evasion charges, Leonard?"

"I suppose we could. But because of the Philadelphia police investigation, that doesn't take out the suspicion of murder. You see, Mr. President, even though the case was turned over to the CIA, there must still be interest in the case back in Philadelphia. Burying the tax problem only solves one part of the puzzle. You see, the Philadelphia police might now suspect him in the shooting. I can easily control my guys, but there's no way to know how the Philly police will react if we try to sweep the entire thing into oblivion."

"Let me see if I understand this thing correctly, Leonard. You're saying that Jeff doctored his tax returns without his accountant's knowledge and that this eventually led to a murder investigation?"

"Yes, that's about the size of it."

"So, if the murder were solved, then the tax evasion charge could then be isolated from everything else. Right?"

King nodded warily.

"In that case, the suspicion of him having murdered this Mike Lane disappears, and the deaths of his wife and his aide would become nothing more than matters of bad timing and coincidence! Hell, the press has already had their feeding frenzy on his aide. He was just another fucking queer who couldn't handle his emotions. As far as his wife is concerned ... shit, the public feels sorry for the poor bastard! He lost his wife, after all! Does that all make sense? Do I have a grasp of the situation? Isn't that the way it falls together?"

"Yes, sir. But that would mean that we'd have to find the real murderer."

"Or give the Philadelphia police a murderer."

"Okay," King said, "let's say we fabricate a murderer. Then how do we handle the tax evasion?"

The president shrugged.

"What are you talking about? What tax evasion?" he said. He knew that Senator King could easily clean up Wheatly's tax situation.

"All right, but what about Philly?"

"Do you have the Philadelphia file, Leonard?"

"Yes."

"Including the evidence of tax fraud?"

"Yes."

"Great," the president said casually, "we have the file in an ongoing investigation, and they have an incomplete investigation."

"Well, Mr. President," King hedged, "we did take the file and were sure to ask the Philly captain to give us all of the related notes and material, but ..."

"Good," the president interrupted, nodding. "Then destroy the fraudulent tax records at the IRS and replace them with appropriate tax returns. Can you do that, Leonard?"

"I'm sure we can, sir."

"Good. Once you've done that, there'll be no evidence of tax fraud, and it becomes a lead that didn't pan out. Anyhow, we can't afford to go probing into the tax returns of senators—trust me, that would be disastrous. Hell, everybody has unreported income in this town!"

The president stood and walked around his massive desk.

"Senator King," he said, "I want you to finger someone for the shooting of Wheatly's accountant and clean up his tax problem." He made a motion suggesting that King was dismissed. "Some day, you'll know what this is all about, and I'll make sure that you play a significant role in it. And Leonard, leave me the file—everything except what you need to clean up the tax problem."

After Senator King's departure, the president, deeply troubled by the entire ordeal, summoned Senator Wheatly to the White House. He appeared at the Oval Office a couple of hours later.

"Have a seat, Jeff," the president said sternly. "We need to talk."

Wheatly felt a bit bewildered and on edge. He wondered what the president might have to say that could not have waited until their next scheduled meeting.

"Jeff … a couple of hours ago, Senator King from the Senate Ethics Committee was here to discuss a few things about your behavior." Annoyed, he baited Wheatly. "Do you know why he was here?"

The senator's heart started thumping madly. He wondered whether King had found out about his dealings with the mob—or worse. He tried to think of where he might have left a loose end dangling.

"No, sir," he said and shook his head.

Disgusted, the president said, "He says that you're guilty of tax evasion, Jeff!" He pounded his fist on his desk.

"God almighty, Jeff! *Tax evasion!* How the hell are we going to pass Point Guard into law if the author of the damn thing is breaking the law himself?"

Wheatly tried to conceal his sigh of relief. Thoughts of murder, theft, and a good number of other things faded. He knew that the ethics committee usually did little more than give politicians warnings when it came to tax problems.

"Come on, sir," he said. "I'm not the only politician in this town who's bending the rules when it comes to money. Hell, Congress is rife with the misappropriation of campaign funds, bogus expenses, overdrawn Senate bank accounts, tax loopholes—"

"*Legal* tax loopholes, Jeff!" the president shouted. "When you commit fraud, it's a federal offense. Hell, you could go away for three years if someone wanted to make an example of you. For God's sake, what the hell were you thinking?"

After giving the president's warning some consideration, Wheatly realized that his tax dilemma had the potential to undermine his position with the Point Guard program. He felt relieved, in one sense, but he was still concerned about how this disclosure could affect his future.

"What do you want me to do?" he asked.

"I'm going to take care of it, Jeff. But before I do, you need to hear the extent to which your bad judgment has affected things. Leonard King came here today to tell me that he's had to use the CIA to protect me from my relationship with you."

The senator started to respond but was silenced by a gesture from the president.

"Like I said, Leonard came in to tell me that the Philadelphia police have been investigating you for tax fraud. As if that in itself weren't bad enough, he tells me that the only reason they were investigating you for tax fraud is that your accountant had been murdered." The president leaned across his desk and raised his voice in order to drive home his point. "*And* ... because you were a client of his, it was discovered during the investigation into his murder that you were committing *tax fraud*, which then made you a *murder suspect!*"

The senator leapt to his feet. "Murder! I didn't—"

"Sit down, Senator."

Wheatly dropped back into his seat, lowering his head.

The president took a long, hard look at Wheatly before resuming.

"I'm going to have the evidence of your poor judgment on the issue of tax evasion eradicated. And as far as you being a suspect in the shooting ... well, we're not going to talk about that right now."

Wheatly nodded as the president stood up to end the meeting.

"You just keep your mouth shut, I've been assured that a shooter *will* be named very shortly. That should square everything up for you, and we can get back to work. Now get out of here. I'll be in touch."

Upon leaving the White House, Wheatly decided to celebrate his incredible good fortune by taking a stroll down Pennsylvania Avenue on this bright, sunny day. He could hardly believe this turn of events. First, no one suspected him of the theft of the Point Guard document, and second, the president promised a shooter would be identified in the Lane murder case! The case would be closed, and all ties between him and the stolen document would be gone. He felt drunk with power and confidence. It was amazing what a senator could get away with! There would be no limit to what he could do if he were to become the Point Guard.

After several lengthy meetings with Senator King, agents Andrew and White had their orders. They secured the services of a top expert in covert operations—an operative by the name of Neil Dugan. Dugan, a loner, was an expert in computers, counterfeit documents, and tax records and had been involved in more covert operations than he could remember. He was forty years old, balding on top with thick brown hair at the sides, and wore thick wire-framed glasses. He was thin and looked essentially like a nerd. His unassuming appearance was very important to his job, as was the fact that he had no family or close personal associates of any kind. He was a perfect cipher.

This was certainly not the first time he had worked on a case of this magnitude.

Dugan got to work immediately on the cover-up. Posing as an IRS employee named Joseph Yserman, Dugan entered the IRS building with a false badge and passcard. He wore a black suit and toted a black leather briefcase. He rode the elevator to the customer service floor. After arriving at an empty cubicle on the outside edge of the busy call center, Dugan made sure that no one was watching and slid into the seat. He began pecking furiously at the computer keyboard on the desk. He thought that it would be relatively easy to locate Senator Wheatly's tax file in the IRS database.

The harder part of his task would be locating the senator's physical tax return among the millions warehoused in the building's basement.

Using his alias and the IRS security clearance he had received from King, he began to tackle his first challenge. He changed Wheatly's tax records in the computer files to reflect what had been salvaged from Lane's smashed computer. It soon became apparent to Dugan that the senator's tax details had been altered some time after Lane had prepared the senator's legitimate returns.

Dugan pulled from his briefcase hard copies of the senator's tax returns, which had been printed from Lane's files, and compared them with those on file with the IRS. Line by line and item by item, he checked and changed each discrepancy between the two returns. From time to time, he looked over his shoulder for any intruders. Gradually, the IRS files began to look identical to the ones from Lane's records. Although Dugan's task was a simple one, it was also very tedious and nerve-racking. But he did it with relative calm.

Nearly forty minutes later, Dugan had completed the first part of his mission. He typed in the command to save the changes he had made, logged off, and stuffed his papers into his briefcase. Now with the senator's electronic files clean, it was time to switch hard copies. Dugan phoned the record storage department. An IRS security guard answered almost immediately.

"Hello, this is Joseph Yserman. My security code is E255J225. I'm an auditor on the fourth floor. I need permission to come down and pick some hard copies for an audit."

"Yes sir, Mr. Yserman. I'll just need your ID and security pin when you arrive in the basement."

The Yserman alias was an identity concocted by the CIA years before, and it was often used in hands-on covert operations. The name had been programmed into the IRS database as that of an IRS auditor. When the alias was needed, an operative's photo was simply placed on a counterfeit ID card featuring Yserman's name and security clearance.

In the basement, Dugan approached a slack-jawed guard who slouched on a folding chair outside the record storage area. Dugan presented his security code, and the guard took a quick peek inside his briefcase and checked his ID. Dugan was then granted access to the hard-file storage area. It was a massive room—it covered the area of a city block and was filled with racks of file boxes, stacked twenty-five feet high. After searching for nearly forty minutes through the untidy mountains of files in the dimly lit basement, he located a box with Wheatly's file inside. He pulled it off the rack, placed it on the floor in the middle of the aisle, and rifled through it for copies of the documents in question. Hunched over the file box, he soon located the appropriate files and made the swap. He swiftly closed the box and placed it back in the rack. Wheatly's paper returns now matched the IRS's electronic files. All Dugan needed to do now was deliver the senator's fraudulent tax documents to Agents Andrew and White.

Dugan left the cavernous room, and after another listless inspection of his briefcase by the slouching guard, proceeded to the elevator. In the elevator, he contacted Agent White via cell phone and told him that the job had been completed. Outside the building, Dugan climbed into the backseat of the agents' dark sedan as they pulled up alongside the curb. The entire operation had taken less than two hours and had come off without a hitch.

All proof of Senator Wheatly's tax evasion was gone.

The agents' car sped past the IRS guard shack and weaved into the busy DC traffic. Instead of heading back to the operatives' office, they headed north on I-95. Dugan had been accustomed to constantly changing plans and agendas, so he sat unaffected by the diversion. After diving awhile on the interstate, Dugan— now stretched out comfortably across the backseat—asked the agents where they were going.

Keeping a close eye on the road, Agent Andrew looked through the rearview mirror into the backseat and answered, "To do some more of the same shit. Wheatly's state returns need some cleaning, and we want to check out some of the Philly police files."

"Beautiful," Dugan responded sarcastically. "Is this an overnight trip?"

Before Andrew could answer, White tapped his shoulder and pointed at an exit sign in the distance—EXIT 100, Northeast, Rising Sun, FOOD, LODG-ING.

"What do you say we get something to eat?" asked White.

Dugan thought that sounded like a good idea.

"We'll tell you what the next assignment is over a sandwich," White said.

The car turned off the exit ramp onto a quiet country road.

White faced Dugan with his arm slung over the seat back as they talked.

"Neil, wait until you get one of these sandwiches here. We stop in here every time we're up this way. They make the best damn milkshakes."

Dugan rubbed his stomach. "Sounds good to me," he said.

White faced forward again and tugged on his jacket as Andrew turned the car into the narrow parking lot in front of the tiny sandwich shop nestled in the woods. Andrew drove beyond a flickering street lamp that offered little illumination to the far end of the lot, to a point where some overgrown bushes and trees hung out over the blacktop. It was dusk, and the dark sedan seemed to fade into the tree line. Andrew parked beneath the forest canopy. The red brake lights faded as the three men got out of the car. They were barely visible as their silhouettes blended into the woods.

Andrew stood next to the car and stretched.

"Hey," White said to Dugan, "grab that briefcase. I don't want to leave it there. We'll put it in the trunk"

Dugan bent down and reached across the backseat as Andrew released the latch of the trunk from beneath the driver's side dash. Holding the briefcase, Dugan slammed the door and went around to the back of the car as White stood off to the side holding the trunk open. Andrew took a quick look around the lot and walked to the back of the car as Dugan bent over the trunk to place the case containing Wheatly's tax documents inside. Suddenly, Dugan noticed that the trunk had been lined with a large sheet of plastic. He turned toward White with a look of terror. Andrew leaned forward and fired a single bullet into the back of Dugan's head. A bright white flash lit up the area behind the car as the body slumped over the tailgate. In one fluid motion, White snatched the briefcase from Dugan's hand, lifted his legs off the ground, and spun them into the trunk. Andrew dropped the gun inside the trunk and slammed it closed. As Dugan's body still twitched and gushed blood, the two agents strolled toward the sandwich shop.

"Where are we going, Dugan?" White said carrying the briefcase. "To deliver a patsy in Philadelphia."

The owner of the sandwich shop greeted them at the door while looking inquisitively toward the dark end of the lot. "Hi, fellas," he said. "Did you hear that? It sounded like a gunshot!"

Andrew shrugged and said, "I guess a car backfired."

There wasn't a car in sight.

"Sounded like a gunshot to me," the shop owner muttered.

After their dinner, Andrew and White headed for Philly with Dugan's body lying cramped in the trunk. It took them a little over an hour to get to their destination—Lane's house. They parked in the driveway and entered the still-untidy house—everything looked pretty much the same as it had after the Philadelphia police had conducted their investigation on the night of the shooting. The agents examined the ground floor and exterior to be sure that it was empty and that there was no surveillance going on inside or out.

King had made it clear to be very careful. He emphasized to them the importance of taking extreme precautions. If their cover-up were discovered, it would precipitate a scandal of huge proportions. After ensuring that the house was secure, the agents removed a leather flight jacket from a hall closet and several of Lane's business cards from his desk. They placed the cards in a pocket of the jacket and the jacket in a brown paper bag, which they took with them when they left. They drove back onto the interstate and continued north to an area known to Philadelphians as "the Northeast." By now, the sky was completely black—it was overcast and not a star was visible. The agents drove to a secluded part of a Northeast neighborhood and parked on an empty lot next to a highway support column under a raised section of I-95. They both donned latex surgical gloves. Andrew opened the trunk, and White immediately grabbed hold of Dugan's body and jerked it upright into a sitting position. Andrew yanked Dugan's jacket off, emptied his trouser and shirt pockets, and dumped the contents into the paper bag. He then dressed Dugan in Lane's flight jacket. The job was a bloody one, but they didn't seem to mind—they moved as casually as if they were working in a kitchen butchering meat. They pulled Dugan's body out of the trunk after a quick check to see if anyone were watching and simply dropped it on the ground. After they took off their gloves and tossed them in the trunk, Andrew reached in and carefully gathered the corners of the blood-soaked plastic liner and rolled it up tight. He then retrieved from the spare tire compartment a hidden pistol that had the same caliber as the one that had shot Lane. As White started the engine, Andrew placed the gun in Dugan's waistband and placed a wallet in Dugan's back pocket. Andrew climbed into the car, and the agents drove away.

The entire procedure had taken less than two or three minutes.

As expected, the Philadelphia police contacted the CIA agents the next day when they discovered a body in the Northeast with Lane's business cards in a jacket pocket. Also inside the expensive leather flight jacket were the letters M.L. written in marker across its label. Identification found on the corpse revealed that the dead man's name was Nicholas Scorali. He had been a small-time thief from Baltimore.

Scorali's identity had been plucked by King's men from the CIA database of John Does who had died with no evidence of family or friends. Often, these nameless men were illegal immigrants or vagrants. The CIA would secure their records, fabricate new identities for them, and use them for operations like this one. Typically, it was preferable to use the body of a John Doe as a patsy, but because of the magnitude of this cover-up and the direct involvement of the president, Senator King felt it best to have as few people involved as possible. It had been decided that after he completed his work at the IRS, Neil Dugan would be more valuable as a dead Nicholas Scorali than as a living operative. All traces of Neil Dugan's identity would be destroyed.

After an investigation of this new murder scene, Captain Carr called Andrew at CIA headquarters.

He leaned back in his chair with his feet propped up on the center of his desk. "Agent Andrew, this is Captain Carr, Philly PD. I have some news in regard to the Lane investigation," he said.

"Is that so, Captain? What is it?"

"It looks like we have the shooter. It looks like it may have been a simple case of burglary, but we'll let you guys decide on that. It's your case now, ain't it?"

"How do you know he's the shooter?" asked Andrew smugly.

"We've identified a man that appears to have been killed gangland style and dumped under the interstate in the Northeast. Nicholas Scorali, from Baltimore. Background check shows he has some small-time break-and-enter priors. He was wearing what appeared to be Mr. Lane's coat and was carrying some of his identification."

"Hmm …" Andrew acted as though he were distracted.

Carr was growing fed up with this character.

"Hey, Andrew, … this is your investigation now. We have the body and the report available for your people to pick up whenever you want. It sounds to me like you might have two separate cases on your hands: burglary and tax evasion. And as far as I'm concerned … we're done with both of them."

This was what Andrew had wanted to hear.

"Alright, Captain. Thank you for the information. We'll add it to our file. I should tell you that the tax evasion matter has been passed on to the IRS and is no longer a concern for either of us anymore. And let me just make one thing clear again. Neither you nor your department is authorized to release any information about the senator or his relationship to Mr. Lane. You *do* understand that, right?"

"Yeah, fine. You can pick up the body at the city morgue." He could take no more and hung up without saying good-bye.

The commotion surrounding the discovery of Scorali was typical in that the usual outlets were clamoring for information to report to the public. After briefing Agent Andrew, Captain Carr released to the press statements about the discovery of Scorali in connection with the Lane shooting. Once again, one of the big stories in the papers and on television in Philadelphia was the Mike Lane case. A story on the local news confirmed that a Baltimore drifter by the name of Nicholas Scorali—reportedly responsible for the shooting of Philadelphia accountant Mike Lane—had been found dead after an apparent execution-style shooting under Interstate 95 in North Philadelphia.

Agent Andrew phoned Senator King with the results of the mission.

He included only what King needed and wanted to hear.

"Hello, Senator," Andrew said. "Everything went as planned. The Philadelphia police have contacted us and have assumed that they have the body of the thief who shot Mr. Lane. The Philadelphia police have told me that they will close the book on the case, and they are aware that the investigation into tax evasion is a separate case being handled by the IRS. That's all, sir."

King thanked Andrew for the report and then slowly placed the phone receiver on the hook while he sat on the edge of his chair. Rubbing his lips with his hand, he sat for a few moments and stared at the phone, as though he were considering the events of the last twenty-four hours. He took a deep breath, picked up the receiver, and made a call from his secure line.

"Hello, Leonard. How did everything go?"

"As planned, Mr. President."

"What's the report?"

King's heavy breath pushed into the phone. "An undercover operative by the name of Neil Dugan has rectified the senator's tax problem. Mr. Dugan has been secured, and the senator's situation has been taken care of. Everything went as planned."

"Fine job, Leonard. And the tax documents?"

"Under lock and key."

"Thank you, Leonard. I'll be in touch."

The president was pleased at having been able to contain any potential damage done by Senator Wheatly's tax problems. They could now continue their work on the Point Guard program.

As he breathed a sigh of relief, Senator King sat quietly and stared at the phone receiver in his hand.

Chapter Twenty-Five

Detectives Lewis and Farrel had learned that a body had been discovered that was connected to the Lane case, and they headed back to Philadelphia to find out more. It was no secret around the precinct that the CIA had taken over the Lane case. However, only a few people in the department knew anything about the case. As they drove north on the interstate, Farrel's cell phone rang.

"Hello?"

"Frank, it's Billy."

"Hey, Cap. What's up?"

"Frank, find Lewis and get in here right away. I've got news on the Lane case."

"Yeah? What kind of news?"

"Just get in here! I'll tell you when you get here."

"Sounds like the captain's bent out of shape," Farrel told Lewis.

Lewis took out his phone and dialed his friend and fellow detective Mark Hannon. "Let me see if Mark knows anything more than we already do."

Hannon answered after a couple of rings.

"Detective Hannon."

"Hey, Mark, it's me George."

"Hey, George, what's up?"

With a predictable and trademark response to "what's up" Lewis cracks, "A chicken's ass when he's eatin' ..." Keeping his sense of humor about him seems to help ease Lewis's nerves in tight situations. Glancing over at Lewis as he drives, Farrel shakes his head and chuckles to himself having heard that line from Lewis hundreds of times.

"What's going on up there, Mark?" George asked.

"Where the hell you been, George? A lot of talk about the Lane case is what's going on."

"Yeah? The Cap called Frank and me to come see him. What's it all about?"

"You're kiddin' me, right? Do you sit at home and watch soaps all day? A shooter and a weapon were found in the Lane case! Damn, George, it's been all over the station. Where the hell have you been, man?"

"A weapon? Where?"

Farrel was frustrated with his inability to hear the other end of the call. He struggled to keep his attention on the road as Lewis fed him tidbits of information.

"In Northeast, under I-95? When? What time last night? Do you have any other particulars?"

"I don't know much," Hannon said. "That's the weird part. All I know is that this guy was from Baltimore and that he was shot in the head. He was supposedly wearing Lane's coat and had some of his belongings; other than that, it's all hush-hush. No one is saying anything. It's as if it's some sort of huge secret around here. All I know is that the body was found last night and that the CIA has already showed up and taken it away."

Lewis wondered why the CIA was so quick to pick up the body.

"All right, thanks, Mark. We're on our way in. We'll see you in awhile."

"What's goin' on, George?" Hannon asked.

"I don't know, buddy. I'll see ya later."

Lewis shut the phone, and Farrel could tell that something was eating him.

"What's up?" Farrel asked.

"I don't know, Frank. Considering what we know about this case, I can't see where this dead guy fits in."

"Well … listen, we don't know enough about it yet. Let's not do any speculating until we get some more info."

"Maybe you were right. Maybe this guy was hired by Senator Wheatly to knock off Lane?" Lewis suggested.

"Like I said, George, let's wait for more information."

But Lewis felt compelled to try to make sense of the whole thing. "Maybe the senator had this guy wiped out, too," he said.

"George!" Farrel snapped. "Stop! Where would it all end? The way you're going with this, Wheatly would have to wipe out each person after he wiped out the previous one. Like I said, let's just wait until we get some more information."

One thing they were sure of was that the senator had not personally killed anyone in Philadelphia the previous night—they had been watching him in Washington.

Within the hour, Lewis and Farrel appeared outside the captain's office. Carr waved them in and told them to take a seat.

The captain got right to the point.

"It appears that the CIA will be closing the lid on the Lane investigation. Last night, detectives in the Northeast discovered the body of a man who's being linked to the Lane shooting."

"You two are back on duty as of now." The captain seemed somewhat despondent. "And don't ever hide police business from me again, understand?"

Disgusted with the way his detectives had handled the case and with the CIA's arrogant and puzzling participation in the investigation, the captain found himself with his nose out of joint. Regardless, the chief had ordered him to move on and not discuss the case any further.

Turning away from the detectives, he waved his hand and said, "Now, go to desk sergeant and get your new assignments."

Before following the order, Farrel scratched his head and seemed surprised at how easily the captain was willing to throw in the towel, especially after a body had mysteriously appeared in his city. Farrel waited in his chair and kept a steady eye on the captain as Lewis started for the door. Shaking his head, Farrel looked like a man with something on his mind.

"Now, wait a minute, Cap ... where did this body come from? Why was he killed? And what about ballistics? Was it the same gun that was used to shoot Lane? And what about the CIA? Why are they so damned interested in all this?"

Lewis froze just inside the doorway and waited to hear the captain's response.

These same questions had been running through the captain's mind. He had answers for some of them, but the ones that bothered him the most ate at his gut. *Did* ballistics prove that it was the same weapon? And why was the CIA investigating this? The captain felt compelled to respond, even though he had been ordered not to.

"Okay, Frank, I'll tell you what I know." He pointed at Lewis. "Sit down ... this is to stay in this room between us three. Understood?"

Farrel and Lewis nodded.

"I don't know any more than the officers that found the body. His name was Nicholas Scorali—a small-time thief from Baltimore. I did a background check on him, and he's only got priors in Baltimore—nowhere else. It doesn't make any sense why he would be here. I mean, all of a sudden he decides to come to Philly, rob an accountant, leave no traces of being here for awhile, and then turn up with a bullet in the back of his head under the interstate in Northeast? I don't understand that. And what's the motive? He's a small-timer, and there are plenty of places to rob in Baltimore. No reason to come to Philly—it makes no sense. As for ballistics, the CIA goons came right away and took the body—and every scrap of evidence—with them. Our detectives were left to assume that the gun on him was the same one used in the Lane shooting—but hell, there wasn't any ballistics done, so we don't know! I'm not happy about all this shit … but it is what it is. Now you have it."

Carr opened the door and motioned for the detectives to leave.

"Now, get your new assignments," he said.

Farrel had no intention of leaving or giving up the investigation. He crossed his legs and shook his head again. He was about to speak when Lewis stood up.

"It's a fucking cover-up, Cap!" Lewis shouted. "We should …"

Carr slammed his door shut before Lewis could finish his thought.

"Sit down and shut up!" he yelled. "For God's sake … I'm telling you two to forget it and move on to the next case. It's a federal matter now!"

Lewis started to speak again, but Farrel held out his hand to quiet his partner.

"Wait … wait, George." Farrel turned to address the captain. "When did you start to roll over on investigations, Cap?"

Carr gritted his teeth.

"Since whenever the CIA and the chief fuckin' tell me to, Frank! And what the fuck is it about this case that has you so obsessed with it?"

Ignoring the question, Farrel asked more.

"Cap, shouldn't there be something more to this? Shouldn't we take the steps to confirm that the senator is guilty of tax evasion and check some of this out ourselves?" Trying to persuade the captain not to roll over, Farrel pressed his buttons. "Why bury this thing, Billy? You *know* it doesn't smell right!"

"Look, do you guys think I *like* what's going on?"

Carr had obviously been frustrated by the orders he had received—especially by the fact that he had been expected to roll over for the CIA.

Farrel sensed the captain might be weakening and ratcheted it up a notch. "What about the tax evasion?" asked Farrel.

"What about it?" the captain responded.

Purposely getting under the captain's collar, Farrel raised his voice.

"The fucking tax evasion! We turned this case over based on the fucking tax evasion!" Farrel said, as veins popped in his throat and forehead. "Now there are dead people showing up left and right, and suddenly the CIA has some shooter from Baltimore wearing the victim's clothes, and that's that? This isn't just about fucking tax evasion any more!"

"Lower your fuckin' voice, Frank, or you'll be back on suspension!"

"I don't give a fuck!" He pointed a finger at the captain. "There's something very wrong here, and you should want to know what it is!'"

"Calm the fuck down, Frank. Tax evasion is a federal matter. The CIA has turned it over to the IRS."

"What?" Farrel yelled.

Farrel got up and circled the captain's desk, got within a foot of his massive boss and friend, lowered his voice, and looked Carr straight in the eyes.

"Billy," he said, "tell me that you honestly believe that Wheatly will be properly investigated and that he'll get his due, and I'll drop it. But I swear to you if he walks, I resign."

Lewis stood. "Me too, Cap."

The captain sighed. He knew he couldn't assure them that the senator would get what he had coming to him. Carr knew that he was dealing with two good, clean cops.

"Listen, you two ... sometimes it doesn't come down the way we want it to. No, Frank, I can't tell you that he won't walk."

"What happened to you, Billy?" asked Farrel softly. "When did you stop caring about the truth?

Unaccustomed to feelings of shame, the captain stood silently.

"Before we walk out this door," Farrel said, "I think you'd better listen to what we found out about the senator this week."

"Damn it, Frank," Carr said weakly, "what the hell are you ..."

"Just hear us out. Then you can do whatever it is you think you should do, all right?"

Carr sat down, and his red face slowly drained of color as he tried to calm himself for long enough to listen to what Farrel had to say.

"George and I have been pursuing the investigation on our own since you gave us some time away. Wait until I'm finished, Billy! Then you can bust us, if you want. But before you do, you're going to want to know what we know. Now, maybe the CIA's working to cover up the senator's tax evasion by closing the book on the Lane shooting. Maybe they're trying to cap a scandal before it gets started. Who knows how those people work? Everything is classified top fucking secret. But let me tell you what we *do* know.

"What we do know about the senator is that he's working on a legal reform bill—something that's supposed to change the judicial system as we know it. It's supposed to be a very powerful tool, and it's captured the attention of the president. The kicker is Mike Lane actually wrote the document describing the system, and we believe that the senator might be trying to pass it off as his own! Right now, we have proof—a credible source has helped us substantiate the fact that the document is really the work of Mike Lane. What we don't have is concrete evidence that the senator is claiming to be the author. You see, Billy, our source has told us that Wheatly was very interested in this reform document and was kind of chasing Lane down in an effort to get involved with it.

"The long and short of it is … our source received a package from Lane, right after he was shot. It contained a computer disk and a note that essentially requested the disk be kept in a safe place. The disk had Lane's research and the manuscript on it. We found no traces of his work at the house, and we have since come to believe that the theft of his work was the reason for the break-in. That, in addition to everything else surrounding the senator, makes him our prime suspect in this entire mess."

"How credible is your source?" the captain asked.

"*Very* credible, Cap," Farrel said seriously.

The captain rubbed his face and shook his head. He looked both annoyed and exhausted as he tried to settle back in his chair.

"All right," he said. "Go on."

"Anyway, we have no way of knowing whether the president knows that the document was stolen, and it would be suicidal at this point to try to find out. It's premature to go in that direction anyhow. The stakes are high—the one who brings this Point Guard system to the table and gets it passed into law becomes a powerful man."

"What *is* this system, Frank?"

"I'm not all that clear on it, Cap."

Lewis had a better grasp on it and described it to the captain as best he could.

"You see," said Lewis, after he had explained the point system, "we feel strongly that the senator is involved in the Lane shooting somehow. If this is true, then we should have some concern about the death of his aide … and his wife, for that matter. What we don't know is just how much of this the CIA knows and how deeply they are involved. For all we know, they could be behind the entire thing, or maybe they're just lackeys. Maybe they're only focused on the tax evasion angle. I don't know. There's only one way to find out, Cap, and that's for you to let us continue our investigation unimpeded. We'd keep it all confidential, of course."

Lewis looked excitedly at the captain, like a kid standing at the top of the stairs on Christmas morning. Farrel, however, was all business.

"Come on, Billy," Farrel said, "what do you say?"

Still annoyed, the captain took a deep breath and pushed himself away from his desk. He took a quick inventory of his police career. He looked at the framed medals and awards hung on the walls.

"You two are askin' me to put my job on the line."

"*All* of our jobs, Cap," Lewis said. "Isn't that what we do? We're cops. It's the right thing to do."

Carr stood up and paced for nearly thirty seconds. The room was dead silent.

"All right," he said simply.

Lewis punched his fist into the air, and Farrel smiled calmly while breathing a sigh of relief.

"What's the next step?" asked the captain.

"We have our contact help us bug the senator's office."

"Is there any other way, Frank?" Carr asked. "I mean, are we really talking about bugging a senator's office—in another jurisdiction—and possibly recording discussions involving the president? We'd find ourselves in deep shit regardless of the outcome."

"It's the only way, Cap. We need concrete evidence."

After a bit more discussion, the captain was reluctant, but he knew that they would have to break the rules to get at the truth.

"All right, guys, this is between the three of us," said the captain. "But you tell me *everything* from here on in, deal?"

Farrel and Lewis agreed.

"Once we have what we need on tape," Farrel said, "we'll turn it over to the attorney general's office and tell them what we have. What do you think?"

The captain gave Farrel an odd look. He was unsure why at this point, after all his posturing, Farrel would even consider turning the investigation over to the attorney general's office, or anyone for that matter. Especially, considering how hard he and Lewis had been working to control it themselves.

The captain shook his head. "Let's wait to see what happens next, Frank. Then we'll see if it needs to go to the attorney general." He escorted the detectives to the door. "Now, try not to get our balls in a sling. And I want minute-by-minute reports! Every day! Do you understand me?"

They did, and the captain ushered them out.

"Bug a senator ..." Carr said, after the door was closed. "I must be losing my mind."

Farrel returned to Washington alone and spoke to Kathy at her condominium about the meeting with Captain Carr and their plan to move ahead.

Nixon purred happily on his lap.

"Nixie's really taken a liking to you, Frank."

"Yeah. He sees me often enough these days."

"Well, we *both* like seeing you," Kathy said, smiling. "So, Frank, tell me about the plan."

"It's not much of one, but it involves you taking another risk. It's okay if you don't want to do it."

"Thanks," she said.

"No, really … if you want out of any of it, just say so."

"I trust you, Frank. I really do. What do you want me to do?"

They looked into each other's eyes for a moment. Farrel cleared his throat and glanced down at Nixon.

"Like I said, it's not much of a plan. You have the lay of the land, so to speak, so we'd like you to place a listening device in the senator's office. That's about it."

The senator's office had been recently getting some attention from the Secret Service since the president and senator had started talking regularly, so planting a bug even after office hours would probably be difficult. However, Kathy would, on Farrel's instruction, have the opportunity to plant a bug early in the day—after one of the occasional unscheduled surveillance sweeps—and remove it when Farrel would tell her.

"When?" Kathy asked.

"Day after tomorrow."

"Let's do it!" Kathy said confidently. She held out her hand.

Farrel shook it firmly and smiled. "You're something else, Kathy," he said.

The phone rang, and Kathy looked at the ID display.

"It's George."

"I need to take this," Farrel said.

He spoke with his partner for nearly twenty minutes and apologized to Kathy after he hung up the phone. "Sorry, we had a lot to talk about. Well … I guess I'd better get going."

"All right, Frank. Will we talk tomorrow?"

"Yeah. I'll call to go over the details."

He reached out to shake her hand, and she surprised him by leaning into him with a warm embrace. Farrel gladly accepted it and held her tightly against his chest for several seconds, and then he left.

Two days later, Kathy arrived at work thirty minutes before the rest of the staff, as she normally did. After carefully inspecting the entire office for anything unusual, she went into the senator's private office and placed an electronic listening device about the size of a small shirt button under the drooping leaf of one of the plants close to his desk. Only on days when Farrel instructed her to, she would time her spy routine and remove the device to avoid the occasional presunrise electronic sweeps done by the Secret Service. Outside in their car, the detectives would listen through earpieces hooked into a small receiver/recorder. They did this for many days that followed.

Fatigued from the long, lonely hours of surveillance, Lewis sat alone one day in the parked car only a half block from the senator's office. He had maintained this position for weeks, except for when he shifted locations to avoid the Secret Service presence during one of their surveillance checks. For the most part, Farrel was absent except for those days that Kathy placed the bug. On those days, he would visit Lewis to pick up the tapes at the end of the day. Otherwise, Lewis sat alone for endless hours. On the days when the senator was being taped, he would listen to details of the Point Guard program and all of Wheatly's other daily communications. Despite the dozens of hours of conversation that had been recorded, there was nothing on the tapes yet that could incriminate the senator as the Point Guard thief. Occasionally, Farrel phoned Lewis to inform him that all was going as planned and he was keeping an eye on CIA Agents Andrew and White. Meanwhile, Kathy did her job splendidly, managing the listening device without a problem.

One particular evening, Farrel phoned Kathy and instructed her to place the bug. On the following day, he and Lewis had switched duties. After sitting on a park bench across from CIA headquarters for most of the morning, Lewis spotted Andrew and White jogging down the building's front steps. Keeping a safe distance, he gave pursuit. The agents walked briskly to Senator King's office, which was several blocks away, and disappeared into it. Lewis took a seat on another park bench across the street. Only minutes later, the agents reappeared with Senator King and started off in the direction of Senator Wheatly's office, which was only a little over a block away. Lewis followed again, and before long, he realized they were heading right for Farrel. Lewis pulled out his cell phone and called Farrel to warn him.

"Frank, they're coming right at you!"

"Who?"

"King and the CIA."

King and the agents were fast approaching Farrel's parked car.

"Where?"

"Behind you!"

Farrel looked in his sideview mirror and saw the three men coming up the sidewalk about a hundred feet away. He leaned across the seat, yanked out his earpiece, and tossed it and the recorder under the passenger seat. He grabbed his newspaper, folded it, and stepped nonchalantly out of the car. He then walked down the sidewalk in the same direction as the men and only several feet in front of them. He crossed the street as King and the agents climbed the steps to Wheatly's office. Once they were inside, Farrel doubled back to the car, where Lewis was already sitting in the passenger seat, looking relieved. Sliding in behind the steering wheel, Farrel shook his head as Lewis let out a sigh. Saying nothing, they just looked at each other and listened to the meeting going on inside Wheatly's office.

Up to this point in their surveillance, there was plenty of tape that captured Wheatly's side of conversations with the president. All of those discussions focused only on strategy relating to Point Guard. There had been absolutely no dialogue about anything else.

This day would be different. As the detectives listened to the meeting—that lasted under an hour—they heard even more than they had been hoping for.

Senator King ended the meeting, and the detectives hurriedly removed their earpieces and pulled out of their parking spot. As the detectives drove past Wheatly's office, they saw King and the agents step out the front door accompanied by Senator Wheatly. Farrel immediately phoned Kathy.

"Good morning, Sena …"

"Kathy, get the bug outta there."

A few moments later, Wheatly found Kathy inside his office.

"It's a great day, Kathy!" he said. He was in unusually high spirits.

"I'm just cleaning up these coffee cups," she said, startled. "Don't mind me!"

She cleared the empty coffee cups, put them on a tray, and slipped out. Her hands perspired as she made her way to the small kitchen down the hall. She placed the tray on the countertop, took a deep, nervous breath, and looking over her shoulder, glanced down at the bug in her shaking palm.

Once again, she had come through.

Chapter Twenty-Six

At the end of each day, Farrel phoned the captain as instructed and gave him the day's report. On days when he had Kathy place the bug, he collected the tape from Lewis and made sure that it found its way to the captain in a confidential package. Although there had usually been very little to report, there was always a lot of detail on the tapes relating to Lane's work. The captain always listened to the tapes in full, paying special attention to any conversations dealing with Point Guard.

Today, however, there was a break in the case. Lewis burst into the captain's office interrupting a phone call. Hardly able to contain himself, Lewis stood there as the captain made a face and cut short his call.

"I'll need to call you back. What the hell, Lewis?"

"We've got something!" he exclaimed. He waved a cassette over his head and grinned.

Farrel followed close behind.

"You ever heard of the Senate Ethics Committee, Cap?" asked Lewis.

"Yeah."

"Well, Cap," Lewis said, greatly amused, "it should be called the Senate Cover-Up Committee!"

He handed Carr the tape.

"You look like you just saw your first prom dress hit the floor, Lewis," said the captain.

"Just listen to the tape, Cap," Lewis said as he placed a player on Carr's desk.

The captain turned to Farrel, who appeared much more serious.

"I've got to tell you, Frank, from what I understand … mind you I only hear Wheatly's side of phone conversations … this Point Guard system is the most incredible thing I've ever heard! Hell, our conviction rate would skyrocket! I love how the system puts convicts to work to manufacture products and …"

"Yeah, yeah, Cap," said Lewis, "are you going to play this tape, or are we going to just sit here and talk politics?"

"Listen to Nipsy," Farrel said. "I thought you wanted to get out of this thing as quick as possible. You told me it was bad news."

"I know," said Lewis, "but now we got him by the balls, the little fuck."

Farrel grinned, inserted the tape in the machine, and fast-forwarded past some irrelevant business. He finally arrived at a meaty part of the taped conversation.

"So tell me, Leonard," Wheatly's recorded voice filled Carr's office, "why are you visiting? Am I being investigated by the ethics committee or something?"

"Not anymore, Jeff. You've been cleared."

"Cleared of what?"

"Don't play stupid with me, Jeff. I know better. We took care of your tax situation. It seems pretty important to some people that your improprieties not be made public. Let's face it—a senator of your ranking evading taxes—that would look bad, Jeff." Then, unexpectedly, he said, "We also took care of the shooting mess in Philadelphia. That would have looked *really* bad, wouldn't it?"

There was a brief but noticeable pause on the tape. Carr sat forward as his eyes darted between Farrel and Lewis.

"What shooting mess?" said Wheatly.

King had arranged the meeting at the request of the president. Its purpose was to inform Wheatly that extraordinary favors had been extended to him and that he should take special care to stay out of trouble in the future. This entire meeting had been conducted under the standard protocol of confidentiality, which meant there would be no mention made of the president. King quickly got to the gist of the meeting.

"It came to our attention that two detectives assigned to the Mike Lane case came across some information that could possibly have linked you to the murder. In their report, they wrote that you were under suspicion of murdering the man because he may have found out that you were filing fraudulent returns. We don't know what the investigators were thinking, but the bottom line is that they suspected you in the shooting of the accountant. Jeff, you should be thankful that this entire thing has been turned over to me. Let me make this as short and sweet as I possibly can. Jeff, you're clear."

"Clear of what, tax evasion?" Wheatly sounded confused.

"Yes. And murder."

"Murder!" Wheatly shouted.

"Yeah, Jeff! *Murder!"* King had raised his voice above Wheatly's.

At this point, the tape became briefly indecipherable as the senators talked over one another.

"Jeff, Jeff, Jeff!" King finally said. "Listen, I don't care if you did or didn't kill anybody. We dumped a patsy to take the rap for the murder of Mike Lane. That issue is closed, and you are clean. That's all I'm here to tell you."

Lewis turned off the machine. A couple of seconds passed.

"So there it is, Cap," Farrel said. "It's a cover-up. Scorali's a patsy, and it sounds like they covered up the senator's tax problems."

"Do you think we can get that body back?" asked Lewis.

"No way," said Carr. "They probably already incinerated it!"

"What about a copy of his tax return?" asked Lewis.

The captain shook his head.

"I already tried that, fellas. I was gonna tell you that, according to IRS records, the senator's taxes are squeaky clean. I checked into it when you started bugging Wheatly's office. This tape is all we have."

Farrel tapped on the captain's desk as he appeared to give some thought to the situation. "We're going to need some help on this," said Farrel. "Cap, do you remember when I said maybe we should contact the attorney general's office when we got enough on tape?"

"Yeah. What's up with that, Frank? I mean, one second you're putting your ass on the line to keep control of this case and the next you're suggesting we turn it over to somebody else ... before we have an inch of tape. How come?"

Lewis seemed to find the question intriguing as well.

"Well," said Farrel, scrambling for words, "uh ... I figured we needed something else to help persuade you to let us keep investigating the case. So I tried thinking a step or two ahead, and frankly, I thought that it would help if you knew that I was willing to involve someone like the attorney general. Do you guys disagree with that?"

"Disagree with what?' asked the captain.

"With contacting the attorney general's office for some help."

"No ... I don't, Frank. But I'm not sure I understand your answer."

Farrel shook his head and seemed confused. "What's your question?"

The captain looked totally flummoxed and raised his hands. "What is this, Frank, Abbott and Costello? I don't even know what the hell we're talking about anymore! Are you trying to confuse me? Because if you are, you're doing a great job!"

"Look, Cap ... bottom line here is, are we going to bring in some help, or are we going to keep investigating this ourselves? I think that from the sound of the tapes, the president and Wheatly are close to revealing this Point Guard program. So, if we suspect that the senator stole it from Mike Lane, we'd better get some big guns in here right now!"

Captain Carr stared curiously at Farrel for several seconds before responding.

"All right, fellas," he said, "we can't contact the FBI—they sent in the CIA—and obviously we can't contact the CIA. Judging from what's on that tape, we can't contact the Senate Ethics Committee." Nodding at Farrel, he continued, "So I guess you're right, Frank—the United States Attorney General it is."

A day later, Attorney General Delores Yocum appeared in Philadelphia at the request of the Philadelphia police chief. Due to the sensitivity of the subject matter, the chief hadn't discussed the case over the phone. He had stressed that the problem was very urgent and involved government security. She was not overjoyed at having to travel so far for a meeting on an unknown subject. She arrived in the middle of the afternoon. Waiting for her inside the captain's office were Carr, the detectives, and Walter Ludwig, the Philadelphia chief of police.

"It's a pleasure to meet you, ma'am. I'm Captain Carr, and this is Chief Walt Ludwig. These are Detectives Farrel and Lewis."

Without telling the detectives, Captain Carr had kept Chief Ludwig in the loop ever since Farrel and Lewis had been discovered at the precinct house interrogating Anthony Kane. After learning about the allegation, the chief had decided that he should be personally concerned with an investigation as sensitive as this.

Chief Ludwig had just become chief of police in Philadelphia. He was a highly decorated police officer and the first African American police chief in Philadelphia's history. Only in position as chief for about a year, he was a big man and a solid leader with a great sense of fairness and justice.

Attorney General Yocum smiled thinly as she shook their hands. They all settled into chairs.

Delores was five feet, three inches tall, with short, brown hair and glasses. She was an attractive, slightly overweight woman, wearing a brown tailored skirt suit and high heels. She took a seat in front of the captain's desk and crossed her legs.

"Now," she said, "what's so important that you gentlemen can't tell me about it over the phone?"

"Well, Ms. Yocum, we've uncovered a situation which we believe your office should be involved in. It involves some pretty heavy hitters and ... well, frankly, dirty politicians."

She raised her eyebrows. "Captain, you know as well as I do that this type of thing should go through proper channels. You should be taking this to the FBI. Whatever you give me in regard to a political investigation, I have to share with the Federal Bureau of Investigation."

"Well, ma'am," Carr said, "that's part of the problem. We *did* send the matter through the proper channels once before, and they seem to have covered up the whole thing. Frankly, we don't trust them with it any more. You see, Ms. Yocum, we've uncovered a case that involves murder, tax evasion, and a cover-up of all of it. It involves a couple of senators, the CIA ..." He closed his eyes and took a deep breath, hardly believing what he was about to say. "And maybe the president. What we're looking for from you are two things. First, we'd like you to look at what we've found and to keep it in confidence until you see the whole picture. And second, we want to be involved. We don't want to be pushed out. Frankly, we've had enough of that shit. Uh, excuse my language."

Yocum surveyed the others in the room. Each man's face was stiff and rife with anticipation. Giving no immediate response, she studied each face for several seconds before turning back to Carr. Being sure she understood the accusations and the pickle his staff was in, he continued.

"Ma'am, I know what might happen to all of us if you decide not to help us. We know that we'll probably lose our jobs. You see, we understand fully what we're doing. We're so confident that some serious laws have been broken that we feel we have no choice but to put our jobs on the line."

There was a moment of silence. The attorney general looked a little incredulous.

"You guys must think you have something big," she said.

"We *know* we do," said Carr. "And if it ain't handled right, the shit will hit the fan ... Pardon the expression."

Delores smiled at the captain's colorful phrase. "Okay," Yocum said, "show me what you have, and I'll tell you whether or not I think I can follow it up. I can't promise you anything."

The others all sat a little more comfortably, thinking that this could be a big step in the right direction.

"If you decide to take this on," Carr pursued, "you won't turn it over to the CIA or FBI? And you'll keep us involved?"

"Like I said, Captain, let me see what you have. If I think it's something my office should handle, I'll do my best to keep you involved. If not—I have to warn you—it is my obligation to turn it over to the FBI. Do you understand that?"

They all nodded. It was a chance worth taking.

"Okay," said the captain. "What we have is—"

Interrupting Carr, Farrel said, "Ah, Miss Yocum …" Farrel looked over at the captain, who started to squirm in his seat. Carr looked both annoyed and surprised, but Farrel ignored Carr's body language and continued, "Would you like to hear what we have so far?"

"Yes, detective, that would be fine."

Farrel immediately launched into a briefing for the attorney general, as the captain eyeballed him and passed a copy of the case file that had been prepared for her. Farrel painted a colorful and complete picture of the entire investigation, explaining the complicated details to Yocum as clearly as he could.

She listened to him for forty minutes without interrupting.

At the end of the briefing, she rubbed her temples, then lifted her glasses, and wiped her burning eyes.

"So let me see if I understand, Detective Farrel. You and your partner were taken off a case that involved the shooting of an accountant. You had strong suspicions during the course of the investigation that Senator Jeff Wheatly was responsible for the shooting. Knowing that this made it a federal matter, you continued your investigation anyway."

Everyone else sank in their chairs. They could sense where she was going.

"After your superior found out about your actions, he contacted the FBI, who turned the case over to the CIA. But you withheld from the case file any information pertaining to the Point Guard document, which you decided in your wisdom to keep to yourselves. You were then suspended. Do I have this right?"

Farrel and Lewis nodded. Yocum addressed the entire room.

"Then, you continued your investigation by *illegally* bugging a U.S. senator's office! Do you people know what the hell you're doing? You're accusing senators, the CIA, and maybe the president of covering up murder, theft, tax evasion, and God knows what else!" She stood up and began to gather her things. "I'm telling you, you guys are either nuts or—"

Chief Ludwig interrupted her. Until now, he had only been an observer.

"Excuse me, ma'am." He spoke deliberately, eloquently, and with an authority that couldn't be denied. "We have already disciplined our men for their behavior. We are not here to have you discipline or browbeat them. We called you because we believed that a person of your stature and obvious interest in truth and justice would be able to look at this situation with open eyes and offer a solution. We believed that you would be able to see past the excessive exuberance of two police detectives and look at the underlying facts they uncovered. Those facts tell us that we have some very dangerous people in some very high places. I think that because we are paid servants of the people, who expect us to keep a clean house, we should act in their best interest. I would just like to ask you once more—respectfully—will you help us in this matter, or will we have to find someone else? You can be sure that we will not be giving it up."

The men stood in quiet awe of their chief's speech. Yocum studied their faces for a moment.

"If what your men have uncovered turns out to have merit," she said, "then, yes, I will help you. However, I will need some time to go through this file and have some things checked out before I commit to anything specific. Understand me, Chief; I *do* want to see the right thing done. I *do* want a clean house." Glancing over at the detectives, she continued, "But I will clean it by the book—with subpoenas and warrants. If it seems as though I'm hesitant, it's because I have to consider the law above all else, and the law is complicated. I also want to be sure that the only people who get burned by this are the ones who deserve to be burned and that whatever we accuse them of sticks to them like glue! Do you understand me?"

"Fair enough," said the chief. He smiled and shook her hand.

"I'll be in touch after I look through this file," Yocum said.

Yocum placed the file in her briefcase and then shook everyone's hand before leaving. As the others started for the door, Carr said, "Frank, I need to talk to you."

Nodding his head, Farrel stepped off to the side as Lewis and the chief walked past.

"Close the door," said Carr.

"What's up, Cap?"

"Frank, what the fuck are you doing?" Farrel cocked his head to the side as if he were confused. "Who asked you to brief the attorney general? I wanted her to read our file first ... then later, we could give her verbal clarification. I wanted to avoid being scolded like schoolboys before she was able to read an official file!"

"Sorry, Cap, I was trying to be sure she understood the severity of the case. I wanted to be sure she would—"

Carr interrupted him. "Frank, shut up! I know what I'm doing, and you know I do. We've been working together for ... shit ... God knows how long. I don't know what you're trying to do, but I want you to knock this shit off. I get it; you want to be involved in this case! But if you keep doing this kind of shit, I will pull you off. Do you understand me?"

Without a response, Farrel simply nodded."Now get out of here, and let's wait to hear what the attorney general comes up with over the next couple of days."

*   *   *   *

The next day, after eating his brown-bag lunch, Farrel swept the crumbs off his desk, grabbed his coat, and headed for the door. Kathy's identity as an informant was still secret, and Farrel knew that if the attorney general's office became involved that would have to change. Knowing that Yocum would want to know the identity of his informant, Farrel decided it would be best to tell Kathy about the situation in person.

"Hey, Frank, where you going?" Lewis asked as he ran into Farrel near the top of the stairs.

"I thought I'd drive down to Washington and let Kathy know what's going on. We'll have to reveal her identity if the attorney general's office gets involved."

"Well, shit, let me get my coat," said Lewis. "I'll ride with you. There isn't anything to do around here until we hear from Delores Yocum, anyhow."

Farrel hustled down the stairs and shouted back brusquely, "Why don't you stay here, George? I know there's nothing to do, but if Yocum calls, one of us should be here."

Lewis felt a little left out but agreed to stay. However, leaning against the railing at the top of the stairs he did wonder for a moment why his partner didn't simply phone Kathy.

Farrel pulled off I-95 near the Maryland state border and ordered a cup of coffee at a crowded highway rest stop. He sat at a booth in front of a window facing the parking lot and sipped coffee as he watched travelers bustle in and out. One particular passerby wore a dark suit and red tie. He and Farrel nodded to each other, and a moment later, the man slid into the seat across from him. Placing his cup of coffee on the table, he smiled and reached across to shake Farrel's hand.

"Hey, Frank, how's it going?"

"I'm throwin' lefts and rights and duckin', Paul. How 'bout you?"

"Pretty good. Can't complain."

"Good to hear. How's Mrs. Miser?"

"She's great. So, what did you need to talk to me about, Frank?"

After an hour-long meeting with Paul Miser, Farrel returned to his car and continued south to Washington.

Kathy's solitary dinner was interrupted by a knock at the door. She was glad to see that it was Farrel.

"Come on in, Frank! I thought I wasn't going to hear from you for a couple more days. Where's George?"

Farrel smiled. He was just as glad to see Kathy as she was to see him.

"He couldn't make it this time."

"Oh ... Can I get you some dinner?"

"Uh ... Yeah, I'd like that."

"Grab a seat. I've got plenty."

Kathy soon appeared with a dinner plate loaded with spaghetti in one hand and a cold beer in the other. She placed them in front of him and briefly rubbed her hand gently against his back before sitting down again.

"What brings you all the way down here?" she asked.

"Well," he winced a little, "let's talk about that after we eat. What do you say?"

"Okay, that's fine," she said with a smile.

Kathy opened a bottle of white wine for herself, and Farrel guzzled several beers with the delicious meal. After dinner, they moved over to the living room sofa.

"It's great to see you, Frank. It really is. But why the surprise visit?"

"Listen, Kathy, ... this case is picking up momentum. The United States Attorney General's Office is looking into our allegations, and I feel pretty certain that Delores Yocum will take up the case."

"Well, that's great, isn't it?"

"Yeah. But it also means that your identity may be revealed. I'm not comfortable with that."

Kathy knew that she would eventually have to come forward. Suddenly, that time was at hand, and she felt scared and insecure. Though she had been comforted by Farrel's support, she still found herself rather confused by everything that had happened since Mike was shot. It seemed as though all the emotions she had felt since then now rushed into her head at once.

She placed her wine glass on the coffee table and covered her face with her hands.

"Oh my God ... what's happening here? Mike ... Anthony ... Jane ..."

Farrel reached out his hand toward her. She stood and turned away, trying to hide tears of fear and confusion that were welling up in her eyes. Farrel stood and placed his hands on her shoulders. He felt a little ashamed of himself, knowing that if it hadn't been for him Kathy would never have found herself in this predicament. Kathy stepped away from him and toward a window. She pulled back the curtain and stared aimlessly outside. A tear trickled from one of her eyes.

"I'm a little scared, Frank."

She turned to face him. He walked over and wiped the tear from her soft, rose-colored cheek. He looked directly into her eyes.

"You don't need to be."

As she gazed into his eyes, Kathy felt that this was true. He seemed to exude an inexplicable confidence. She fell forward to his chest and wrapped her arms around his waist.

Holding her tight, he felt her warm body press against him. Suddenly, she leaned back to gaze up at him. Keeping her in his embrace, he looked down and met her sultry eyes. Unexpectedly, he leaned forward and softly kissed her lips. Kathy pulled away, hesitated, and then, as though she had lost control, made a passionate advance and violently pressed her supple lips hard against his. She drove him backward with the long and powerful kiss and frantically ran her fingers through his hair. He had been taken a bit off balance, but a second or two later, he spun her around and slammed her back against the wall. All the while, their lips never parted. He tugged at her tight silk skirt. She tore at his Oxford shirt and savagely unzipped his swelling trousers. Emotions they had kept penned up since shortly after their first meeting were finally released.

Grinding her against the wall, she let out a groan of pleasure as he pulled her skirt up above her well-toned thighs and shapely hips. He pushed her even harder against the wall. Panting like wolves, they pawed one another as he leaned back to glimpse her covered breasts. He ran his hand beneath her blouse. Firmly massaging her full breast with one hand, he reached around with the other and tore at the clasp of her bra. She breathed hotly and stared down at his crotch while pushing his trousers below his knees. They were intoxicated by the rough, forbidden passion, and there would be no gentle foreplay. Frank stepped out of his pant legs while pushing Kathy's panties down to her knees. Letting the panties fall to the floor, she kicked them aside and pressed her lips even more tightly against his. He wedged his knee between her strong legs and spread them apart while grabbing her just below the buttocks. He raised her off the floor with his strong arms and pushed his head between her breasts, which were soon found by his probing mouth and tongue. She gripped his waist with her powerful thighs. He lowered her as she clutched his shoulders. She bucked wildly as he furiously thrust himself into her, jamming her repeatedly against the wall. She moaned and screamed as she bounced madly. She rode and clawed at him until they both climaxed and fell to the floor in a heap of sweaty limbs.

Later, they lounged on the sofa, saying nothing about either their ferociously passionate encounter or the investigation that had brought them together.

Chapter Twenty-Seven

Over the next several days, Attorney General Yocum studied the file. When she finally thought that she had a firm enough grasp on it, she called Captain Carr and asked to meet with him and the detectives once more. She wanted to offer her opinions on the sensitive case.

Sitting in front of the captain's desk, Delores took a sip of her coffee and winced through the rising steam at Farrel and Lewis seated near the door. After swallowing the burnt, black coffee, she placed her cup on the desk and turned to the captain.

"At this point, Captain, I feel confident that we have a case that needs to be investigated further by my office. Of course, a case like this would normally go before the Senate Ethics Committee. However, in light of what you've discovered about Senator King and his associates, I think that it would be best to keep *all* federal entities, aside from my own, from investigating this for now. I believe that our best course is to try to get one of the players in this cover-up to turn against the others. In other words, we need to give someone a reason to save his own hide.

"That means we'll eventually need some concrete, firsthand evidence and credible testimony, so that we can get this in front of a grand jury. The illegal bugging you two orchestrated renders any information on those tapes useless in any legal proceeding." She shot Farrel and Lewis a withering look.

Yocum moved to the end of her chair and reached for her cup. She looked down at the scorched coffee and made a sour face before pushing it away.

"Now, I know Senator King, and I've never had much respect for the man. When he was in the business world, he operated on the very fringes of propriety. He was immensely successful there, so I can only imagine the kind of skeletons he must have in his closet."

It seemed almost as though she had a personal score to settle with King.

"I've always suspected him of something crooked, and I'm sure that he's abused his position as the head of the Senate Ethics Committee prior to this. Therefore, I'd like to start with him. Let's see if we can smoke him out. He's never struck me as much of a hero, so I don't think it'll take much pressure to get him to crack. But you never know. Guys like him sometimes hang on and try to make deals ... and we don't have anything to offer him, at least not yet."

Carr, Farrel, and Lewis liked her attitude and listened very carefully as they slurped down their coffee.

"I've got to say that this entire case—this Point Guard plan and everything surrounding it—is a real bombshell. Fortunately or not, there's no indication—at least as far as I can see—that the president knows that it might have been stolen, so let's leave him out of it. We'll just assume that he's been suckered by Wheatly.

"But, I can see," she raised her eyebrows, "why there would be such competition to be the one who gets the credit for the Point Guard system."

Lewis interrupted her monologue.

"Where do we come in, ma'am? What do you want us to do?"

"I'll need you guys to fill in the gaps," she said. "You'll have to work with a very small, personally selected staff of mine and get them acquainted with the investigation. I realize that this isn't terribly exciting, but it's what I need you to do."

Lewis didn't try very hard to conceal his disappointment.

"Look," Yocum said, "I'm holding up my end of the bargain by keeping you involved. So just do what I need you to do. Okay?"

Yocum picked up her briefcase and laid it across her lap.

"I'm going to interrogate Senator King myself," she said. "I promise you that'll get his attention. I'll explain to him that he's currently under investigation for conspiracy regarding the cover-up of Senator Wheatly's tax fraud. There is nothing on any of the tapes that leads me to believe he knows anything about Point Guard." Pursing her lips, she glanced at the ceiling as she gave her strategy some more thought. Turning to face Carr she continued, "I'll do my best to find out whether he knows anything about Point Guard. I'll make it perfectly clear to him that I'm willing to take this investigation as far as I need to in order to get the truth. I'll go so far as to let him know that it stretches beyond tax fraud to multiple murders and federal conspiracy. That should shake him up. We'll see if anything falls out. Then we'll keep an eye on him and see what he does after that."

Carr nodded. "That sounds like a plan. You're awful quiet today, Frank. Is everything okay?"

"Yeah. No, I'm fine," Farrel said. "Just thinking."

Yocum snapped her briefcase shut.

"Oh, Detective Farrel," she said, "sooner or later, I'm going to have to interview the source who gave you the computer disk and any information about the Point Guard document. Whoever it is needs to be credible and must be ruled out as a suspect."

"A suspect?" Farrel couldn't help but laugh. "Our informant is hardly a suspect, ma'am."

"I don't think that's for you to judge," she said.

"I'm just saying," Farrel insisted, "that our informant is aboveboard, credible, and *not* a suspect. I don't think it's necessary to reveal or interview the informant at this point. George and I can vouch for her."

"Detective, it's my job to examine all the players. What makes you so sure that your informant … she's a she, I take it … isn't involved in the theft of the document? If she runs in political circles and understands the power of the thing, then there's as good a chance that she's involved as not."

Farrel was annoyed but said nothing as Yocum took her leave.

"Detective Lewis," she said from the doorway, "when you meet with my staff and our investigators tomorrow, I'll need you to give them the identity of your informant."

Early the next morning, Senator King thumbed through a newspaper at his desk while drinking coffee and munching on a bagel slathered with cream cheese. His office was larger and even more elegant than Senator Wheatly's. It was one of the benefits that came with being the chair of the Senate Ethics Committee. As he chuckled at a cartoon that poked fun at his friend the president, he was interrupted by an announcement from his speakerphone.

"Sir, Attorney General Yocum is here to see you."

"Show her in," he mumbled through a bagel-filled mouth.

Led by King's secretary, Yocum walked through the walnut double doors to find King wiping cream cheese from his lower lip and not bothering to stand.

"Come on in, Delores! How are you?" Although his tone was hospitable, he actually had little regard for her. And he knew the feeling was mutual. "Have a seat. To what do I owe the pleasure?"

Lacking the small talk gene, Yocum got right to the nitty-gritty and rejected his offer to sit. She stood at is desk, front and center.

"I'm not here for pleasure, Leonard. This is business."

"Aha, business, you say?" His tone was condescending. "What kind of business?"

"You're under investigation by my office, Leonard."

King gave absolutely no indication that he was the slightest bit concerned. He again motioned for her to take a seat as he stared right through her.

"*Me*, Delores?" he said. "What would you want to investigate *me* for?"

Yocum stepped closer to the desk.

"Leonard, you're being investigated for conspiracy to cover up tax fraud and murder in the case of a man from Philadelphia named Mike Lane. The case that had been turned over to the CIA by the Philadelphia Police Department has now been taken over by *me*."

Although the news made his heart drop to his stomach, he appeared outwardly not to have been fazed in the least. He kept his stare locked on Yocum and raised his eyebrows as if to say, "Is that it? What's the big deal?"

"Leonard, do you have any reaction to the charges? Or anything else to say? Or are you just going to sit there like an idiot and stare at me? Face it, Leonard; you're really not all that intimidating."

"You know, Delores," he finally said. "I never did like you. It's beyond me why the president would appoint a *woman* United States Attorney General—what with the monthly mood swings and all. Or are you too old for those now?"

"Is that all you have to say, Leonard?"

"No. How about you've got to be kidding me!"

"You know, Senator, it's been a pleasure after all," she said. "For your own sake, you'd better hope that you've covered your ass on this one." She planted her fists on his desk and leaned toward him. "Because I don't like you either, and I'm going to try my best to nail your balls to the wall!"

King tried to laugh but could only manage a smirk. His feet fidgeted under the desk as she turned away and walked toward the doors.

"Take a good look around, Leonard!" She waved a hand extravagantly. "I don't think you'll be here much longer."

In the doorway, she turned to face him. "And by the way, I hope your goons are as calm and cocky as you are. You wouldn't want one of them to serve you up, would you?"

King only stared as she briskly walked out without bothering to close the door behind her. As he pushed his coffee and bagel away, his secretary appeared in the doorway and opened her mouth to say something.

"Leave me alone!" he screamed. "And close that door!"

After a couple of minutes of deep thought, King phoned Agent Andrew to warn him and Agent White about the attorney general's intention to investigate their cover-up. King had used Andrew and White many times over the years, and he was confident that they could handle Yocum perfectly well. But since the attorney general had never before personally conducted an investigation into his affairs—and because of the president's involvement—he was deeply concerned and wanted to proceed with great caution. After his call to warn the agents, King immediately called the president.

The president sounded glad to hear from King.

"Hello, Leonard! What can I do for you?"

King dispensed with pleasantries and sounded rattled.

"Delores Yocum just left here. She's become involved with the Philadelphia Police investigation into Senator Wheatly's finances."

"Sit tight, Leonard," said the president as he took on a sudden and serious tone. "Give me a few minutes. I'll call you back."

"I didn't like this from the start."

"Senator, I said I'll call you right back."

"Sir, I'm not ..."

Interrupting King, the president raised his voice.

"Calm down, Leonard. I will call you right back."

The president immediately placed a quick call to his Secret Service director and called King back right away.

"Leonard, listen to me. We're prepared for this. What I need you to do is to sit tight and not talk to her unless she serves you with papers. I doubt she's ready to do that. By that time, the entire thing will have been taken care of. Do you understand me?"

"Yes. Uh ... when will we ..."

"Senator," the president interrupted the anxious King. "I need you to listen to me right now. Do you understand me?"

"Yes sir, I do."

"Now—those classified tax documents of Senator Wheatly's—I need you to give them to the Secret Service agent who is on his way to your office. We'll put that file and the one you left with me from the Philadelphia investigation into a single file and do some creative paperwork. I'll get back to you with the next step."

The president's confidence seemed to ease King's anxiety only marginally.

"Leonard, do you understand me?"

"Yes, sir. I give your agent the Wheatly tax file and sit tight."

"That's right, Leonard. I'll speak to you soon."

Not long after the end of the conversation, a Secret Service agent arrived at King's office to retrieve Senator Wheatly's tax returns. King handed over a large manila envelope with the text "TOP SECRET—Classified" stamped on it. Only thirty minutes passed between King's call to the president and the delivery of the envelope to the White House. The president now had in his possession the entire Wheatly file, which included not only what had been discovered by the Philadelphia police, but also both the fraudulent and original tax returns. He placed another call to the Secret Service director. The phone was answered on the first ring.

"I've got the tax documents."

"Good," a voice responded, "give me five hours, and we'll meet you at the White House."

The president hung up and settled back into his chair. He looked at his watch with a confident grin.

Detective Lewis had spent many hours on the phone, talking with the attorney general's staff. He gave them all of the pertinent information regarding the investigation.

After a long phone conversation of his own, Farrel rose from his desk and grabbed his coat off the back of his chair. Lewis snapped his fingers and gestured for Farrel to wait a moment as Lewis finished a call.

"Where you headed?" Lewis said when he was done.

"Washington. I think I'd better get down there and touch base with Kathy."

"Yeah? How is she?"

"A little shook up."

"I'll bet."

"Well, I'd better get going. It's a long drive." Farrel looked as though there was something on his mind, and Lewis tried to guess what it was.

"Listen, Frank, it's not your fault that Kathy got caught up in this thing. You only did what you had to."

"Yeah, I know, George. That's not what's bothering me."

"So what *is* bothering you, pal?"

To Lewis's surprise, Farrel reached out and shook his hand warmly.

"You're a good man, George." Very sincerely—almost sadly—he added, "You're a good cop."

Farrel let go and walked away.

Chapter Twenty-Eight

Almost exactly five hours after the president's phone call, Secret Service Director Paul Miser and one of his associates sat in the Oval Office. Miser was a tall fifty-six-year-old Texan with short, dark hair. He typically wore dark suits, red ties, and expensive, well-shined, black wing-tipped shoes. He was the highest-ranking official in the Secret Service and a specialist in covert operations. He had advised the president since learning about the Philadelphia investigation and was working with him to accomplish one objective: to bring the Point Guard system into law with no controversy attached to it.

Waiting for the president to arrive, Miser sat comfortably with his legs crossed as he scratched at some lint on his red tie. His associate seemed a bit on edge when the door to the office opened and the president appeared. The president smiled and placed a manila envelope on his desk.

"How are you, Paul?"

"Great, sir! Not much sleep lately, but great!"

The president turned his attention to Miser's associate.

"And you must be …"

"I'm sorry, Mr. President," said Miser. "We've all spoken on the phone so many times that I forgot you two have never met in person. This is Frank Farrel, sir."

"It's a pleasure to finally attach a face to the voice, Frank. We really appreciate your help with this." He glanced at Miser and added, "Paul keeps telling me that without you the operation wouldn't be running nearly as smoothly as we need it to."

"Thank you, sir," Farrel forced himself to smile. "It's a pleasure to meet you as well."

The president sat down and gestured for Miser and Farrel to do the same.

"All right, Paul," said the president. "Go ahead."

"Sir," Miser said as he moved to the edge of his chair, "I think it's time to make some moves. First, I think that the time to unveil the Point Guard program is close at hand, which means that we need to tie some things up in a pretty big hurry. It might be a good idea to review what's been done so far and get a baseline for this meeting, so that we can talk about what we need to do from here forward."

"Where do we start?"

"Let's start with Frank. You should know, sir, that Frank has performed commendably throughout the entire operation. If it weren't for Frank's ability to drive the investigation in the direction we wanted, we'd be having a significantly different discussion right now. His success in steering the Philadelphia police investigation has been nothing less than spectacular. As you might expect, sir, I haven't given you every minute detail regarding this operation, but I do want to go over a few things—to give you a bit of detail about what's been done, so that you can fully understand where we need to go."

Miser moved his chair closer to the desk.

"Due to some twists of fate that don't need to be rehashed at the moment, I met and recruited Frank to work with us at the very start of this operation. As a covert Secret Service agent, under my supervision, Frank was able to effectively steer and manipulate the Philadelphia police investigation. In the beginning, he exposed Wheatly's tax fraud and then successfully steered the investigation toward the theft of Lane's work. Eventually ..." Miser stopped himself. "Listen, I don't think it's necessary to go over every detail that's led us here. Suffice it to say that Frank either knew in advance or set in motion everything that would eventually happen in the Philly investigation—from the bugging of Wheatly's office to breaking policy and taking the investigation interstate so that we could ultimately intervene through King and his CIA agents and all the way to the suggestion to bring in the attorney general. Obviously, we learned more things as the investigation grew, but for the most part, we controlled the information and drove the direction of the entire case through Frank. And because he's done such a masterful job, we have all the players in place with all the right motivations."

Farrel sat without moving and blindly stared at the floor as if he were off in another place.

"Let's talk about where we are," said Miser. "Let me ask you, Frank. Where exactly are we in the Philadelphia investigation?

Farrel snapped out of his catatonia, retrieved a worn file folder from his briefcase, and placed it on his lap. He thumbed through an untidy stack of papers as he responded.

"Uh ... everything seems to be going as planned. Just as you had expected."

He seemed a bit nervous and cleared his throat.

"I've been able to get my partner, George Lewis, to go along with all the questionable tactics that we were employing to maintain control and steer the investigation. As a result, we were able to investigate Senator Wheatly secretly and were able to confirm that he had stolen Lane's Point Guard work. At first, we didn't let our captain know exactly what we were investigating. At Paul's instruction, I led the investigation across state lines, resulting in my captain contacting the FBI, who in turn contacted Senator King. Eventually, because of our influence and perseverance, we attracted the attention of the attorney general, and she took on the case, as Paul thought she would. I guess we could talk about the details, but for the most part, you already know what they are." He shrugged. "That's about the size of it."

"The Philadelphia police completely bought into the bugging of Senator Wheatly's office, right?" Miser asked.

"Um ... yeah. The captain listened to all the tapes I sent him. When he heard the tape with Senator King and Senator Wheatly talking about the taxes and the patsy Scorali, the captain was convinced we had something big."

"Sir," Miser explained to the president, "Frank was able to persuade Wheatly's assistant to bug his office. Obviously, we could have bugged it ourselves, but having Frank's source do it gave Captain Carr the comfort, confidence, and sufficient information he needed to continue to support Frank's investigation ... and ultimately supporting our operation."

The president approved.

"Frank," he said, "you've done an outstanding job, and your participation will not go unrewarded. *Thank* you, Frank. Now, Paul, tell me again about these tapes."

"Sure, sir. Frank had Kathy Nolan bug Wheatly's office. Of course, our agents were aware that there was a bug in the office and were directed to leave it alone if they were to discover it. We bugged only on occasions when we wanted something in particular recorded. Like when you and I sent King to talk with Wheatly about his tax evasion and King's cover-up. Of course, King stuck to protocol when he met with Wheatly and never mentioned your involvement. Having them on tape talking about the cover-up eliminates any possible suspicion of your involvement. The other reason was that we wanted to be sure that we had *you* on tape talking about the Point Guard program."

The president pushed away from his desk and looked up at the ceiling. He shook his head and moved back toward the desk with a puzzled look on his face.

"Paul, I appreciate you bringing me up to speed on the details. I have always understood why it's so important to get Wheatly and King on tape, ... but explain specifically, why it's so important to have Wheatly talking to me on tape."

"Certainly, sir, ... first of all, your voice was never recorded on tape. I want to be perfectly clear about that. We bugged Wheatly's office, not his phone." Miser leaned forward on the desk. "So we only have Wheatly's side of the conversations with you on tape. I thought it was vital to get a little insurance in the event that anyone—particularly Jeff Wheatly—has any misgivings about your involvement in the Point Guard program—the potential for which *does* exist. We have the Wheatly tapes to prove your honest, well-intentioned participation.

"I found it interesting," he continued, sidetracking, "curious, even, that Wheatly's thirst for power is so great that he never—not once during the entire operation—noticed how oddly fortunate he had become. Everything he needed appeared, and any problems—like his tax evasion, among other things—disappeared.

"Anyway, the conversations and meetings you had with him focused mainly on the logistics and provisions required for the suitable presentation of the document to the Senate and House. Obviously, he never noticed that he wasn't much more than a gofer for you. You gave him all the information and the changes and additions to the document, and he properly positioned it all into an acceptable format for the House and Senate to review before taking it to a vote. He never questioned how you were so well versed or who might have been helping you. As you've said on occasion, sir, there's no one in Washington better at bird-dogging and getting things done than Jeff Wheatly. But the truth is there's no worse individual to have involved in legal reform. Hell, look at all the mayhem he's caused up to this point! Imagine what he would do if he were involved in the day-to-day operation of the program.

"Anyhow, when we start making moves and Wheatly doesn't like the direction we take with Point Guard, I don't want any blackmail or threats coming from him. And, sir, before Frank mailed the tapes to his captain, he handed them off to us, and we edited out any questionable content. As I just mentioned, Wheatly never recognized that he was just doing everything you asked, and after we did our quick edit, it almost sounds like he's nothing more than your assistant. So I think he's limited to the amount of noise he can make about his participation. Sir, if anything, the Wheatly tapes make *you* sound like the Point Guard author." Miser paused and seemed to give his last statement some more thought before continuing. "Bottom line—everything that Captain Carr, the Philadelphia police, the attorney general, or anyone else heard on the tapes was what I wanted them to hear. I wanted Carr to be intrigued enough to keep the Philadelphia police in the game long enough for us to get Delores Yocum involved—we're going to need her to make a deal with us."

He winked at Farrel. "Good job, Frank."

"You see, sir," Miser went on, "keeping the Philadelphia police in the game has given us the distance we need. As they stay focused on their desire to stay involved—thanks to Frank—it allows us to do our jobs. While they have been investigating tax evasion, murder, legal reform, and whatever else we had Frank steer them toward, we've been able to continue to work on Point Guard without interruption. Otherwise—without Frank's participation and the tapes—who knows where this all would have ended up. Fortunately, we've been working with Frank, and so far … none of Wheatly's destructive behavior has impacted our progress on Point Guard."

Miser walked to a small serving table draped in white linen and poured himself a glass of cold water.

"Now," he continued, "we taped Senators King and Wheatly so that we would have a couple of guys with the proper motivation to participate. And now that the Philly police have contacted Delores Yocum—and now that she is aware of what's on those tapes—we have three people who *have* the proper motivation, all of whom should help get this whole thing wrapped up.

"Having King and Wheatly on tape discussing tax evasion, the cover-up, and a dead patsy gives us the upper hand in anything we need to negotiate, and it gives them more than enough motivation to *want* to negotiate. What I want to do is let them know we can protect them if they do what I say. Even though the Philly police have been involved, I can spin this whole thing to protect them … provided we get Delores to go along with everything."

The president raised his eyebrows.

"That's a tall order, Paul."

"Well, sir, I think that she also has a certain motivation."

"Really? What would that be?"

"The Point Guard work itself. And a shot at Wheatly … and possibly King. She's a smart woman, sir; I think that if we lay out a reasonable deal for her, she'll take it."

"What kind of deal?"

"We ask her to let us keep moving forward uninterrupted and without scandal on the Point Guard program, and we let her have at it with Wheatly and maybe King. If she understands the Point Guard system, and I know she does—Frank tells me that she's copied the Point Guard disk they got from Kathy Nolan and has been studying it—she'll understand its power, and I believe that she'll be willing to deal with us. Hell, she knows how badly this country needs legal reform, and she knows that the Point Guard program is perfect! We need her in on this deal; if we can get her to deal with us, everything controversial that's connected to Point Guard gets swept under the rug. Besides, I'm going to spin this thing so hard that she'll never be able to uncover the truth."

"Maybe, Paul, but I don't want Wheatly hung out to dry. He gets things done for me that no one else can. I want to protect him and King. They're too valuable."

Miser shook his head and glanced at Farrel, who had been sitting quietly and by now listened to the conversation with great interest.

"Um … Why don't we talk about this in private, sir?"

The president nodded and agreed to move on, but not before he took notice of Farrel's inquisitive look.

"All right then, Paul, it sounds like you have most everything under control. What needs to be done now?"

"We need to take care of the situation between Delores Yocum and Leonard King. I knew that Delores would jump all over this thing the minute she learned about what King and Wheatly said on the tapes. She absolutely despises Leonard King and has little or no regard for Jeff Wheatly. It's time to start wrapping this thing up. Did you get the tax file from King like I asked, sir?"

The president slid the manila envelope across the desk.

"Just as you asked—Senator Wheatly's tax file."

Paul Miser slid his briefcase out from under his chair, placed it on his lap, and twirled the combination dials. He snapped open the locks and raised the lid. From the briefcase, he retrieved a stuffed lime-colored file folder with the name "Senator Wheatly" printed on the tab and placed it on the corner of the president's desk. He then carefully opened the manila envelope and removed Wheatly's top secret tax papers. He slid these documents into the already stuffed green folder and tidied the thick stack of paper within.

"Now this thing is coming together," he said while pointing at the file. "This file has everything I want in it—Wheatly's tax files, the case file King secured from the Philly police, the fraudulent returns Wheatly filed with the IRS, and copies of the originals that were prepared by Lane."

He withdrew a file marked "Classified" from his briefcase and presented it to the president. Miser seemed to ignore Farrel as he appeared to focus only on the president. Farrel moved forward in his chair and listened closely.

"Sir, here's your copy of the same file, minus the taxes." He then handed the president a second classified file. "And here is your copy of what is about to actually happen, as well as what we will present as our official Secret Service investigation file when we meet with Delores Yocum." He hesitated and glanced at Farrel. "Sir, this file will stay in our possession until we need it. It's not only our spun version of what we will claim to have discovered in our investigation, but it's also the blueprint for what is going to happen from here on in."

Farrel noticed and felt uneasy that there was no copy of the file for him.

Hell, he thought, *what's going on here? Why are they excluding me from the plan to finish this thing? Shit, this isn't good. Am I no less expendable than Dugan? For all I know, I'm the next dead man described in that damn blueprint.*

He was concerned but not willing to verbalize his insecurity. He tried his best to listen as doubts inundated his mind.

"Frank," Miser said, "I'll give you a briefing on our spun version of the investigation a little later today. As for the *entire* plan to wrap this up … at least for now, for security reasons, I'll only brief the president after we've finished here with you. But before I do that, I want to go over what needs to be done right at this moment."

Farrel had grown anxious and suddenly appeared doubtful as he looked at Miser with a suspicious eye.

"Don't worry, Frank, this is all normal procedure," said Miser as he noticed Farrel's look. "You only have need-to-know clearance. You'll have to trust me and do what I tell you to do. Do you understand?"

Farrel gave no indication that he bought into Miser's assurance. He sat quiet and uncomfortable for several seconds before he shifted his steady gaze from Miser to the president. After another second or two, he looked back at Miser and slowly nodded. He had taken a sobering hold of the fact that he was an outsider, and he knew that he had better be very careful from this point on.

Seeming to believe that he and Farrel had an understanding, Miser took out his copy of the blueprint, put on his glasses, and made some notations in the folder as he described what should happen next.

"Gentlemen, we will deal with Wheatly a little later, but the situation with Yocum investigating Senator King needs to be dealt with immediately. We need to get Yocum out of Senator King's shorts and off the hot seat. Lately he's been getting a little squirrelly with Yocum on his tail. We know he doesn't know anything about the Point Guard program, but he obviously knows we're working on something big. So let's not let him become a liability. Let's get Yocum off his ass." He looked at the president over the top of his glasses. "Like I said, we expect Delores Yocum to go after King—so far, all is going as planned. If everyone does as I direct them, I'm certain that the Point Guard reform will get voted on without any controversy attached to it."

"Sir, I'll need you to call Senator King and inform him that you have the entire Wheatly file and the plans for the next step in the operation. I want you to tell him to have his agents, Andrew and White, rendezvous with my agents at our confidential meeting spot and then …"

Miser continued with detailed instructions for the call. Taking a break, he asked, "Mr. President, sir … are you with me so far?"

"Yes," the president answered.

Farrel unconsciously nodded and tapped his foot nervously on the floor.

Miser stood up and returned to the service table, this time pouring himself a steaming cup of black coffee. He took a sip and continued to outline the King call.

"Be as brief as you can, but be sure to relay to Senator King that we'll be turning Wheatly and the entire tax evasion case—minus any incriminating mention of King's involvement, of course—as well as the Philadelphia investigation file over to Delores Yocum. And be sure to tell him that he will be protected as usual and that we will go over the details of the plan the moment the agents deliver the file. Also, be sure to tell him to have the agents drive into his garage. We don't want all of these guys being seen together, just in case Yocum is having King watched."

"Paul, I told you I want Wheatly protected."

"I'm aware of that, sir. I'm going to need to talk to you about that in private."

The president nodded, although he was obviously concerned about Wheatly.

"Okay, Paul. What about Leonard?"

"Sir?"

"Do we protect Leonard?"

Once again, Miser glanced at Farrel, who again stared and waited for a response to the same question that Miser had dodged earlier in the meeting.

"Sir, I'd like to do that, but for now, I only want to get the file over to Senator King and have him meet with Yocum and see if there is a deal to be made. At that time, we can assess everything again and see just where we stand."

The president appeared to be considering a response when Miser interrupted his thought.

"Sir, we need to be sure that the Point Guard work is the priority here. We'll get to King and Wheatly later."

The president nodded. "Fair enough."

This exchange did little to comfort Farrel. He realized that the stakes in this game were high and that anything could happen to anyone at any time … including him.

"If all goes as planned," Miser said, "Yocum will make a deal. I feel pretty certain of that." He seemed to be thinking aloud. "I don't think I'm leaving her any choice. There will be nothing else for her to do. There shouldn't be much to deal with when I get done with this."

"When do we get started?" the president asked.

"Right now. With Yocum digging around, we don't have much time. She's sharp, and we don't need to give her any more time than she's already got."

The president immediately lifted the phone receiver to call Senator King at his suburban Washington home.

"She is sharp," the president said as he dialed. "Damn sharp. Honest, too. Ha … she'd make a great president, don't you think?"

Miser raised his eyebrows and agreed.

Farrel considered the president's comment. *"Honest president?" Could there even be such a thing?*

King answered, "Hello?"

Glancing back and forth between Farrel and Miser, the president had started the next stage of the operation.

"Leonard, listen very carefully to me."

"Yes, sir." King focused on the president's every word.

"I want your two agents to meet my men at the Crystal City Marriott parking lot on level four, near the elevators."

"Yes, sir."

"My men will have the tax file. I want your agents to escort my men to your house."

"Yes, sir."

"Leonard, Jeff's going to have to deal with Delores Yocum. She has her sights set on him for conspiring to defraud the IRS as well as whatever else has been uncovered in Philadelphia. As usual, you will be insulated. Do you understand?"

"Yes."

"How long will it take your agents to get to the Marriott?"

Anxious to move the process along and remove himself from Yocum's cross hairs, King answered, "Give me thirty minutes."

"Good, phone me the moment our agents arrive, and we'll go over the plan and the contents of the file real quick. And Leonard, be sure that none of you are seen together. Take whatever precautions necessary. Let the agents drive into your garage. I don't know if Yocum is having you watched. Do you understand me?"

"Yes, sir. I understand. How long will we need to go over the plan?"

"Ten minutes at the most."

"Sounds good, sir. Talk to you soon."

The president instructed King as Miser had suggested.

"It's done," the president said to Miser. "He'll have his agents meet yours in thirty minutes at the Marriott parking garage."

"Good. My men have their orders and have been briefed on the tax evasion case … nothing more."

Miser stood up, gathered his files, placed them inside his briefcase, and locked it.

"Now, if you'll excuse me, Mr. President, I'd like a minute with Frank."

The president nodded, shook Farrel's hand, and said good-bye.

Miser escorted Farrel out of the Oval Office and found a nearby spot just out of earshot of an armed marine guard.

"Frank, everything's going as planned. As you can see, Senator King will accommodate the president's request immediately. I want you to go to King's house and keep an eye on it; make sure no one else is watching it. I don't want King to leave his house until all of the agents arrive and deliver the file. If he leaves or if something doesn't look right, I want you to phone my agents in their car. Do you understand?"

Farrel nodded and took from Miser a scrap of paper with a phone number scribbled on it.

"Here is their number. Park where you can keep a close eye on the house. Don't leave until my agents show up with Andrew and White. I want you to drive them back to Washington. They'll phone you on your cell when they're ready to leave King's house. You got me?"

"Yeah, I think so. Um … anything else I need to know about this meeting?"

"No. Just keep an eye on the house and drive my agents back here."

Miser looked at his watch, said that it was time to go, and shook Farrel's hand.

Wary, Farrel watched Miser return to the Oval Office. As the marine started to close the door behind him, he could barely hear Miser say, "Sir, here's what's going to happen—"

And the closing door cut off the sound of his voice.

Chapter Twenty-Nine

Farrel drove past King's spacious three-story colonial house. As he examined the property, Farrel was struck by the wealth that King and politicians like him have amassed. The lawn was finely manicured, the garden groomed, and the home meticulously kept. He parked about two hundred feet away, atop a slight rise on a street that dead-ended into King's driveway. He tucked the car in beside some high bushes. He could see King's house and property quite clearly. Realizing that it could be some time before the agents showed up, he slouched down behind the steering wheel and lifted the lid off a cup of lukewarm convenience store coffee. He tried to get as comfortable as possible. He phoned Lewis at home.

"Hey, George, how are you?"

"All right. I'm watching *The Rockford Files*. I love this show. He makes you look like James Bond."

"Yeah, okay, Shaft."

"Oh no, here we go with the black shit. Why do you always got to go there?"

"Ah, lighten up, Nipsy."

"I'll lighten your ass up."

"Listen to me. I'm still here in Washington." He paid close attention to King's house as he spoke. "Kathy is fine, and I expect to be headed back by tomorrow."

"Hey, my man, where you stayin' down there? Don't tell me you're tappin' Kathy!"

"Nah, nothing like that."

"You are tappin' her …"

No, I'm not. Knock it off. There's nothing to report here, so I'll talk to you tomorrow. Okay?"

Lewis was preoccupied with the television. "Yeah, man, I'll catch you tomorrow."

Farrel stared straight ahead and reflected on his actions during the case. Deceiving George had been emotionally difficult, and he found himself troubled by the thought that his friend might never forgive him. For the time being, he knew there was nothing he could do but continue with the charade. He tried to shake the regretful thoughts from his mind and focused on the task.

Meanwhile, in Crystal City, Miser's Secret Service agents sat inside their car near the elevators on the vacant fourth floor of the Marriott parking garage, waiting to rendezvous with Andrew and White. As King's agents prepared to carry out their duty and deliver Senator Wheatly's file, they remained acutely aware that Dugan, an operative like themselves, had been murdered in the course of this cover-up.

Tires squealed on the concrete and echoed across the poorly lit lot as Andrew and White pulled up alongside the only other car on the floor. Miser's agents quickly stepped out of their car and slid their large-framed, dark-suited bodies into the backseat of the CIA men's Chrysler. Saying nothing, one of the agents placed a briefcase on the backseat between himself and his partner. They each took a long, hard look at Andrew and White as they pulled away and started on their way toward Senator King's house, which was only minutes away.

"I'm Andrew; this is White."

The Secret Service agents barely acknowledged the introduction as they looked out into the empty lot through dark tinted windows. White raised an eyebrow toward Andrew as he kept a suspicious eye on the backseat through the rearview mirror. As White wound the Chrysler down the narrow spiral ramp to street level, an uneasy quiet was impossible to ignore. Professionals capable of unspeakable aggression, they were on edge in each other's company.

"Do you guys have the file?" Andrew asked, as White steered out of the garage and onto the street.

"Yeah," the man behind him said.

"Let's see."

The agent popped open the case, and Andrew was able to identify some classified documents bearing Senator Wheatly's name.

"All right," Andrew said, "we all know where we're headed; we'll receive our instructions at Senator King's house. But first, we have to call the senator and tell him to be ready **for us**. We were told to do the transaction as inconspicuously as possible—to pull **directly** into the garage, so that no one sees us all together."

It was 8:30 PM when Senator King received the call.

"Senator, it's **Agent** Andrew. We'll be at your house in five minutes."

"Right. See you then."

"We're all set," Andrew told White.

King hung up his phone, opened the door leading into the garage, and tossed a bottle of Tums into a deep rubber trash barrel. He then went to his study, where Mrs. King was relaxing with a novel.

"Honey," he asked, "I'm going to have a short meeting and really need some Tums. Do you mind running out and picking some up for me? My stomach is really acting up again."

"I think we have some in the kitchen."

"No," he said, "we're out. I ate them all."

"I need my dry cleaning for tomorrow. Do you mind picking that up, too?"

She had been worried about his stress level, and she needed to buy some things herself. So she smiled and agreed to run the errand. After grabbing her jacket and purse, she kissed him good-bye and walked toward the garage and her white Lincoln Town Car. He followed her through the kitchen trying to hustle her along.

"Thanks, hon, I really appreciate it."

"Okay, sweetheart. I need to get a few things myself. I'll see you a bit later."

Farrel saw the garage door slowly rise. He sank down deep into his seat and spied through the bottom of his windshield as the Lincoln backed out of the garage and turned up the street toward him. Under the circumstances, Farrel's car would look suspicious to King if he were to notice it sitting out on the empty affluent neighborhood street. So he ducked down behind the door as the car passed. Unable to confirm that it was King at the wheel, he craned to get a better look after the car passed. He was fairly certain it wasn't King, but he couldn't be sure.

"Shit!" he muttered to himself in disgust.

He couldn't decide whether to contact the agents. He started his engine and rolled toward the end of the street to get a closer view of the house. He was now less than a hundred feet from the King property and could see straight down the throat of driveway to the garage. He tapped nervously on the steering wheel and reached for his phone.

Andrew turned around and tried to ease the tension.

"You guys from around here?"

"Baltimore," responded the agent seated behind White.

"How about you?" asked Andrew.

"Chicago."

"I'm from St. Louis, and this guy," he pointed to White, "is from Baltimore, too. Maybe you two guys know each other."

"I doubt it," said the Secret Service agent.

"Oh, come on," said Andrew. "Are you guys going to be hard-asses for the rest of this thing? I mean, shit, it looks like we're working with each other whether we like it or not."

The agent behind White was reluctantly receptive to the overture, while the other agent ignored the offer of friendliness entirely. The man behind White reached forward to shake Andrew's hand. "Mike Carlin," he said. "This is my partner, Bobby Coyne."

"Now, *that's* better!" said Andrew. He shook Carlin's hand and then reached over to Coyne, who shook but continued to stare out the window.

"Now, we can get on with things," said Andrew. "Are you guys always this tight?"

"I guess it depends on the circumstances," said Carlin. "Besides, this is a pretty charged-up program we got here. It's not exactly a stress-free situation. We've read the file, and we've been briefed. We know what's been going on with this thing, and we know what role you guys have played." He glanced over at Coyne. "It makes us a bit edgy."

Andrew nodded. "I can understand that ..."

"I hate to fuck up your meet-and-greet," said White, "but we're here."

Chapter Thirty

Only moments after Farrel's car rolled to a stop, he noticed the agents' arrival. He hastily reached into his shirt pocket and pulled out the scrap of paper with the agents' cell number on it. He slouched behind the wheel and peeked over the dash as Agent White turned into the driveway. Farrel could hear the gravel crunch under the slowly rolling wheels of the agents' car. He gripped his cell phone and wondered whether he should make the call. The Chrysler approached the two-car garage, and the wide door began to screech as it rose. Farrel suddenly realized that Senator King must still be at home due to the timing of the garage door opening and the agents' arrival. Sure enough, Frank saw shoes, then suit pants and a belt, as King appeared inches at a time. Relieved, Farrel closed his phone and watched as King waved the agents in. Once inside, the door reversed ever so slowly as Farrel's heart quickened. Sitting up, he draped his body over the steering wheel to get a better look.

As the garage door made the slow descent, Farrel saw the rear doors of the cruiser open first. From each side, identical legs dressed in suit pants and wearing polished black shoes slid out at once and stepped solidly onto the concrete floor. With the brake lights still visible and the garage door only half open, Farrel saw the rear passengers rise up as they continued to disappear behind the falling door.

He turned away to swiftly survey the area to be sure he hadn't been noticed. Again, he focused on the garage and watched as the two men moved forward toward King as the door slid shut, sealing them inside. Instructed to keep an eye on the house and return Miser's agents, he let go of the wheel, settled back, and waited.

Inside, King smiled and nodded at Carlin as the agent approached with the briefcase in his hand.

White unbuckled his seat belt, turned to Andrew, and mumbled, "I'm glad this fucking thing is coming to an end."

"Tell me about it," said Andrew.

Andrew was reaching toward his door handle when Coyne stopped, swiftly drew his weapon from inside his dark suit jacket and fired a single round that smashed into the side of Andrew's head.

Startled by the gunshot, Farrel sprang up behind the wheel and locked his eyes on the garage door. Instinctively, he began to compute his next move.

By now, Carlin's pistol was trained on King's face as he swiftly advanced toward the petrified senator, who was beating a rapid retreat toward the kitchen door. White fumbled frantically for the gun underneath his suit jacket as Coyne fired another bullet over Andrew's slumping body. It found its mark, pounding into White's shoulder with such impact that it knocked his hand away from his holstered weapon. Carlin continued toward the senator, watching him fall backward into the group of rubber trash barrels next to the kitchen door. White desperately groped again for his gun as he tried to open his door and escape. In a primal effort to protect himself, he lifted his leg and lowered his head just before a second shot found the meat of his hamstring. As he finally grabbed hold of his weapon, a third shot struck him in the rib cage with such violent force that the gun flew from his hand and landed on the seat beside him. Finally, his door swung open, and he made a feeble attempt to push his way out when one last fatal shot pounded into his back.

Farrel threw his car into gear, gunned it down the driveway, and stopped some fifteen feet from the garage door. He pulled out his gun from under his coat and quickly ensured that it was ready for action.

Inside, Carlin jerked a numb King to his feet and dragged him back toward the driver's side door. Coyne calmly reached inside Andrew's coat, pulled out the dead agent's holstered revolver, and briskly circled behind the car. Carlin released King and stepped aside as Coyne approached. With his own gun stiff and steady in his left hand by his side, Coyne raised Andrew's gun in his right hand and walked to within five feet of King. He fired two rapid rounds into King's chest, knocking him to his knees. After firing, Coyne briskly continued moving forward past King to the kitchen door as the senator gasped and clutched his chest. Coyne struck the garage door button on the wall with his elbow as King crumpled heavily to the floor.

With adrenaline coursing through his veins, Farrel crouched behind the driver's side door of his car and pointed his gun at the garage. Having been activated, the garage door slowly started to rise.

Inside the garage, Coyne pulled a handkerchief from his pocket and wiped down the weapon as he hurried back to Agent Andrew. He reached inside the car for Andrew's hand and forced the dead man's grip onto the gun. He raised it and shot one round into the driver's side door and one past the door into the garage wall. He then dropped the dead agent's hand while Carlin opened the briefcase and tossed it on top of King, spilling Senator Wheatly's tax forms onto the bloody floor and corpse.

The garage door was not yet fully open, and Farrel could only see so much. But he could make out the Secret Service agents moving about very quickly. He could also see the two bodies lying on the floor.

The agents opened the back doors of the car, and Farrel anxiously waited for the garage door to fully open. They swiftly and meticulously wiped down the door handles and the insides of the back doors. After wiping down his side, Coyne reached across the backseat and handed Carlin his gun. Carlin pulled a handkerchief from his pocket and quickly wiped the piece down.

Now with the garage door fully open, Farrel could clearly see the agents tidying up the assassination scene. He swallowed hard. The agents pushed the car doors closed with their hips. Carlin then took his partner's pistol, placed it in King's hand, and fired a shot into White's body.

No more than two minutes had elapsed from the time the car pulled into King's garage. The agents, their job done, emerged onto the driveway.

"Freeze!" Farrel yelled.

Carlin and Coyne slowed their pace slightly but continued in Farrel's direction.

"Frank Farrel?"

"Yeah?" Farrel answered nervously.

"Stop pointing that thing at us! We're with Paul Miser. We're Secret Service!"

After a moment of confusion and indecision, Farrel lowered his gun slightly and then stood up straight and pointed his gun at Carlin's head.

"I said *freeze*, or I'll shoot your fuckin' head off!"

They stopped dead in their tracks. They looked over their shoulders at the carnage they had created. A gust of wind sent bloodied papers swirling about the car and the bullet-riddled corpses.

"Listen, Farrel," said Coyne, "we don't have much time! Now, do you want to lower that thing and get us the hell out of here, or do you want to wait for the police and King's wife to get here?"

Farrel stared at them and said nothing.

"Listen, Farrel," Coyne tried again, "we're with Paul Miser. He told us that you'd get us the hell out of here! Now, what's it going to be?"

The agents were growing impatient and irritated.

"Are you going to get us the hell out of here, or are we going to have to shoot our way past you?" asked Coyne. "Either way, we're getting the fuck out of here!"

Farrel blinked. It was all sinking in—he was part of it all. Not only of what had just happened here, but also of *everything*. He slowly lowered his gun as the two agents rushed over to the car and jumped in.

Farrel felt a sudden urge to get away from King's property—fast. He got in and slammed the car into reverse. He peeled out into the street, shifted gears, and roared away.

Farrel punched the steering wheel as he picked up speed. "Fuck! Fuck!" he shouted. "Why didn't you people tell me this was going to happen? Shit, you pricks set me up so that I'd be a part of this! Damn it! You …"

"Farrel!" Coyne screamed from the back seat. "Shut the fuck up and slow the fuck down! We don't want to be stopped by the police!"

A moment of silence passed as Farrel eyed Coyne through the rearview mirror and Carlin in the passenger seat. Coyne pulled on his collar and calmed himself. "Now, slow down, act normal, and get us back to Crystal City with as little to say as possible."

"Look, Farrel," Carlin said, "we have nothing to do with how things come down or who does what. Sorry, but it is what it is."

Farrel noticed a white Lincoln passing in front of him at a stop sign. It was Mrs. King, heading for home. He tried not to think about what they had left behind—what she would find.

At the Marriott parking garage in Crystal City, Farrel drove where the agents directed him. After winding his way up a steep spiral ramp, he pulled into an area of the garage where there were no other cars but one—a massive, black Chevy Suburban with tinted windows which was backed into a parking spot. He anxiously wondered if perhaps he was the next hit. He swallowed hard and looked at the agents. But he knew that it was really too late to wonder. He gave himself a false sense of security by feeling for his gun under his jacket. He nosed into the parking spot next to the solitary SUV. As soon as the car stopped, the agents stepped out of the car without saying a word and disappeared into a stairwell only a few yards away. Farrel watched them closely until they were gone and then focused his attention on the smoky windows of the massive truck beside him.

Its driver's side electric window—that was directly next to his own—hummed as it glided down to reveal Paul Miser. Farrel lowered his own window and prepared to tell Miser exactly what was on his mind.

But before he could say a word, Miser nonchalantly asked, "How did it go?"

Farrel could hardly believe his ears. How callous *was* this man?

"How did it *go*? They're all fucking dead! *That's* how it went. Why didn't you tell me I was the getaway driver?"

Miser looked out across the empty parking lot.

"If I did, would you have gone?"

Farrel jerked his head away from Miser and stared at the concrete wall directly in front of him.

"I didn't think so. Frank, you need to be committed to the cause. You're a good man, but now you're one of *my* men—a Secret Service man. You *had* to be a part of this; you have to have something at stake. You've become more trustworthy—more committed. It's the price of membership. I know it's a hard pill to swallow, but you have to trust me. This will all be worth it. When this operation is done and the Point Guard system becomes law, it'll be because of this—because of *us*, Frank. Because of *you*!"

Farrel nodded shamefully and resigned himself to the fact that, at least for now, he was in as deep as anyone could be—as deep as Miser wanted him.

It's what's best for the families of all Americans, Frank thought to himself. The problem was he couldn't help but think that this was *not* best for King's family or for the families of all the other victims of this cause.

"Go get some rest, Frank," Miser said. "I'll call you when I need you."

Farrel chuckled sarcastically.

"Do you have something you want to get off your chest, Frank?"

"Ha ... where ... where does this all end?"

"What do you mean?"

He turned to face Miser. "This shit. Killing ... killing people like King and ..."

"Listen to me, Frank," Miser interrupted. "King let Yocum get under his skin. He became a liability. Based on the way he reacted from her very first contact, we weren't sure he wouldn't give in under the type of pressure she could eventually bring. So we had to be sure that he and his agents wouldn't ..."

"Wouldn't what? Talk?"

"Yeah, talk! Frank there is a lot at stake here. Do you realize that Wheatly is one of a only few people who can take the Point Guard plan and get it positioned in the right way with the right people? Our job is to get this thing done with no controversy attached to it. So if we need to cover-up Wheatly's ... or anyone else's actions for that matter, we will."

"What about me? Aren't you afraid I'll talk?"

"No. I'm not."

Farrel glanced into the rearview mirror.

"What makes you so sure?"

"I just know," said Miser confidently.

Once again, Farrel turned to face the concrete wall. Miser patiently waited for him to collect his thoughts.

"Where does all this shit end? When do we stop ... killing?" Farrel asked.

"Now."

Farrel looked at Miser as if he didn't believe him. Miser started his car.

"Frank, ... now go get some rest, okay?" Miser put his Suburban into gear. "I'll call you when I need you."

Shortly after being notified of the shooting, Delores Yocum appeared at the King property, which was now surrounded by yellow crime scene ribbon. Investigators and police swarmed over the property. Mrs. King laid on her bed in shock, guarded by a police officer until her relatives arrived.

After inspecting the scene, Yocum returned to her office and spent a long, black-coffee-drinking night trying to piece things together. She phoned Lewis at around 4:00 AM, waking him from a sound sleep.

"Sorry to wake you, Detective, but I can't get a hold of Farrel."

"Yeah?" He was still trying to wake up. "Yeah, what's up?"

"Senator King is dead. So are Agents White and Andrew."

"Shit!"

"Get hold of Detective Farrel and get to my office as soon as you can."

On hanging up the phone, Lewis found that he was now wide-awake. He tried to reach Farrel but was only able to leave a message on the cell phone that rang on the dresser of Farrel's empty hotel room.

"Frank, as soon as you get this, I need you to call me. Some serious shit is happening, and Delores Yocum wants us in her office right away."

Unable to sleep, Farrel paced the empty streets near his Washington hotel. He walked into a twenty-four-hour convenience store and poured himself a cup of coffee. As he stared at the coffeepot, he tried to remember why he had stopped attending church more than thirty years ago.

This is as good a time as any, he thought.

He found an old Catholic church he had remembered seeing earlier in the day and walked up its broad granite steps only to find the doors locked. Alone, he faced the doors, took a sip of his coffee, and began to pray where he stood.

God, I know you haven't seen me here in some time, but … um … please forgive me for all that I've done. Please don't let all that the others and I have done be in vain. I know that there's no excuse for my actions, but I really believed that I was doing the right thing. I'm not so sure anymore.

Stepping back from the doors, he leaned back and looked up at the cross perched high on the steeple.

He turned and walked down the steps.

"Sorry, Kathy," he said, "None of this should have happened."

By 7:00 AM, Farrel had made it back to his hotel room and phoned George.

"Frank, where the hell have you been? The attorney general wants to see us as soon as possible."

"What's going on, George?"

"She said that King was found dead in his garage, along with those two CIA agents who took over our investigation. This is fucked up, Frank!"

"Yeah, I agree. Where are we supposed to meet her?"

"At her office."

"Okay. How long will it take you to get down here?"

"Maybe three hours or so."

"All right. I'll meet you at Yocum's office at around eleven."

Farrel showered and dressed, and then he went to intercept Kathy on her way to work. She smiled as she saw him standing on the platform when she stepped off the train. Farrel forced a smile as she wrapped her arms around him and gave him a healthy hug and a kiss on the cheek. They started walking toward Senator Wheatly's office.

Farrel wanted to tell her everything that was going on, but he couldn't. It was apparent to Kathy that he was feeling uneasy. Putting her arm in his, she smiled and asked him whether he was all right.

"Yeah. Yeah, everything's fine," he said unconvincingly, as they walked in the bright sunshine.

"What's going on, Frank? Guys like you don't beat around the bush. Tell me what's on your mind. You'll feel better."

They stopped a half block from the office. Farrel took Kathy by the hand and turned her to face him. He gazed into her eyes and tried to smile.

"Kathy, I can't tell you what's going to happen or what I've been involved in. I know that from here on in everything will be okay, and you have nothing to worry about. Just like I promised. I just want you to know that, no matter what, you're very important to me."

Kathy was confused, but she found relief in the man she trusted most telling her that she had nothing to worry about. She started to speak.

"No, no, listen," said Farrel, "you'll understand later. For now, I just want you to know that you're very special. Some things are going to happen, and you may not like me for what I've done. But trust me, it will all work out."

"What are you saying, Frank?"

He kissed her on the cheek, gave her a firm hug, turned toward the street, and started to walk away.

"You'll see me again soon," he shouted. "You'll understand then."

Frank weaved through the morning traffic, and Kathy just stood there wondering what he meant.

Chapter Thirty-One

At eleven o'clock, Farrel joined Lewis at the attorney general's office.

"Have a seat, Detective." Yocum pointed to the chair next to Lewis.

She had been thumbing through the King murder scene report.

"Last night," she said, "Senator King and the two CIA agents, Andrew and White—who, as you know, had taken over the Lane/Wheatly investigation— were found dead in Senator King's garage. It appears that there was some kind of shootout between King and the agents. The details are yet to come, but it appears as though they shot one another. Why, I don't know. The weapons all match up, and the folks down at ballistics pulled an all-nighter to get the report to me this morning."

Yocum leaned against her desk and rubbed her tired eyes.

"Senator Wheatly's tax documents were strewn all over the place. I spent most of the night trying to make sense of that as well as of why these guys would get into a gunfight in King's garage. I don't even want to get into the odds of Leonard King knowing what end of a gun to hold, let alone the odds of him killing two elite CIA agents. As for the tax documents, we recovered two sets: what appear to be the originals as they had been prepared by Mr. Lane and the doctored ones that had been filed fraudulently by Wheatly." She paused and shook her head. "I don't buy into a confrontation that just so happened to kill everyone involved in the cover-up. And I know that Jeff Wheatly is a heartless prick, but he doesn't have the kind of pull it takes to put together a hit of this magnitude. However, finding these guys and the tax documents all together certainly substantiates what we heard on the tapes. The question is—why? Aside from Wheatly, who would want these guys dead?"

She tossed her pen onto her desk.

"Any ideas, fellas?"

Lewis—who appeared rattled—shook his head.

Farrel shrugged.

Yocum pitched the file onto the desk.

"Me neither," she said. "After trying to make sense out of this all night and half the morning, I get this phone call from the president. He asked me if I was involved in an investigation that had to do with Senators King and Wheatly. Of course, I told him that I was. He then told me that his office and the Secret Service were also involved in a top secret investigation that involved the senators as well."

Lewis squirmed and loosened his tie. "Ah, shit, I knew that this ..."

Yocum continued on and ignored Lewis as he tried to fire off one of his famous doom and gloom sentiments.

"He told me that he wanted to see me and the investigators involved in the case this afternoon at one o'clock." They all looked at their watches simultaneously. "That means the three of us. Gentlemen, we've got about an hour and a half before we see the president. What do you say we get some lunch first?"

Lewis rolled his eyes. "Oh, boy, here we go, Frank. This ain't gonna be good."

Farrel reached across and patted Lewis on the leg. "Don't worry, Nipsy. Everything's going to be okay."

Not in the mood to fire off a colorful comeback to the Nipsy dig, Lewis slowly pulled himself up from the chair and followed Yocum and Farrel out of the office.

While Yocum and the detectives ate lunch and discussed the case at a nearby deli, the president and Miser sat in the Oval Office having a private lunch of their own while discussing their strategy. Miser was prepared to spin the investigation as hard as needed to ensure that the Point Guard plan had an unobstructed path to the House and Senate. He knew that it was only a matter of time before Yocum started to piece things together. It was imperative that they try to work out their deal with her immediately. However, they had no illusions. Even though the president had appointed Yocum, they knew not to expect her to rubber-stamp anything, let alone something that had to do with King or Wheatly. In fact, since he knew her so well, the president was certain that they had a difficult negotiation ahead.

Miser opened a large, phony file he had created on Senator King.

"Sir, you need to come to grips with the fact that we need Wheatly as bait, at minimum. The truth is you need to be prepared to see him crash and burn if you want a clean path for the Point Guard program."

"I hear you, Paul, but I need this guy."

"Sir, Wheatly's all we have to bargain with. I didn't want to get into this with you when we were with Frank Farrel, but hell, sir, it's what *has* to happen if we're to strike a deal with Delores. She's going to want something if and when"—he pointed to the King file—"she ferrets through this thing."

Unresponsive, the president stared vacantly at Miser.

Miser opened the file and pointed to the top of the pile with his index finger.

"Sir, this is the story we are giving Delores. Every detail has been taken care of—bank accounts have been opened, deposits have been made, tax and financial reports have been fabricated. This file is complete, down to the last detail. We'll present it to her, and it will facilitate a deal. I'll do my best to limit the damage done to Wheatly, but like I said, you need to be prepared to see him go down."

"Listen, Paul," said the president, "let's just see what happens when we meet with Delores. I know how to work with her. Trust me"

Delores Yocum ate the last bite of her sandwich and washed it down with a large mouthful of bottled water.

"I've given this a lot of thought since the president called. I know Paul Miser—he's a sharp guy. If the Secret Service is involved, then Miser is orchestrating whatever it is that's going on. He's not bringing us in just to find out what we're doing—he wants to know what we *know*. He's got something for me—I don't know what it is, but you can bet that it could be anything—from genuinely helping us with the investigation all the way to trying to derail it completely. One thing I feel pretty certain about—in fact, I'd bet on it—is that he wants something. Otherwise, he wouldn't have the president bring us in. He'd have waited for us to come to him."

After lunch, the detectives and Yocum walked over to the White House. Waiting outside the Oval Office, Delores leafed through some case documents while Farrel sat watching Lewis pace the floor.

"Relax, George," said Farrel. "Sit down, before you pass out from exhaustion."

"Yeah, right. Why are *you* so calm, Frank?"

"Calm, my ass," Farrel mumbled to himself.

Oblivious to their conversation, Delores continued to read the case file on the King shootings. She was trying to see whether there was anything she hadn't thought of—anything she might have missed.

The doors to the Oval Office opened. Miser appeared in the doorway and waved them over. He stepped outside the office and gestured for the sentry to close the door behind him.

"I'm Paul Miser, Secret Service director."

He extended his hand.

"George Lewis."

"Nice to meet you, George." Miser turned to Yocum, "Delores, how have you been?"

"Pretty good, Paul. I knew I'd be seeing you when the president told me that the Secret Service was involved."

Miser and Yocum had met on many occasions and had a mutual respect for one another's abilities. Yocum was well aware of Miser's talents as a covert operator and master deceiver. She knew that if he was personally involved that it was a big deal.

Miser finally turned toward Farrel, smiled, and shook his hand.

"Frank, can you give the president and me some time alone with the attorney general? We'd like to discuss a few things before you and George join us."

Lewis and Yocum were stunned by the notion that Miser knew Farrel by name. They each shot Farrel a look that unmistakably asked what the hell was going on.

Miser led Yocum inside, closed the door, and left Farrel and Lewis alone outside. Farrel slid his hands into his pockets and tried to avoid George's piercing stare. Looking like he had just ran a marathon, Farrel crossed the floor, dropped into a chair, and expelled a sigh. Frozen in place just outside the Oval Office door, George continued to size up Farrel. After a moment of observing Frank's uncomfortable tics, Lewis started across the floor. With each strike of his heel against the terrazzo, a clap echoed from the massive domed ceiling and off the curved atrium walls. Farrel leaned forward with his elbows on his knees, resting his face inside his cupped hands. As Lewis drew closer, Farrel could see each deliberate footstep through his fingers.

"What was *that* all about?" asked Lewis.

Farrel pulled his hands away from his face.

"Frank?"

Farrel's face was red; his eyes were bloodshot. He could only hope that George would understand. He had known this would be difficult. He knew the trust he and George had developed in their partnership had been betrayed. Farrel had wanted to tell George what he was doing from the beginning—to tell him about his dual role with the Philly police and the Secret Service. But he couldn't. On one hand, he was glad that it was finally time to come clean; on the other, he was afraid that George would feel let down by his partner—by his friend. Even now, he could not tell George everything, only what Miser had told him he could say. Although Farrel had known that this day would come, he was no more prepared for it than he would have been had it come as a total surprise.

"What's going on, Frank? How does this guy Miser know you?"

"It's a long story, George."

"Well, fuck, Frank!" Lewis gestured toward the closed doors of the Oval Office. "It looks like I got some time to burn. What the fuck is going on?"

Farrel mindlessly tugged on his tie and rubbed his thigh.

"All right, George, ... I've been working for Miser."

"The Secret Service?"

"Yeah, the Secret Service. I have been since ..."

"The fucking Secret Service, Frank? You work for the Secret Service?" Lewis turned away from Farrel, wiped his lips, turned back, and pointed a finger at Farrel's face. "I trusted you, you motherfucker!"

The nearby marine paid close attention to the scene as Farrel tried to calm his friend.

"Keep it down, George! I *wanted* to tell you ..." Lewis turned away from him again. "George, do you want to hear what I have to say, or not?"

Lewis avoided eye contact and sat in the chair next to Farrel. Farrel leaned forward and stared at Lewis as he waited for him to simmer down. After a long silence, Lewis spoke.

"How long?"

Farrel shook his head. Lewis's nostrils flared.

"How long you been with the Secret Service?" he repeated.

"Since the beginning."

"What beginning?"

"At the hospital."

"What hospital?"

"When I left the Lane crime scene ... when you stayed at Lane's house to complete the investigation and I went to inspect the body. That was when I met Paul Miser."

"*What?*" Lewis could hardly believe what he was hearing.

"Mike Lane had done some tax work for Miser. They knew each other."

"So how did Miser get into this? Start from the beginning, Frank."

"I can't."

"What do you mean, you can't?"

"I can't, George. I'm not cleared to talk about it."

"Not cleared? Man, you really are his boy now, ain't you?"

"It's not that simple."

"Not that simple? You got to be kidding me, Frank. Are you going to tell me what the fuck is going on here, or not?"

"No," said Farrel. Disgusted, Lewis turned away.

"What I *can* tell you is that the Point Guard program is moving ahead and that your participation in the investigation will be recognized as an important part of ..."

"Don't tell me a fuckin' thing, Frank. If you can't tell me the whole story, I'll just sit and wait for your man to tell me. You can tell me anything you want at this point. I have no reason to believe you." He faced Farrel again. "Is that why I'm here? You got something else you want to pull over on me?"

Farrel shook his head; his eyes drifted to the floor. The two friends had nothing left to say to one another.

Inside the Oval Office, Yocum started the meeting off by opening her briefcase and pulling out a file jacket containing her notes on the investigation.

"What do we have, gentlemen?" she asked as she laid the closed file on the president's desk.

Miser liked her no-nonsense approach.

"Delores, why are you investigating Senator King?" he asked.

She laughed at the question.

"Why are *you* investigating Senator King?" she shot back.

He hesitated. "We're investigating him in connection with a tax fraud cover-up."

He noticed that her face was expressionless. She didn't believe it for a second.

"Anyway," Miser continued, "*you* were personally out investigating Senator King's house last night after the murders, and we wondered why. The president tells me that you're conducting an investigation. True?"

She rolled her eyes and nodded. "Come on, Paul, give me a break! I wasn't born yesterday! It's obvious that you know what I'm up to. Hell, you obviously have something going on with Farrel, so why don't you tell me why I'm here?"

Yocum moved to the edge of her seat and looked hard at the president for a moment before turning back to Miser. The president nodded for Miser to continue.

"Listen, Delores, I don't want to play cat-and-mouse."

"Good! You know I despise games." She settled back in her chair. "Why did you bring me here?"

Miser leaned forward and grabbed his coffee cup from the corner of the president's desk.

"Delores, we've been investigating a rogue cover-up operation conducted by Senator King in connection with Senator Wheatly and tax fraud."

Miser sipped his coffee and got comfortable. He was well prepared and launched into his version of the case, as Yocum produced a pad and started to take notes.

"We have been investigating Senators King and Wheatly, along with CIA Agents Andrew and White, for ethics violations in regard to tax evasion, blackmail, fraud, and a number of other things."

Miser fanned the pages of the file he had prepared. Delores took notice of the movement and read the print on the file jacket: "King—CLASSIFIED."

"Now, understand, Delores, that we learned much of this during our investigation, but much of it we're also piecing together right now, just like you. What we know is that after Senator King learned that Senator Wheatly had filed fraudulent tax returns, King dug into the case through the usual method of pulling Wheatly's household expenditures, receipts, bank statements, tax returns, and so on.

"King discovered—as did we, eventually—that Wheatly had been accepting very large amounts of illegal campaign cash for many years. My guess is that King saw this as an opportunity to make some substantial money himself. From the best information that we're able to piece together, we think that King confronted Wheatly and told him that he could make the Philadelphia tax fraud investigation go away—which would put to rest any suspicion of campaign misappropriations—in exchange for a cut of the money Wheatly was collecting and not reporting. We know that they came to some kind of an agreement because we acquired records from the IRS database that clearly indicated activity on Wheatly's IRS account on the same day we tailed Andrew and White to the IRS building."

Yocum dropped her pen onto the notepad. "Do you have these records?" she asked.

"Yes, they're in the file."

Yocum was suspicious. Miser could read the guarded look on her face. He explained.

"Delores, we've had our eye on King since shortly after the start of the Lane shooting investigation in Philadelphia. That's when King launched his own illegal cover-up—when he sent Andrew and White to Philadelphia to take over. When we learned that King had basically hijacked the Philadelphia investigation from the FBI and personally involved himself without the authority to do so, we saw a red flag and launched our own internal investigation. And because the Lane case had been turned over with strong implications of tax fraud, we immediately did to King what he did to Wheatly. We wanted to know what his motivation was for taking the case from the FBI and handling it himself, so naturally, we pulled his taxes, his recent cash expenditures, newly acquired assets—everything. The long and short of it is that he'd recently made a couple significant cash purchases and had opened an offshore account at the same bank Wheatly used. We estimate that King's cut for the tax cover-up and keeping his mouth shut was about thirty percent of Wheatly's annual unreported income and campaign funds."

The attorney general placed her pen and pad on the corner of the president's desk, sank back into her chair, and clasped her hands above her head. Recalling what she had already learned on her own, she now tried to understand this complex new angle. The president noticed a puzzled look on her face as Miser continued.

"We're sure that when King made the arrangement with Wheatly to cover up his tax fraud, he didn't account for the CIA agents' greed. We believe that they somehow learned, during the cover-up, that Wheatly had significant unreported income. They must have figured that if King was willing to put himself so far out on a limb to keep Wheatly's tax records from being investigated, there must have been a lot of money involved. So, the agents jumped in and demanded a cut in exchange for keeping their mouths shut—just like King. As the rest of the information related to the King shootings comes in, we'll be able to confirm all of this."

Miser casually pressed the creases on his suit pants.

"Bottom line? King and the agents were all blackmailing Wheatly at the same time without one another's knowledge. When Wheatly started getting squeezed from both ends, he simply stopped paying, ... and the shit hit the fan."

Yocum's eyes narrowed. "How much of this do you know is fact, and how much of this are you piecing together based on the circumstances, Paul?"

He tapped on King's classified file. "It's all in the file."

"No. I mean ... how do we *confirm* all this?"

"Oh, we had a fair amount of it on tape. We bugged King's office."

"Had a fair amount?"

"Yeah. We had the tapes destroyed for security reasons." Miser shook his head casually. "They would have been inadmissible, anyway. We didn't get a warrant."

Perplexed, she motioned for him to continue.

"We think that King decided to threaten Wheatly with the reversal of the tax repair—that would have maintained the blackmail and the flow of money. However, when King got together with the agents, they might not have been agreeable to the strategy ... we're not sure. We think that they were all negotiating what to do next. That's why they had Wheatly's tax file and the entire Philadelphia investigation file over at King's house. Your guess is as good as anyone's as to how they ended up killing one another."

Miser stretched and took a quick look at the president.

"This is why we've been investigating Senator King. Our conclusion, as it relates to Wheatly, is that he was and is involved in tax fraud and the misappropriation of campaign funds. Evidence of that was scattered all over King's garage. But clearly, he is isolated from the actual shootings at King's house. He had simply been paying off extortion demands and using exceptionally poor judgment. He had a lapse in judgment and fell victim to King's, Andrew's, and White's greed—as well as his own."

Yocum raised her eyebrows and nodded slowly. This was certainly a twist she could not have foreseen. Suddenly, this had become the most complicated case she had ever encountered. Nevertheless, she never forgot that she was dealing with Miser—a master of deception and deal-making. This was not her first negotiation, and she was not naïve enough to believe that he and the president had asked her to come to the White House just to explain to her their conspiracy theories. She also knew that if they had simply wanted to find out what she knew, they could have easily bugged her office, tapped her phones, or placed an informant in her camp—as they had done with the Philadelphia police. She believed that they had brought her in to make a deal.

"Well," she said, "that's a good story, Paul. But I find it strange that both versions of Wheatly's documents—the originals *and* the fakes—were strewn all over the place. It seems a bit too fortuitous; it was as if they had been planted there."

Miser shook his head. "No, I don't see that, Delores. I just see some greedy people taking advantage of Senator Wheatly's bad judgment. Their greed blinded them, and we had good fortune in our investigation as a result of their poor judgment."

She wasn't exactly sure of Farrel's role, but she was confident that Miser had recruited him specifically for this case. Her gut told her they must have been aware that she knew there was a connection between Wheatly's tax evasion, the shooting of Lane, and the Point Guard document. After all, if Farrel was on his team, then Miser knew at least as much as she did—and probably a lot more.

"Is Frank Farrel on your team?" she asked.

Miser nodded.

Delores now knew, that she was there to make a deal.

"What is it that you want from me?" she asked.

"Delores," the president said, "you know that I have great respect for you, so I don't want to beat around the bush."

She acknowledged his sentiments with a brusque nod.

"I want to be perfectly clear. We know everything you do and then some. We're aware that you know about the Point Guard document, about Jeff Wheatly's tax evasion, and all the mayhem surrounding it and the shooting of Mr. Lane. We also know that you know about the patsy Scorali. The fact is we know *exactly* what you know. We spoon-fed it all to you and the Philadelphia police. But frankly, I don't care about any of it except Point Guard. If you wish—and I'm only going to offer this once—I'll give you Wheatly on the tax evasion; in exchange, you stay away from anything that could have a negative impact on the Point Guard program. This is the only time I'll offer this deal."

Caught off guard by the president's direct approach, Miser turned toward Delores with a serious look on his face that successfully masked his surprise. He was shocked that the president was suddenly willing to turn Wheatly over. He was even more surprised that he had told Delores the truth. The president had said that he knew how to work with Delores—now that the truth was on the table, Miser could only hope that she chose to take his offer.

"I'm sure that you feel the same as I do about the Point Guard document," the president continued. "I'm sure that you can see that this system could dramatically and swiftly change the face of American justice for the better." He stood and leaned over his desk with as serious a look as any world leader could possibly possess. "I don't want anything to poison this program." He burned a hole through her with his glare. "I will do whatever it takes to get the Point Guard program voted on in record time."

Yocum sat for a moment and appeared to contemplate the president's grave tone and one-time offer. With rebel blood bubbling in her veins, she took a quick look at Miser and then returned her focus to the president.

"What about murder?" she asked.

The president offered no response.

"With all due respect, Mr. President, what about Mr. Lane? I think that his death was extremely suspicious. And for God's sake, what about Wheatly's wife and his aide? Don't you guys have a problem with all these dead people?" She stood and faced the president. "And this bullshit you're feeding me about the King shootout? Where do you guys think you're going with all of this?"

"I guess I'm not making myself clear," said the president. "This is not a nego-tiation." He lifted the King file off the desk and waved it in front of her. "You can have Wheatly on tax evasion, and we get to move on with our Point Guard pro-gram. If you think that our investigation of Senator King is bullshit, fine." He tossed the file down in front of her. "We have our story now. You can try to refute it, if you like. As for Mike Lane, Wheatly's wife, his aide … *go for it.* It's all closed business, but you have the power to reopen it."

The president slipped his hands into his trouser pockets.

"Delores," he said, "Mike Lane is alive."

"What?"

The president reiterated.

"You heard me right. Mike Lane is alive and has been continuing his work on the Point Guard system."

She stared incredulously at the president and then at Miser; then she plopped down into her seat. She thought about how her entire investigation centered on the murder of Mike Lane. It was the base on which every aspect of her case was built—the tax fraud, the murder, the senate ethics violations, and probably a dozen other charges. She needed to rethink everything she knew, and fast. She needed time to sort it all out, but she also knew this president well—if he told her that this was a one-time deal, then this was a one-time deal.

"How can he be alive?" she asked, hoping to buy just a little time.

"I can't tell you," Miser said. "It's classified."

Cloaked in secrecy, Mike Lane had been contemplating and writing changes to his Point Guard document with the protection and support of the president. As Lane worked, Miser and the president took the lead in one of the most exten-sive and complicated covert operations Miser had ever been involved in. The gen-esis of the operation was rather unorthodox and rather serendipitous.

It all began when Lane was shot in the throat during Anthony Kane's botched attempt to steal the Point Guard document.

Frank Farrel went to the University of Pennsylvania hospital to examine Mike Lane's body. Farrel's partner, George Lewis, stayed behind at Lane's house to secure and investigate the crime scene. To Farrel's surprise, the emergency room doctor informed him that Lane had somehow survived the gunshot wound to his throat. However, the doctor was not completely sure that he would live. Farrel decided to try to get a statement from Lane. He was acutely aware that time was of the essence, so he didn't pause to contact Lewis with the news that Lane had survived. He went straight to the intensive care unit, where he met Lane for the first time.

From across the room, it was obvious that Lane was unable to speak. He had a wide gash at the base of his throat with a thick white tube protruding from it and snaking its way down through yards of tangled intravenous lines to a ventilator that pushed each breath of air into his lungs. Faced with the prospect that the patient might expire at any moment, Farrel quickly approached the bed carrying a pen and notepad.

Farrel leaned forward over Lane and touched his shoulder.

"Mr. Lane?"

Lane's eyes lazily opened.

"Mr. Lane, my name is Frank Farrel. I'm with the Philadelphia Police Department."

Lane's eyes widened slightly and slowly moved up to meet Farrel's eyes. Farrel heard the beeping sound of Lane's heart monitor speed up as Lane's heart started to race.

"Mr. Lane, do you know who did this to you?"

Lane did his best to focus on Farrel and keep from slipping into unconsciousness. Farrel held his pad and pen near Lane's face. Lane started to wiggle his fingers. Farrel took hold of his wrist, lifted his arm, and placed the pen in his hand with the pad beneath it. Worried that Lane might die at any moment, Farrel bent down closer and asked him again, "Do you know who did this to you?"

Tears leaked from the corners of Lane's eyes as he summoned what little energy he had left. His trembling fingers caked with blood beneath the nails scribbled ten barely legible letters.

"SECRETSERV"

Unable to make out all the letters, Farrel tried to sound them out.

"Secre Sev, Secre Sev, Secret Sev, Secret Serve … Secret Serve?"

Lane squeezed his eyes shut and wiggled his fingers again.

Farrel placed the pen in Lane's hand again and held the pad in front of him. Lane drew a large "S" on top of the previous letters and across the entire page.

"S?" Farrel said. "S? I don't know what that means." He looked back down at the pad and sounded it out again. "Secret serve … S."

He quickly picked his head up from the pad.

"Secret Service?"

Again, Lane squeezed his eyes shut. This time, he was nearly unable to reopen them.

Farrel raised his voice.

"Mr. Lane, are you trying to say Secret Service?"

Lane's eyes opened and blinked again, this time more slowly. He tried to lift his arm but couldn't. Farrel lifted Lane's arm again and placed the pen back in his hand. Turning the page, Farrel asked, "Does the Secret Service have something to do with this? Do you work for the Secret Service?"

Again, Lane moved the pen slowly, forming letters like a child. He had written the letters "PAULMISER," when his eyes rolled back into his head and he lost consciousness.

Farrel rushed to the nurses' station and told the first person he saw in white scrubs that Mr. Lane had passed out. Two nurses and a doctor hurried into Lane's room. Farrel reached over the counter and grabbed the phone. Before long, he was connected to the Washington office of the Secret Service. He identified himself to the operator as a Philadelphia detective involved in a life-and-death situation, and he said that he needed to talk to someone by the name of Paul Miser, if there was anyone there by that name. Moments later, he found himself speaking with the director of the Secret Service, although he was completely unaware of Miser's status at the time.

Paul Miser and Mike Lane had met after Tina's death, when Lane was doing research for the Point Guard project. Miser had no idea what Lane was working on when Miser had contacted him for tax advice. Like a dozen other politicians and bureaucrats, Miser had been referred to Lane for his tax preparation and accounting services. Miser eventually met with Lane at Lane's home office and became a client. It wasn't long before Lane had learned that Miser was the top gun at the Secret Service. Soon afterward, Lane suggested that he would waive his accounting fees if Miser would consider answering some questions and allow Lane to seek out his advice from time to time for a project on which he had been working. Miser agreed to the barter arrangement, as did a few other political clients of Lane's. They would occasionally answer his questions regarding the law and judicial process. However, none of them knew—or even cared—about what Lane was doing with the information. Over time and multiple phone conversations, Miser and Lane eventually got to be professional friends of sorts. Miser guessed that Lane's project had something to do with legal reform, but he was never privy to the details. However, during the course of their conversations, Miser did come to believe that a very intelligent man was doing serious work.

"Hello, this is Paul Miser."

"Mr. Miser, my name is Frank Farrel. I'm a Philadelphia detective investigating the shooting of a man named Mike Lane. Do you know Mr. Lane?"

"I do."

"Sir, I'm sorry to have to tell you that Mr. Lane has been shot. He has also written your name down." After a brief recap of what Farrel knew, Miser decided that the situation warranted his attention.

Miser thought it curious that Lane would write his name on the pad for Farrel that night in the hospital. He figured that Lane would rather have wanted to contact someone he knew better. However, the fact that Lane knew that Miser worked for the president made Miser wonder—even worry. He couldn't help but think that perhaps Lane was trying to tell him something—something important. Why else would he write his name down? As head of the Secret Service—and therefore charged with protecting the president—Miser couldn't help but read into the situation, nor could he gamble on the chance that this had anything—as remote as the chance might be—to do with the president's security. So—not on a hunch, but as a precaution—Miser took Farrel's call very seriously.

"Detective, do you know what I do here with the Secret Service?"

"No, I don't, sorry."

"I'm its director."

"I didn't know that, sir. I'm not trying to accuse you of anything. I assure you. I just have a man dying here, and if there's anything you can tell me, it would be helpful."

"I understand that, Detective. My concern is that Mike knows that I'm responsible for the security of the president—and that it's my name he wrote down. My job doesn't give me the luxury of ignoring things like that. Chances are that it's nothing related to my job, but for the life of me, I can't understand why he would write my name down. In any case, I'm going to fly up there right now. I'll be there in less than an hour. Because of my position in relation to the president, I want you to listen to me very carefully, Detective. We take everything here seriously these days. I want you to lock this thing down. Do you understand me? I want you to keep your mouth shut for sixty minutes. I don't want you to talk to anyone—and I mean *anyone*—until you hear from me. Understand?"

"I do, but I'll need to check in with my partner and brief my superiors."

"Detective, you're not listening to me. Talk to *no one* until I get there. I know very little about Mike's background, but I do know that he works with a fair number of politicians in his accounting business. However, my primary concern is for the president, so I want to get up there and learn whatever I can, fast." Miser hesitated, as he had expected Farrel to respond. "Do you understand that this is now *my* investigation and that I'm ordering you to put a lid on it until I get there?"

Farrel digested this stern mandate. He was annoyed, and he paused as he considered telling Miser to back off.

"I'll wait till you get here," he said angrily.

"Good. I'll get you some help as soon as we hang up. Listen, Detective, I have to do all I can to protect the president from any threat. Why Lane wrote my name down, I don't know. But I *do* know that he is aware that I work for the president and that I'm the director of the Secret Service. The bottom line is that I need to read into things that may seem harmless on the surface. If I've offended you, that wasn't my intention. I'm just doing my job. I'm sure you can understand that. I just need you to keep quiet for sixty minutes or less, for the sake of the president's security. Are you with me?"

"Yeah, I got it." Farrel softened his edge only a little.

Farrel hung up on him. He then checked in with Lewis at the scene as he routinely did during an investigation. Lewis had nothing new to report. Although Farrel made no mention of Lane's condition, Lewis assumed, as did everyone else, that he was dead.

Miser headed to a private government jet and contacted the head of the Philadelphia division of the Secret Service. He instructed his lieutenant to remain on call and had a couple of undercover Secret Service agents with phony Philadelphia police ID dispatched to the hospital to ensure confidentiality in the event that the case posed any threat to the president.

When Miser arrived, just under an hour after Farrel's call, Lane was comatose and showed little sign of improvement. The reason for his shooting was still a mystery, as was his reason for writing Miser's name down. Miser could only speculate that Lane was trying to tell him something. But what? He considered what he knew about Lane. He knew only that he was an accountant and that he was working on something to do with legal and judicial process. That gave him hardly anything to go on, but he still needed to be vigilant in order to protect the president. That was what brought him to the hospital.

Shortly after arriving, Miser assumed control and started making decisions without consulting Farrel in any way. They talked at the foot of Lane's bed.

"Detective, I ..."

Upset at being pushed around on his own investigation, Farrel was still annoyed with the tone Miser had taken with him earlier. "You need to listen to me."

"No, I don't, Detective. The longer we sit around here and wait for Lane to wake up, the more nervous I get. I want to go ahead and announce that Lane is dead."

"What the hell are you talking about?"

Miser knew that the faster he decided on a plan, the faster he could get some answers.

"Tell the press and your department that Mike is dead. I'll utilize my local resources to write up whatever reports are needed—death certificate, hospital reports, delivery of the slug for ballistics—everything! Whatever makes Mike's death look authentic. Maybe if whoever did this thinks that Mike is dead, they'll get sloppy, and we can get a quick lead. Let's hope that Mike comes out of this coma soon and tells us something, but in the meantime, we'll take this approach."

Hardly able to contain himself, Farrel turned to face Miser.

"Hey! I can appreciate your power and position, but I don't work for you!"

Miser motioned for Farrel to follow him into the hall.

He kept his voice low, since the hall was filled with hospital staff.

"Detective, I'm going to need you to work with me here. Right now, only you and a select few of my staff know that Mike is alive. In a short while, everyone is going to think that he's dead. It may seem to you like too much confidentiality and control, but we have the president's life in our hands every day, and we have to take every possible precaution. Like I said earlier, I'm doing my job."

Farrel checked his watch as Miser spoke.

"We need to know that you'll work with us on this, Frank."

"What do you mean?"

"You're the only one who knows that Mike is alive."

"Look, I don't like how you come in here and throw your weight around. You're turning my investigation …" He leaned into Miser and his nostrils flared. "And I stress *my investigation* … into a federal case! I don't give a shit if you *are* the director of the Secret Service. There is a right way to go about this, and you're not doing it."

"All right, think of it from our position. If Mike were trying to warn us about something related to the president, wouldn't you do everything in your power to find out what it was? Wouldn't you do your job?"

Farrel offered no response.

"I'm not asking much—just to work with me until I learn more or until Mike can give me something more to go with."

Farrel stepped away from the wall. "I recognize that you want to do your job, but I'm not sure that you recognize that I have a job, too. I have a partner and a boss who expect me to report this to them. I work for the Philadelphia police, not the Secret Service."

Miser seemed to consider Farrel's position.

"What about my partner?" Farrel asked. "I want to tell him what's going on."

"No. I want to keep a lid on this."

"What about my captain?"

"Frank, this is just for a short time."

"Short time, my ass ... I don't like keeping my partner out of this."

Miser started to lose patience.

"Don't make me force this on you, Frank—because I can! I have the power of the president and unlimited resources behind me. All I'm asking you to do is to start your investigation with the notion that Mike Lane is dead and to tell me everything you learn. When Mike wakes up and can tell me why he wrote my name down—or when you learn something that makes me satisfied that the president isn't in any danger—we'll call it quits. Is that so damn difficult? You have to investigate the case anyway! Hell, take your ego out of this for a second and listen to the logic."

Farrel turned and walked to Lane's doorway.

"What about my captain? I could lose my job over this."

"You won't. I'll take care of that. Ultimately, we both want the same thing. We both want to know who did this to Mike."

Farrel paced as he considered Miser's logic. After a few moments, he nodded and agreed.

"All right, Frank, let's get this done. If you're okay with it, I'd like to compensate you for your service. And if this lasts for more than two weeks, we'll call it quits—how does that sound?"

"I want George to get the same compensation as me, even if he's not involved."

"Done."

Although Lewis didn't know it, Farrel considered him to be his best friend—perhaps his only friend. Farrel struggled with deceiving him and Carr, but once he was over that and was able to remove his bravado from the equation, he could see the importance of presidential security. Eventually, he found that working with Miser was quite agreeable.

Lane's condition improved even as word of his death was released to the public and reported on the Sunday morning news. The Secret Service did its job, skillfully preparing documentation to prove Lane's death while it worked quickly to cover up and create an alias for Lane during his care at the hospital.

Farrel informed Lewis of Lane's death and asked him to withhold any details of the shooting from the media as Miser had instructed. Lane steadily improved, and on Saturday—fourteen days after he was shot—he was able to sit up and communicate. Lane's communication in the first couple of days of consciousness was crude and difficult. Limited only to writing, he had quickly begun to help Miser and Farrel unravel the mystery. At that point, there was suspicion only of Wheatly's tax fraud, which at the time only made him a *potential* suspect in the shooting of Lane. Although Lane was unable to identify the man who had broken into his house, he was able to relate how fascinated Wheatly had been with his Point Guard work. As soon as Miser had learned of the senator's interest in Lane's work, he suspected Wheatly. Miser knew that the president had met with Wheatly often to discuss NAFTA and that Wheatly had recently presented the president with a legal reform project of some sort. Then, Kathy revealed to Farrel the computer disk that she had received unexpectedly from Lane. All things pointed to Wheatly as the prime suspect. He became the main target and a pawn for the president and Miser's covert operation to gain control over and protect Lane's work. Miser immediately recruited the influence of the president to convince Farrel that he needed to become a full-time, covert Secret Service agent. The president reminded Farrel of his patriotic duty and made him aware of the power and importance Lane's work would have on American judicial reform. In the end, the president's influence convinced Farrel to commit to the operation and join his Secret Service.

Chapter Thirty-Two

Delores Yocum considered the president's deal and Miser's version of the King shootout. Pointing her pen at the president, she asked, "How is the King shooting going to play out?"

"Easy," said Miser. "It is what it is. They killed one another because of their own greed. Wheatly will take some heat because he's guilty of tax fraud, but he's not responsible for any of the deaths."

"And if I prosecute him for tax fraud?"

"We'll cooperate with that as much as possible. We won't place any roadblocks in the way."

"What about his wife and his aide? Their deaths are more than just suspicious; I want time to investigate them."

"No, Delores. They are what they are: a suicide and an auto accident."

"Mr. President," Yocum said, "since Mr. Lane is alive, I'm going to need some time to look at everything again to ..."

While she spoke, the president gestured to Miser to open the private back door of the Oval Office. Distracted, Yocum stopped talking and turned to see a tall man enter the doorway and casually walk across the room. He wore a pair of khakis and a blue Oxford shirt.

"Delores," the president said, "meet Mike Lane, author of the Point Guard document."

"It's nice to meet you, Mr. Lane." She found herself fascinated.

He looked fit, as though he had healed well. He reached into his back pocket, smiled easily, and withdrew a palm-sized notepad and pen. He wrote something on the pad and then turned it over to show her. "Thank you," it said.

"You've had time to study Mike's work, Delores. Do you think it's worthy enough to replace the current system?"

"Yes, I think it is."

"What are you willing to do to make it law?"

"I'm sorry, sir, but it's not my job to get things passed into law. It's my job to uphold the laws we already have."

"I understand—and you're the best in this country at doing that. That's why I appointed you attorney general."

The president paused and buttoned his jacket.

"Delores, we live in a changing world. Respect and common decency are things we take notice of now, whereas they were once qualities we took for granted. Hate and violence surround us all, and it is our job, under the current laws, to make things safe and just for all Americans. The problem is that there has been no way to insure that justice is fair and swift in this modern world. I know that you would agree that it's time to overhaul the system and work *for* the people, not *against* the people." He pushed his chair in under his desk. "Keeping that in mind, is it yes or no to my offer?"

Yocum contemplated her position for a moment. She had to make a decision and needed to make it in the next few seconds.

"Other than anything related to Lane's work, I get Wheatly on tax evasion and anything else I can prove," she said.

"Fair enough." The president reached across his desk and shook her hand.

"I'll be indicting Wheatly for tax fraud as soon as I can."

"Delores, we'll need a few days to sort through the files and get things in order. We want to go over all of your files and make sure that nothing in the records will show any involvement with Point Guard on Wheatly's part."

"Yes, sir. How long will that take?"

"I don't know just yet. Just give me a couple of days to get everything sorted out before you take a run at Wheatly. And be sure to get the Philadelphia investigation shut down. Understood?"

"Yes, sir," she said reluctantly.

Farrel and Lewis were invited in. Yocum, feeling no need to go over the investigation again, decided to take her leave, but not before taking Farrel by the arm, ushering him to the side of the room, and whispering in his ear.

"Enjoy your career in the Secret Service, Frank. Believe it or not, I know why you did what you did here. I, like you and everyone else, think that the Point Guard system will work. But I also think there was a better way than to lie and murder and deceive all of us. You're no better than the Kings and Wheatlys of the world, Frank. I hope you can stomach murder and deceit for Old Glory because that's what you're going to get, working with Paul."

Despite the lingering sting of these words, Farrel turned to join the others in the Oval Office. Lewis had already been introduced to everyone and was shocked to be speaking to Lane. After an abbreviated select debriefing on the case for Lewis, Miser reached for a briefcase that had been standing unnoticed at the side of the president's desk and handed it to Lewis.

"This is yours."

Lewis had been stunned and confused by what he had heard during the debriefing, and he didn't know what to make of this new mystery. He placed the case on the edge of the president's desk. "Do you mind, sir?" he asked as he cracked it open. He was amazed to find it filled with orderly rows of banded twenty-dollar bills. He looked at Miser, mystified.

"You'll need to talk to your partner about that," Miser said.

Closing the case, Lewis looked suspiciously over at Farrel, who said nothing.

"George," said Miser, "I briefed you on this case because I want you to understand the importance of the operation. It's top secret. I also briefed you because I want you to join us—to become an agent for me. We're going to need your help to wrap a number of things up—most importantly, to make sure that we have everything taken care of with the Philadelphia police. If you decide to take my offer, your salary will double, and you'll get to keep Frank as your partner—at least, for now."

"I don't think so," Lewis said. "I'm not going to work with Frank anymore."

"George, ... I'm not sure you completely understand the position Frank was in. He was ..."

Farrel interrupted.

"Paul, you don't need to explain this to George. I understand how he feels. I let him down personally. I can't change that."

Farrel rose and stood still for a moment to look at all the players in the game.

Like a lost soul, he slowly turned to leave the office as they all watched.

"I have some fences to mend and some soul searching to do," he said.

"Take a few days off, Frank," said Miser. "I'll call you, and we'll start back up at the beginning of the week."

"Nah. I don't think so," Farrel said. "This is it for me. I'm retiring. I've had enough."

Lewis watched him as he left the room. His eyes slowly drifted to the floor.

After a moment, Miser turned to Lewis and asked, "Are you on board?"

Lewis looked up at Miser but didn't answer.

"George, … your participation, though you weren't aware we were steering the case, has had a tremendous effect on our ultimate goal. Everything in this case was done for the sole purpose of moving Mike's Point Guard work ahead. Now that you know most of what Frank knows, you can play a greater role due to your knowledge of the Philadelphia investigation and exactly where it stands with the Philly brass. Your knowledge of that—combined with what you'll be learning from us—will position you as a vital part of the operation, particularly as it relates to closing out the case once and for all in Philadelphia."

Lewis seemed to be considering Miser's offer.

"George, we need you on this! The most important piece of judicial reform in recent history is on the line!"

Lewis thought about all the information Miser had presented during the debriefing. He thought about the truths he'd been told and the truths that had been left out. He looked at the floor, the president, and Lane before finally locking eyes with Miser.

"Did you kill King and the agents?" he asked.

Miser just stared back as the president and Lane looked on.

After two or three seconds, the president responded to the question.

"Yes," he said.

Lewis faced the president. "Did Frank participate?"

"Not until after the fact."

"There's a lot more to this case than what we've told you," said Miser. "If you come on board, you'll learn everything—and I mean *everything*." Miser pressed once more. "Are you on board?"

After a couple of seconds, Lewis nodded and spoke softly. "Yeah," he said.

He looked toward the door as though he were waiting for Farrel to return.

"Great! On the bottom of that case are some classified documents. I want you to look them over. I'll meet with you later today to discuss them. In the meantime, why don't you wait for me outside? I'll be done here in a few minutes."

Lewis picked up the case and shook the president's hand.

"It was a real pleasure meeting you, sir."

"Likewise, George. Welcome aboard!"

"It's a pleasure to meet you as well, Mr. Lane."

Lane showed Lewis his pad. "Thank you."

As Lewis turned to leave, Lane wrote another note on his pad and showed it to the president. "I'm tired. May I go?" it said.

The president nodded and patted Lane on the back. "This will all be over soon, and you'll be able to go home."

Flashing a tired smile, Lane left the office the same way he always came in— through the private back door.

Only the president and Miser remained.

"Great job, Paul! Your spin on this is outstanding! Delores knows what she's up against and took the deal like you said she would."

"Yes, sir, that *is* good news. I have to tell you, though—I didn't expect you to throw the truth out there like you did."

"Well, like I said, I know how to work with Delores."

"Sir, what are we going to do about Wheatly? He won't keep his mouth shut if we hang him out to dry with Delores."

"No … you're right. I have a plan for that. After we have everything together, we'll bring Jeff in and make a deal with him."

"I think it would be better if we got rid of him, sir."

"No. He's too valuable alive. He's like King, but better. He can do almost anything. He has no conscience. Right now, he's not expendable. I need people like him to do things like what he just did with Point Guard. No, Paul, we need to use him to do things that no one else could or would do. We need to figure out a way to save his ass, regardless of what we told Delores."

Chapter Thirty-Three

Over the next couple of days, Miser and the president labored over the files and the mounds of paperwork in an effort to complete the operation and tie up any loose ends. They put Lewis right to work. Miser had him study the case file and gave as much detail about the operation as Farrel had. He then prepared Lewis for a scheduled call with Philadelphia Police Chief Ludwig and Captain Carr.

Miser sat at the stainless steel, glass-top desk in his spacious, modern, glass-encased office with a view of the Capitol. His newest recruit, Agent George Lewis, sat in front of him in a black leather chair. Miser had been working with Lewis for a couple of days to prepare him for the call that would aid Miser and the president with the final steps of their plan.

Right on schedule, Captain Carr's phone rang. The chief was beside him, puffing on a large cigar in the smoky, dimly lit office.

Captain Carr leaned into the speakerphone. "Hello?"

"Hello Captain … Chief," said Miser. "I wanted to talk to you about the Senator Wheatly case and your detectives, Lewis and Farrel."

"Okay."

"I suppose the best place to start is to thank you for your efforts on the case and your willingness to turn it over to the CIA awhile back. As you know by now, the CIA agents who took over your case shot Senator King. That was unfortunate. But it seems as though they were blackmailing the senator, and they all ended up killing one another. Anyway, the reason for my call is that I want you to know what we're doing with this case, and I want to see if we can't agree to close it up … at least as far as you guys are concerned."

"All right," Carr answered.

"I'm sitting here with Detective Lewis." Captain Carr sat up and exchanged surprised looks with the chief. "He has explained to me that your department remained involved in the case with the attorney general's office even after you passed it off to the CIA." He waited for a response but got only silence. "I'm not calling to discuss your attempt to maintain control of the investigation nor about how Lewis has come to be here with me right now; I'm calling to talk about closing down the investigation. Gentlemen, this case is now a federal matter that has been and will continue to be investigated by my agency. I know that the attorney general's office has already told you to cease and desist. Nevertheless, to make sure that the case is handled properly from here forward, we're going to need the services of both Detectives Farrel and Lewis. They both have an intimate understanding of the case and know everything that has transpired from the start of the investigation. Do you have a problem with that?"

"Are you asking for permission to use our detectives?"

"No. I'm telling you that they are no longer working with the Philadelphia police. They are now working for the Secret Service. They will need to close down the Philadelphia investigation and continue it with us. I'm going to dispatch Agent Lewis to Philadelphia to brief you on the King murder and Senator Wheatly's unfortunate yet, aside from taxes, innocent connection to the case."

Carr looked over at the chief, who shrugged.

"Captain? Chief? Should I surmise from your silence that you understand and agree?"

"We've already been contacted by Delores Yocum," said Carr, "and she told us to turn everything over to her office and get off the case. I'm a bit confused as to why you're contacting us now to tell us the same thing."

Miser put his feet up on the desk and lounged comfortably.

"Courtesy," said Miser as he raised a brow. "I thought it would be proper to tell you that Wheatly will be indicted on tax fraud and that Farrel and Lewis will be recruited and utilized by my agency to work on the Point Guard program. I know that you guys have been privy to everything related to Point Guard, and we need your confidentiality and cooperation with Lewis and Farrel in the future, if required."

Disgusted with being bowled over like this, the captain reluctantly agreed. The chief tossed his hands into the air and folded his arms across his chest, shaking his head in disgust.

"Okay," mumbled Carr.

"Good. This Point Guard program is classified, and we need it to stay confidential in order for us to move ahead. Agreed?"

"Agreed," came another mumble.

"That will be all, gentlemen, unless you have something to add."

"No," said Carr.

"Chief?"

"No."

"Then that will be all. Thank you, gentlemen!"

Miser sat up and hung up the phone.

"George, it's all yours! You'll go to Philadelphia tomorrow and present the same spin we gave Delores to the captain so that we can shut the thing down. Understand?"

Lewis nodded slowly; he appeared somewhat unsure of himself.

"You okay, George?"

"Um ... yeah."

"You look like you've got something on your mind."

"Not really. It's just that I have worked with Captain Carr for quite some time, and ... he's a good guy and ..."

"I understand how difficult this is for you George," said Miser. "You have a role to play in this thing, ... and we need you to play it well."

Lewis nodded.

"George, if you can't do this, I need to know right now. All the pieces of the puzzle need to fit together. Do you understand me?"

Lewis nodded again, this time more confidently.

"Okay, then," Miser responded. "Go take care of business!"

The time had come to deal with Senator Wheatly.

At the request of the president, Wheatly arrived at the Oval Office for a meeting with him and Miser. After a few pleasantries, the president got down to business.

"Thanks for coming down, Jeff. Paul and I need to talk to you about the Point Guard project. Your involvement with it, specifically."

"What about my involvement?" Wheatly asked proudly.

"Jeff, you're going to have to listen very closely to what I have to say. Do you hear me?"

Wheatly nodded warily as the president's eyes nearly cut through him.

"Jeff, ... I know that you're not the author of the Point Guard document."

Instantly, the senator moved to edge of his chair and raised his voice to refute this allegation.

"What? I *am* ... "

"Shut up, Jeff, or I'll have Paul handle this!"

Wheatly glanced over at Miser, whose expression sent a shiver up the senator's spine. He knew very well of what Miser was capable.

"Jeff, I know that Mike Lane is the author. So don't waste my time telling me he isn't. You also need to know that he is alive."

The shocked senator scowled and shook his head as he tried to digest the president's words. So secure was he in the knowledge that Lane was dead that the senator was convinced that he was being set up. His expression soon settled into one of heavy doubt.

"I don't believe that," he said.

Miser stood up, folded his arms, looked down at Wheatly, and chuckled.

"He can't be!" Wheatly insisted.

Miser walked over to the private back entrance and opened the door. Appearing in the doorway, his face tight with anger and his lips pressed tightly together, was Mike Lane. He walked across the room with his bloodshot eyes fixed on Wheatly. The president came out from behind his desk and placed a hand on Lane's shoulder.

"Meet the Point Guard, Jeff."

Instantly, Wheatly felt the room spin as his dreams and ambitions crashed down around him. The sudden despair was almost unbearable. He felt frozen. He struggled to believe his own eyes. His stomach tied itself in knots; he felt as though he was going to lose control of his bladder and bowels. In that instant, he knew that he was back on the hook for everything he had done. Jolted to the root of his dishonor, the senator held on for the ride.

The president began to describe just what that ride would look like.

"Tomorrow, Jeff, we are going to unveil the Point Guard System in a news conference. Because my friend Mike is the author and founder of the system, I am going to appoint him as the head of the program. He and I will choose a Supreme Court justice to take care of the legal aspects of the system. Together, Mike and that justice will co chair as Supreme Point Guards who will oversee the legal operation and implementation of the program. We still have a lot of work to do, and it may take some time, but I know that the system will be voted on and pass."

Having been kept in hiding ever since the shooting, Lane was pleased that things were coming to a close, but he was disgusted by all the horrible things that had happened because of Wheatly's actions. After a long, hateful stare at the senator, Lane took out his pad and jotted something down. He tore off the note and laid it down in front of the president. After glancing down at it, the president smiled.

"Yes," he said.

After one last, unyielding, scornful look at the senator, Lane turned to leave the office, this time—for the first time—through the front door. As the president and Miser watched Lane proudly make his way toward the office door, the senator strained to read the note that lay in front of the president. He was just able to make out the scribble:

"Can I go home now?"

The door closed firmly behind Lane as he went back to his life. Now, it was time to lay out a plan for Senator Wheatly.

For perhaps the first time in his political career, Senator Wheatly had nothing to say. Stunned and mute, he watched the president return to his chair.

"Jeff, we made a deal with the attorney general, who has been investigating you in conjunction with the Philadelphia police. We've agreed to turn your tax evasion case over to her, and she has agreed—at least for now—not to direct her attention toward all of those sudden deaths that seemed to follow you around. She has agreed to this for a couple of reasons. First, we have confused or covered up everything as best we could—at least anything that could tie you directly to any murders. And second, she is a patriot and wants to see legal reform; therefore, she is willing to participate in clearing a path for the passage of Point Guard.

"I'm not going to get into all the bullshit we went through because of your tax evasion and the theft of the Point Guard document. I'm just thankful that we are where we are now. Jeff, I want you to keep your mouth shut from here on in. Delores is aware of your involvement with the document's theft but will stay away from anything related to it that would incriminate you. Do you understand?"

Though the senator was scared, his cockiness was never far below the surface.

"Yeah, I understand!" He stood and raised his voice. "You want me to commit suicide!"

"No, Jeff. I want you to commit self-preservation."

"No fucking way! If I go down, so does everyone else!"

"Jeff, we've already made our deal!" the president warned.

"Then change it!" Wheatly yelled through quivering lips.

The president's temper boiled over.

"Do you want to end up like Leonard King and those agents, Jeff?"

Wheatly wiped sweat from his upper lip, and his eyes darted back and forth.

"Well, *do you?*" yelled the president.

The senator offered no response.

"Who do you think you're fucking with, Jeff? Some country hayseed? You're going to do what I tell you, or I'll have your fucking throat slit and your body dumped in a landfill."

The president's face turned red, and his eyes bulged. There was no mistaking the seriousness of his threat.

"We've gone to a lot of trouble to arrange things so that you don't go to the fucking electric chair! So you do what I say, or I *will* have you ripped apart!"

The president took a moment to calm himself.

"Look, Jeff, you're going to be okay if you do what we tell you. I need your talents. No one could have pushed and bulldogged this thing along as you have. You have the practical knowledge and the right political connections for getting this reform positioned. Besides, Mike was in bad shape early on and only able to pass bits and pieces of information to us. We passed that information to you, and you added it to the document.

"By the time we learned about your tax evasion … and the suspicion of murder, we had already initiated a covert operation that, among other things, freed you of suspicion in the Philadelphia investigation. Our goal was to keep anything associated with the Point Guard work confidential and to eliminate anything we deemed controversial. If anyone were to ever learn about everything you have done, Point Guard would crash and burn."

The president took a deep breath and paused.

"Jeff, we had you do all the work, … and we covered up all your troublesome behavior." He hesitated again. "Although I made a deal with Delores, I'm going to protect you. All right?"

The senator found himself with a new motivation. He could either take the deal with the hope that the president would protect him—or he could end up like King.

"Suppose you can't protect me and Yocum gets her teeth into the tax evasion?" He thought about what he had done to Jane. "What if she persists and tries to connect me to the King or Lane shootings … or anything else?" He thought of what might happen if Jane's body were exhumed and an autopsy performed.

"Jeff," said the president, "trust me. I want you around. I need your talents. I'll do the best I can."

"But just suppose she digs deep? Or says that she'll expose the Point Guard operation if she's unable to get what she wants?"

"You're going to have to trust that I will protect you, Jeff. That's all."

"I understand that. But, let's—"

"We'll take care of it. Now, are you going to back out and keep quiet on Point Guard?"

"I guess I have no choice," said Wheatly.

Kathy hadn't heard from Lewis or Farrel in a couple of days. She was sitting on her sofa trying to read, but she was distracted by curiosity about the status of the case. She wore a silk nightgown and matching robe and sat quietly with her legs tucked beneath her. There was a knock at the door. She was happy to see Frank's tired, worn face through the peephole.

"Hi, Frank! How are you?" She held the door open and smiled.

He looked into her eyes and, with a tone of regret in his voice, said, "Kathy, please forgive me." He reached his arm out beyond the edge of the doorway and guided Lane into her view. Kathy was stupefied. Speechless, she quickly turned to Farrel and then, confused, back to Lane. Her eyes filled with tears, and she threw her arms around Lane's neck. She pressed her body against his warm chest and nestled into his inviting arms. Tears of happiness trickled down her cheeks. She leaned back and examined every inch of his face. She touched his lips—his familiar smile—and cried aloud.

Farrel silently turned and walked away as Kathy watched from Lane's embrace. Before Farrel got too far, she called out to him. He turned to face her, but words seemed to escape her. A sort of sad smile crossed his face when he turned back around and continued on his way.

Farrel had fulfilled a promise he had made to himself—to make right what he felt he had done wrong. He hoped that he would be able to make things right with Lewis as well. But for now, he knew that they could not be friends. He did not return to Miser's office the following week. Instead, he cashed in his retirement plan and bought a cabin in the woods. Living modestly off his police pension, he spent his days fishing and his nights alone on the porch or by the fire. One day, months after he had left Lane at Kathy's door, he returned from fishing to find a large package on his doorstep. Inside the package, he found a short, unsigned, handwritten note. Accompanying it were banded packs of twenty-dollar bills, neatly stacked and totaling one million dollars.

"We could not have done it without you," the note read.

Lane and Kathy picked up where they had left off. Very much in love, they married, sold their homes, and built a house in Virginia—close to DC and Lane's work. Kathy quit working for the senator and stayed home to enjoy retirement and charity work while Lane worked with the president and his Point Guard program.

Though a lot of work was still ahead, the Point Guard System was now well on its way to reforming the current violent crimes judicial process. The country was elated with the prospect of having a system that dealt with violent crime and appeared to be swift and just—as the Founding Fathers had intended *their* system to be, over two hundred years ago. The president was easily reelected and was well on his way to being recognized—along with Lane—as a political icon.

Attorney General Delores Yocum continued her spirited efforts to indict Senator Wheatly, who had been conducting congressional business as usual, having received no more than a slap on the wrist.

She requested a meeting on the subject of Wheatly with the second-term president and Miser. At the meeting, she made it clear that she had been more than disturbed by Miser's lack of cooperation.

"Sir, it's obvious to me that there is an ongoing policy of protecting Wheatly."

"If that's how it seems, Delores, I can assure you that it's purely coincidental."

"May I speak candidly, sir?"

"Of course."

She glanced at Miser.

"Quit creating roadblocks, sir."

"What do you mean 'roadblocks'?"

"Mr. President, it's obvious that you are trying to keep me from getting an indictment. It won't work. We made a deal. If you don't stick to your end of it, I'll tear down the facade and expose all the lies and murders that paved the path for the Point Guard program."

"It's a little too late for that, don't you think, Delores?"

"To expose everything? No! The Point Guard reform process is well underway now. Nothing will derail it—not even the public knowing what happened behind the scenes. Although Point Guard will remain, they might see *you* in a different light."

She paused.

"Sir, I don't need to go over all the people who have died for this, nor do I need to remind you that Mike Lane is alive and kicking and that no one has been charged with his shooting. I had agreed to go after Wheatly for tax evasion and stay away from anything that could derail the Point Guard process. But if I can't get him on taxes, I *will* go after everything else. There is nothing to lose at this point."

"Careful, Delores. You're crossing the line."

He and Miser had expected that she would erupt eventually, but they had hoped that it wouldn't be until after the Point Guard reform had passed.

"You're an intelligent woman, Delores," the president said. "I know you don't want to do this."

"You're right, I don't. But if I don't get some cooperation, I will. I want this pig Wheatly to get what he deserves, and if I think that you're not allowing me to do my job, I'll have to take matters into my own hands. He's an evil little bastard. He can't continue in politics."

"All right … give me some time to see what I can do. Okay?"

"Sir, with all due respect, it's *not* okay."

Not appreciating the confrontation, he abruptly gestured toward the door.

"That will be all, Madam Attorney General."

After she left, the president discussed the situation with Miser.

"Paul, at this point, she's more of a liability to us than Wheatly. At least I know that he'll keep his mouth shut to save his own skin. She worries me— there's no telling what she'll do. We need this to go away right now."

"What do you want me to do?" Miser asked.

"If she doesn't get something soon, she may try to blow the top off this entire operation. I can't let her do that. I need to think about this."

There was a long silence. He took a sip of coffee and then slowly placed the cup on his desk.

"Paul, I'll contact you later," said the president as he gestured toward the door for Miser to leave.

Miser headed for the door as the president picked up the phone and dialed it. The president held the receiver as Miser closed the door.

"Mr. Barletto," he said, "how are you?"

✳   ✳   ✳   ✳

Several days passed, and Yocum grew angrier as she watched the senator go about his business. Wheatly had regained his confidence and was feeling quite secure with the president's protection. He was confident that everything was under control.

In Senator Wheatly's office—where a new girl had taken over Kathy Nolan's duties—the game was being played at full throttle. Wheatly visited the University of Pennsylvania—to give a speech, but also to scout recruits to replace Anthony. After a short lecture, he met with several upperclassmen to screen them informally as possible candidates for the job. One candidate stuck out, a slender kid named Robert Tecco. As Anthony had been, he was at the top of his class. He lettered in hockey and had an outgoing personality.

Impressed by him, the senator invited Tecco to join him for drinks at a bar called the Campus Casino—the same bar he had taken Anthony to when they had first met. Sitting alone at a booth at the far end of the bar, the senator explained to Tecco the tasks and responsibilities he would be taking on if he were to get the job. Tecco required little persuasion, and it was agreed that he would intern part-time in Philadelphia while he finished his senior year. After that, he would come to work full-time in Washington.

Tecco raised his glass as the senator proposed a toast.

"Well, son, welcome aboard! You're going to enjoy ..."

Wheatly was distracted by a figure appearing suddenly at the end of the table. He looked up to see Delores Yocum standing there in an unbuttoned tan overcoat.

"The senator and I are going to need a moment alone, son," she said.

Slightly confused, Tecco slid out of the booth.

"Someone from my office will contact you in the next day or so, Robert," Wheatly said. "Delores! What brings you here, of all places?"

"You."

"Me?" he asked smugly. "Well, have a seat, then."

"That won't be necessary; I'm not going to be long."

"Suit yourself," he said arrogantly.

Wheatly looked beyond Yocum as if her presence was not significant.

"I know that you're aware I've been investigating you for tax fraud, but it seems you have some friends in the right places."

"That I do." He nodded and smiled.

"I'm here to make a deal with you."

He laughed.

"Wow, it must be a pretty good deal! I know that you've been having me followed for quite awhile, but to have you actually show up in person ... it *must* be big!"

"Like I said, Senator, I'm going to make you a deal. After I leave this table, you'll have thirty-six hours to accept it. I know that you're being protected. But I can't help but think it must bother you that the most comprehensive and significant reform on violent crime in the history of the American judicial system is going to be voted on soon—and will probably pass—and you will get zero credit for all your work. It's obvious to me that you played a large role in the program—

one as important as the president's, even. But your name will be nowhere on the thing. Doesn't that bother you?"

The senator's smug smile quickly disappeared; he cleared his throat and squirmed a little. "Not really."

"Oh, come on, Senator! If the American public were to know about your participation, you'd become an American hero—like the president and Mr. Lane will be. You'd be a very powerful man."

Wheatly tapped on the table anxiously. "What do you want from me, Delores? I'm a busy man."

"Simple—you work with me and confirm what I think I already know, and I give you amnesty from prosecution. I get the truth, and you get the credit you deserve for your participation on the Point Guard program."

"That's suicide! This is much more complicated than that."

"Maybe. But although I've put all of my resources into this case and I'm already able to expose everything and get what I want, your participation would make it much easier and would keep me from risking the derailment of the Point Guard process. Of course, if you decide not to deal with me, I'll go ahead anyway."

"What exactly do you want?"

"Justice. It's my job."

Wheatly recalled the reason he had been willing to commit such terrible deeds in the first place. He fantasized about the immense power he could brandish as one of the architects of Point Guard reform.

Delores buttoned her coat.

"Day after tomorrow," she said. "Nine AM, in my office. If you're not there, you'll go down with the rest of them.

"Chew on that, you little shit," she mumbled as she left the table.

Giving her offer serious consideration, Wheatly asked for the check and left the bar shortly afterward. He crossed the quiet street under the dark sky and walked briskly toward the nearly empty parking lot and his new pearl-white Mercedes-Benz. He weighed the risk of turning on the president against the power he might seize if he were to take Yocum's offer. She gave him little to go on, but much to think about.

As he approached his car at the back of the dimly lit lot, he reached into his pocket, took out his cell phone, and dialed. He stood alone at the back of the lot, between his car and a row of bushes that lined a dark alley.

"Good evening, Mr. President," he said. "I'm just touching base. How is everything going with Yocum?"

He reached into his pocket for his keys when the thunderous blast of a single gunshot echoed across the parking lot. Wheatly suddenly lurched forward against the car and then slid limply to the ground with a gaping bullet hole in the back of his head.

Out of the darkness of the bushes, a wisp of gun smoke rose toward the sky. O'Mally stepped out of the camouflage into the drifting gun smoke and cocked his pistol. A single shell ejected and fell with a gentle ping to the macadam at the feet of the massive assassin.

O'Mally stood for a moment with his gun pointed at the senator's still body. Then, as quickly as he appeared, he slipped back through the bushes and vanished.

978-0-595-40559-6
0-595-40559-2